Land of My Fathers

Bully boys and pickpockets eyed me from the dark corners, the Rodneys of a town bleeding to death: tarts sidled along the slushy roadway, or sold their wares shrilly from top windows. This, I learned later, was the running sore which some called Pont-Storehouse and others called China. Only the dissolute – thieves, vagrants and prostitutes – called it home.

Merthyr was not alone in this disgrace: the rich Sodoms and Gomorrahs of Birmingham, Liverpool, Nottingham and London challenged each other for new depths of degradation in which to plunge the labouring classes. Park's Cellars, known to the Welsh in Merthyr as Sulleri, related the abyss of total greed; the inhumanity of its iron-master – a crime on the body of Mankind from which the town will take a century to recover.

'A marvellous story-teller, writing straight from the heart . . .'

Daily Express

**Also by the same author
and available in Coronet Books:**

Land of My Fathers

Alexander Cordell

CORONET BOOKS
Hodder and Stoughton

Copyright © 1983 by Alexander Cordell

First published in 1983 by Hodder &
Stoughton Ltd

Coronet edition 1985

British Library C.I.P.

Cordell, Alexander
    Land of my fathers.
    Rn: George Alexander Graber   I. Title
    823'.912[F]   PR6053.067

ISBN 0–340–36650–8

Printed and bound in Great Britain for
Hodder and Stoughton Paperbacks, a
division of Hodder and Stoughton Ltd.,
Mill Road, Dunton Green, Sevenoaks,
Kent (Editorial Office: 47 Bedford
Square, London, WC1 3DP) by
Richard Clay (The Chaucer Press) Ltd.,
Bungay, Suffolk

For my friends Geoff Thomas, librarian, and
Arthur Morris, teacher

I am again indebted to the following for making available to me books of research, original documents, letters and maps, some of antiquity:

Mr. G. A. Dart, F.L.A. and Mr. E. Goulden, F.L.A. of Headquarters Central Library, Cardiff; the Departmental Record Office of the Home Office; The National Library of Wales; Mr. J. Bowring, B.A., A.L.A. of Douglas Public Library; Mr. D. G. Edwards, M.P.S.; the Gwynedd Archives Service and Mr. S. C. G. Caffell, B.A., A.L.A. of Gwynedd Library Service, Llangefni; Mr. D. Francis, B.A., A.L.A. and Mr. G. James, B.A., A.L.A. both of Merthyr Public Libraries; Mr. Wilfred Bowden, J.P. of Abercynon; Mr. T. Iowerth late of Bangor Branch Library, and not least to Mr. Geoffrey Thomas the Cultural Services Officer of Libraries, Archives and Museums, Dyfed, to whom this book is dedicated.

Idris Davies's *Gwalia Deserta* is quoted by permission of Mr. Ebenezer Morris and the Estate of the late Idris Davies.

To many others I am also grateful for help, especially to John A. Owen whose *History of Dowlais Iron Works* was a constant companion in the writing, and to Jim Robinson and Deryck Brown for research: also to Ian Stuart for his encouragement, interest and suggestions.

Lastly, my thanks to Mam-gu, my first love, for being of the Rhondda.

AC

*In a certain part of the Island
there is a people called* Welsh,
*so bold and ferocious that, when
unarmed, they do not fear to
encounter an armed force; being
ready to shed their blood in
defence of their country, and to
sacrifice their lives for renown.*

Gerald of Wales—*c.*1146–1223
—quoting Henry II of England

I stood in the ruins of Dowlais
And sighed for the lovers destroyed
And the landscape of Gwalia stained for all times
By the bloody hands of progress.
I saw the ghosts of The Successful Century
Marching on the ridges of the sunset
And wandering among derelict furnaces,
And they had not forgotten their humiliation,
For their mouths were full of curses.
And I cried aloud, O what shall I do for my fathers
And the land of my fathers?
But they cursed and cursed and would not answer,
For they could not forget their humiliation.

Idris Davies
Gwalia Deserta

Book One

Anglesey
1831

1

My tenth birthday, I remember, was one of those early up flying April mornings when even churchyard corpses were dreaming of high-buttoned girls, parasols and kisses.

Certainly it was a day when the clergy from Petter to Wesley Street were sitting ducks.

At six o'clock most mornings the privy ten-holer on Turkey Shore was occupied by bright-faced boyos who always got up first – deacons, the leaders of the community. And here the business of the day would be discussed – as to who would be on what 'bargain' that week, who would be carting, and the quality, or otherwise, of the sermon given by a travelling preacher a week last Sunday.

"First up, first served," said Andy Appledore, my mate who sat next to me with the *copar ledis*, and he lit a rag, dropped it on to a board and floated it down the gully-way of the big ten-holer, and you couldn't see deacons for dust. The language coming up from that privy was enough to singe the tail off Satan, let alone deacons.

Andy went one way, I went another.

It becomes clear to me, said my father at the inquest, that this particular Englishman is a bad example to a well-mannered Welshman, and I didn't sit down for a week.

I ran fast that morning up to Costog Spinney, then down to the beach where old Joe Herring, my friend the black-faced gull, was waiting for his breakfast.

Dear me, I was in love with the world that morning; it was full of sun, wind, birthday greetings, and all the sweetness of

April. Panting on the edge of Ogof Fain I saw the sea below me dancing in spindrift, and he was a marvellous blue with him that week, frothing up his white-topped breakers and smashing them against the harbour wall where the copper carriers spiked the sky with cobwebs of rigging. Far away to the north was Ellan Vannin they call the Isle of Man: to the south was snow-capped Snowdon, and great bedsheet clouds were lumbering across the caverns of the wind.

Ach, I do love the bright springtime days when the mutton chops do handsprings across the meadows. The birds play leap-frog, the lads are all polished and quiffed – putting years on the girls, my mother used to say. Aye, there is something in springtime that gets everyone frisky, and it is a hell of a thing when you're ten years old, to see folks billing and cooing in hedges and knees up in haylofts, and Satan himself in the back pews of Calfaria, looking for clients, according to my father.

Tall and wide-shouldered is Dada, his head higher than any man in Amlwch . . . with our dead mam's hymnal on the pew between us. The most eligible widower in Town, I'd heard say, with fat women fanning themselves in flushes at the sight of him.

"Please keep away from that English Andy Appledore," said he.

"Yes, Dada."

'Rock of Ages' it was then, full blend of soprano, contralto, tenor and bass, with my piping treble coming up beside my father's voice. In shafts of sunlight from the Chapel windows the dust-motes dance; a blue bottle is wheezing among the polished boots and black-stocking knees.

"Never been near that ten-hole privy," said I.

"Accepted," said my father. "And there are a few in Amlwch who may need heating up. In due course all will receive their just deserts, Taliesin, as did Samson for setting fire to the tails of foxes. So take the hiding just to please me, is it?"

"Yes, Dada."

Wasn't me. It was that bloody Appledore.

Sweating, me. In this mood he could rend a lion.

*

On the other side of my father was my Cousin Poll, aged fifteen. All peaches and cream was she under her poke-bonnet, a face all innocence and very flourishing in the breast, being in milk.

It always set the congregation staring when we took my Cousin Poll to Chapel on Sundays, and she always did herself up gay in colours, contrasting the bombazine black, said she, and the women, creaking and corsetted, gave her the eye. A crying scandal it is, said one: with his woman scarce cold in her grave, said another, that Gwyn Roberts brings a harlot in to share a pew with decent people . . . But my father did not appear to hear this. Through the Chapel door he came, standing politely aside while Polly took her seat. Radiant was my Cousin Poll; a primrose in a bed of deadly nightshade.

A bit more about my father and Cousin Poll, while on the subject.

Large was he, as I have said, with thick-muscled arms where the hairs grew like forest trees: Iberian Welsh to the marrow, the people used to say: so tall that he ducked his head under the back of Three Costog, and that was six foot two. In he comes from the Smelter with funnel dirt upon his face, and there, in the kitchen, sits our Poll feeding my little sister Meg, with a wicked little smile . . .

After my mam died, having my sister Meg two months back, my father brought this Polly into our house.

The death of Gwyn Roberts' missus is a tragedy, they said in Town, and he will be a long time getting over it.

O aye? they were saying now.

For about this time my Cousin Poll brought forth, too, and her baby was dead. So my father took the dead baby from Poll's breast and buried it with my mother: then he took our Meg and put her on the breast of Poll. Naturally, the people in Town had opinions on it, and Mr. Dafydd Owen, our deacon, said:

"Your niece's child was born out of wedlock, Gwyn Roberts – how can you bear it – a baggage suckling your child?"

My father went about his business as if he hadn't heard.

"You will show Cousin Poll due respect, Taliesin, you hear me?"

"Yes, Dada."

"Her mother, like yours, is dead; her father is at sea. She is alone and of our blood. It is right and fair that she should come and live with us, you understand?"

"Yes, Dada."

"And do not heed the gossip in the Town."

"No, Dada."

"Your Cousin Polly's milk will taste as sweet as Mam's. If in doubt, ask little Meg."

"Yes, Dada."

"And Poll is in need of us, poor little soul."

Mind you, I was coming a bit sore these days about this 'poor little soul' business, for she do not look so poor to me, this Cousin Poll, and make sure she has an egg for her breakfast every morning while she is on the feed, and no bloody egg for me.

"I know where she'd finish up if she belonged to me," said Mrs. Dahlia Sapphira.

We were at table, I remember. I suppose I could have chosen a better time to raise the subject. Poll was upstairs putting Meg to bed; Dada and me were together after a hard day on Turkey Shore.

"Born out of wedlock, is it?" I asked, getting into bread and jam.

My father blew his tea. "To what are you referring?"

"Poll's baby."

I could never get the hang of this birthing baby stuff, with Andy saying she'd gone swimming among tadpoles.

"And who stated that?" asked my father.

"The *copar ledis* do say so."

Mam's bread board, warped by years, was beside me on the starched, white cloth. She was a noble little thing, my mam, with Welsh-dark hair and the face of a housewife, with little fat hands for cutting bread and butter on her little fat tum. What that big handsome Gwyn Roberts do see in her I do not know, said more than one, but I knew. Gone? Not to us. She walks this house. Now my father said:

"Is that a fact? Then tell these *copar ledis* to stick to chipping copper, or I'll be down to have their tongues out for measuring. It's the good girls who get caught for babies, Tal."

"Old Poll's always at it, mind," I said.

"At what?"

"Don't know, but Andy Appledore do say so."

"One more mention of him and you are straight to bed."

I did not fear him. He rarely laid a hand on me: to strike a child is to assault the child, he used to say, except when blowing up deacons.

"Anyway, we can manage on our own," I said.

My father gave me a queer old look, and a sigh. "We cannot manage on our own, Meg needs her – her milk, I told you."

"We can get milk off Dulcie Brown Cow."

"We cannot. Your sister is not a bull calf. Now, do you think we could have an end to this?"

The kettle was grieving on the hob. My mam used to swing it off with a smile. I wanted to run upstairs and cry on the bed. Ever since Poll had come he had taken less notice of me. Now he said, his hand in my hair:

"Be generous, Tal – she had nobody in the world but us."

Serve her bloody right.

Mind you, there were some happy compensations in having a harlot in the place, and a happy little soul was old Poll, give her credit; coming in, crying, "Morning, Uncle Gwyn, how you doin', Cousin Tal? (she couldn't even speak English, never mind Welsh) Make a good breakfast, both of you, and a bottle for my darling Cousin Meg – steak and kidney one side, rice pudding the other . . . There, there . . ." and she opens the front of her bodice, whispering as mothers do, "Hush you, hush . . . old Poll's got plenty," and our Meg crowed delighted in her tears and clamped herself on like a navvy on to a pint.

My father said, his voice low, "A good boy you are, Tal,

not staring. Ladies are entitled to privacy and respect when feeding babies."

So everybody was happy at such times, including me, for I could see old Poll at it in the cracked mirror of the kitchen. And a good old set she had on her, too, smooth and white, the colour of lotus flowers. Beautiful are women, I think, possessing such lovely things.

"She is taking it, Polly?" my father asked his pipe.

"Yes, Uncle Gwyn."

"She is a lusty baby. You have no pain?"

"No, Uncle Gwyn."

Mind, this was the daughter my father always wanted, for once I heard him talking about this to my mam. "A son for you and a daughter for me, eh, Peg? A little poke-bonnet in the house, woman, and I'll be doubly blessed . . ."

Now he said, "If pain comes, Poll, you'll tell me, yeh?"

"Doin' fine, Uncle Gwyn, really, Uncle Gwyn."

Dear me, Uncle Gwyn.

I still say we could have got it off Dulcie Brown Cow.

About this time I received a lesson in the sweet mystery of life, as Dada called it: trust my mate Andy Appledore not to be behind the curtain, either, when Cousin Poll was handing out religious instruction, though the way she was acting now butter wouldn't have melted in her mouth. And my father would have had fits with his legs up if he'd seen the way she behaved in our barn on Saturday Fair Night, the week after Easter.

Mind you, it's on summer nights mostly when grown-ups start getting frisky, I find, when the moon sits smiling on the sea and warm winds come fanning in from Snowdon. The animals are at it, too, I've noticed, with Bill, my ferret, knocking hell out of Milly, and Ben Rooster, our cockerel, rousting up his women, to say nothing of the lads in Town.

About the hottest male in Amlwch that year was my mate Appledore. Rising sixteen was he, with ambitions to do his utmost for Welsh womanhood, said the *copar ledis*, who spent most of the day fighting him off, and these days he was breathing down the neck of my Cousin Poll.

"Your night in, Tal, Poll's night out – and don't forget to shut up the hens, there's foxes about," said my father, on his way out for his Oddfellows pint.

"And don't have any women in, mind," added Poll. Done up in her Fair Night braveries was she, all pink and flouncy, and she fluttered an eye at me.

"And where might you be off to, Madam?" asked Dada.

"Band of Hope."

"A good girl you are," said he, kissing her. "Here's a penny for the South African missionaries. Back at half-past nine, remember."

"In bed by nine, Uncle Gwyn, if that suits you better."

"And keep away from that Andy Appledore."

It appalled her. "O, shame and damnation on you, Uncle Gwyn, for such a suggestion!" and she wriggled and went coy, melting him.

O aye? I thought. If that penny lands in the Fund for Missionaries I'd be mistaken; more likely a couple of gin tots for her and Andy Appledore, for I knew they were on the booze, and turn our barn near Three Costog into an abode of love.

No wonder our hens were off the lay; such things can have a bad effect on chickens.

When I went out that night to lock up the henhouse I found our Ben Rooster and his wife Betsy absent. So I went into the barn to look for them. And in there came Cousin Poll hand in hand with Andy Appledore, and what happened then took the shine off cassocks. I just lay there in the shadows, sweating cobs, my hair standing on end and breaking my neck for a closer look. Faint, I crept out of that barn and came face to face with Dada.

"Well I never!" said he. "I thought you were abed. I was just coming to find Ben Rooster and lock up the henhouse."

"Just done that, Dada," I lied.

"And Cousin Poll? Where's she?"

"Came home half an hour back."

He would have asked more, I think, but did not; behind the barn door old Poll giggled in the dark, but I don't think Dada heard. Instead, he did a strange thing: reaching out, he held me against him, saying:

"A good little lad you are, Tal. Home then, the two of us?"

It is funny, I think, that grown-ups don't catch on so quick.

Everybody in Town knew what old Poll was up to, but I suppose that's difficult to understand when you're hoping she's your daughter.

"Come," said Dada, and took my hand; together we climbed the little hill back to Three Costog. So everybody was happy, including old Poll: two hours later she came through my bedroom window like a witch on a broomstick.

That night a fox knocked off poor old Ben Rooster, who was supposed to be locked up in the henhouse, yet my father never even mentioned it.

Strange, really, come to think of it.

Two years later, when our Meg was two, I was still working with the *copar ledis* on the tables along Turkey Shore.

There is a size for you are some of these copper ladies! – and enough gas in them to light the flares come market. Six to a table we were, women and girls one side, kids like me opposite, and it was *chink chink chink*, the little hammers rising and falling; twelve hours a day, six days a week – chipping the rock away from the copper vein before it went into the Smelter.

The miners dug out the 'bargains' up on Parys Mountain, the carters brought it down to the harbour and tipped it close to us. And then we were at it, chinking, chinking, chinking, and you've never heard such a gabbling since they raised the Tower of Babel: girls and women in their home-spun tunics and red scarves, with spotted yellow handkerchiefs on their heads – chattering like magpies, leg-pulling and shrieking laughter.

But that was in summer, with the sea calm and blue and the gulls soaring in the harbour wind above us.

Come winter it was different.

Then the wind would tear in from the sea and bite us to the bone, and the copper ladies under the tent roof were tied up like bales of rags for warmth, with their blue noses sticking out of their mufflers and their fingers like claws of ice. But still the copper ore would pour down from Parys Mountain and still the hammers would chink away in the dark, with children as young as six years old dancing to broken fingers. Then snow would come and frost the land and our breath would smoke in the tent, and the moment the overman's back was turned we would dash in twos and threes for the warmth of the Smelter where my father worked.

Pretty quiet were our *copar ledis* in winter, but they were sitting newspapers when a new spring came sweeping over the earth.

Wonderful it is to get a whiff of the scandal when you are twelve years old: as to how Dora Jewels, the Jew girl, has had the Sailor's Farewell off Mr. Ifor Bach, the skipper of the *Mona Queen*, and if Ida Promise, the ugliest woman in Amlwch, isn't inching up Shoni Bob-Ochr, the Welsh Dutchman, they were very much mistaken: but musical, too, as well – singing Welsh folk-songs in full harmony – beating time with their hammers. And the sound of their voices would drift over the sea in a sulphretting musical scarf; the sailors coming into Amlwch harbour cocking an ear above the thunder of the rigging.

The following year, when I was thirteen, two things happened to change my life. I got promotion and was sent up to the Precipitation pits; also, I fell in love.

In love with Miss Prudence Ichabod, aged sixteen, and to hell with copper ladies.

Dark and slim was Pru Ichabod, with eyes as big as saucers, dark-lashed and flecked with green, and her cheeks were high in her small-boned face; white were her teeth in the curved, red smile of her lips. And she walked with a pretty swing to her hips that drove me damned demented.

Aye! The moment I set eyes on this Pru Ichabod in the Welsh Wesleyan she drove me spare; three months she sat on my bolster back home in Three Costog and it took me a year to get her off. We used to sit behind her in Chapel, and the perfume of her fluttered me down to my socks. See her now, coming out of Chapel with the sun on her face; summer, full and splendid, was into us.

"Well, well! Good morning, Tal Roberts. Fancy seeing you!"

Dear me, she smelled even sweeter outside in the sun.

Most women, I find, smell as sweet as nutcake, even old

Dahlia Sapphira with lavender water under the arms, but none smelled like Pru Ichabod that Sunday morning after Chapel.

"Ay ay," said I, moochy, for off comes my father's cap and he bows deep, sweeping up the pavement:

"Good morning, Miss Ichabod! A fine June day it is going to be, I'm bound."

Why can't I talk like that?

"Lovely indeed, Mr. Roberts," says she, silky.

"Did you enjoy the sermon? Mr. Owen at his best today?"

"Aye, Mr. Roberts – a marvellous tonality, mind."

"But sincerity, too, Miss Ichabod – sincerity is the essence," and he elbowed me to keep me upright.

The congregation, glum, pressed about us in smells of moth balls and whiffs of polished mahogany, God now being on his way to St. Eleath, Church of England.

"And how is little Meg, and Poll?" Pru dimpled a smile at me. "Taliesin in long trews, too – working the Precipitation, is it?"

God help her if she hadn't noticed. I stood on tiptoe with my hair quiffed up and the crutch of my new trews cutting my throat.

"Two men in the family now," said my father, and he touched my head. "But old before his time, this one." Which was the standard joke about my pure white hair, and I hated him.

"Grown inches since I see you last, Taliesin," said Pru.

Two months she had been ill with the chest, poor soul – two months of agony for me: wandering around Brickpool hoping for a sight of her, stealing up to her window in Sixteen Methusalem. And every time Dr. Griffiths Thomas Davies of Bryn-y-fryd came out I examined him for news. His smile would send me off with daylight under my boots; his frown of worry painted pictures of crow-clad funeral directors in serge and dubbined boots: love in its purest form I held for Pru Ichabod.

"Are you managing better these days, Mr. Roberts?"

My father replied, "Perfectly now, Miss Ichabod."

"If Poll wears badly, do not be afraid to ask, mind, for I

am better now."

"You would be the first I would come to for help, Ma'am." Down she goes again and her dress spreads wide in her curtsey: up with her then and a fluttering wink at me; it is good to know when you've made an impression on a female.

"Come, Tal," whispers my father, replacing his cap. "Quick!"

For Mr. Dafyyd Owen, the head deacon, is approaching with the Book under his arm, and he is afflicted with bodily odour, poor man, says my father. Away with the pair of us up Smelter Hill to Three Costog, our cottage.

Those were the early weeks I spent working at the Precipitation pits, and received seven shillings a week, the wages of a man.

Marvellous are the works of humans to take red water from a mountain and turn it into copper.

See them digging the new shaft on Parys – red-core Parys that is riddled with copper – working as did the Romans. Down, down goes the shaft into the bowels of the mountain: fill the shaft with water and leave it for nine months: then pump it out into Precipitation.

In come the ships carrying scrap iron for the stew.

Aye, this is the stew of copper – old bedsteads, old engines, wheels and nails – scrap of all description from the iron industry of the North comes surging into Amlwch on the ships. The carters unload it and carry it to the pits: and in it goes, iron scrap into the sulphate stew, the blood of Parys. And we, the stirrers, worked the brew with wooden poles – wooden ones, since metal ones would melt in the acid – even copper nails in our boots. Stir, stir, stir – nine months it took to melt the iron into a liquid. And the sludge that dropped to the bottom of the pits was copper. Break this up cold and cart it like biscuits down to the maw of the Smelter for refining.

This was the process; a job for men, not boys.

"You are growing up, Tal," said my father one Sunday morning after Chapel. "Thirteen years old, is it? You're the height and width of a man."

I did not reply, knowing that my father had something under his waistcoat that was bound to come out.

"You are aware, I suppose, that Miss Prudence Ichabod is a beautiful woman?"

"She's all right," I said, chewing at a straw.

"Also, that she is pledged to marry Mr. Dick Evans, the landlord of the Oddfellows, Market Place?"

This stopped me in my tracks. Dick Evans? God, I'll kill him.

"A bit of a surprise for you, is it?" My father glanced at me as we walked together over the short mountain grass.

"Her business," I replied, dying inside.

At this, he stopped and slipped easily to the ground; crossed his thick arms around his knees and stared at the harbour. I thought: Tonight, at high tide, I will get up in my nightshirt and walk into the sea. My father said:

"You know something peculiar – something almost unbelievable? When I was about your age I fell in love with a girl called Prudence – an English girl – as fair as Pru Ichabod is dark."

I thought: And when the tide goes out they will find my body on the sand. Already I could hear the tolling of the bells, the congregation sniffing and wiping; me boxed in cedar and brass handles.

"She was twenty-two and I was thirteen," said my father. "She married a butcher, I remember." He turned, gripping my arm. "Look, look, Tal, there is little that happens to you that has not already happened to me. And little you do that I have not already done . . . no, do not turn away, son – men face each other in difficult conversations."

His eyes, I remember, were blue in his strong, square face, and he continued:

"Women are weaker than us, Tal; true love protects. Pru Ichabod is frail. Further, she is in love with Dick Evans, the landlord of the Oddfellows. Do not make it difficult for her. The choice between the two of you is hard enough as it is . . ."

Oh God, let me die . . .

"You are fast growing up, Tal. All in Town speak of

it – Taliesin Roberts, who is a man at thirteen years. But when your body moves in manhood, do not always trust it, for bodies can betray."

A strange time to talk of such things, I thought, and on a Sunday.

Hot to set alight I sat there, my eyes lowered before his steady gaze. He added, "Let Pru Ichabod be, Tal. To pursue her at this time would be to put her into an impossible situation. Be generous."

We sat together in silence. The wind whispered and I smelled the salt tang of the sea.

My father said:

"Home now, is it, and see what Cousin Poll has for dinner?"

3

Saint Peter was in a perky old mood when he fashioned my
Cousin Polly. My father said he was getting his own back on
the Roman hordes who used to play hell with the Welsh. She
is one of the beautiful Goidels who kept the centurions
tossing and turning around 50 B.C., said he.

I don't know about Romans, but she started to have a
terrible effect on me, especially after Pru Ichabod betrayed
me with Dick Evans of the Oddfellows. And when my father
was on night-shift at the Smelter, I got it worst of all.

It is the good girls who get into trouble, Tal, mark me, said
Dada.

Generosity, like wisdom, can be the biggest fool of all.

"You all right, Cousin Tal?" asked Poll.

The night was black with him, the wind doing doh-ray-
me in the chimney and only me and Poll in the kitchen. I was
shivering to have my teeth out. It was the week of my
fourteenth birthday, and the way Poll was behaving it looked
like being my last.

I'd just got in from the Precipitation and walked the three
miles down from Parys. My trews were soaked with sulphate
water and I was anxious to get them off.

Being a stirrer (Shallow Enders, we were called) we used
to wear a rum barrel on each leg above the clogs, to save us
from the splashes – but now I could feel the copper water
heating up my shins.

It was only when I found the tin bath steaming hot by the
fire that I remembered about Dada being on night-shift, and
by the look on Poll's face I had only ten minutes to live.

The sight of that tin bath do bring back memories!

Time was, when I was a nip, Dada and me used to bathe by the copper out the back. Marvellous, it is, to share a bath with your father. In with him first, rubbing for bubbles, and I can see him now – shoulders on him like Barney's bull: down goes his head; come up blowing like a whale: up on his feet now, eight feet tall, rubbing for a glow with the towel, his fists thudding against the packed muscles of his stomach. "Here we go, *cariad*!" he shouts to my mam, and reaches out and hooks me in, aged six.

"Right you, Tal!"

But it was different now I was growing up.

Give Poll credit, mind, she didn't come in while I was bathing by the fire. I left my trews to soak and put on others she'd laid out ready.

"A pretty boy you are, though," said she, coming downstairs from Meg, and taking the lobscouse off the hob.

"Aye, woman, let's have it," said I, and waited, staring at the starched white cloth while she ladled from the saucepan. Mutton stew she smells of, and a pink petticoat sweetness. And I sat there with my knees knocking.

"How old are you, Tal Roberts?"

"Fourteen, Missus."

"Gawd! Ye'll be eight feet up by the time you're twenty." And she put the saucepan back on the hob and came back and stroked my hair. "And such lovely hair you do have, too. But fourteen's too young for a decent dinner, or I'd eat you with spuds and cow cabbage."

I got into the stew, packing the bread in after it and wishing her to the devil.

"Never mind, small acorns do grow into very large oaks," said she. "You marry me, Cousin Tal, when you grow up?"

"I'm not particular, Cousin Poll."

"Meanwhile, while I'm waiting, I'll take a snip o' that lovely white hair for me locket," and she made big eyes and pulled it up the front of her.

"Ach, lay off!"

Snip, snip went the scissors.

Judges 16, verse 19. Try having your hair cut while you're

eating lobscouse. Samson got himself into the same predicament.

But real trouble started coming in the spring I was fifteen.

I suppose, thinking back, it had started long before that. My mam (before she died) owed Greathead's Truck Shop for a couple of pounds of candles, they reckoned. And five years she had been gone before the debt was discovered. So they put it on my father's debit when he came for his six weeks' pay.

"Two pounds of what?" he asked.

"Two pounds of candles, Mr. Roberts."

"Not for us, Tasker, we burn oil."

"Here's the entry, Mr. Roberts. In your wife's name."

"And the woman dead these past five years? Talk sense!"

"Don't know about that, Mr. Roberts."

"I do," said my father, "give it here," and the clerk of Greathead's Shop gave Dada the account and he tore it into pieces.

"Debt paid," said he.

But you don't so easily get rid of a debt to Greathead's.

Every six weeks' pay night it was the same now – the Robertses still owe for two pounds of candles.

"I'll tell you what I will do," said my father. "I'll buy another two dozen candles and push them up the agent."

Now, you do not talk like that about the agent of the Marquis.

"They'll have you for it, Mr. Roberts," said Mr. Dafydd Owen.

"I am not paying a debt my wife did not incur," said my father.

I ran fast that spring morning to feed Joe Herring, my friend the black-faced gull, then dropped to my knees and scrambled to the cliff edge: and I saw, a hundred feet below me, the mighty swirl of the sea. There, standing on one leg awaiting me, was Joe, his beady eyes winking in the sun. Clearly, I heard a voice, my mother's voice, calling me above the wave-crash in the plaintive wailing of the gulls:

"Taliesin!"

Aye! As clear as day I heard her voice whenever I climbed down the cliff to feed old Joe; but knew that it was the daft old wind playing his flutes in the thickets above, and the crying of the oyster-catchers from the sea. Down, down, down I went, toes and fingers scrabbling for a hold, down the hundred feet to the beach, and dropped the last two yards.

"Night-shift," I said to the bird. "You hungry?"

I had been feeding him since my mam died. Once, wandering, loosened with tears, I had seen him flapping in the bay below me hooked like a fish on the breast of the sea. And I had stripped off my clothes and dived in naked, swum to him, cut the line, and dragged him ashore, breaking his wing.

I had taken him home to my father, who fashioned a feather quill and prised out the hook in his throat; then we fed him on sprats and oil.

His broken wing he reckoned was my fault, and he'd had me on toast ever since.

So every third evening, winter, summer, wet or fine, I would come down to the beach after shift and fetch him out a mackerel. He was awaiting it now, and I pulled in the line with a flounder wriggling on the end of it, and Joe had him down without showing which way he went.

"Greedy old bugger!"

He just watched me, his breast feathers ruffling in the wind.

Another, another. God knows where he put them.

It was on this particular evening that I saw my father coming along the sand towards me.

Very strange, this, since he was supposed to be at work.

Stranger still was the heliograph signal flashing out at sea.

True, as a lead-refiner under the Smelter boss, Mr. Edward Rees, my father came and went almost as he pleased. Even as I stared at his approach I heard the whine of the Smelter and saw its yellow smoke gathering above the harbour. The heliograph message stopped winking, obliterated. Then the prow of a cutter made shape, and a shark's-fin sail cut the smoke. The cutter appeared, shaking herself like a terrier and I saw her mains'l bellying in the slanting wind. Now, in a confusion of jumbled water she came inshore, her prow spraying water . . . making directly to the beach where my father was standing.

Looking back, my father was sailing pretty close to the wind in more ways than one about then. He made no bones about who he spoke his mind to. And I'll always remember the night we collected our six weeks' pay.

The copper agents always paid out in the ale-houses, a different house for every trade: the tutworkers who worked the bargains got theirs in the Old Glastonbury; the halvaners who dug the waste were paid at the Blue Bell in Amlwch Port (fourteen ale houses within three hundred yards down by there). Dressers received theirs at the Farmer's Arms, Smiths at the Two Frigates and Carpenters at the Windmill, School Lane.

Dada and I pocketed ours at the Oddfellows where old Dick Evans, now the husband of my dearly beloved Pru Ichabod, held court.

A queer old lad was this Dick Evans, with a body like a lath and the face of a thrashed dog, and God knows what my Pru saw in him; but he be privately endowed, see, said Bill Bopper, the tasker of Greathead's Truck Shop; as plump as a market pig was this Bill Bopper, with an expression to match.

This came out as my father and I were going into the public.

"What does he mean?" I asked.

Dada glanced at the debt collector and thumped the bar for ale. "Pass such eloquence unheeding, my son. It is an intellectual leap for some to lift a pint," and he smiled at Pru, who came up to the bar. "A quart for me, Ma'am, a half for Taliesin."

I could have wept.

Where had gone the bloom that I had loved?

Two years now Dick Evans had been at her, the bed and the tub: twins first, now she was carrying again. But she smiled at me and I saw in that smile the woman she might have been. My father glanced at the pair of us, then lifted his pewter and blew off the froth: like most good Welshmen, he liked his ale. "Drink deep, Tal, but never drink drunk," he used to say. "Hops, like love-making, is a pastoral activity of the Celtic mind."

"You all right, Pru?" I whispered amid the thunder of shouts and chinking glasses.

"Doing fine, Tal!" and she mopped up the bar.

"Come on, come on, woman!" shouted her husband, and I stiffened.

"Easy, lad," said my father.

Oh God, I thought, one day I will flatten Dick Evans and take you from here. And, as if reading me, he raised his bloodhound eyes to mine.

"Very obedient, isn't she, mun!"

After a couple of pints I forgot about Pru Ichabod.

Dandy it is to be drinking ale with your father. Don't swallow – just open the gullet and pour it down. Everybody in the public was at it; parting their whiskers and tipping up quarts; quarrelling, soothing, paying debts with promises, grumbling about wives. And in every voice lay the eternal threat – to empty Amlwch of Cornishmen. Always it is the same – a couple of glasses and they're marching on Plas Newydd, my father used to say – then back home to the grouses of their half-starved wives.

Men drowned themselves in the fumes of ale that pay night: the drained sulphretted faces of the smelters I saw, their lips cracked by the poison that ate their lungs.

Copper beat everything flat with its production: laying waste the country, killing animals and humans. Rees the cripple was there, I noticed, a man spawned on the farms, but now a tributor who had dug out his heart on unfair 'bargains'. Gory Blood, too – he who mined the shafts up on Mona; his mate, Alfie Cromwell, was beside him, a man of warts and a vacuous sense of humour; also Old Cog Costog, the tiny husband of Betsy, who lived next door to us up above Brickhill. She used to hit Hell out of him when he came home plaiting his legs; a rancid disposition had Betsy; no kind of wife for a scholar like Old Cog, who worked the engines up on Mona.

"Wales, O Wales," he would cry after a whiff of the hops, "'Thou who hast the fatal gift of beauty . . .'"

"Get the poet right," my father used to say. "'*Italia! Italia!*' it is, and he was down the Po Valley, not up bloody Snowdon."

"Is this an inference that I do not know my Byron?"

"It is. Next we'll be having Shakespeare for Plato."

"Died in the Greek war of independence, I heard," said Old Cog.

"Dear God!" groaned my father.

Very happy I was to have this straightened out, having assumed that he got an arrow in the eye at Agincourt.

"Who?"

"Plato."

"Another quart, and quick," said Dada.

"I hear that you and your father are going into the carting business, young man," said Old Cog.

A travelling newspaper, this one, and your business was all around Town.

"Are we?" I asked.

"Aye, and if I had a son six feet up, I'd loosen me engines and start carting – money there, mind."

The pay was chinking now, and the babble was like a Muldoon picnic. I saw Pru watching me from the bar as Bill Bopper, the tasker, pushed his way to the front.

"Is it true ye have shop debts, lad?" Old Cog jerked his thumb at my father who, eyes closed, appeared lost in a dream.

"Our business," I said.

"Your father has a bone of contention in this respect, I understand . . .?" His pink eyes, those of a rat, inspected me.

"Has he?" I'd always been doubtful about bones of contention, and Cog said:

"And, what is more, I understand he is airing his grievance tonight."

"Is that a fact?"

"It is, and I take issue with it. If the debt has been incurred the family pays."

31

"If my mother incurred it."

"And, in taking on Tasker Bopper by refusing to pay, he is also taking on the Marquis of Anglesey."

"That doesn't bother my father much," I said.

He regarded me, head on one side. "We don't get a lot out of you, do we, Taliesin?"

"Not a lot, Mr. Costog."

"Pray silence!" roared Bill Bopper, then. "In the name of the Marquis," though God knows what he had to do with it. Yet, as always, it silenced them. There was no sound now but breathing and the chinking of paymasters' money.

"Joe Oldfield!" bawled Bopper, and poor old Workhouse Joe came up, his clothes burned to holes by copper water.

A Bradford man, he had a missus and five kids in the House of Industry down Narbeth, the first workhouse in the country, and he had tramped North into copper to bail them out. Bopper slapped down money.

"*Jesus!*" whispered Joe, staring at it. "Is that all?"

"How is that made up?" called my father.

"Oldfield's business, man – stick to yours!"

"How?" Dada came to the bar, and the tasker said, sighing:

"Forty-two-day period at six shillings a week less shovel hire time and candles; less fourpence for the doctor and ten shillings shop debt – draws twenty-four shillings."

"Proof of shop debt?"

"Sure, Holy God, would ye audit the account personally, Gwyn Roberts?"

Bad Irish, this one. The only thing we had against the Irish in Amlwch was their stomachs, it was the Cornish we wanted out, but Tasker Bopper was the dregs.

"Leave it, Mr. Roberts," whispered Joe Oldfield, in the silence. "I need the loot."

"Any more palaver and he'll be out on his arse," said Bopper. "Next!"

"Have a sight of it each week, Mr. Oldfield," said Dada, "before you sign your six weeks' cross."

The names were called. One by one the men went up for their pay, and this day, for some reason or other, we were mixed in the trades, with deductions for the Truck Shops, fuses, candles, gunpowder, hire of tools, and often rent. And the tutworkers and tributors on the 'bargains' got it worst that pay night, I recall.

These were the men who worked in teams of four, who got a face of copper and rock on an auctioning system called 'bargains'.

In St. Eleath's square these 'bargains' were struck, and the team-leaders bid against each other to the agent, who would strike with a pebble the leader who won. And so, with their income tuned to the rate of copper per ton of rock shifted, their stomachs were dependent on the luck of the 'bargain'. The standard was five per cent copper; if less than that, their pay was lowered; if more, it was raised. I have known tributors work for a week on an auctioned 'bargain' and draw no wages at all, so God was very popular with the teams – every dig up on Parys Mountain being dependent upon the Deity. Keep Him sweet, was the cry, or the agent will drop the rate. Down on their knees morning, noon and night, these 'bargain' workers, in the name of Jesus.

And the Cornish agents of the Marquis – men like Jimmy Liar and Billy Spy – also made a profit out of us on the mine stores – a practice they had brought from the Cornish mines. They'd buy candles and powder in bulk when times were bad and sell them to us when times were good.

A deputation to the Marquis? somebody suggested. The place is in rags, folks are starving – a deputation, for *God's* sake – go over the heads of these pilfering agents.

Blame the Marquis, said my father, also the rotten Welsh gentry; not only those who rule us now, remember, but those who sold Glyndŵr to an English king. If I had my way, said he, I would hang these parasites from a Parys whimsey – death by ritual strangulation.

I had gathered the impression that my father didn't think much of the Marquis of Anglesey.

"Gwyn Roberts!" bellowed Bill Bopper, the tasker.

My father stood before him, and I groaned, sensing trouble.

"Last pay day, eh, Mr. Roberts?" called a man.

"Aye," replied Dada. "This time next week we'll be carting."

"Thirty-one-day week," said Bopper. "Four shillings a day, agreed?"

"Agreed."

"And no stoppages?"

"Correct."

"But a little matter of eightpence for two pounds of candles."

"Oh yes, I forgot – can I see the bill?"

Bopper showed it and my father took it and tore it into pieces. "Debt discharged," said he, again.

"You know what this means, don't you, Gwyn Roberts?" asked one of the paymasters, handing over his pay.

"I do. The Marquis will be eightpence short."

"You'll regret it."

"No, he will. The loss is his. Come, Tal," and he put his arm around my shoulders.

The stars were big; donkeys and horses stood statuesque in the moonlight of Pritchard's fields, and I remembered their begging eyes when under the whip.

I said, "There's going to be trouble, isn't there?"

"Of course," came the reply. "Eightpence to the Marquis is the difference between life and death: he was born with the ethics of a vulture."

We walked on. The copper-dusted trees were night hags brooding on the starved earth: two skeletons who called themselves mules were grazing on the garlic-tasting grass.

"The men thought you ought to pay. I could see it in their faces."

Said he, "The men there tonight sickened me – eternal gratitude possesses no pride."

We took the old path that went over the bridge by the Old Brewery. The night glittered with cold air and light. And, at that moment, a man stepped out of the shadows. It was Skipper Rowlands, the captain of the *Amlwch Queen*.

This was a man I had often seen with my father. Big and heavily-booted was he, wearing a blue jersey and yellow neck scarf. Talk had it that he was bad company; up to his neck in running rum and guns to Ireland.

"A word, if you please, Gwyn Roberts?"

I left them together, glancing back as I reached the cottage gate: they were no longer there. It was as if they had disappeared into the night.

Poll was asleep by the grate with Meg in her arms. I went back outside. A light was dancing on the waves inshore.

4

That summer my father retired from the Smelting and I gave up the dirty old Precipitation pits. We went into carting.

This was before the coming of the railway, and carters were in demand. With Parys Mountain three miles distant from the harbour, everything dug up there – ore, ochre and brimstone – had to be horse-pulled down to the harbour. Smelter coal had to come from even more distant places.

Carters contracting under Mr. Hughes were paid by him at a shilling a ton; we hired the cart, but were expected to buy our own horse, and for this my father had been saving.

So now there was five of us in Three Costog Cottages – my father, Cousin Poll, Meg my baby sister, me, and Dobie.

Lovely was this Welsh cob, Dobie, bought at Llangefni Fair. Great in strength, standing fifteen hands with big brown muscles down his back and thews; his hooves were as large as dinner plates, all ragged with white hair; his mouth was as soft as the inside of a thigh.

He was a grandad and often bad-tempered; his teeth said he was nearly as old as me, but lithe and gay was he that summer day we walked him back from Llangefni, with the hired cart grinding along behind. Done up in our Sunday braveries, my father and I were up front with the reins; Poll, with Meg on her knee, sat on sacks behind.

And, as we came down Llaneilian Road, the doors came open and curtains went back. But my father looked neither right nor left as we came through the sulphur-ridden country of Brickpool: the evening sun was setting, the sea lay before us like a corpse stained with blood.

*

My little sister Meg was growing up.

Aged five now, her wrist bangles were disappearing with her bubbles and coos: nobody could have brought her up as fresh and clean as did our Poll. And now Poll said when we'd done our first shift at carting:

"Old man Greathead's agent came today, Uncle Gwyn."

My father was kicking off boots. "O, aye?"

"About the debt."

"What debt?"

"The eightpence for the two pounds of candles."

His expression did not change. "What did you tell this agent?"

"To get about his business, like you said; that the last thing he'd get off us was two pounds of candles."

"Well done, Poll; a good girl you are," which was a change; lately he had been cool with her.

That first day had been hot on the brimstone, with all the sounds of summer as we came down from Parys. It was a tough old business, this carting.

The loading was done mainly by immigrant labour; a ragged army of men, women and children swarming like red ants. But since we were expected to lend a pound it was shovel, shovel, shovel into the bowels of the mountain, with buckets from overhanging whimsies swaying high, tipping into the waiting carts. And the air was filled with the bawled commands of overmen and tutworkers, the neighing of horses, grinding wheels, and the ragged labour yelling wild Irish oaths.

We ate in a deathly silence that night, with a threat of an eightpenny debt in everybody's heart.

"What did the agent say to that?" I asked, blowing at my tea.

Poll took a breath. "That the Robertses wanted to watch out, so they did; that there was more than one way to skin Welsh rabbits."

We ate in a silence of tinkling knives and forks: currant cake for afters; no wife in Amlwch could turn out currant cake like Poll.

37

After supper I went out the back to the tub for a real wash; pulling off my shirt it ripped at the seams.

Nothing could be kept decent, working in copper: skin chafes, blisters, sore eyes, burned clothes. Most of the working population of Amlwch was in rags – the clothes they wore, once they'd been in copper, were never worn decent again. So, the streets of our town were filled with tattered, broken-booted folks, a rag-tag, bob-tailed army of gaunt neighbours full of burns and chafes; half naked in summer and muffled up in holes come winter.

These were largely the immigrants from the Irish and Black Country hungers. Flooding into Anglesey at a time when we could scarcely feed our own (copper was dying on world markets) they ate their way like locusts across the turnip and potato fields, at the mercy of the Guardians of the Poor.

I looked up at the sky that night.

Moonlight, they say, is the sunshine of the dead.

"How much did the agent ask for, Poll?" I came in and sat at the table again. My father was smoking his pipe in a holy quiet; there was no sound but the singing of the kettle.

"Eightpence, of course."

"Best pay it." I put eightpence on the table, but Dada reached out and swept it on to the floor, saying:

"Listen to me, Tal, I will not pay it. It is not your mother's debt or I would have known of it. She and I starved together; we knew the date of every coin in the house, we wrapped up every crust of bread. I will not pay it, neither will you, or you are not your father's son," which was a bit of a speech for him, and I didn't forget it. I replied:

"But the debt is written. If necessary they will whip it out of us at the Quarter Sessions."

He got up noisily. "They're welcome to try."

God Almighty, I said to myself, and went down to the barn for a look at Dobie, for he was sweating badly: after a while I returned. My father was still smoking in his chair by the fire, his herb tobacco a perfume in the air. Poll was clumping around the kitchen, Dada was white-faced, and I knew they'd been having words in my absence.

It is sad, I think, when loved ones fall out of love. Time was, when Poll first came to us, she was his darling, a goofey for sitting on his knee. But lately she had grown into a woman and perhaps he had lost the daughter he had longed for. With Andy Appledore still in the offing, perhaps Dada was wondering what else she might bring home.

Summer was into us, warm and green; another June Fair came up, with Poll all frills and fancies, being her night off.

"And where might you be off to?" asked Dada.

"Band of Hope," said Poll, sarcastically.

"Very funny. But you'll be back and abed by ten o'clock, girl, or you'll have me to account to."

"To Hell! D'ye think I'm a child? I'm turned eighteen!"

"Act like a child and I'll treat you like one. And keep away from that Andy Appledore!"

They had forgotten, I think, that I was there; getting up from the table I mooched out to the back, and heard Poll reply:

"Christ! There's some dirty old minds round by 'ere I'm thinking . . ."

"Yes, and more than one," shouted my father. "So bring home another and you can find somewhere else to live."

"Perhaps I'll do that anyway," said Poll.

I think I knew then that the rift between them was too wide to be healed, and that no good would come of it.

5

About the time I was rising sixteen I was coming a little warm with me about women, with queer things happening around the lumbar regions. And it was clear that this new comrade possessed something more than an academic interest in girls. So, most hours off, I used to limp with him into the Cemaes woods in the hope of showing him off, since a few stockinged legs had started wandering, with garters of bright ribbons. These, it appeared, possessed for him the same common interest, and it is only right and fair, Andy Appledore used to say, that you should share your manhood with the world.

Here, above the sea, the beech trees stood firm and strong to the wind, a heritage of greenness contrasting Amlwch and its stinks of sulphur garlic.

Nature luxuriated here. Lying beneath a bush with a halfpenny bag of Slip-down ju-jubes I used to contemplate the world, and if Siân Fi-Fi, aged fifteen, happened by I contemplated her in tempestuous breathing. She was the cushiest little fourpenny this side of the market, the lads said: her thighs were of silk, her breasts tipped with honey, and she'd come pretty pliable for a penn'orth of ju-jubes. And I can see her now through the mist of years, lying there in the refuse of the autumns, her face patterned with sunlight. She said, Irish:

"You'm a terrible fella, you, Tal Roberts," for she was as murphy as a spud, though named with the Welsh.

"Hold your hat on, Siân Fi-Fi," said I, "I'm only just started."

"Put me in the family way as sure as Fate, you will."

This appeared to be the general hope, for she was a great talker on the *copar* table where she was employed. And I soon got a name for a sort of Lothario, with sheaves of females following me in the hope of similar treatment. To this day I do not know why I never fathered six out of Siân Fi-Fi (and why she was called this nobody seemed to know) for she married Joey Belcher, the cobbler, at the age of eighteen and in seven months had premature twins.

Sometimes, when the weather was cooler, we used to gather *gwymon*, which the English call flat wrack, from the rocks – a sort of seaweed – and take it up to poor old Erfyl, aged ninety, her great-grandad, for rubbing into his rheumatics. Rub rub rub – hours we were at it, with Siân on his left shoulder and me on his rear, for it do not seem decent for ladies to see the genitals, he used to croak, turning over. He needn't have bothered for Siân had seen most. And, while we were rubbing he used to tell us tales of his youth; of how he was handed an empty sack by his dad and told not to return home till it was full of sheep wool. It took him a week to fill the sack, he said, poor old Erfyl, and he lived off the land, begging his food, sleeping like a tramp, aged five. "And that, I reckon," he used to say, "is why I got the screws today." But he still lived to a hundred and two, which is more than you will, said Andy Appledore, if you keep giving ju-jubes to Siân Fi-Fi.

But there was more to her than garters.

My memories of her are hand-in-hand roamings; chewing, with her, the *delysg*, a weed we found on the shore; eating the leaves of the hawthorne in spring, gasping to the bitter tang of sorrel. Bumbledores we caught between thumb and forefinger, too, extracting, with barbaric joy, the sacs of golden honey.

Down to the fair we'd go. Sailors from the West Indies danced the hornpipe to whooping roundabouts and blasting German Bands; organ-grinders cranked for dancing bears and monkeys. The flares hissed, the caulking hammers rat-tatted from the shipyards on the quay. Blacksmiths struck their anvils, carpenters sawed, riggers climbed like cluster flies against the sun-shot sky.

And best of all was watching the ships coming in and the sailors flooding ashore with ships in bottles, sea shells, fabulous coral, love-spoons, the shrunken heads of cannibals, love-birds, love-fruit, beribboned guitars and mandolins.

All the wealth of the Orient came leaping into Amlwch these days; mulattos with cockatoos and parrots on their shoulders, looking for ale and women, and most Saturday nights there was a 'blow-up down Town, with men like Bob Butt and Dico Canaan in the thick of it with their pointed clogs and fists. And then a race along the shore to Cemaes to get the garters off old Siân; a midnight bathe, or just a solitary laze in moonlight.

Here, according to my father, had trod the early Celtic saints: here had camped the Roman legions under Suetonius and King Egbert the Saxon, eight centuries later; also the Normans under the banner of Lupus and the Earl of Chester. And I would lie on my belly on the soft, brown breast of Mona, and press my face deep into this mother and draw from her tales of her past.

Diawl! Lie on your back in the glades of Cemaes; watch the tracery of black branches cobwebbing the sky. Touch the ancient oaks, feel beneath your fingers the vibration of centuries – the chanting, the lutes, the harps! How many lovers have lain like this and seen this same Welsh sky?

Here the first bluebells, the first wild daffodil! Llaneilian and Porthwen, Dulas, Moelfre! These are the magic names of Anglesey, old when Europe was young. *Ogof Sant*, the cave of holy men; Ffynnon Bwstri, its waters a cure for blindness . . . the sparkling brook of Safn Ci tumbling down to the sea! Here the court of Caswallon Law-Hir, the northern prince my father revered: there the nest of the linnet.

Sometimes I used to sit naked above Porthwen, seeing the Skerries to the west and Ellan Vannin to the north. Sea-pink and golden gorse decorated the summers; Welsh catchfly and sea lavender, lady-trees and moonwort grew in profusion in the woods of Cemmaes.

Lie still. Do not lift a finger. Here comes old Brock Badger, poking at the earth for nuts. He knows I'm here, of course; and he bawled down his set, no doubt, informing his wife and family that here comes this white-haired Welshie from Amlwch, the boy with the old man's hair.

Not the least interested in badgers, me.

I lay on my back watching the stars doing handsprings over the branches, and spare time squinting around to see what this old wood-pig was up to; snuffle-snuffle, snort-snort.

He was old, this friend. Once his teeth were white and strong, now they were but rotting stumps in still vice-like jaws – he could sever a terrier's paw or wrench the spade from the hunter's hand. Give a cudgel to a badger, my father used to say, and you wouldn't see red stockings for dust: give a fox a gun and you wouldn't coax the cowards into donning red coats.

"You'm a greedy old badger," I said, as he licked the last of the sugar off my hand, and I got up.

It was then that I saw my father walking along the edge of the wood.

6

Now, sitting in the wood within a few yards of him, I saw my father lift a telescope and look out to sea. In the moonlight I saw a little boat with a slanting jib-sail tacking for the shore. She came fiercely, with foam on her prow; her keel scraped sand and a man jumped out – instantly I recognised him – Skipper Rowlands of the *Amlwch Queen*. Turning, he put out his hand to another man standing in the prow and helped him into the shallows while my father caught the boat's painter and dragged it to a shore anchor.

Rowlands led the third man up the beach to a sandy track. I watched, and saw my father join them: suddenly the lighthouse beam swept the sea, brightening the world. Although they were now in shadows I saw Rowlands and Dada help the man up the track and then they disappeared from my view. That he should need assistance was in itself strange, for the man they were helping was possessed of a fine athleticism.

Without knowing why, I found myself following them.

The three of them – Rowlands leading the way and my father following with his hand on the big man's shoulder – took field tracks up to Parys Mountain, they did not keep to the carting road. At a discreet distance I followed, always keeping out of sight, for Dada kept turning, almost as if he suspected they were being watched. Past the loading bays of Parys Mountain we went and down the lane to the Precipitation pits, where I once worked. Then, turning abruptly into the shelter of trees, the three of them descended into a hollow that led to the farm of old Iorri Ifan, a ramshackle building being reclaimed by Nature. At the entrance to the farmhouse gate Rowlands turned and deliberately looked about him while the stranger and my father went forward into the house. Sinking lower in the undergrowth, I watched until he, too, turned and followed his companions.

Indecisive, I sat down in the bushes: the silence of the wood, the very loneliness of the place was filling me with a portent of coming disaster.

This was not mere smuggling: none of these men had been carrying anything and the strange behaviour towards the incoming stranger intrigued and frightened me; it was almost as if they were protecting him, and would do so even at the cost of their lives. It was sheer curiosity that took me onward, stealthily towards the entrance to the derelict building, and from its kitchen I heard muffled voices. The entrance door, however, was stout, as if recently repaired: as I approached it down the path night-cobwebs blew across my face; involuntarily I shivered, not with fear but with anticipation, and rose from my crouched position. From the darkness of surrounding trees came a man. He was broad and squat and had the shambling gait of an ape: upon his head he wore a cockade hat and about his shoulders a heavy rug, and in his hand was a pistol; the hammer, clicking back, halted me before him.

"Right you, boyo – inside!"

Through the muffling scarf that half covered his face I recognised the valley sing-song of the Southern Welsh; a long way North, this one, I thought. Then his fist came out and he struck me in the back, forcing me on. Through the door I went with the pistol in my back and through another door into a dimly lighted room of covered windows.

Here some twenty men stood or lounged on the broken floor: at a little table my father and the stranger I had seen were standing; all heads turned as I stumbled in with the sentry behind me.

"For God's sake!" My father's voice broke the stunned silence. "Tal!"

"Who's this?" demanded the stranger.

He was a big man and younger than my father. His brown

hair hung in shining waves to his shoulders, over these was thrown a black travelling cloak, and this enhanced his size. He sat as he asked the question and thrust out long legs, his big hands folded on to a hickory stick, one curved at the top like a shepherd's crook; he appeared suddenly like a giant raven perched upon a bough, and his eyes, bright blue, seemed to burn into mine. My father said softly:

"It is my son."

"But uninvited."

"I apologise to you, Gideon." My father approached me, saying softly, "What the Hell's the meaning of this?"

I took off my cap and screwed it in my hands; the men moved awkwardly in soft-breathing attitudes of disassociation.

"You followed us?"

The sentry said, "Found him skulking outside, Gid Davies," and the other said curtly:

"Bring him to me, Gwyn."

My father, his eyes furious, jerked his head and I stood before the table as the man behind it raised his face to mine. His eyes, I noticed for the first time, were strangely opaque, the pupils fixed and dilated; then I recognised the whiteness of his stick. Blind. He said, and his voice was deep and tuneful:

"How old are you, Taliesin?"

"Sixteen, Sir."

"Then you are no longer a child. You followed us, did you not?"

Earlier, he had spoken in English, but now it was Welsh. "Why?"

"I . . . I was afraid."

He leaned forward, smiling up. "Of me, you mean?"

I looked at my father. "Of the smuggling."

The men chuckled behind me, some whispering. The blind man said, "Oh come! What is a little bottle of brandy between friends? Or an ounce or two of tobacco – the quality's good, is it not?" He laughed bassly, lifting a hand to an attentive audience. "Everybody's at it, are they not? Even the Bishop, they tell me, is a connoisseur when it comes to

46

Irish port!" He beamed around the room. "My young friend Taliesin, if you are as sensible as your father claims, you'll see small harm in a little bit of swag on the side when half the county's queueing up behind the rummy gentlemen!"

"But it is not smuggling," I said.

It silenced them: had a mouse run the floor I would have heard it. The man before me rubbed his chin, his smile dying, then said:

"You deal with this, Gwyn, he is certainly not a child."

My father came closer.

"I'll be responsible for him, Gideon." To me he added, "Take a seat at the back, Tal, and grow a few years older."

Obeying, I sat on the floor at the back of the kitchen: the men whispered among themselves, disturbed, casting glances at me over their shoulders.

Joe Oldfield was there, his skinny arms projecting through the rents in his coat; Ikey and Alby Sapphira, the Jewish twins, and Mr. Appledore, the father of Andy, also Mr. Ifor Owen, a sidesman in the Wesleyan, the brother of the Elder and Mr. Ichabod, the father of my Pru. Others were there whom I knew also, but not by name, and several more whom I had never seen before – men from as far south as Menai, some said – Southern men, too, the followers of Gideon Davies who had settled in the North for other reasons than work. Now Gideon was speaking, his deep voice quiet and purposeful, and I had to strain my ears to hear him:

"As I said," he continued, "the Southern towns are going on fire, and it is only a question of time. Plans are being laid up and down the country from Liverpool to London; the industrial towns and cities plan for war. And war it will be unless these robber barons share their wealth with us, the makers of that wealth. But they will not share despite all the threats, since they had never shared before. Can ye hear me, you at the back?"

We called assent, and he said, "For a thousand years we have lived in servitude – in earlier times in abject slavery under the English. But it is not only the English who exploit us now, it is our own, remember. The wealth of the industrial aristocracy is derived from the labour of factory children –

aye, ours and yours, you who are English here. It is on their blood that float the great estates!" He rose, his voice growing stronger, and he stared down at us with his sightless eyes. "So force will be met with force, we have begged enough. And it will be a struggle to the death with our allies, the down-trodden of the London slums and the labourers of the Forest of Dean. It is a crime, and it will stop."

The audience mumbled aggressively, staring around in dull anger, and Gideon rose to his full height.

"But would you leave it all to your Southern cousins? When the first blow is struck a million men will be under arms in the Chartist cause. Will it be said, when victory is gained, that you in the North sat on your backsides while other Welshmen fought for the Charter – so listen to its aims. Secret ballot at the polls, the right of every man to vote, equal electoral areas – for the boundaries are being rigged – no property qualifications for M.P.'s, and paid Members, too, ones we can kick out annually if they don't suit us. Listen to me!" and he leaned down, swinging his fist before them. "I repeat – will you be under the bed when the time for retribution comes, and still call yourselves Welsh? For we will sweep them down in a thunderstroke, and up here you could be part of our victory!" He was breathing heavily. Not bad for a blind man, I thought; Hell would blow up were he sighted.

"Gwyn!" he called.

"Aye, Gid." My father touched his arm.

"When is the printing press due up from Dinorwig?"

"There's always talk of it but the bloody thing never arrives."

"I will try to hasten it." He unrolled a bundle of literature. "Get these pamphlets out within a week. Pin them on the lodges, on the Works' gates, on trees – nail them to the door of Plas Newydd itself. Let them have fair warning that the North is taking to arms."

The meeting closed soon after this, the men dispersing silently into the night; I was standing at the kitchen door, waiting for Dada when the blind man called, "Taliesin!"

He was seated now and I stood before him. He said,

"Draw closer, lad, that I may touch you," and he beckoned: stretching out his hand he touched my face, then ran his fingers over my features: I shivered, for his fingers, though long and slender, were at the tips curiously deformed; the thumbscrew; the nails were missing. Now these fingers were in my hair.

"The colour?" he asked, staring up at my father.

"White."

"Albino?"

My father said, "Peg, you remember, was Iberian dark – a blackbird's wing, it was said: Taliesin, in her line, is a throw-back in the lineage."

Gideon Davies grunted. "Ah, I remember – Dafydd ap Owain!" He gripped my hand. "That is a glorious line – can you tell of him historically?" He turned his face up to mine.

I said carefully. "It . . . it was he who laid waste the province of Tegeingl before the armies of Flanders attacked us in the hills of Llangollen."

"Excellent! And the year?" Arms folded, he surveyed me blindly.

I replied, "It was the twelfth century, Sir, but I do not know the year."

He rose, pressing on my shoulder. "And now we fight again, eh? It is our Welsh curse, always to be fighting. See that you serve your father well and your country better. And die for her if needs be, eh, Gwyn?"

My father said, "Oh come, Gid, he is still a lad."

The reply was instant. "If he is sixteen he is a man. The responsibility for freedom is ours, his, and all who come after, and he is old enough to know it."

If this one had his way I'd got about another fortnight to live, by the sound of it.

7

Strange is God's behaviour, I think, that he makes mountains of iron, ochre, brimstone and gold; then says: "Now sort that out. Fight over it, dig it, stamp misery on the faces of the poor with it, make the rich richer . . . and put it back into the soil again."

So it was with the copper of Parys Mountain; Welsh copper for minting the head of a foreign queen; copper for sheathing ships' hulls the better to ply the slave trade; copper for tears.

But all Parys Mountain provided for us, the workers, was God's water, as Amlwch called it. In the bubbling red springs that scampered down the hills were gifts of Nature: a detergent, excellent for leg ulcers, a cure for the itch, mange in animals, a killer of worms in sheep and children; good for dropsy, internal bleeding, and the bowels. A cup of Parys Mountain water was as good as a physic from the bal doctors if your tubes went tight.

Not that the bowels were tight that winter, with my father down on the beach every weekend with Skipper Rowlands and still refusing to pay the bill for eightpence claimed by Greathead as a debt for candles.

Eightpence, eightpence, *eightpence*.

The winter went by, though, with scarcely a nudge of trouble in our house, though some were not so lucky. The *copar ledis*, now under a tent, chipped away with their hammers, their hair and eyebrows mantled with frost. Mr. Small, a tutworker, was killed in a fall on Mona Mine and four others with him; we didn't know their names, since they were only Irish. I remember seeing poor Mrs. Small, her black-stockinged legs skinny in the wind, weeping in a feast of indigo.

Andy Appledore, my English mate, got the molten copper over his arms and legs in the Smelter; learning the trade was he, and never rightly got the hang of it, and his Lancashire mam and dad used to carry him round town on a board. Yet he was as handsome as a young lion the previous summer, showing it to the girls. Mrs. Ida Promise went into the family way under Shoni Bob-Ochr, the Dutch Welshman, and Dora Jewels lost her second with a mismanagement.

Also, my little Pru Ichabod died of the chest, and was laid in the warm earth of April; put there by Seth Morgan. Wheedling, nobbly-knuckled and sparse was old Seth, his staff like a flock of carrion crows, and for God's sake get her under quick.

But it wasn't all mine falls, copper burns, politics and undertakers.

There were nights when Dada had the three of us in the kitchen with firelight on our faces while he told us, in Welsh, the four branches of the great *Mabinogi* and other tales from the Red Book of Hergest.

I can see old Poll now, shivering, enwrapped in the weirdies and ghosties, while the night winds sang soprano and hammered in the chimney.

My father's voice was deep, his thick, strong hands held out to us, the fingers curled up into claws. But it was his *eyes*. Like bright jewels they shone in the masked darkness of his cheeks. He said:

"Towards a valley rode Peredur where great pines stood, and saw, on one bank of a rushing river a flock of black sheep, and on the other bank a flock of white sheep nearby. From its roots to its highest branches, a tree was on fire, one half glowing red with tongues of flame, the other half bright green with summer leaves. And, even as Peredur watched, he heard a white sheep bleat, and a black sheep crossed the river and turned white. Then a black sheep bleated and a white sheep crossed and turned black. And Peredur, fearful because this was magic, saw an exhausted deer plunge into the river beside the burning tree, pursued by hounds. And the hounds pulled it down, tearing it, and the whiteness of the river turned to the colour of blood . . ."

"*Diawch*," whispered Poll, shivering more.

I said, "But this we have heard before, Dada. Tell us, instead, 'The Tale of Delwyn'."

"We," said he then, "are direct descendants from bards who sang from the book of Taliesin," and he touched me. "This is why you are so named."

"From Iolo Goch, the bard of Glyndŵr."

"From him, a direct line in my blood, he who told of Delwyn, the tale which I read now."

Taking a tin box he drew from it a little book in manuscript, adding:

"When I am no more, preserve this in our line, Tal, giving it to your son and your son's son, as it was handed down to me by my father, and to him by his father before that, and before that also. Cherish it. But if no son springs from you, then bury it in the soil of Wales, for it is hers, and no foreigner has claim to it." My father then opened a yellowing parchment with care, and read:

" 'Listen. When first King Maelgŵn was crowned, the gods tested him, sending across the Irish Sea waves of hated Goidels, hairy monsters sunk to the level of beasts . . .' " he stared at our intent faces. Meg stirred in sleep. Above the hissing of the kettle I heard wave-crash from Costog beach and the wailing of gulls. My father continued:

" 'Until now kept in check by the Romans, these Goidels came in swarms of coracles, to ravage the fair land of Gwynedd; but Maelgŵn sent a billow of fire over the ocean, and the sands of Deganwy were littered with charred corpses. But twelve Goidels remained alive, and King Maelgŵn, being merciful, set them free to roam at will, first cutting out their tongues so that they would not corrupt the Celtic speech.' Are you listening?"

Later, he replaced the manuscript in its tin box.

The debt is eightpence, for two pounds of candles in your wife's name. Please settle it at once, or you will hear of this further.

Once a week now this note from Greathead's Truck Shop came regular; as regular as clockwork my father tore it up.

"Would it not be best to pay it, Mr. Roberts?" suggested Mrs. Dahlia Sapphira, now teaching music spare time and putting years on herself at the very sight of him. "No point in asking for trouble, *bach* . . ."

Young Dahlia, her figure returned since her chap flew south, was suffering, her mind kicking up its heels now it was spring again: ravished by erotic dreams was she, promising her fancies to get Dada behind the sofa or under the piano by Christmas, and the very sight of her hovering around Three Costog worried me to death, never mind him.

The debt has been outstanding for over six years now, said the final Greathead note. Legal action will be taken unless it is settled at once.

"Oh, God," I said, tossing it on to the table, "Pay it and have done with it."

Dada did not reply, and I pushed away my plate, disgusted. Haricot bean soup, it was, worse than donkey's brains, though Poll did what she could.

The slump of 1838 was upon us now and things were getting skinny. Ore production from the Mona Mine up on Parys was down to seven hundred and fifty tons that year, less than half what it was five years earlier: the 'bargains' were getting poorer, and so were the workers, and Mr. Treweek, our manager, was sending his Cornishmen over the hill, never mind the Welsh; the Marquis of Anglesey, dining off silver plate down in Menai, was losing weight.

"I'll give him bloody Marquis," said my father. "Pining to death, is he, for a few pounds of candles?" Rising, he added, "Ah well, let's get on shift," and he tightened the big belt at his waist. "Coming, Tal?"

We always worked night-shift at weekends, but Dada insisted on doing the final run up to Parys and back alone, and I knew why.

But we didn't go on shift that night. Bang bang on the back, and I opened it. Jacki Scog, the pig murderer, stood there.

"What the Hell do you want?" I demanded, for I hated him.

"Dear me," said he. "Long trews, big balls, is it? It is your father I am interviewing; kindly send him."

Dada pushed me aside. "Yes?"

Jacki Scog said, "Mr. John Hughes, contractor, do send me. Kind of you to report to him at once, Mr. Roberts," and he pulled off the black cap he wore for pig-killing and screwed it in his hands.

"No notion what he wants, Mr. Scog?"

"Just come, and quick, yeh?"

John Hughes the Carter was the darling of our Cornish masters and the ripest Welsh saint in Amlwch, with twice to Chapel every Sunday and beating his wife on Saturdays. A bull of a man was he; bald as an egg and bellowing bass in the Psalms, he had a chin on him like a navvy's arse. Talk had it that his mam saw faerie marks on the butter an hour before she had him.

Five feet up, filling his doorway, he eyed us with intent to kill.

"You asked us to call," asked my father, quiet.

"O, aye!" Mr. Hughes clutched the velveteen lapels of his smoking jacket, staring up. "You enjoy carting for me, Gwyn Roberts?" He had a voice like a cinder under a door.

"Passably."

"Then pay Mr. Greathead his eightpence."

"And what has a Shop debt to do with carting, Mr. Hughes?"

"Nothing. But pay it just the same, or you're out on your arse."

"In the situation in which we find ourselves, it will be a pleasure, Mr. Hughes."

"Right. Now bugger off."

On our way down the garden path of the big house, I asked:

"Who won that round, Dada? Did we have our backsides kicked, or am I mistaken?"

There was an ash beard on the bars of the fire when I got home that night. My father had said he had another engagement, and was not yet back. An ash beard, the old ones said, betokened the coming of a stranger.

With Meg upstairs in bed, Cousin Poll looked washed and perky with a spirited coquettishness, and the Devil himself, I reckon, was down in the cellar trying on pink-lace spacers.

"You like my dress, my lovely?" asked she, her fingers pinching out its scarlet skirt, and she pirouetted around the kitchen. Weeks now, she'd been making this old thing.

"It's all right," I said.

"All right, is it? Is that all? Eh, Lover, you do send me all goofey!" She pouted red lips.

"Look at the grate," I said, changing the subject.

She obeyed, her hands creeping slowly to her face. "*Diawch!*" she whispered, "Bad strangers comin'!"

"Any time now."

The ash beard grew longer as we watched.

"Where's Uncle Gwyn?" asked Poll, fearfully.

"God knows. The whole damned world's lop-codded."

"The world's all right, it's the people living in it," said Poll.

Never having heard her speak wisdom, I sat down and stared at her in the firelight. Most beautiful she looked standing there with her black hair down her back. Of Latin blood was she that night, her eyes sparkling, her cheeks high in her small-boned face.

Until then I do not think I had recognised her beauty: she was in full bloom.

Smiling down at me, she clutched her hands, saying softly, "You think anything about me ever, Tal Roberts?"

"O, ah!"

"I don't mean cooking and washing, an' all that. I mean, like walking me out Sundays for others in Town to see, and have us over – you know – proper goofers."

"Sparkin'?"

"Well yes, really speaking."

"Never given it a thought, *cariad*."

"Dear me," said she, and held herself, "the way you say that do send me shivery. A lovely voice you do 'ave, Tal. I'm too weak now to carry a clek."

I got up. I was worried about my father and she was a pester to me.

"You're a good old girl you are, Cousin Poll," I replied, "but I am too young for women."

"You'd fill a bed though." Dark and sultry she said this, like Cleopatra when the light went out, and she was getting me into a sweat, with shivers under the armpits. She whispered, coming closer:

"Ach, Lover, looking at you I feel like last week's rhubarb. You'm a fine set-up chap, my darlin', my mopsy, my pearl. You do send me all love-sick and spooney," and she reached out and drew me into her arms. "Come to bed for two minutes and I'll show ye which end up ye are."

I thought of my father fine and upright, now perched tranquilly on a pint, while I broke the ropes of Hell by frolicking with a blood relation. I said, desperately:

"Hey up! You've got other chaps on the go, for I've seen 'em . . . there's that Tom Merv Williams and Dai Mount . . ."

"Ach, come on, Lover!" cried she, and pulled me, skidding my boots on the floor. "The other chaps don't mind as long as they don't miss it. Be a Rodney, Tal, shiver up ye shanks."

Bang went the garden gate as I was halfway through the door for the stairs. It was my father, thank God. She'd nearly had me.

Entering with happy gusto, Dada stared at us with mild surprise. "Ay ay!" said he. "The trouble with virtue is that it never knows when it's coming or going. Those who suffer, conquer – remember that." Saying this, he tossed sixpence and two coppers on to the table, adding, "Take that to Greathead's in the morning, Poll, and settle up for these," and he pulled out of his pocket a bunch of candles. "You, Tal, put them up in Nellie's room behind the clock," which meant that I was to hide them.

I said, "What have you been up to?"

"Thrice blessed am I with children who do what they're told – get rid of them, I said."

Clutching the candles, I took them upstairs and put them under Meg's bed and stood there in the moonlight, watching her sleeping face: her eyelids flickered a couple of times, but I was certain she was asleep.

The strangers, not one, but two, came to the house a little earlier than we expected.

Special Constable Mostyn Morris was a six-foot scowl of a man and going up in the world, said the people of Amlwch, for he wore high heels to raise his stature in life. Advertising for a female companion, he got a reply from his wife, so we called him Casanova.

But Morris was no joke on the night he came to Three Costog as Arresting Officer. We eyed each other on the doorstep, Morris and me, cats of a different breed.

"Grown some for sixteen aren't we, Tal Roberts?"

"Gone seventeen now," I said.

"Aye? Well, I'm after the organ-grinder, not the bloody monkey, yeh?" and this he said in Welsh.

"Who is it?" called my father from the kitchen.

"Casanova."

"Ask him in. I've always wanted to see him with his trousers on."

There was no point in taking it seriously.

Like me, I think my father knew that the die was cast.

It was close to midnight. I shut the door on a night of stars and the stink of an acrid, bitter land.

Dada nodded towards a chair and Morris sat. His great bulk in constable blue seemed to obliterate the room.

"You come at a convenient time," said my father. "Say your piece and go."

"I will, Gwyn Roberts." The policeman took out a book and opened it on his knee. "Where were you between the hours of nine o'clock tonight and now?"

"Do I account to you for my movements?"

"You do now. You called, with your son here, on John Hughes Carter at six o'clock, did you not?"

"You're well informed."

"Aye, mun. It's my job. Then you went to the Oddfellows?"

"I did."

"And drank there for an hour?"

"God bless Dick Evans."

"And left there at ten, he says." Morris consulted his notebook. "What did you do after that?"

"What's all this about?" I asked.

Poll opened the door to the stairs, peered around it, and went out again. Morris rose, throwing it wide. "Oh no, girl, come you in! Let the family know what's happening," and Poll entered, made large eyes at me, and sat down. Morris said:

"You arrived back here at eleven, did you not, Gwyn Roberts?"

With the air of an Old Testament prophet, my father said, "I did, and to save you asking, I walked down to the harbour for an hour before that. Is there a law against taking a walk?"

"There is about breaking and entering."

"Breaking and entering where?"

"Greathead's shop."

"What kind of fool do you take me for?" My father rose. "I who've had a quarrel with Greathead's for a debt I did not owe?"

There was a silence, then Morris said, "A fool who will break and enter for a couple of pounds of candles."

"And you hope to find them here?" I asked. "We use oil. There's not a candle in the house."

"You're welcome to search, yeh?" said Poll, but her face was pale.

"No, he is not," said Dada, and opened the back door.

The stars walked in with the moonlight; never will I forget the beauty of that night. My father shouted, "Come on, *out*! We've had enough of you. Arrest me if you have the evidence, if not, shift!"

The door of the stairs came open then and Meg stood

there, her eyes gummed with sleep.

"The quarrelling awoke me," said she drowsily. "Is somebody wanting candles?" and she put them into my hands.

Then the second stranger, Red Bracer the gaoler, came to arrest my father, and he and Morris took him away.

8

Ten minutes after my father was in gaol the Guardians of the Poor Committee arrived in the interests of morality; they hooked Poll and Meg out of our house, and put them next door.

"The chapel Elders have suggested it, Taliesin Roberts."

"Of course," I replied.

"It is no reflection upon your integrity, you understand?"

"Perfectly."

"Will I be back when Dada returns, Tal?" Meg, her hand in Poll's, shot a grieving look at me as she went next door to Old Cog Costog and Betsy.

Bending, I kissed her. "The moment he is home. Do not cry, my precious."

I had been three weeks on night-shift since my father was taken: now I awoke to an afternoon girt with light, for summer was in the hedges with a shine of blackbirds, and oyster-catchers and curlews were shouting demented. I was in the barn with Dobie when Poll came visiting.

Old Dobie was sick and wounded. A whimsey bucket up on Mona Mine had caught him in its swing, and his side was red raw and congealed with blood. Morning and night I had to bathe and bandage him, which meant putting a twitch on him – a cord twisted with a stick on his upper lip to quieten him – for he was as touchy as a housewife owing rent. Then I'd cleanse him with carbolic and soapy water and put on Horses' Ointment, also a cure for breast ulcers.

I glanced up as Poll entered the barn. "Mind his rear," I

said, for he'd flatten a rhino if it came within range, a trick my father had taught him.

I knew Poll had something up her apron the moment I saw her.

"I got a letter," said she, and preened.

"O, aye?" I went on bandaging.

"Come last night while you was on shift." She raised her face with a strange, infantile assurance. Fishing down the front of her she fetched the thing up.

"What's the odds?" I spoke lightly, but I was worried. "For Dada, is it?"

"Same letter as always comes month end, Tal. What you goin' to do?"

"Take it to him in Beaumaris."

"To the prison? Don't be daft! Perhaps he's adventurin'."

"And perhaps you're right." I took the envelope.

"You go to Beaumaris, likely I'll come, too?"

"Ach no, woman. You stay and mind Meg."

She raised her chin in opposition. "O, aye? That be my job in life, ain't it – minding your old Meg! Well, now your pa's gone I'm afinishin' wi' that, Tal Roberts. Likely I'll cut loose and find meself a fella." She sent me a wink. "I could do better'n here, ye know, for you're throwin' stones at it, when I ought to be up an' sparkin'."

"Who will care for Meg, then?"

"Likely you. I got me own life to live, Tal Roberts, so I'm not bothered hot."

"She is of your blood."

She did not reply, but put herself jaunty, and there grew in me a great sickness for my father. Had Poll and Meg not been weighing on my shoulders I'd have left this place that moment.

Not a lot can be had talking of it, but I was hollow with his going. Upon the little cottage rooms had fallen a mantle of grief that I could touch, and I used to stand by his empty bed, fighting tears.

Meanwhile, Poll was stepping it jaunty around the barn, picking things up and putting them down. Now, pouting in a piece of broken mirror, she said at nothing:

"Your Meg anna my business, Tal Roberts, I didn't born her, yeh? She do come from another womb. Moreso, trouble's on its way, and I reckon to be gone before it arrives."

"Trouble?"

It turned her. "Don't you come so stiffin' coy, you know what I mean. Every night I dream it, cold as a witch's hand."

"You're mad."

"Mad, is it? I'm the only sane chap in Three Costog. What with you goin' mooney over badgers an' your dada out nights with rum gentlemen . . ."

"Rum gentlemen?"

"Smugglin' fellas – come on, Tal Roberts, I weren't born yesterday."

I was relieved. For a moment I'd wondered if Poll knew more than was good for her; if so, she'd have put it around Town.

Finishing off poor old Dobie, I left her without a word and walked down to the harbour across Turkey Shore where the *copar ledis* were belting it out and the Smelter rolling her sulphurous smoke over the blue-tinted sea. The sun was hot, the wind kind, and I knew comfort in the bedlam of the quay unloadings; in it one could bury the sense of loss and biting fears.

The scrap-iron tramps were in; cranes were swinging, carts and horses thronging in hoarse commands, chain-clatter, wheel-grinding, whip-cracks: iron for melting into the sulphate Precipitation pits up near Mona, where I once worked.

But more than scrap iron was coming into Amlwch that morning, for it was on that day that I saw Rhiannon for the first time.

The mail packet from Ireland was in harbour, too: a little wide-beamed sloop with brass ventilators and binnacle, snow-white decks and a touch of class.

I straightened, watching, because from her rail gentry were coming ashore.

Every so often we got the gentry in, mainly the Quality from County Cork and Ellan Vannin: coming to do us over here, my father used to say, after skinning the poor Irish of their wit and turnips over there.

Walking daintily in their summer dresses and big hats, the ladies came first, handed down the gangplank by a chap in blue and gold: with their skirts held up and their heads inclining politely to the ragged Welsh workers, they were followed by their gentlemen in morning coats, top hats, and airs of authority: bound for the tour down to the South, I thought, after a couple of days rest at Dinorben Hotel, recovering from the voyage.

Mr. Treweek and his two drunken sons were there to greet them; also Sanderson, the agent of the Marquis. And all around them, as this retinue proceeded, the mob of scorched and tattered copper workers doffed their moleskin hats or tugged their Welsh forelocks.

What has happened to my country? I wondered. Gideon Davies was surely right.

Time was, sprung from princes, we raided English castles and burned the English occupations: at the time of Cunedda and Maelgwn we laid full strong against the Romans and fought from Carlisle to Chester, along Sarn Helen to Neath. Now, hundreds of years later, we were a people in thrall, bowing and scraping to an invading aristocracy put here by the Church, our old Traitoress, and apologies for Welshmen who despised their heritage.

God help us. Our nationality had gone out like a smoking candle.

Rhiannon de Vere walked alone.

She approached where I was standing like an acolyte in white; her long, lace-trimmed gown, well bustled, reached to her feet; a pink, summer hat was lying on her shoulders.

No Cousin Poll was this one; no Pru Ichabod matched her: she was like an Iberian princess bred of a distant age, and moved within my racing thoughts.

Nearer, nearer she came.

I was standing on the cobbles of the Britannia public,

unaware of the waiting chaise and its two white mares stamping before me.

Nearer; now on the arm of an elderly gentleman, she approached, and delayed in mounting the steps of the chaise as her eyes found mine: dark-lashed in her Celtic face, they drifted over me in quiet assessment.

How to tell of her smile, with only words to use?

I was still staring as the chaise drove off; Rhiannon raised a hand to me, but I did not make reply, for she had taken my legs with her.

A quick half pint at the Britannia and I got news of her.

Her people, the landlord said, were up from Dowlais in South Wales, where they were in trade – iron, he thought: her mother was Welsh, her father Irish, and they had property in County Clare.

Let loose a captive butterfly and it will mate with a rare species, I thought.

Dowlais, eh? That's where my Aunt Mellie Williams lived . . .

As fresh as a little girl's pinny, I went back to Three Costog in a world changed from despair to expectation. And in this mood I opened the letter again – the one Poll had brought me – and read:

Rendevous for scrap iron. Menai Ferry.
Midnight. June 10th.

If this kind of thing continued, I thought, I'd never see the skies over Dowlais . . .

9

I thought I'd find Skipper Rowlands, my father's accomplice, in the Oddfellows that night, and I did.

I also found Dick Evans, who had buried my Pru Ichabod and had now come up with another.

She was a perky piece, this new barmaid they called Alicia, with the face of a schoolgirl and a bust full of erotic problems; a splash of crimson was she, serving up the jugs to the beery men. I slapped down money and she poured a pint.

"You got the same colour hair all over, my charmer?" she asked, pouting over the bar.

"Not under the arms." I sank my teeth into the amber flood and stared around the room, I had scant respect for her, having known Alicia since she was aniseed balls, all-sorts and weenies.

"Oho, upperty-upperty are we now, Tal Roberts?" It was like a raven's squawk.

I turned away, and Dick Evans cried above the hubbub, "Tell him you don't give a monkey's arse, girl, including the monkey. Don't you fret, my beauty."

It was said of Dick Evans that he never allowed a virgin in the place and I believed it.

She shouted more, but I didn't hear her words; pushing my way through the men I stared back at Skipper Rowlands who was perched on his pint like a big, jerseyed raven. He nodded almost imperceptibly; I nodded back, and the banter of the pay night beat about us in foul language and curses. Yes, I thought, Gid Davies was right – it was a hell of a place, this copper town, and it needed cleaning up.

Ale was most of the trouble in Amlwch these days.

With a population of some seven thousand, there were over sixty beer houses in Town. And the women took the rub for it, as usual, with black eyes and broken noses most nights, and Saturday a Roman holiday when it came to wife-beating, one of the local sports.

Aye, they took it hard in Amlwch, like in most industrial towns. Skinning the pennies to make ends meet, they were chained at home with children, wading to the shops in a foot of filth and washing raw sewage off the kids. Typhoid and cholera snatched at their children, pigs and goats wandered at will. Never did I hear women cry like I heard them cry in Amlwch, rocking themselves in their windows, surrounded by their tattered, howling kids.

Don't blame the men, said my father; blame Treweek, the manager, and his tipsy sons; blame Sanderson, the Plas Newydd agent, blame the Marquis, but do not blame the men: if St. Peter himself was a tutworker in Amlwch he'd be on the tipple.

I'd got my own views on that: nobody pours ale down a working man's gullet.

We were lucky up on Costog, but down Town rats were scuttling over sleeping babies.

Years after I left, the Education Commissioners said that Amlwch was the poorest place and with the lowest morality in the whole of Anglesey. No hospital existed; most doctors who called themselves surgeons were habitual drunkards who didn't know a scalpel from a saw. The dregs of the Cornish medics, they drew their fourpence per week per Welsh worker under false pretences. One of them, Dan Sleep-Late, they called him, was doffing up the whisky in the Oddfellows even as I watched.

Skipper Rowlands raised his face and flickered an eye. Sinking my pint, I followed him out into the night.

Wider than me, this one, with a strong, square face burned brown by sea-wind; the moment he opened his mouth I knew him for Irish.

"It strikes me you've had a letter, me boy," said he.

"Aye."

Taking it from me he held it up to the moon, whispering, "Honour to their houses, the sweet souls, but they'll get us bloody hung."

"Who's sending these? My father gets one regular."

"Ye don't know?"

"I do not."

"Then keep it that way, so they can't beat it out of ye in Beaumaris."

I said, bitterly, "As they are doing to my father?"

"Ach, lad, you cotton on quick. Somebody talked, d'ye see?"

"Who?"

He stared about him. The harbour lights of the port were glimmering glow-worms in the rising night mist: the lighthouse at Lynas was dousing the blossoming stars. Rowlands said:

"Would I be tellin' even if I knew, ye numbskull? But there's a donkey travelling the area putting all the mares in the family way, and it's either him or Dick Evans." He stared up at me. "Is that enough, or do I write it down?"

"Are you certain?"

"Jesus, I'm not! But in this game there's always a bloody conjuror with his hand in the till and the trick is to find the rabbit."

"And my father? Please tell me."

He smiled at me and his eyes were good. "You'd best know, son, so you can see what you're into. Two whippings on the frame so far, a fortnight on the treadmill, another whipping round Town soon, then seven years transportation."

I bowed my head. "God, what for?"

He laughed softly. "Formally arraigned, formally sentenced. For breaking and entering Greathead's shop and stealing blutty candles."

I breathed a filthy word.

"Aye, so call it names, lad, but it's our current justice. He won't open his mouth so they've got to have him for something."

I raised my face. "An appeal . . . to the Marquis?"

"Appeal to him? Don't make me laugh. Now this letter. It's about a printing press. They call it scrap iron for security reasons, but the lads need it for the pamphlets and posters. Just meet it at Menai and wheel it up to Iorri Ifan's farm, yeh? I'll do the rest."

The night wind was suddenly cold. I was thinking about Meg. Rowlands said, "Christ, mun, they'll not bloody hang ye if you're found wi' it, you know. A month or two on the treadmill at most. Anyway, it'll be crated – how should you know what's in the box?"

I nodded.

"Ye'll do it, son?" He clapped me on the shoulder. "God speed ye, Tal. Roots are there to hold on to in a stiff breeze, you're the son o' your father."

He'd had a few, by the look of him. I stood watching as he rolled off down to Town. Funny, for although my father dealt with him, I never really trusted Skipper Rowlands.

I got old Dobie out into the night-shift carters and began, with them, the long sleepy procession up to the loading compounds. The stars were big above Parys Mountain and the naphtha flares were dousing the moon: instead of waiting my turn for the loading, I went straight on as if heading for Precipitation, and nobody appeared to notice me.

Soon I was alone in the summer night with Dobie: the activity of the mountain died behind me.

An hour or so later, taking east, I went through Talwrn. The wayside cottages were toads ready to spring, their blinkered eyes watching, their roofs shining quicksilver in a weird grandeur. A baby cried faintly; someone loved in a squeak of bedsprings.

Through Llangefni I went, and here Dobie snorted and looked over his shoulder at me, as if recognising his home; on to Brynsiecyn on the back road for safety and I reached the gate that led down to Foel ferry by Menai Inn, which I assumed was the rendezvous: here I got down off the cart and stood at Dobie's head watching the ferries coming and going from the Caernarfon side and listened to clocks chiming midnight. After that I didn't wait long. Not a sound I heard, not a whisper, but a man suddenly leaped from the dark, spinning me sideways into the berm, and the point of a knife pricked my throat.

"Who are you?" A whisper.

Only a professional works this way. Lying in his arms, I whispered back, "Taliesin Roberts, the son of Gwyn."

Another loomed above me. "Where is your father?"

"Beaumaris gaol."

"*Christ!* When?"

"Weeks back."

"Who sent you, then?"

"I've had a letter."

"Your father's letter. You opened it?"

"With Skipper Rowlands, my father's friend."

"Beaumaris, you say?" The man gripping me relaxed. Rising, he pulled me up beside him. "On what charge?"

I told him.

The moon blazed and I could see them clearly now.

One was tall and slim, a man of education and good breeding; his companion was short and squat, his voice high and thin, like a mountain fighter's. I said:

"My father has been taken, so I have come in his place."

"What for?"

"A printing press."

I saw them exchange glances and one sighed with relief, saying, "How old are you?"

"Seventeen."

"You know the punishment for this – printing pamphlets?"

I stared back at them. The other said, "Hanging, drawing and quartering our gracious Queen reserves for treason, lad, and you are pretty near it. Your age will not save you, remember. Skipper Rowlands knows of this, you say?"

"It was he who sent me."

The bigger man shrugged. "Up to you, but die, if need be, to save anyone getting this printing press, my son," and he went to nearby bushes and pulled out a trolley and on the trolley stood a packing case.

"It weighs a ton, or nigh it. Give us a hand, boy."

I did so, and we lifted the case and trolley on to the back of Dobie's cart, and covered it with brushwood from the berm. They faced me.

"Now where to, tell us?"

I replied, "The old farm behind the Precipitation."

"And who is to receive this printing press?"

"Skipper Rowlands."

"He will be there to receive it, because you need help unloading."

"He will be there."

The smaller man groaned. "God help us, they will be snatching them from the cradle soon." Reaching out, he gripped my shoulder. "Go in God."

The other said, turning away, "He'll get a lot of bloody help in that direction – away with it, lad, and get it under cover."

I reined Dobie in and he strained to the greater load; some printing press, I thought; big enough to print *The Trumpet of Wales*.

Dawn was fingering the sky with hope when I got back to Parys Mountain; the ramshackle farmhouse of Iorri Ifan raked burned rafters at the paling stars.

At the farm entrance two men were waiting in the shadows. They started forward when they saw the cart: one was Skipper Rowlands, the other Joe Oldfield.

"You're late," said Rowlands. "Quick, give a hand," and Joe took one end and we carried the case into the kitchen and laid it on the floor. I made to go but Rowlands stopped me.

"No, see this," said he, and prised open the lid of the box.

Muskets, pistols, sabres and two-piece pikes: arms of every description – the things I'd seen in gentry museums: bags of shot were there, too, even mining black powder. I stared at it: beneath it was a little printing press.

"Best you know, Tal Roberts," said Rowlands. "Now you're in this up to your neck."

10

Next morning I saw Old Cog Costog and his Betsy in Town: he was sporting the black eye she'd handed him for tippling it with Alfie Cromwell, the English: she'd warned him a couple of times about his doubtful friendships but Old Cog, the rebel, never took heed of it. "I'm the man of the house," he used to say, "I snap my fingers and she jumps six feet. Aye, a good wife should be on her knees to her husband – 'come out and fight, you bloody little coward,' and she's there on all fours raking under the table."

One thing about Old Cog; like most Welsh poets he was light in the attic, but he never lost his sense of humour.

With them, outside Greathead's shop that morning, was my little sister Meg.

Good neighbours were these two, mark me: since I could remember we'd lived next door to each other and never a dull or ditchwater word over the wall between us. Just the usual popping in and out for caddy tea or a bit of lard for rubbing on someone's chest or liniment for rheumatics; otherwise we kept our distance, like good neighbours should. And she kept quite a good table, too, did Betsy, for Cog earned good money on the engines, though he put a lot of it up against the wall, too, said Dada.

I was up to my elbows in my trews, mooching over the Square when I heard Meg's little shriek of delight and her face was bright with sun and her head fair curls.

"Your Poll's gone, Tal," said Betsy, flat.

"Walked out without a word," added Cog.

"*Gone?*" I couldn't believe it.

Down Market Street that morning the carts were end to end, with stalls going up in St. Eleath's square and gentry carriages queueing at the bank. Beggars were crying for alms, mostly the riff-raff refuse of the South Wales ironworks; legs off, arms off, many soldiers from the Napoleonic wars. And they raised their drum-stick limbs to us as we stood there talking. Meg sidled up and put her hand in mine.

"Aye, Tal, Cousin Poll has made off," said she.

"When?" I asked Betsy, and she eyed me.

"Dirt to dirt, anna it, Tal Roberts? Never did like her, never approved of her. Told ye so, didn't I, Cog? Best off without her."

"God!" I raised my eyes to the sky. It was one thing after another. Betsy added:

"Gone for some fancy chap, more'n likely; very hot under the tails the likes of that Poll, beggin' ye pardon."

"Took one-and-fourpence from the tea caddy, mind," said Old Cog, glum. "Saving it for the rent, we was, wasn't we, Mam? And two china dogs and the bread board."

"*Heisht* you, darlin'," whispered Betsy, elbowing him, "he anna got that kind o' money."

"I'll pay, though," I replied. "But what about Meg?"

"O, loveliest of children!" cried Old Cog, his arms wide to the sun. "'And on that cheek, and o'er that brow, so soft, so calm, yet eloquent . . .'" Bending, he kissed Meg's face.

"Quiet, you!" said Betsy. "Greathead's it is this mornin', not Byron," and she smiled into the sun. "Can't mind her, see, son? Things are tight now with my Cog up on the Mona engines, so I'm due out scrubbing."

"You mean you can't have Meg now Poll's gone?"

"Sorry, Tal Roberts."

We stood in the confusion of Amlwch's sun and wind, the scurrying people, their shouted greetings, the scrape of hobnails, the clopping horses; everybody was in Town that morning, I reckon: racked, undecided, we stared at each other. And Meg's eyes were filling with tears.

"Especially with your dada in Beaumaris, an' all that . . ." added Betsy.

I said, lifting Meg against me:

"We've got an aunt and uncle down Dowlais way . . . I've written them a letter."

"O, aye! We forgot! Aunt Mellie, *Boppa* Williams, isn't it? Sister on your dada's side?" Betsy mopped and flourished, being on the change, and Old Cog shouted at nothing, eyes closed:

"'A mind at peace with all below, a heart whose love is innocence. She walks in beauty, like the night . . .'" and he reached out, stroking Meg's cheek. His missus said:

"Sorry in my heart I am, Tal Roberts. But folks 'ave to eat, see, that's the trouble," and she eased her great fat legs along the pavement, giving Old Cog one in the ribs. "Home, you," said she. "Faggots and peas it is this morning, not Welsh poets."

I stood watching as they went into Greathead's.

Farther down Market Street, in a raven-black clutch of Chapel worshippers, I bumped into Mr. Dafydd Owen, our Wesleyan Elder.

Parsimony in frugality was he, with a brass-bound Bible under one arm and under the other the books of the Slaughterhouse. Seeing Meg and me, he raised his eyes to Heaven and gathered us against him in grievous pain.

"Oh, Taliesin!"

"You ill, Mr. Owen?"

"Sick to my heart, lad. This morning your father was brought back from the prison at Beaumaris; he is incarcerated now in the gaol in Wesley Street."

"For the whipping around Town tomorrow? Yes, I heard, Mr. Owen."

"Have you yet seen him?"

"Red Bracer, the gaoler, would not let me in."

"May God grant you strength." He wrung his withered hands.

I raised my face. "They did the same to Jesus."

"Oh, no!" Censure, deep and pure, lay on his ancient face.

I said, "After my father has gone, we're going from here, too, Mr. Owen. Down south to Dowlais, likely. We have an aunt . . ."

The happy crowds pushed and shoved us in the sun's nonchalant brightness: I thought of my father . . . the third whipping in a month; this time before his own people, and said, with an effort. "No . . . no point in us staying . . ."

"I understand. And that little harlot, Cousin Poll, she has also deserted you, I understand?"

"Her business, Mr. Owen. She's been good to us till now."

Megan sneezed at the sun and I wiped her nose. "No place for her here, either – Poll, I mean."

But he was not listening. Racking his brains for memory, he said:

"I have a brother in Dowlais, you know – a deacon in the Welsh Wesleyan – he serves in the same Chapel as Mr. John Guest, the ironmaster, whose wife is Lady Charlotte, the best blood in England. My brother tells me that they are looking for an assistant schoolmaster there . . ."

"Kind of you, Mr. Owen, but my English is peasant."

"Perhaps so, but you are beautifully educated in the Welsh classics. Would you like a letter of introduction?"

"Thank you very much, Mr. Owen."

I said it to get rid of him, for the mouth often says one thing and the heart another.

It do beat me how Chapel deacons are appointed: this one managed the Amlwch Slaughterhouse, and six carcasses of veal pumped up for the Dinorben gentry come Sunday, plus fifteen ox-tails.

Passing Pritchard's fields the doe eyes of the little calves always raked me; one day we will pay for this, said my father. Mr. Owen's question tore me from my thoughts:

"When will you be going, you say, Taliesin?"

"When my father leaves Amlwch."

"So you will be walking in the whipping procession?"

"Of course. Mrs. Costog's having Meg."

"Then we will walk together, you and me, and I will give you the letter I promised you then. Meanwhile, remember, I beg you, we Welsh should grovel for crumbs from no employer, least of all to the tenant of Plas Newydd. How old are you, Taliesin?"

"Seventeen, sir."

"May I speak personally?"

I nodded, and he said:

"If you believe that your father is being whipped for the theft of a few candles, you're a larger fool than I took you for."

I nudged Meg and down she went in her little bobbed curtsey, while I bowed.

Patriots were all over the place, I thought; one never knew where they'd turn up next. And Mr. Owen bowed back, a man of impeccable loyalty, religion and tolerance: God knows how he ever got mixed up with a slaughterhouse.

11

They brought my father out of the gaol in Wesley Street and tied his wrists to the back of our cart, his arms outspread; starched blood was still upon his shirt from the earlier whippings in Beaumaris, and he moved like a man still on the treadmill. He looked for me among the crowd and I raised a hand to him. Red Bracer, the Amlwch gaoler, after fixing a scold's bridle over my father's face, turned Dobie, our horse, and the whip, moving fast, slashed down.

Walking next to me in the procession behind the cart was Mr. Dafydd Owen, and he said:

"You are worthy of your father, Taliesin. For one so young it is an ordeal, walking behind the cart of a relative's punishment. You consider the punishment unjust, I take it?"

"For the theft of a few candles? Of course."

"Have you considered – I asked you this before – that a greater charge might be involved?"

I did not reply to this.

Outside the Dinorben Hotel were standing the Quality; English mainly, but with a sprinkling of Welsh gentry. These were the people I had seen disembarking from the Irish mail sloop a week or so before. And all about them stood the smelters, carters, tributors and tutworkers; the miners, spraggers, coalers and hewers, also a score or so *copar ledis*, with whom I once worked. And Mrs. Dahlia Sapphira, who once had designs on my father, raised a fat fist as the cart went by, and shrieked:

"Stick it, Gwyn Roberts. Stick it, mun!"

Rhiannon was not on the street.

She was standing by a leaded window of the hotel, with her hands over her face.

Most felons were whipped or put in the stocks on Fair Days. It was a change of entertainment from the bull and badger-baiting, cock-throwing, wife-beating and endless pitch and toss. Also, it instructed incoming paupers of the inadvisability of staying too long in Amlwch, and informed the Quality of our Welsh respectability.

Social conditions were going from bad to worse around then, in 1838. With the ore running out on Parys Mountain, the copper boom was over, yet still the immigrants flooded into Amlwch.

With them came the starvers from Ireland and the North Country, bringing in their ranks the blacklisted workers of the rioting southern towns.

After the Bread or Blood riots of Merthyr seven years back, hundreds of wanted men escaped to North Wales. Under assumed names they had streamed with their families into the copper trades, running from the Usk House of Correction. Undercutting Welsh copper wages, the immigrants would crowd the pavements to see the whipping carts go by, cat-calling, whistling, jeering, the blind fools.

"Go on, Bracer lad – give 'im a penn'orth!"

"That's right, make the bugger dance, my lovely!"

"Put one on his shanks for me, old lad!"

But not today.

Today they were silent.

Irish, North-country men, Midlanders, even Cornishmen, stood with downcast faces; their eyes switching at those around them, the hostile, fuming Welsh.

Returning past St. Eleath's gate I saw the Church of England clergy, black-gowned and twittering like rooks at a conference.

Here the cortège halted because the mail coach from Bangor was coming through. Red Bracer, tiring, gave the whip to Cross-Cut Jack, once an old Landore mountain-fighter, with shoulders on him like a barn ox and a face for chopping firewood.

On our way up to Quay Street my father fell to his knees, finding it difficult to breathe. So Red Bracer removed the scold's bridle from his mouth and gave him a spell.

The sun burned down. There was no sound in my ears but my father's gasping and the cracking of the whip. And in a sudden silence a man bawled with a voice like a siren:

"Is this the best ye can do, Dafydd Owen? Ye bum-faced bloody Pharisee! Is this in the name of the Welsh Wesleyans?" and Mr. Owen, beside me, cried back:

"What can I do? Have I a monopoly on the law?"

"What about a monopoly on God, ye boot-faced, bloody puritan? We'd ne'er stand for it in the Catholics!" Irish was Jobie Quarts, the landlord of the Red Bull in Pig Market. "Ye're luxuriatin' in pastures of devotion while a decent man is whipped for nothin'! Do your job, mun, shout your authority, or we'll come in there an' take it from ye!"

"When the law is the authority the Chapel has none – be reasonable!" The Elder beside me shook with anger.

"Ay ay? Mind, ye did the same thing two thousand years ago, did you not? Anointment don't come in half pints, Deacon, it's penitence or nothin'."

Another bawled, "Hold hard there, Owen, and I'll fetch ye water to wash your hands . . ."

Standing bowed at the cart my father raised his head at this, saying:

"Be silent, Jobie! The Elders can do nothing. The trial was fair, the punishment just."

Halfway up Machine Street, on the way to the harbour, Mr. Owen questioned me on this:

"You heard what your father said?"

"Yes."

"And what have you to say to it?"

"I have nothing to say, Mr. Owen."

"There is more in this than meets the eye, isn't there . . . ?"

I closed my eyes.

The sun stood still.

I was walking on splashes of my father's blood.

A woman broke from the ranks of the people along Machine Street and lay down in the road in front of Dobie;

others joined her, legs kicking, petticoats flying as the gaolers tried to pull them away.

Soon the road was filled with kicking, shrieking women; grandmas, rosy-cheeked girls in poke-bonnets, old hags, the Fair pickpockets; large-hipped worker-women, too, the *copar ledis*, tougher and more courageous than their men. If Robespierre had done the knitting and left the Revolution to Madame Lefarge, said my father, the chances are he'd have kept his head.

Amid shouts and shrieks, they cut my father free of the cart and bore him away, but he fought them and was standing alone when policemen came running to the assistance of Red Bracer: from Turkey Shore they came, men of Beaumaris Prison, and among them was Special Constable Mostyn Morris of Amlwch. With their big hobnails stamping on the cobbles and their hardwood truncheons stuck out before them, they came in a phalanx, scattering the people with short, sharp blows. Retying Dada to the cart, they positioned themselves about it and the whipping continued, until we reached the harbour.

Here they loosened him and he stood bloodstained and swaying. I went to him.

"No, Tal, leave me."

"Dada . . . !"

"*Leave me!*"

Those who had brought a cutter began to escort my father aboard, but Mr. Dafydd Owen cried:

"*Wait!*" and climbed upon a bollard. "It is the entitlement of a felon to address the town before transportation, and I would hear what this man has to say. I myself am dissatisfied with the justice of his sentence."

After much nodding and whispering among the crowd, this was agreed.

My father said then, leaning against the cart:

"Earlier, I asked you if you were patriots, and got no answer. Now I ask if you call yourself Welsh?"

He wiped blood from his face. "Listen! We have the misfortune to be sitting on copper, and it is needed for the

English trades. So our gentry bring in Cornish experts to teach us how to dig it; how to mint it with Victoria's stamp – the Royal Pimp who feeds her penal settlements with our Welsh heroes and makes whores of Welsh women. And we, whose copper this is, have known no profit from the greed save hunger.

"Where goes the Welshman mutilated on a whimsey – home to his wife and children – treated by Cornish doctors I wouldn't let near a horse. Where goes the refiner with molten copper over his shoulders? To the earth floor of his hut – and not a sovereign, mark you, from the Marquis in Plas Newydd."

The crowd thicker, massed before him now; the constables moved uncertainly; Red Bracer fingered his scold, and my father cried:

"Think ye that Anglesey's pensions are adequate? He who makes more out of larceny than Dick Turpin? Silas Bach of Petter Street lies blinded by copper sulphate – a shilling a week after twenty years up on Parys. Cornelius Solomon, now eighty, breaks stones along Machine Street on parish relief!" He raised a fist. "Out of a hundred and five petitions from the halt and maimed, his lordship has granted six pensions, and from these the Guardians have stopped the parish shilling! Are ye standing for all this, or are you fighting for it, like me?"

They made no answer: disconsolate, they hung their heads.

"All right!" Dada shouted. "Whine for alms, then, you apologies for men, but you'll get nothing from Treweek or his ale-soaked sons. You'll get nothing from Sanderson, unless you take it!"

Insulted now, they grumbled among themselves like bulls at a manger, and Dada cried:

"You're being swindled at the 'bargains' and diddled in the Truck Shops – the agents run hand in hand with their master – yet you'll sit on your backsides after I'm gone, because you're a broken people." He levelled a finger. "Have you forgotten Hywel Dda and the hundred tribes? Upon the head of Llewelyn a new body grows in English dust and he'll come and take the streets if you start being Welsh! Can't you see the ploy, for God's sake? The way to kill a people is not to drive them into slaughterhouses, but make them forget who they are!"

He glared around.

After they had taken him to the prison in Beaumaris, I stood there until darkness, looking at the sea. Then I collected Meg from Betsy and took her into our cottage, fed her, and put her to bed.

"Our Dada is gone, has he, Tal?" she asked.

"Aye – natural, isn't it, being his birthday?"

"His birthday, is it?"

"Yes."

"Do folks go off on birthdays?"

"Grown-ups, usually."

"Well I never," said she at her fingers. "Coming back soon, is he, like our Poll?"

"Just as soon as his party is over," I said. "Our Poll's got one on the go as well."

"Will I go off when me birthday comes round?"

"You and me going off soon."

She wept and I held her. Strange are children. She was only seven years old, but I wondered who was kidding who.

After I'd got her abed I went into Dada's room and collected up the things he had left; papers, chiefly; some love-letters from my mother tied with scarlet thread.

Strangely, the little tin box in which he kept 'The Tale of Delwyn' had vanished: I presumed that he had taken this with him, the only real treasure he possessed.

"Goodbye, Dada," I said at the door.

There was growing within me a cold, shivering anger.

Book Two

Dowlais
1838

12

A hunter's moon, fat-bellied after a banquet of summer, rolled his backside along the rim of the Brecon Beacons when Meg and me, jogging on Dobie, clip-clopped up from the plains of Brecknock, heading South.

Above us flashed the cosmic fires of chaos; Pleiades of red and silver; the Milky Way streamed tails across the Universe.

For the last five days we had been at it. From Amlwch town, over the ferry at Menai we had reined old Dobie; down, down south through the forests of Penllyn and Dyfnant we had come, Meg dozing in the saddle before me. Then through ancient Rhayader to snoozy Builth, where the great Howell Harris preached: sleeping in wayside barns and thickets, working our passage on the tin whistle: Meg dancing, me telling the tales of the folk-lore *Mabinogi*, that my father had passed on to us.

At every little market-place we rested I'd tell the *Mabinogi*.

Beginning on the tin whistle to raise a crowd, Meg would dance; then, with her sitting cross-legged at my feet, I'd give them the folk-lore of King Arthur.

Hunched together, squatting on their hunkers, they would listen, and it took them back to the bedtime stories of their childhood.

I told these stories by declaration, striding before them as my father had done in Three Costog, my fist swinging an inch from their faces.

When I'd finished, Meg would go round with my cap.

Thus we worked our way through sleepy old Brecon. On

to Libanus then, and a climb through the pine forests of Tal-y-Bont, along the Redcoat Road, past the Drovers' Arms, through Coed Taff to Garn.

Here stood the cottage of Aunt Mellie Williams, my father's sister; married to a woodsman on The Top rough shooting, was she, and ten years past his grave was her husband, Sam, though still fit and able.

Sitting with his boots up on the settle in the kitchen he regarded me from under shaggy brows.

"You're not the first to come, ye know, Taliesin. Your Cousin Poll was here a while back."

"But she didn't stay," interjected Aunt Mellie, cold.

"And if she had, it's me guess we'd have seen her off by now," said Sam, and he ran his fingers through his mop-gold hair; for a man of eighty he looked fifty.

"No better'n she should be, mind," explained Aunt Mell, "though we be open-minded, b'ain't we, Sam? Down with the Rodneys in China, we heard tell, an' ye know about them!"

I said I did not, and held Meg closer against me in the mild hostility.

Sam stared at me in the flickering fire-light: gin-traps and snares of poaching were stamped upon his face, the cruel lines of pegged crows: I'd like to have known what my father thought of him, and said:

"I'm sorry Cousin Poll's been a bother."

"No bother, but ye've got political trouble up at Anglesey, I heard tell, and we're not askin' for more."

"Ach, lad," said Mellie, plump and motherly, "our Tal's too young for the politics, anna you, son?"

"Cousin Poll was too young for gentlemen, but she collected a few," said Sam.

"Dear me, Husband, mind the little one," whispered my aunt.

To break the silence, I said desperately, "You . . . you got my letter, Uncle Sam?"

"Aye. But the police'd been into it; ripped and torn, it was."

"They're intercepting mail?"

"Aye, so learned about your pa, didn't they! Breakin' and entering?"

"That was the charge, Uncle Sam, but there's more to it than that."

"I bet there was."

Rising, he tapped out his Turk's Head pipe on the grate and I saw the full size of him; a man of great dignity and sinewy strength. Age had left its mark on his riven features yet granted him an extraordinary presence. Turning from the fire, he said:

"Listen. Blood to blood, it is, and relatives are welcome under this roof. But we've enough trouble in Merthyr without begging for more. You heard about the Bread or Blood?"

"The Merthyr riots seven years back?"

"Aye, but still not over, lad. Spies are everywhere. The Chartists are gathering in every iron town on The Top between here and Blaenafon. Trouble's comin' and we can do without scruffs and felons. So let me say this – stay in Dowlais, if you must, but keep out of bother. The pot-houses and taverns are packed full of unionists, socialists and tub-thumping anarchists."

"I'm not staying," I replied. "I am only asking you to care for Meg for a while."

It stilled him and he moved uncertainly: his wife said, swiftly, "There now, Sam – 'tis only the little one, see? Dear me! Wonderful it will be to have a little bonnet in the house again. Soften ye'self, is it?"

Sam moved his hobnailed boots uncertainly. "How long?"

"I'll be back for her as soon as I can."

"You're certain sure o' that?"

"Aye, just hold her for me till I get a start. I . . . I've got a letter."

"You'm stack full o' blutty letters, son!"

"From Mr. Owen, our Elder, to John Guest, the iron-master."

It raised his grizzled face. "For employment? In what capacity?"

"Assistant to the headmaster at the Stable Free School," I said.

"A Free School, is it? D'ye hear that, Mell? Free my arse! Listen, you! Guest builds a school, all right? Then he stops fourpence in the pound from his workers' wages if he's got no children – single men, remember! If a man's got kids he pays more – twopence a week each child. Education, ye call it? For a couple of hundred in a working population of thousands? Let's get this bloody benevolence right, nincompoop! So there's a profit, isn't there – and where does that go? – on sick relief, since they're too bloody mean to build a hospital." He was sweating and breathing hard.

It was an astonishing outburst.

"Sam," pleaded Aunt Mell, "*let it be?*"

"Aye, let it be! Everywhere I hear talk of Guest benevolence! Nothing is free in Dowlais, son, take my word for it. Burn off a leg at the furnace and they trim the stump on your kitchen table; it'll be another twenty years before we get a hospital. They soak iron scalds with whisky here, and take us home on boards!"

Aunt Mellie said, with plump homely charm, "A scholar we have in the house now, is it, just like your da?" A diplomat, this one.

"Good on the Welsh poetry, mind," added Meg, warmly.

"And a situation with the Guests might make a difference, eh, Sam?" said Aunt Mell, slyly.

Sam was rubbing his chin; his mood had changed with astonishing speed.

"Aye, and well it might, Missus. I never gave that a thought . . ."

There was a smell of *cawl mamgu* on the hob; afterwards, whenever I thought of Sam and Mellie, I smelled granny's broth, and now their blood called to me, the unpretentious kinship of true relatives, and Mellie said, suddenly examining Meg's cheeks:

"This child, ye know, has a suspicion of agnes. I'll have to clear that up."

"Acne," said Uncle Sam, at his pipe.

"Agnes," said Mellie. "You think I don't know agnes

88

when I see it? I've been clearin' it up all my life."

"I am sorry. I apologise to you," said Uncle Sam, and raised fierce, shaggy eyes at me. "Meanwhile, the small one stays, agnes and all, but the big one goes."

And Mellie said, "And now, get Meg to bed, Tal. I want to hear about my brother . . ."

It was the look that her husband gave me then; a strange look of triumph mixed with pride: one thing was sure, this one wasn't exactly what he appeared . . .

A couple of days later I saddled up Dobie, left Meg in the care of Mellie, and rode past Grawane Houses into the crazy, criss-crossed roofs of Quarry and the clanking of the Cyfarthfa ironworks; taking this road to escape the cluttering cottages of Tydfil's Wells and Fishpond.

I regretted the decision because the road grew narrower immediately, the cottages thicker. And here, as if barring my approach, a cinder tip behind a brook rose up before me, a sulphretting mass emitting plumes of acrid flame: worse than Amlwch at its best, this; a Devil's paradise of windowless habitations from which peered faces through the smoke. Wan and ill, these; human refuse dropped out of the rectum of the sky into a labyrinth of alleys and filth.

Whispering to give Dobie confidence, I reined him on through the narrow streets and unpaved courts, past whole families clustered together on broken doorsteps, getting occasional glimpses of sticks of furniture and unmade beds.

From these rooms new smells arose to challenge the stink of Crawshay's Works: the scent of newly baked bread, boiling fish, lobscouse. It was an appropriation by the owning rich of poor men's decency: the penury and deprivation of Cyfarthfa stood as a monument to a man defiled.

Bully boys and pickpockets eyed me from the dark corners, the Rodneys of a town bleeding to death: tarts sidled along the slushy roadway, or sold their wares shrilly from top windows. This, I learned later, was the running sore which some called Pont-Storehouse and others called China. Only the dissolute – thieves, vagrants and prostitutes – called it home.

Merthyr was not alone in this disgrace: the rich Sodoms and Gomorrahs of Birmingham, Liverpool, Nottingham and London challenged each other for new depths of degradation in which to plunge the labouring classes. Park's Cellars, known to the Welsh in Merthyr as Sulleri, related the abyss of total greed; the inhumanity of its ironmaster – a crime on the body of Mankind from which the town will take a century to recover.

Yet quite early, with the sun just setting, it was nevertheless dark, as if a mantle of pestilence had fallen upon the town. I saw eyes watching me as through a sun-glass hazed with smoke, soot and acrid air. And now came a roar from the nearby Cyfarthfa ironworks. A furnace went into blast, the ground beneath me trembling and scything into the rhythm of ceaseless hammers. Simultaneously, a nearer furnace was tapped, its molten iron flowing in incandescent flashes – a fizgig of light, gorgeous in variegated colours of red and gold. This blaze lit the world, illuminating squalid places, sending light shafts into the fog, etching into shape the topsy-turvy town.

China, in those seconds of scintillation, was written indelibly upon my mind.

As Dobie plodded on in a foot of filth, beggars, maimed and ill, called to me. Skeleton children waylaid me, shrieking from wizened faces. A relay of drunks now, reeling four abreast along the decaying walls, bawled unintelligibly; one pausing to dance to a drunken Irish tune on a whistle, his hobnails clattering. And, as the sparks of the furnace tapping flew above him, I heard the blasting engines shriek; the clanking of chains, the whirring of the Big Wheel.

Alongside the canal now, its murky waters reflecting the glow, I saw a girl watching me from the tumbled entrance to a court.

Bent nearly double, she was about fifteen, but a cripple aged seven by the size of her, and her eyes, bright in the hollows of her starved face, stared up into mine. Bare-footed, in rags, she was supporting herself on a ladle. And in that radiant moment of furnace glare we saw each other, before our world again subsided into darkness. It was as if she had been plucked out of my sight, but I knew, with a strange certainty, that I would see her again; that our futures were linked.

Now a tattered procession of people were following me: thugs and layabouts hastened out of doors; roughs were shaking their fists. And, as I spurred Dobie, some ran alongside, trying to grip my stirrups: another, braver than the rest, flung himself at the reins, but Dobie shook him off. Ploughing forward, flinging up mud, we galloped now, scattering a band of men who had linked a human chain across our path. Followed by threats and stones, we skidded along the bank of the canal, turned left down Jackson's and over the bridge to the Morlais tram-road, where trucks, heaped high with glowing slag, were being hauled down from Pen-y-darren.

Sounds of pursuit died behind us. It was the first and last time I would go into China, I promised myself, but the face of the girl told me that this would not be so.

And, as I rode away I thought of the ditty about copper-making which my father used to tell, when I was young:

> It came to pass in days of yore,
> The Devil chanced upon Landore.
> Quoth he, 'By all the fume and stink
> I can't be far from home, I think.'

I don't know about Landore down Swansea way, but this old doggerel certainly applied to Cyfarthfa.

13

It was dusk; the stars had killed the sun by the time I reached Dowlais market, and the moon, wondrous in the heavens, banished the hissing naphtha flares above the stalls.

These, stretched with canvas, were end to end across the square in front of Dowlais stables; a sea of billowing roofs decked with flags.

I slowed Dobie to a halt and tied him in a hollow beside the road.

Wool merchants were here, auctioning their bales; pack-men from Pontypool and Swansea opened their black boxes and displaying their wares – silk from Gascony, embroidery from Flanders, ivory from the East. Tanners and saddlers were here, throwing up their musty smells: coopers making barrels worked like demons, their hammers rising and falling in piercing clouts. There were necklaces and beads, amber, sharks'-teeth bangles, bracelets of beaten gold: black men, brown men, Orientals with eyes like cobras', brayed and postured, their hands clutching ornaments of marvellous colours. Chickeners had come, slapping up the small, cold carcasses.

After gathering a crowd at the entrance, playing on my tin whistle, I began to give them part of 'The Lady of the Fountain', for anything to do with King Arthur always entertained them. And I'd just got to where Luned, Owain's lover, was about to be cast into the flames when there was a disturbance at the market entrance.

A lady had alighted from her carriage on the road behind

me. Seeing her arrival, the people hushed. Tall and straight, the lady walked. It was her dignity that encompassed me, not her beauty; yet she was heavy with child.

In a long, white dress, smiling under her broad-rimmed hat, she came, and the crowd parted. A man ran up with a chair.

The lady sat.

"Pray continue," said she, politely, smiling up.

With an effort, I said, ". . . And when Owain came to a forest clearing he saw a bonfire blazing there, also two young men who were leading a maiden towards it, to cast her into the flames, and Owain cried, 'What charge have you laid against this one, that she should die?' and the men replied, 'Owain has failed her. Therefore, under the law, we are taking her to be burned.' But Owain commanded, 'This shall not be so. Let me stand in her champion's place and I will do battle with you both for her.' And the young men, hearing this, left the maiden and attacked Owain, shouting, 'By the one who fashioned us, we will kill thee, too,' and Owain was hard pressed . . ."

I stared around their faces; gentry, roughnecks, drunks. And in front of them, quite composed, was the lady. She said:

"You tell a fine tale, White Hair, but why not in English? Come, I do not comprehend all your beautiful Welsh."

"There is no English version, Ma'am." I took off my cap.

"Why not? Such a classic?"

"Being primitive prose, it is not easily translatable."

"Who says this?"

"My father. He was a bard."

"And he taught you well, for that is correct. Do you know other tales?"

"I know eleven, Ma'am."

"But there are twelve!" Her chin went up.

"Twelve with the 'Tale of Delwyn', but few know of this."

"'The Story of Taliesin', you surely mean?" She peered, frowning. "How informed you are! Come, let us test you in the classics," and the people laughed softly. "What law, for instance, governed Luned's punishment in 'The Lady of the Fountain'? – can you answer that?"

I said carefully, "Under Hierosolym's Law a woman shall be burned and her champion hanged, if he be defeated in combat."

She opened her hands in a gesture of disbelief, saying softly, "Did . . . did your bardic father also instruct you in this – these are annotations."

I nodded.

"A Welsh law, was it not?" It was a trap. I said:

"No, Lady, it was the law of Europe."

"And burnings outraged Cobbett – you know of him also, I suspect!"

"No, Ma'am."

"Shame to Christianity! Shame to chivalry! Shame to England!" She laughed gaily then, and the people took up her laughter. I remember the hissing of the flares and the laughter of the people, and the lady said:

"Well done, White Hair! You are truly blessed. I have need of Welsh scholars, and would certainly like to meet your father."

"He is dead."

"Then to his son I say this – love Wales and she will repay you. One thing's sure – you've made a good start – but love learning better. You are passing through Dowlais?" She peered at me.

"I have come for work, Ma'am."

"Then work you shall have, for there's labour in plenty here, is there not?" She smiled around the faces about her.

Activity in the market appeared to have ceased; the coopers had stopped their hammering: pack men, their wares clutched against them, had drifted in from the stalls, and I wondered who this lady was. She said, turning to Dobie:

"This one is your friend?"

"Yes."

"Like you, he looks in need of a feed. What is your name?"

"Taliesin Roberts."

"And your father's bardic name?"

"Gwyn Mynydd."

"White Mountain!" It delighted her and she rolled it around her tongue. "There now! I knew you for a Taliesin or a Delwyn because of your hair, Radiant Brow." She pointed. "Over there are stables. Take your horse to the ostlers, feed and bed him. And if you yourself have no pillow tonight, go to Dowlais House and say I sent you!"

"What name shall I say, Ma'am?"

"Lady Charlotte Guest."

14

Autumn faded into winter and the Top Town cobbles were glazed with ice: back-door snows were ten feet high, heaped around the clustered terraces leaning shoulder to shoulder against the cold. East winds howled Irish banshees down the alleys of the Dowlais poor. Then spring, elbowing winter out of it, came dancing over the Beacons. Bright and hot came she with cowslip bracelets in her hair and bluebells on her feet; her thighs were cloths of gold, her hair of swansdown cloud.

I love this Wales when she dresses up for springtime! In winter she's frizzed and sad, an old hag wailing among the sodden branches; summer sees her as a garlanded woman, desiring, desirable. But Wales, in springtime, is a maid all dancing, red lipped, with skirts of green rushes and a bodice of blossom.

What place can compare, in spring, with my beautiful country?

The sun was high; warm winds fanned the mountain grasses as I reined old Dobie along the hedgerows of Dowlais Top, talking him towards Pontsticill, and up to Dolygaer.

Here the forest firs and pines formed a block as solid as Napoleon infantry, their tops speared with blinding light. Little waterfalls squirmished in the rock outcrops, spraying arms of joyous water. It was a sun-burst morning of dew wetness, every leaf sparkling from night downpourings of rain. We went slowly, Dobie and me, savouring the scents of spring; bob-tailed rabbits scampered before us, curlews shouted curses up in the blue.

I was at peace, save for memories of my father.

Never had a job come so readily, nor was so easy: six shillings a week all found (and two for Dobie's feed): a little fat cook in a kitchen to feed me on a table corner, a little room over Dowlais House stables, and five Welsh cobs to look after – that was all. Oh, and part-time help to Old Joe Hitherto, the Dowlais warden. One night-shift at the Company stables I did, too; this was no hardship.

Two hundred horses they kept in the Dowlais Stables off Market Square. Hereford shires, these mostly; they dwarfed my cob Dobie, big though he was: horse-power for the ironworking loads on the tram-roads, coal up from Gethin to the furnaces, clay from the brickfields, finished iron and ingots down to the Cyfarthfa canal wharf, all bound for Cardiff and the ports of the world.

John Guest, the ironmaster, hadn't given my letter from Mr. Owen a second glance; things were all cut and dried by Lady Charlotte, by the look of it.

"Name?"

"Taliesin Roberts, Sir."

His agent, Mr. Clark, hovered nearby, but the ironmaster saw to this himself; something he always did, apparently, with a house employee.

"Where from did you say?"

His speech had the right intonation; no trouble with his phonetics, this one: rub him down with a Welshcake and he'd have been a Taff. I answered:

"Amlwch, Sir, up Anglesey way."

He nodded and his eyes were blue in his brown, square face. Handsome beggar; I think he knew it.

I liked him, but not much. He said. "My neighbour, Sir Richard de Vere, knows it well; I do not. Where are your people?"

"My parents are dead." I told him about Meg and work in copper, and he nodded, attentive, saying:

"Right, then, Roberts. Industry will be paid for with money, laziness or dishonesty with discharge. You understand? And if your horse eats too much, he's out – tell him that."

Nearly thirty years older than Lady Charlotte, John Guest was the grandson of a Shropshire yeoman farmer who emigrated to Wales and, with partners, rented land from Lord and Lady Windsor. Useless land, thought they, so they charged him thirty pounds a year. A century later the owners raised this rental to twenty-five thousand guineas, such was its mineral wealth. And even at that figure they were out of their minds, said the locals where I took a pint.

Now the owner of the biggest ironworks in the world – bigger, even, than the nearby Crawshay empire – John Guest the Younger married into gentility; taking the hand of Lady Charlotte Bertie, who claimed she was of the finest blood in England. Soon she brought forth his first-born, a son.

But all was not as clean as it looked concerning Guest, I'd heard. Dai Tomorrow, landlord of the Vulcan and Friendship in Market Square, reckoned that he was like the rest of the ironmasters when it came to wages. He had seen him, he said, with his hands full of sovereigns, holding them under the noses of starving Welsh. Even William Crawshay, his competitor, had claimed that Guest's Truck Shop in Dowlais gave him a ten per cent advantage in trade, for the prices there had gone up as iron went down. "Give me Crawshay," said Dai Tomorrow (who would never do today what could be done next week) "you know where you stand with him."

But the best blood in Wales that fine spring morning was up on Dolygaer, I reckoned: this, the battlefield where gallons had been spilled in the name of Welsh freedom. With bone-cold fingers I reined in Dobie and looked about me.

Here was the country of Tydfil the Saint; there the grass-covered palace of the Prince of Brycheiniog. All Wales seemed alive to me at that moment – Cunedda and Maelgŵn – heroes who had fought the barbarians of Bedd y Gwyddel, the Irish giant who had come from the sea, and been flung back to Ireland by the stubborn Welsh.

The honour of my country rose in me as I stood in that

bloodstained place.

It was then that I saw a horse and rider coming towards me out of the forest:

"'Morning," said I, and removed my moleskin hat.

Tell me that God and Fate are not in service to lovers! *It was Rhiannon.*

So still she sat on the white mare, staring: then recognition came and she smiled.

"We've met before, haven't we?" she said in Welsh.

It was a celebration of love just to sit there looking.

Dobie nuzzled her white mare, quicker than me on the uptake. I said falteringly. "You . . . you live here?"

She gestured with her whip. "Kierton Manor. Between Pontsticill and Vaynor, but you're a long way south, aren't you?"

"You remember me?"

"Of course. Last autumn, up in Amlwch!"

The hubbub of the Amlwch unloading clattered in the ear of my memory. I saw her again, coming off the packet from Ireland; beautiful then, the year had flourished in her, bringing her to a new womanly shape and dignity. I made to pass, reining Dobie up, for he was becoming too intent on her mare, but she delayed me.

"What's your name?"

"Tal Roberts."

"Tal?" Her eyes questioned, laughing.

"Taliesin."

"How beautiful! Fair brow? Radiant brow?"

"Reckon I was white-haired at birth. Started off aged sixty."

She laughed softly, regarding me. "I remember your hair." The mare tossed, and she steadied it, coming closer. "You work down here now?"

"Aye." I screwed my hat, feeling unequal, dying to be gone: dry in the mouth and wordless now that she was near. "For . . . for John Guest – well, Lady Charlotte, really speaking."

"Good gracious, she's my aunt!"

"Good God," I said, faint.

"Well, not an aunt, exactly. I'm a cousin to Mary Pegus, Lady Charlotte's half-sister. She's sixteen, a year younger than me. I stay at Dowlais House with her, when she comes from London." She raised her olive-textured face. "Where are you going now?"

"To the shooting lodge. You know it?"

"Only from the parties given by the Guests. Can I come?"

Above her a hawk was flying in a stormy pentecostal sky; the sun had vanished over the tree-fringe of the forest. Earth smells arose in a sudden coldness. It was as if a hand had placed between us in a mosaic of peering eyes. But Rhiannon, unconcerned, wheeled the mare expertly, smiling over her shoulder.

"Come," I said, and reined Dobie in; and she followed me along the track that led to the lodge.

Rhiannon left early on, but I stayed with Old Joe Hitherto, the Dowlais warden, cleaning guns till dusk, and then took home back to Dowlais, with the pale moon rising up from a savagery of pines.

At a ford in the bottom of Dolygaer forest a man was standing, barring my way: waiting apart, but a little way off, were three more.

"Down off that nag, Tal Roberts," said a voice, and I recognised it instantly. It was Sam Williams, Aunt Mellie's husband.

He looked younger in the red light of coming dark. His tattered shirt was open to the waist; around his mop-gold head was a bright red scarf and his scarlet sash betokened Union affiliation. On high buckled shoes he sauntered towards me, a fine arrogance for one so old, and tipped back his head at a marvellous angle of conceit.

He said, and it was a surprise, "We meet again. Your Meg sends love to you, but I do not, for this is business. Now prove who's best, nephew, you or our fighter, by here."

I got down off Dobie. "What are you up to, for God's sake?" and for answer he pushed up one of his comrades, who complained:

"Christ, Sam, he's your nephew?"

"Yes, so do 'im quick and 'ave done wi' it, Knocker," said Sam, adding confidentially to me, "He'll just bust ye beak, son – it's in the line o' business, so to speak – no offence intended. We want to see if you're made like your da."

"I'm obliged," I said.

"So we can enrol ye official, understand?"

"Enrol me?"

"That's it." He turned to his fighter, "Empty him and have done with it, Knocker, like I said, I'm starvin' for supper."

I weighed the man before me for size; with his bunched fists cocked up and his slits of eyes peering from a ring-battered face, he circled me flat-footed in the graceless stance of the old Mendoza.

"Come on, Knocker," shouted a man from the trees. "He's only a lad, ye know – don't take all day," and the fighter spat on his hands and said:

"God help me. It's the first time I ever served knuckle pie to a nip," and rushed.

I had a left in his eye when he swung at me and a right hook over his shoulder as he blinked: then side-stepped like my father had taught me, as he rushed again, blindly hitting air. But it couldn't last, of course. I knew that if he caught me with one of his swings I'd be waving goodbye with my boots. Over his crouching form I saw Dobie glance over his shoulder at the combat, so I circled the fighter again.

"Right, Dobie," I called, as I got him in range, and the old cob's hind legs shot out and caught the boxer square in his moleskins. Somersaulting past me, he hit the ground at the feet of Sam Williams, bawled unintelligibly, and lay still.

"Christ!" said someone as I went back to Dobie, who was now grazing like a spring lamb.

Sam Williams, holding his stomach, was bellowing laughter, and he spluttered, "Well done, Nephew!", and waved high his hat. "The workingman's union had need of your pa, and now has need of you. You've passed the test with flyin' colours."

"Thanks very much," I said.

"You got the job with the Guests, I hear, and spare time

hobnobbin' it with the daughter of Sir Richard de Vere! It couldn't work better." He slapped me on the back. "Bad cess if you let the grass grow under your feet!"

I thought, my God, who could you trust? and said, "What do you want of me?"

"The testing of ye, like now, for good strong brothers are needed for the fight. All good Welsh are in it, mind – your father, Skipper Rowlands, and the most unlikely people, like me. But you're in the hub of it." He flung wide his arms. "Dear God, it's more than we expected to have an ear in Dowlais House!"

"A spy? The Guests have been good to me."

"Good to ye? Christ!" He stared into my face. "What about the rest of the working population? If ye talk of Guest and his woman, then give me Crawshay! Have ye any idea at all about the larceny of profit, mun?"

"The Guests are more concerned with literature, talk sense!"

"Talk sense, is it? You cheeky young bugger! She's more concerned with chandelier Balls while folks are starvin'!" His face was white with anger. "Jesus, can't you smell the hypocrisy? She's tossing pennies into benevolent funds while children are caught in drop-hammers. She's touring the continent while cholera sends down three kids in five!"

He swung back to face me, his face furious. "Do you believe in the Sacrament, Roberts?"

"Aye."

"Then would ye believe that the Reverend Jones refused it to her ladyship, and that the Rector of Dowlais backed him?"

I didn't reply.

"Listen, lad," he breathed. "In the Bread or Blood riots of Merthyr Town, Sir John – the man you're working for – played an active part in selling out the workers. Guest and his missus, like the Crawshays, tipped up their noses when Dic Penderyn hanged, though Guest said he was innocent, mind you – and all turned their faces from the Swansea transportations." He paused, staring at me. "Did your pa ever make mention of a man called Gideon Davies?"

I held my tongue, not knowing what was involved.

"He's our leader, the Chartist organiser in the South. And the military have hold of him and are beating Hell out of him while we're standing here."

Men came up, pestering at his elbow, but old Sam shook them off, saying, "Gid's the only one among us with knowledge of the Chartist plans, and the Redcoats want them badly."

I asked, "And how can I help him, for God's sake?"

"If he talks it's the end of us, for Napier's Hell-bent on breakin' us before a shot is fired." A pulse in his forehead was beating violently. "So we're after springing him, understand? They've got him around here somewhere, probably up in Penywern, and they'll be movin' him to Brecon Barracks any time now. But, it's the date, ye see . . . ?"

"You want the date when he'll be moved."

"Ay ay, we need the date, the route they'll take to Brecon, the number of guards – and the sweet country will be in debt to ye, for if Gid talks it'll spill the blood of a thousand Welshmen."

"And if we get him out?" I asked.

"Then we'll shift him out o' the place. He's blind, did I mention – he's blind, ill, and he knows too much."

The forest glittered with stars and cold air; brandy snaps of cauldron light were playing red on the pine tops.

"Are ye on, son?"

I nodded. "I know Gideon Davies, the blind one, he is my father's friend. Say what you want of me."

Knocker, the mountain-fighter, was now on his feet again, walking unsteadily towards us, and Sam cried huskily:

"Away, Knocker, away!"

"Away ye'self, Sam Williams!" cried the man. "I'm downing that white-haired bastard and having the bones from his back."

"Ach, hop it," said Sam, "while you're still standin'. Amlwch sent us a good one. You were lucky, mun, you only fought the horse."

15

Summer came flying in over the Brecon Beacons and the
brooks sprayed and shouted down to the valleys. The days
were of blinding brightness, I remember, and Rhiannon and
I walked on beds of autumn gold. Our trysts in Dolygaer
forest were a delight to me and yet a treason of the mind,
because I knew it could not continue.

Watch this for summer madness.

Galloping Dobie up the tracks from Tarn, I took him full pelt
along the bridle path leading to the waterfalls, shouting
aloud above his thundering hooves: and I saw, in a duck of
overhanging branches, Penny, Rhiannon's mare, a statue
against white, racing water.

Seeing me coming, Rhiannon dropped her riding-crop
and flew towards me, one hand holding on her hat, the other
hitching up her skirt: shouting and stumbling she came, and
I leaped off Dobie and she staggered into my arms: flinging
her down into leaves of patterned sunlight, I kissed her, and
her hat fell off and her skirt went up, showing her white, silk
pantaloons. Again and again I kissed her until we were
gasping for breath and then we rolled down to the bank of the
brook where I nearly ate her alive.

Personally, on reflection, I'll be glad when I'm past this
ridiculous caper, for it puts years on you. For those early
days of making love to Rhiannon de Vere were a physic of
madness. I'm old now, my youth gone, but I'll always remember that year of hare-brained celebration, when the hills
abounded with blossom, the brooks sang to the rocks and the

earth flung up sweet perfumes. It was a passion of together-
ness that put out the sun.

"Soon I'm telling them," cried Rhiannon, sitting up. "We
can't go on like this!"

One moment a lady, next a village girl; this was her
charm. Her lips moved over my face, my hair. I did not
speak. It was enough just to lie like this in her warmth, and
her breast was soft under my head. She said, leaning above
me:

"I am, Tal, I'm telling them. What matter where you
come from, or I? I'm shouting this love to the world."

I replied, "Yes, then I'll land in gaol and you in a French
convent."

I held her against me. There was no sound on the forest air
but the songs of blackbirds.

"I don't care. I'm telling them!" And she suddenly
pushed herself up and stared down into my eyes.

"No," I said, turning away.

A silence came between us; even the blackbirds cocked up
ears, I reckon.

"No, Rhia," I said, trying to sit up, but she pushed me
back.

"Please, Tal . . . ?"

I fought the tumult, for there was a stiffness in my loins
and great wish to be one with her, my body saying one thing
and my good sense another.

Nothing that had happened to me before had been like
this: no Siân Fi-Fi could invade this pure longing; there was
a dryness in my throat and a forging of my loins in heat and
strength, and Rhia knew of it.

"Please love me, Tal . . . please? Nobody will know."

Somewhere amid the tempest of our breathing I heard a
twig snap and the echo died in my head without recognition.
Footsteps crunching forest leaves I heard next above the
cascading music of the falls, yet still did not heed the warning. Instead, I heard myself say faintly:

"No, Rhia . . . *no!*"

Her hands moved over me.

"*Tal!*"

I thought: I'm taking this one away: she is right, this can't continue. I'll take her to where only time and space exists, under the indifference of a foreign sky . . . somewhere away from class and convention I will take her.

I thought, too: it is my fault, this: I had ensnared her with the poetry of love; I had opened my heart to her, and now she had entered, I was rejecting her. Opening my eyes I stared at the tangleweed of branches above us, seeking escape in light shafts filtering down through the growing dusk: again I heard the approaching footsteps, and again rejected them.

"You all right, Miss de Vere?" asked Old Joe Hitherto, sod him, his boots two inches from my head.

Five feet up, worn with age and care, Old Joe drooped in his moleskin jacket before us, and thank God we were decent. With a pair of conies swinging at his belt, he stared down, then pulled off his cap, and grinned, exposing broken, yellow teeth.

"You restin', you two?" asked he. "I reckon you both look fair done up . . ."

Rhiannon came first to her senses and stood, brushing leaves from her skirt.

"Not resting, old Joe. We were making love – kissin' sweet – like Maypole dancing, you know? – Tal Roberts and me."

"*Rhia!*" I whispered.

"Dear me, that anna right, lady!" He wagged a disapproving finger. "You must 'ave made a mistake, I fancy. You be gentry, he be any ole boot leather."

But she bent closer, for him to get the sense of it, and whispered secretly, "Kissing, Joe, *real kissin'*. Tal Roberts is my chap, boot leather or not. You understand?"

"Well, damn my backside," said Old Joe, scratching it, and stared from one to the other of us.

"Rhia, for God's sake . . . !"

She replied, cool. "Best they know, and the sooner the better. You see, Mr. Hitherto . . ." and she gave him village girl talk so that he would understand the better, "I fancy I'm marryin' ole Tal Roberts, an' going to live wi' him in the ostlers' loft, him on the horses, me doin' the hens."

"*Dammo di,*" whispered Joe, and got going.

I said, "What's wrong with you, for God's sake? Are you mad?"

"Saner than you." She picked up her crop and swung herself side-saddle on the mare, smiling down.

"Maybe you're not havin' me, chap, but I'm havin' you. I anna milking babies on the wrong side o' the blanket."

I stood watching as the mare picked a path through the forest.

16

Ostling nags being a thirsty old business, I used to polish a pint or so some nights down the Vulcan and Friendship in Market Square and listen to the political speeches, like hanging Queen Victoria and bombs under Parliament, all Members present. And I was just killing a quart one dusk when Fanny, our new maid in Dowlais House, came rushing into the tap, telling me I was wanted up there right away.

"Who by?" I asked.

"Her ladyship," said she, screwing up her pinny, and it is astonishing to me how a pair of trousers and a wink have an effect upon them. Lavish in the buttocks, smelling of lavender was Fanny, and blushing red. She added:

"Brainy it do look, mind – Welsh bards and a Justice of the Peace – rather you than me, Tal Roberts."

In the hall of the big house Maria, aged four, came up with Ivor and Katherine in the pram, and I kissed them one by one, Maria being the image of Lady Charlotte.

"Roberts 'as come, your ladyship," announced Fanny, and pushed me in.

Entering the large, ornate drawing-room with its chandeliers and palms, I bowed to three gentlemen sitting before me, and Lady Charlotte said:

"Roberts, this is Mr. Justice Bosanquet, the Reverend John Jones, Fellow of Jesus College, and the Reverend Thomas Price."

Stiff as ramrods they sat, the Judge in the middle.

Mr. Jones I had seen before, the Oxford don famous for his Welsh scholarship, whose bardic name was Tegid: for this man my father had shown the greatest respect. The Judge raised his paunched, sallow face to mine.

But a few years back, at the trial of the Merthyr rioters, this one had sentenced an innocent Dic Penderyn to die, and I reckon he had an eye for a Welsh patriot. Over his shoulder I noticed Sir John Guest and Clark, his agent, poring over books, disinterested.

"You would like to sit, Taliesin?" Milady sometimes called me this.

"Rather stand, Ma'am."

She spread wide her black gown, smiling up at me. "I expect you're wondering why I've sent for you? To learn more of the 'Tale of Delwyn' – does this surprise you?" She warmed to me. "Remember we once discussed it?"

I nodded.

"Tegid and Mr. Price are my Welsh teachers, and naturally interested."

The two bards gave me kindly nods: Justice Bosanquet was staring at me like a ferret at prey. Standing there in my moleskin trews and muddy boots I felt insecure and unequal, and was dying to be away. But more, there was an inexplicable knowledge growing within me . . . that my destiny was linked with the magistrate. Lady Charlotte continued:

"We are planning to publish an English translation of the *Mabinogi* and other stories from the Red Book of Hergest – you know of this, of course."

I nodded.

"These gentlemen will translate it, and I will help – I'm still receiving Welsh lessons, as you know – but we will have a beautiful production. Now, Tal, Mr. Jones here thinks that you are confusing your 'Tale of Delwyn' with the 'History of Taliesin' . . ."

Mr. Price, the younger of the bards, smiled at me. "It's a reasonable mistake; Taliesin meaning Radiant Brow, Delwyn meaning Fair Brow."

"Oh no, Sir," I answered. "They are quite different manuscripts."

"And from where have you heard of such a manuscript? A modern tale, you mean?" The Judge asked this, his manner bored.

"No, Sir. Fourteenth-century."

"Come, lad, don't be ridiculous!" He clapped his hands together in disbelief. "You are close to the era of the *Mabinogi*. Had there been such a manuscript we would know of it!"

I said, "It exists. My father owns it."

It sat them up. Even John Guest and his agent raised their heads, and the former said sardonically, "A few more years, my love, and this one will give performances – like your French scholar Vicomte de la Villemarqué; he also makes up that which he does not know."

But his wife didn't appear to hear this. Staring at me, she said softly, "Your father possesses a fourteenth-century manuscript?"

"Yes, Milady."

"You have seen it?"

"Oh yes."

"How came he by it?"

"It was handed down through our family."

"It is in modern writing – a transcript, you mean?"

"No. It is in the original Celtic script."

Bosanquet rose to his feet. "I do not believe this. Like Villemarqué's *Chevalier au Lion* it will be a copy, and of some modern yarn, I vow. How would we not possibly know of it?" He swung to John Jones. "What say you to this nonsense, Tegid?"

The clergyman was deep in thought. "It is possible."

"But highly improbable," added Mr. Price.

They were momentarily silenced. Beyond the window that faced the Works a furnace was going into blast: pygmy workers danced against a pulsating redness as the bungs were poured: the sudden beating of drop-hammers forbade coherent thought: Sir John was first to speak. "It becomes astonishing, gentlemen, when we have to approach the lower orders of the Welsh *Literati* to discover original manuscripts. Take my tip and send him back to grooming."

Bosanquet added, picking up his hat and stick, "Like the *Mabinogi* itself, I suggest, there's a happy application of wishful thinking in all this." With mock servility he bowed, adding to me, "I take it that we can see this mysterious document?"

"Perhaps," I replied. "I do not know."

"He does not know," the magistrate repeated, and turned to go. "It is in your father's possession, you said?"

"Yes, Sir."

"And where is your father now?"

I took a breath. "In Van Diemen's Land."

All but Bosanquet appeared shocked; he asked, "Where your father at present resides, I assume?" A small, cynical smile was playing on his thin mouth.

I nodded.

"He emigrated?" asked Mr. Clark, the agent. "You . . . you mean that he has obtained a post in Australia?"

I didn't reply immediately and the Judge smoothed his foot on the carpet, saying quietly, "You'd be wise to look a little deeper into this, Sir John . . ."

"You mean he was transported, don't you?" said Lady Charlotte.

"Yes, Ma'am."

"For what crime?"

"For stealing candles."

"Really, and for how long?"

"Seven years." I added. "I have since heard that he has died."

"How many candles, for God's sake?" asked Mr. Clark.

"About two pounds."

They looked at one another. Justice Bosanquet said blandly, "For stealing a couple of pounds of candles he is transported for seven years to the Colonies, taking with him a fourteenth-century manuscript! We are now in the realms of airy nonsense!"

John Jones rose to his feet. "No wait – this is of literary importance and I want some answers."

"So do I," said Bosanquet, and the clergyman turned to me.

"The reason why your father went to Van Diemen's Land is immaterial to me. But this . . . this fourteenth-century manuscript – he took it with him?"

"I believe so, it was not among the things he left behind."

"And this . . . this 'Tale of Delwyn' – do you know it in detail?"

"Oh yes," I said. "My father often read it to us."

"Will you tell it to us now?" asked Lady Charlotte.

"If you wish."

Reluctantly, the Judge resumed his seat: the other five sat on the scarlet-cushioned chairs, staring up at me. I will always remember them sitting there, waiting in a sort of resignation to a coming disbelief.

"Please sit, Taliesin," said Lady Charlotte.

I shook my head, and began:

"Once, long ago, in the castle of Deganwy, Maelgŵn, King of Gwynedd, held a banquet. And while his guests tore venison and swilled it down with mead, one of his bards, after extolling the greatness of his king, told this story, which is the 'Tale of Delwyn'."

My mind reached back to the winter fires of Three Costog: I heard again my father's voice and saw his eyes shadowed in the lamplight.

I continued, "When Maelgŵn was crowned, said this bard, the gods tested him, sending across the Irish Sea waves of Goidels to ravage Gwynedd. But Maelgŵn sent a billow of fire and the sands were littered with charred corpses: only twelve Goidels remained alive, and the king, being merciful, set these free, first cutting out their tongues that they should not corrupt the Celtic speech."

Lady Charlotte gasped, and I said:

"But all this was untrue; the bard was lying. Maelgŵn, of Roman blood, was a despot, and the true Welsh beyond his borders were planning his downfall: the chief plotter was one, Prince Arfon, and Maelgŵn, seizing him, imprisoned him without food in a dungeon after blinding him under torture to reveal the names of his accomplices. Prince Arfon would have died had not bees, hiving near, swarmed through his prison bars and fed him with their honey."

The furnaces simmered beyond the windows; red light glowed within the room. I said:

"Now, among the leaders of the prince's followers were

the bard White Mountain and Delwyn, his son, who was white-haired at birth, hence his name. Travelling to Deganwy, Delwyn entered the court of King Maelgŵn and obtained his favour, for the king had an eye for a pretty youth, as had Marged, his sister, who, seeing Delwyn enter as a page, immediately fell in love with him.

"Because of his white hair the Princess Marged called him '*Fy Machgen Gwyn*', and the two became lovers."

Fanny entered, bringing tea; nobody served it. I said:

"As a spy within Maelgŵn's court, Delwyn learned of Prince Arfon's removal to Deganwy town for public execution, and he and his father and other patriots rescued him from his captors and brought him back to his own people; even Princess Marged helped to secure his release.

"Then the bards, once men of peace and now led by White Mountain, attacked the kingdom of Maelgŵn, to bring it down and restore to Gwynedd the rule of justice, but the rebellion failed. The bards were routed and White Mountain killed: and Delwyn was brought before King Maelgŵn who smote him with an axe, disfiguring him and banishing him to a foreign land for twenty years."

There was a long silence, then Lady Charlotte said, "It is a sad and terrible story. What of the Princess Marged?"

I replied, "To expiate her brother's cruelty she fled to a lowly place, there to work among the villagers, who were suffering from the Yellow Pestilence."

"And her end?" asked Mr. Price.

"She caught the plague, and died. But first gave birth to Delwyn's daughter."

Mr. Jones observed, quietly, "It is a good story and it rings of the truth, were it not for its contrived ending." He stared with large, serious eyes at the window.

"Your opinion?" asked Lady Charlotte of Mr. Price, whose bardic name was Carnhuanawc: he shrugged. "It is typical of the period, bloodthirsty and dramatic, but I doubt its authenticity."

Justice Bosanquet reached again for his hat and stick. "For my part I'd heard enough halfway through it. White-haired boy; it appeared to me that you might have been foretelling your own fate. I am much more interested in the identity of your father's crime. Meanwhile, you should not be employed by the gentle people of this house.''

Lady Charlotte waved a dismissive hand.

The long-pay furnace men were coming off day-shift as I left
Dowlais stables that dusk – the red-eyed ballers, puddlers
and rodders who ran their own furnaces and did their own
accounts; more, they employed their own labour. If these
dropped tools the Dowlais production stopped. Crawshay
and Guest were in constant competition for world markets,
but also for men like these, and the workers knew it.

Things were becoming skinny in the iron trade about now,
and with the lease of Dowlais running out, talk had it that
there was trouble between John Guest and Lady Charlotte.
I'd heard rumours, but discounted them, that he had cut her
out of his Will, and the speculation in Town was why? So
many of these specialist tradesmen were leaving Merthyr for
Rhymney, where employment seemed more secure. Jake
Kilrain, the six-foot seven-inch puddler was one of these,
and he gave me a wink as he passed me down High: behind
him mooched his labourer, Knocker, who was fighting twenty rounds that night with Borer Deal over in Pontypridd, and
was due for a shellacking if he didn't keep off the gin.

"Hey, Tal – old Sam wants you!" he shouted.

"What for? I'm just off out."

The men pushed and shoved along the pavement, their
iron-tipped boots clattering; shouting their banter up at the
windows where buxom wives leaned out, and getting as good
as they got. Children came running down the streets to greet
them. Knocker said:

"It's important, son, get going. The Guests won't thank ye
for tuning up their gentry virgins, ye know, they keep their

pigs in styes. Good news, lad – you'll be better off with Sam – and take that apology of a horse, for ye'll need him."

I gripped his arm. "Good news?"

"You'll find Sam waiting in the yard of The Welsh Oak, and for God's sake don't mention that he's found your blood relation." His battered face puckered up into a smile.

"Who?" I got him by the coat and shook him to rattle. "Who, Knocker?"

"If I tell ye that, son, you'll be as wise as me," and he shook me off. "Meanwhile, if she asks ye to the Ball, send me an invitation?"

The stars were big over Dowlais Top as I wheeled old Dobie over Market Square and trotted him up Charlotte Street to the Oak. Sam was there astride his old Welsh cob, once a barge horse. I cried:

"Knocker said you've found one of my relatives!"

"Bide yersel', wee Tal." He reined up and trotted off, me after him.

"Sam, please! Who?"

"Jesus, mun, would ye have me spill it all over Town? That Knocker's got too much jaw, and the chances are young Borer Deal, the English Terror, will ease it for him."

"Poll, do you mean?"

"Learn to wait and cure impatience. Grief, you're a hot-blood!"

"My father, then?" I was desperate to know.

"Now, how in Hell can your pa rise from the grave in Australia?"

I sat there fuming. "You're a wicked old sod," I said.

"That's putting it mildly," said Sam.

Here, approaching Llangynidr Mountain the land was like the lunar country of the stars, and Sam knew the sheep tracks like the veins in his arm, leading us over broad escarpments and down defiles. Heather abounded, and hunchback trees crippled by the winter gales: nothing moved save the occasional scampering of hares and rabbits, but fierce things were shrieking in the dark, right music for a funeral cortège.

I think I knew where Sam was taking me; whispers had it that renegades and wanted men were hidden in these parts. The moon came out, resplendent and full, lighting the dull forbidding panorama.

"I'm takin' ye to your father, me son. Now then, what d'ye think o' that? Rose from the grave in Van Diemen's Land!"

I reached out and caught his bridle, pulling us to a stop.

"Dada? You're mad!"

"Unless it's a mistake, but I doubt it. The age of miracles, young Tal, is not past – come shake off."

Reaching a cave entrance, one half-submerged in earth and shadow, Sam halted as a sentry came out of the ground like a black apparition; I heard the click of a musket cock.

"Who's there?"

"Sam Williams, and the Roberts lad," whispered Sam.

"Down off those nags, the lads'll take them," and we followed the sentry down an incline into the cave entrance. Here was a light-lock, because, although I could hear distant voices, no light emerged. The man dropped to all fours and called down a hole, "Ifor, are ye on?"

"Aye, Shanco!" came a faint reply.

"Throw the rope in, I'll send the lad first, and there's an old 'un coming after. He'll need a tie in case he gets stuck."

Three men were now standing about us, their features distorted in a faint, wavering light; then a rope snaked from nowhere and struck my legs. The sentry said, "Now listen, you – ceiling to floor is thirteen inches high – are ye a collier?"

"No," I replied.

"Then ye aren't going to like it. Lead with ye arm and the boys'll pull you through, and if the roof grips your arse, don't panic. If you panic and fight it you'll swell, understand?"

I nodded and went full length: my eyes, growing more accustomed to the intense darkness, were fixed upon a distant faint glow of light. As I inched forward I heard the sentry say, "And you anna going at all, old man; we've had younger than you die in there."

"You try and bloody stop me," said Sam.

The men behind me chuckled gutturally: the hole, over three feet wide, gripped my buttocks as I squirmed forward; momentarily stuck, I held my breath, and then a hand gripped my wrist and hauled me through into a cave of blazing light. On my knees I looked about me, shading my eyes, and my father came forward from a group of men and took me into his arms. Unspeaking, he just held me, then said softly:

"No, Tal, no – men are watching."

He was older: the months of his absence had stripped him of his fine presence; he was somehow diminished, his features gaunt, his cheeks haggard. But his eyes still shone with the old substantial fire. Nor had his strength deserted him, though his rags of clothing drooped, and his wrists and ankles, I noticed, were still chafed raw by the manacles and leg irons.

Many men were there, standing in respectful silence or talking together in an air of disassociation.

"But how long have you been here?" I gasped eventually.

"Only a week – I got word to Sam as soon as I could. How's Meg, and Poll?"

Sam, easing through the light-lock, got to his feet and said, "Meg's with us, Gwyn – your Poll's doin' fine – aye, fine – got housework down Pen-y-darren." They spoke more but I did not hear them: the knowledge that he was safe swept over me in waves of intensity. I cried, "But how, Dada, how?"

He told me that he had never been shipped to Van Diemen's Land: of how, after months in Beaumaris, he had escaped along the road to the Swansea Bridewell, where he was to await the prison ship: the Redcoat guard, he said, had been attacked and overwhelmed by Top Town unionists and they had pulled him out of the prisoners' cart and smuggled him up and into the Rhondda through Pontypridd; there, in hiding, they had brought in a blacksmith to strike off his fetters – he and five others, one a woman, he said – and then walked them by night over the hills and into the caves of Llangattock: two days there, and then to Mynydd Llangynidr.

Behind my father, as he talked, I saw a dozen or so men sitting at tables in the cavern; stripped to the belts, they were silently working; balling shot, pouching black powder: two more, a little distance off, were machining pistol barrels – gunsmiths – North-country men by their speech, brought down for the trades. Sam interjected:

"Christ, if Brecon Barracks comes in here they'll swing the lot of us – is there any other way out?"

"Several," said Dada, "providing you know where." He asked me:

"Are you working in Merthyr, Tal?"

I explained about the ostling.

"And he's not mixed up with this lot, Sam?" he asked next.

There was a silence. My father said, "So he is, eh? Sam, where's the sense in it? I've no woman – one for the rebellion, the other for work – that's the rule – or the rest of the family starves . . ." he stared at us, one to the other. Sam said:

"Ach, come, Gwyn, see sense! Did ye expect the boy to sit on his arse when his father's gone to transportation? He told me what Gideon said, and Gid was right."

"And Gideon's been taken now, they tell me."

"Aye, poor Gid – these months back. They say he's up in Penywern, but I've got me doubts. One thing's sure, they'll be hitting lumps off of him." Sam added, "He left for the Forest of Dean and the English picked him up on the road."

A black-maned giant with a fist like a ham came up and barged between us, saying, "Ay ay, perish the privileged orders, death to the bloody aristocracy. Now will you lot put a pin in the arse and let's get back to work?"

"Who the Hell are you?" whispered Sam, pushing Dada aside.

"I'm the foreman of this lot and it isn't a vicarage tea-party – out, old man, and take the lad with ye!" and Sam cried:

"And may I ask who ye think you're talking to?" He jerked a thumb at Dada. "You might be foreman o' this bloody stye, but you're standin' in the presence of the North-ern representative – this is Gwyn Roberts, mun, next in line to Gideon Davies."

"If he don't bloody say, I don't bloody know, do I?" The big man nodded at my father. "You should talk more, Mr. Roberts. I'll fetch ye some decent clothes."

"It's the autocracy of the working classes," said Sam, and gripped my shoulder. "I'll send ye the time and place so you can chair the next meeting, Gwyn. Come on, you," and he turned me. "Are we hanging around here all day?"

My father did a strange thing then; he kissed me.

The night wind was cold on my face. I was glad it was raining.

We hadn't got twenty yards on the horses when a voice called:

"Iestyn! Hurry, they're leaving . . .!"

Sam reined in his cob as we heard running footsteps in the heather, and there came from the dark a young man; broad and tall was he, and in the rain his hair was comically tufted. "Are you happening down Nantylgo way?" he asked Sam.

"We're not, we are Dowlais," replied Sam, regarding him. And then he saw the envelope clutched in the young man's hand. "But, if it's a letter for a dearly beloved, we'll get it through – runners are comin' and going, ye see."

He took the letter and put it in his pocket. The young man said, "Give it to my sister, Morfydd Mortymer, she's with my wife and my mam in the Bailey Houses down Furnace Row – but don't say where it comes from, mind."

"Leave it to us, son," said Sam, and we rode away without a backward look.

But on a ridge I reined in Dobie and glanced back.

The young man was still standing there, watching us in the rain.

The afternoon I had off was cold, as if autumn had blown an arctic breath over the mountains, and amazingly, the hills of Dowlais Top were white and beautiful in the mornings like Church of England brides.

I sat on Dobie in the cobwebbed whiteness of Dolygaer, waiting, and he raised his head and neighed, seeing Rhiannon coming on her mare against brilliant light; the sun had melted the morning frosts.

My excitement increased when I saw her coming and I was dying to tell her that my father was safe, but dared not. Side-saddle, she joined me and we rode side by side, unspeaking in an affinity of silence. But after a bit, she said:

"You're lost to me. What's wrong?"

I was thinking of Dada, but said, "I was wondering if you'd be going to the Dowlais House Ball tonight."

"Of course. Would you turn up if I got you an invitation?"

"Not my line, going to parties."

"Good grief, Tal, you're an old stick in the mud. I suppose you don't approve of gallivanting."

I shrugged. "The Rector of Dowlais doesn't – at least, not the parties Lady Charlotte gives."

"That's because he's an old God-botherer. Mary Pegus doesn't worry about him, either, so we'll be going together."

"When did she arrive?"

"Yesterday afternoon, from Uffington; the rest of her family are coming tomorrow." Her mood was suddenly frizzed and her chin went up and she was pert with me. Dobie was making up to her mare and doing a damn sight better than I was. Rhiannon said, "You can be a stuck up old thing, you know, Tal Roberts. It's a sort of inverted snobbery, you realise that?"

"There's no snobs like those in the working class, mind."

"Now you're being impossible."

"Anyway," I added, "you won't lack for company. You can have the pick of the Brecon infantry and the yeoman farmers."

"I'll give it thought," said she. "What's wrong with you? You've been as dull as an old turnip ever since I arrived."

My mood was vacillating between despair for the future and joy for the present. More than ever before, now my father was in the fight again, I was hopelessly committed, and the love affair with Rhiannon was complicating all my plans. I wondered how she would accept it when the time came to leave her; when the decision had to be made to cut myself off, and I cursed my ineptitude for getting myself into an impossible predicament: in many ways I was beginning to hope that our love would be officially discovered . . . an automatic end to it before her outraged father.

God knows what would happen to us, I thought, if Rhiannon had a baby.

"Aren't we speaking now, then?" she asked.

"Sorry."

She said softly, "I reckon you're getting tired of me . . ."

"God, no!" I reached out and she gripped my hand, her mood changing at the touch; in all but size she was bigger than me.

Now she said, "You're sure, Tal Roberts – quite sure?"

I might have known; her eyes were sparkling; sin and mischief were in her face. Half out of the saddle, leaning down, I kissed her.

"Then take me to the shooting lodge," said she.

I shivered. "It's too damned cold, and you know it!"

"It won't be so cold making love." She made a begging face.

I said, "Honestly, Rhiannon, you're worse than me – you'll get us bloody hung."

"Don't swear, please don't swear."

"But we can't go on like this, it's dangerous." And Dobie looked over his shoulder at me as if I was light in the head.

"Dangerous?"

"Look, love, what if you have a child?"

"Your baby? Oh Tal, Tal!" She closed her eyes and turned up her face in expressive delight.

"Be serious, for God's sake – people are talking . . ."

"Talking?" She was instantly aware, and intent. "Who's talking?"

"Oh come, it's all over Dowlais, and you know it!"

She reined in her horse, suddenly angry. "If it is, I've heard nothing. And anyway, who cares? I don't, because I love you."

"Rhiannon, come on, come on – we've got to face it. We just can't carry on like this."

Her eyes were suddenly bright. We were still now, the horses grazing. "You don't want me, do you?" she said softly.

"I want you and I love you, *cariad*, but we simply cannot carry on in this way. What kind of a chap would I be if I let people tittle-tattle, but how can I deny it?"

"Who's tittle-tattling?"

I shrugged, empty. "Oh, in the pubs – down the Vulcan and Friendship, for a start." I raised my face to hers.

"You talk about me in that dirty old place?"

I retorted, "Now be fair. I didn't say I talked about you. I'm only saying that it's common knowledge."

"And you want to put an end to it, is that it?"

"I didn't say that, either. Just that I think we should be more careful."

"O aye?" She was taking me off. "And that's the difference between us, isn't it? I don't care, and you do – when lovers start being careful they're falling out of love. Oh God," and she wept.

I was off the horse in seconds and lifted her down into my arms; once I'd got her I tried to lever her off because she was bringing me into a sweat. I wanted to talk calmly and reasonably, but it had become emotional, as I'd expected.

"Let's go away, Tal!" Suddenly she held me away, her

eyes searching mine. "Nobody would know – we'd just go. We're both old enough to know our own minds, and . . ."

"They'd bring us back, Rhiannon."

I saw beyond the smooth, sharp curve of her cheek the radiance of the forest; sun-shafts, beaming through the elms, made sovereigns of gold on the leaves of past autumns; wild strawberry and tamarisk, growing in profusion among the tree roots; the wind moved between us bringing scents of the forest and threats of greater cold from the distant mountains.

"No hope for us, is there?" said Rhiannon, flat, and I kissed her, whispering:

"There's every hope. Just that we've got to be cool about it, darling. If anything went wrong, what would we do for money?"

"I've got money."

"Oh, Rhiannon, won't you try to understand?"

She was smiling in tears, as women do, looking up into my face.

"I'll try – if you take me to Old Joe's shooting lodge . . ."

I said, "You just don't care about anything, do you?"

She shook her head. "No, I don't. I told you before – I love you. And I don't care about anything else. *Please?*"

Earlier, I'd heard the rustle of branches; earlier still the clattering panic of disturbed birds, and had buried my fears in Rhiannon's kisses. But now I heard the heavy breathing of a horse and its dull, thumping hoof-beats, and raised my head.

To my astonishment, Lady Charlotte was sitting on her big black horse no more than twenty yards away: seeing us, she approached slowly, reining in: Rhiannon, feeling me tense, turned.

"Good afternoon, Milady," said she, and bobbed a curtsey.

It was as if she had known of her presence all the time. The lady said, her face frozen:

"Good afternoon, Rhiannon, I thought I'd find you here. I'll see you in Dowlais House within the hour. Do you think you might manage that?" and the look she sent withered us. Then she spurred the horse and trotted away.

We stood together, Rhiannon and I, hand in hand. She said, "All right, so it's out officially – why look so glum? We love each other and it's time the whole world knew – her included."

"But your father . . . ?"

"And him."

I said, "They'll skin us alive."

"All right, so they'll skin us – but not in the next half hour," and her arms went about me hard and strong.

We hadn't got time to go to the shooting lodge, but when it comes to what happened next there's not a lot to choose between the workers and the aristocracy.

19

The gourmets of the county didn't go short at a Dowlais Ball; Sir John and Lady Charlotte competed with the Crawshays for splendour when it came to entertainment: they dined off lamb and pheasants' tongues, boar's head and pork rumps, venison, stuffed quails and beef and honeyed hams, and washed this down with port, sherry, champagne and the finest wines mulled and spiced with cinnamon.

And while the Guests vied with Crawshay at table, Maisie Lumpkin reckoned she could make a sheep's head (a penny a time at the back door of the Shambles) do for six. People like us, said Maisie, have an expectation of life of twenty years, and four years less when the cholera comes to town: the disease that could have been prevented had our employers spent a thousand pounds on providing more water than they stole for the Works.

I couldn't settle that night after Rhiannon and I had been caught, and was stupidly jealous that, at the Ball that night, she'd be in another man's arms when she belonged to me. So I found myself wandering around Town: I mooched along High Street towards Pen-y-darren.

Ill-clad children were playing outside their doors, their bare feet stained with the excrement that flooded down the gully-ways: ancient faces peered down from upper windows, a long-since discarded human slag. The slums, row after row of decaying houses, put up in John Guest's early time, had become a sink-pit of deprivation and despair. These children, I reflected, as Maisie had said, would be lucky to reach the age of sixteen while Guest's sons and daughters lived in luxury. Long, long before these privileged few reached adolescence, those I saw now would suffer lientery, small-pox, typhus or consumption; many would die of scrofula and the general wasting of acute malnutrition. On that walk through Dowlais and Pen-y-darren that night I saw the full horror to which these ironmasters had condemned the earners of their fortunes.

Returning to Dowlais House I heard the music of the Ball, so after bedding old Dobie down for the night, I wandered round to the front of the house and stood in the shadows of the bushes beyond the wide lawn, hoping for a sight of Rhiannon through the windows.

All the young bloods of the county must have been there that night, for a legion of horses and traps were waiting; stallions, too, with all the trappings of the Brecon military. Tables lining the walls, white-clothed, were laden with the food and wine; beneath the chandeliers were people I recog-nised – the Vicomte de la Villemarqué, glass in hand, was amiably chatting to Thomas Price, one of Lady Charlotte's *Mabinogi* translators: Mr. Justice Bosanquet was there, Stephens, the Dowlais engineer and John Evans, his mana-ger: Henry Bruce, the magistrate, I saw talking avidly with Mrs. Wyndham Lewis, the friend of Disraeli; William Crawshay was sitting by the window, removed from the others, apparently contemplating the scene before him.

The majority present, however, were not industrialists but the young and dashing former yeomanry, the part-time de-fenders of aristocratic privilege, as my father once described them – ready to gallop their sabres to the nearest workers' disorder: and upon their uniformed arms danced the gowned beauties of Glamorgan.

It was then, at the height of the music, that Rhiannon, hands clasped, moved into the light. And then, as I peered from my hiding-place, she deliberately went to the french doors and stared out on to the garden in my direction.

It was as if she had been called by some unspoken tryst. Had I moved, she would surely have seen me; never have I felt more at one with her; never have I known such a longing for her presence.

"Rhiannon . . ." My lips formed her name.

Motionless, she stood in a long white dress that reached to the floor: upon her head a little tiara flashed its jewels, enhancing her dark, spectacular beauty. I wanted to race across the lawn, fling wide the doors, and take her into my arms.

Suddenly, to my amazement, she opened the doors, closed them carefully behind her and stepped out on to the gravel path. Nobody appeared to notice her departure and I found myself standing on the edge of the lawn.

"Tal!" She called to me as if assured that I would be waiting, and I ran from the shadows and into the light. "Tal, are you there?"

We met in the middle of the lawn, a senseless, stupid act born of desperation; in the light, in such a place, scores in the room could have seen us. Now she was in my arms and I kissed her lips, her face, her hair: but hours before I had actually possessed her; the act had enhanced the magnetism of her presence, not diminished it.

"Oh God," she whispered. "Tal, Tal . . ."

That we would be seen was inevitable. Had we planned it, it could not have been more absolute. The tall figure of Sir John was striding over the lawn towards us: behind him I saw the open door of the crowded room; a group of stilled guests were looking in our direction.

"Rhiannon!"

We were standing hand in hand when Guest reached us. He said:

"Twice now. This is becoming a habit." He touched Rhiannon's arm. "Your parents are looking for you – return to the house." He jerked his head at me. "You – go to the library – I want a word with you. Such behaviour; I'm outraged and appalled."

Rhiannon smiled at me, and said over her shoulder as she went, "I love you, Tal. Don't look so glum! Everything will be all right now, it's far better that everybody knows."

*

As instructed, I went to the library, going through the back door of the house.

The room was wraithlike, ghostly with its great shelves of gilt-edged books; there came to me both the scent of perfume and the odorous tang of decaying paper. Nothing moved. Faintly, I heard the music of the ball, a chinking of glasses, the indeterminate mumbling of voices.

And then another voice made words behind me, and I turned to a man's soft laughter and a woman's soprano protest.

A red velvet curtain moved almost imperceptibly behind me.

I realised that I was trapped, an unwilling eavesdropper.

"Come on, Karen, who is to know . . . ?" said a voice.

"Darling, be reasonable! This is Sir John's library – anybody might come!"

"We've never been caught before, my poppet!"

"But here, dearest, of all places . . . ? Look – I could have sworn I heard footsteps a minute back . . ."

"Somebody passing in the hall . . ."

"Honestly, Johnny, your regiment could come in here and you'd not hear it. *Please* . . . ?"

"Right, when?"

The girl said, hesitantly, "I . . . I could meet you at the inn next Wednesday?"

"God, that's nearly a week!"

"I know. But Jules is taking me on the circuit tomorrow, and I won't be back till Wednesday next."

"On circuit with a judge! And I'm on leave!" He cursed effectively. "Anyway, I'm escorting a prisoner from the police station on Wednesday. Damn these Chartists!"

The girl said, apprehensively, "Is there going to be trouble?"

"There will be if we don't see to this one, he's important. Oh, come on! If I have to go to Brecon as escort commander I won't be back for a month – be a sport, get them off."

I heard the swift inrush of their breathing, the rustling of a dress. The girl whispered, "No, Johnny, oh *no*! This is Lady Charlotte's house . . ." she broke off, and I heard her add, in panic, "*Listen!*"

Footsteps had echoed in the hall. Then the library door came open and Sir John Guest came in, slamming it behind him. Confronting me, he asked in anger:

"For heaven's sake! What's wrong with the pair of you? What are you trying to achieve?"

From behind the curtain I heard more pent breathing. It astonished me that Sir John hadn't heard it, too. He continued, "It's disgraceful! Needless to say, Rhiannon's father is furious, and I feel responsible. His daughter and a groom! For God's sake, how long has it been going on?"

I didn't reply, and he added, "You'll have to go, of course. Frankly, I blame Rhiannon more than you, but you can't stay here now."

He was clearly trying to hold on to his sense of outrage; I liked him better.

"Milady saw you in Dolygaer woods only this afternoon. How far has this gone, Roberts?"

I said, "I'm sorry."

"You will be if Sir Richard gets his hands on you, so you'd best clear out as soon as you can." He hesitated, adding, "Not . . . not necessarily out of my employ – Lady Charlotte doesn't want this – but certainly out of Dowlais House." He was now plainly conciliatory, and I wondered why. "I . . . I'm told that Old Shenks, our tally-man down at Pont-Storehouse, is getting past it. Until you find somewhere else to work, you can share his night-shifts and his pay."

Sir John glanced at his watch. "But before you go there's another matter which Mr. Justice Bosanquet wishes to deal with. Wait." He pulled a bell-cord.

Fanny the parlourmaid entered.

"Give Mr. Justice Bosanquet my compliments, Fanny, and ask him to spare me a moment in the library."

Fanny made big eyes at me, bobbed a curtsey, and went out.

Sir John said, "It is about your father, Roberts. All in all, you're becoming a little intriguing. You'd be advised to answer his questions truthfully and accurately or you'll find yourself in even deeper trouble."

The curtains beside me moved almost imperceptibly; vaguely I wondered what would be the scene if they were pulled; the humour of it touched me, despite the situation.

Within minutes the Judge came, seated himself on a chaise longue and fixed me with his small, sharp eyes.

"You remember me, Roberts?"

"Yes, Sir."

"I'll come to the point. You'll recall, at our last meeting, that you said your father was dead?"

"Yes."

"And that he died in Van Diemen's Land?"

I nodded, my mind desperately searching for answers.

"How came you by this knowledge?"

I said, carefully, "A convict, returning to Amlwch from Australia, said he had seen his grave." This lie was all I could think of.

"Where in Australia?" He was persistent.

"In the Macquarie Penal Settlement."

He and Sir John exchanged glances. "I see. The name Gwyn Roberts – your father's name – is not an uncommon one, you'd agree?"

"Yes."

"Therefore, there's a possibility that the grave the convict saw was not your father's?"

"It's possible."

They were both watching me carefully, I noticed; then the magistrate said, "You tell us that your father was transported for stealing candles – to the value of eightpence."

"Yes, Sir."

His small face peered up. "Seven years in a penal settlement for a couple of pounds of candles? You consider that just?"

"It was unjust."

He nodded kindly. "Unless, of course, there was a greater crime involved – treason, say?"

"Had there been I would have known of it."

"No, not necessarily. For reasons of national security the law sometimes leans on a minor indictment, suppressing the real reason for a heavier sentence."

"I do not understand what you mean."

"I have an idea that you do, Roberts." He smiled. "I am suggesting that your father was transported, not for the theft of candles at all, but for being the Northern representative of these damned Chartists."

Sir John interjected, "Is that indictable? Merthyr's full of Chartists."

"But moral force members, not the advocates of physical violence, or we would put them behind bars." He turned his attention to me again. "What say you to this, Roberts – that your father, while working as a refiner under Mr. Edwards at the Amlwch Smelter – was involved in organising a revolutionary lodge in Anglesey and bringing in arms that would put its violent aims into practice?"

I did not reply to this.

"You heard what I said?"

"Yes."

"Have you no comment?"

I answered, "If that was so, I'd have known about that, too."

"Yet one other person in your family knew of your father's political activities, did she not? I refer to the cousin your father brought into the house after your mother's death."

I prayed for outward calm; within, I was sick at heart and frightened. Clearly, the man before me had unravelled every fact of my father's movements in the North. Soon he would confront me less subtly with the fact – that Dada had never sailed for Van Diemen's Land, that he had been free since his escape. It was like an intricate stage-play that was slowly unfolding my fate: soon, I thought, a bell will ring for another act and I will be confronted with inescapable facts which could only be countered by bare-faced lying, and I was no good at lying. Bosanquet said, quietly, "You knew of his political plans in the North?"

I shook my head.

"And you know, too, that your father never sailed for Australia, don't you – that he escaped on his way to Swansea Bridewell."

I enclosed my eyes to escape the intensity of their stares.

Bosanquet's eyes were almost hypnotic beneath their bushy brows. He cried, "You know that, don't you?"

"I did not know."

"Indeed, your father has been in contact with you, has he not? Every thief and murderer in Wales take to the mountains in the face of arrest. If he has not been to you, then you have been to him?" He rose from his chair, shouting, "Answer me!"

I said, unevenly, "None of this is true. My father is dead. His friend in Amlwch saw his grave."

"And I am telling you that he's very much alive." Coming around a table between us he stood before me, lowering his voice to a whisper. "Listen to me, Roberts. Your father has been found guilty of treason, and for that he was sentenced to be banished from the land. His judge was lenient, but if you come before me for the same crime, I will not prove so. Do you know the punishment for taking arms against the Queen? It is this – and the law has never been rescinded – that you be hanged by the neck until life is almost extinct, then cut down, disembowelled, your entrails burned before your eyes and your body quartered." He shook a finger before my face. "I am warning you, Roberts, lies, either here or in the courtroom, will not save you, nor will your youth. I give you one last chance. Have you, since you last saw your father in Amlwch, been in touch with him in any way?"

"No."

"Had you heard of his escape from custody?"

"No."

"Your cousin – the one who betrayed him – do you know her whereabouts?"

"I do not."

"You swear to this?"

"I swear to it all."

"Before God – if I bring a Bible?"

"I swear it – on a Bible if you like." I was trembling; the trembling grew, spreading to my hands, and he saw it. Sir John said, quietly, "Shall I bring one, Mr. Bosanquet?"

There was a long silence, then the Judge walked past me, touching my shoulder as he went, saying:

"Not necessary. He is telling the truth, aren't you, Roberts? Keep him away from Miss Rhiannon, of course, preferably under your eye, but the lad is perfectly innocent of his father's whereabouts."

He knew I'd been lying, of course; I could see it in his face.

I had to get to Sam Williams at once, to report what I had heard from the other side of the library curtain. It might not be Gideon Davies the hidden man had been speaking of, but there was a very good chance that it might be. Anyway, after the interview with Justice Bosanquet I intended to put a distance between me and Dowlais House.

Meg, hearing the garden gate open at the Garn cottage, came running out to meet me.

What chemistry lies in the tie of blood? I hadn't seen my little sister for months, and there was a new maturity in her talk. I saw my father's face in her face, and the closeness of her, hot from the fire, brought to me a oneness: I kissed her.

"You comin' back for good now, Tal?" she asked.

I nodded, my arm around her shoulders, and we went together into the kitchen and its crying kettle.

"Where's Aunt Mell?" I asked.

"Next door borrowing tea," sang Meg, and smiled her rhubarb smile at me, her teeth missing in front.

Aye, I thought, she had changed; Dada would scarcely know her, with her puppy fat and big knees. Her voice now held the sing-song intonation of the valleys, my mother's people.

"Our Poll's down Town, ye know," she said.

"Poll? Our Cousin Poll? *No!*"

"O ah! Often we do see her on the chat, down Merthyr market, twice last week."

"Did . . . did you speak to her?"

"Aye, but she put her nose so high she tightened her garters. Too good for us now, I reckon." She added. "She were with one of the beehive boys."

"Beehive boy?"

She made a face, shrugging, "He were thimble-rigging and Poll were tacklin' up the gents, said Aunt Mell. Whee!

She were done up fine in frills and fancies!"

"Thimble-rigging?"

"Aye, like they cheat at the fairs, you know. Don't let the magistrate see her, said Aunt Mellie, and Uncle Sam do say she's a Rodney."

It was the infant speaking with a woman's tongue; I changed the subject. A Rodney could mean anything—gambler, prostitute, thief.

"Where's Uncle Sam now, then?" I asked.

"In by 'ere." She opened the parlour door to the front room.

"Why didn't you say?"

Sam, boots up and into *The Cambrian*, had his spectacles on top of his head, dozing: I waited until Meg was out of earshot, and said:

"It's next Wednesday."

"You're sure?" He rose instantly.

"Only that a Chartist is being shifted down to Brecon."

"Any details?"

"The escort's a troop, probably mounted, and they'll be leaving from the police station."

"There's never been soldiers billeted at the police station!" He was adamant. "They're up at Penywern Barrack Row."

"There's some at the police station!"

Sam put down the newspaper and walked to the window. "If that's so, then they'll shift him by night. Gid Davies is too important to move him in the light: these days they wouldn't get a prisoner fifteen yards up High Street without a fight, and they know it." He squinted his eyes at his pipe. "Well, maybe it's Gid Davies and maybe it's not, but he's a Chartist prisoner, an' that's good enough for me." He raised a heavy face. "And how did ye come by this, for God's sake?"

I explained, omitting to mention Bosanquet's interrogation of me; if Sam Williams began to think me a dangerous liability he'd relegate me to some unimportant job behind the Chartist lines. Now he said, with businesslike intent:

"Well done. I were beginnin' to think we'd get nothing out of ye being in the Dowlais stables—that you were keener on sparking with that gentry piece than fighting for the country."

"That's over now," I replied.

"Jesus Christ, am I delighted to hear it!" He lit his pipe, blowing out huge clouds of smoke. "Listen. Be at The Patriot up High Street tomorrow dusk, I'll be gettin' some people together." He rubbed his bristled chin reflectively. "Let me see – a Redcoat troop is four plus one for prisoner escort, usually – we'll jump the bastards before they're clear of the town." He evinced the air of one who has said nothing in particular.

As I went out the back Meg put her hand in mine, saying, "Have you heard when Dada's coming back off the ship, Tal?"

I held her against me in the scullery. Aunt Mell's teeth were in a cup on the window sill, I remember, next to a bowl of floating senna pods, and I knew a small, quietening air of peace and domesticity.

Kissing Meg goodbye, I said, "Don't you worry, Meg Roberts. He'll be coming home soon now – sooner, perhaps, than you think."

God knows what would happen to her if things went wrong, I thought.

20

Shenkin Powell, the retiring checker on the barge canal in 'China,' had all his buttons about him, said Sam.

As old as undertaking was Old Shenks and a confusion of a man if ever there was one.

Foreman on the thirty-eight per cent ironstone, he was lavender water behind the ears on pay day. Of mincing gait and knitting on the side (one plain, two purl, girls – I'm doin' meself a bodice) he once dropped a horse with a left hook for a pint: the right hook he saved for the bruisers, and every pug in Town was frightened to death of him.

No wickedness in Old Shenks who knew his Bible backwards; twice to Church on Sunday, the children loved him (he used to kneel in the street and stroke their faces upwards). Women respected him, though the only one he'd slept with was his mam: three times a week he visited her grave in Pant.

"So you're takin' over me nights, lad?" said he soprano.

"Yes, Mr. Powell. Sorry, Mr. Powell." I stood before him in the canal tally-hut. Behind his wide shoulders I saw the swim of the canal and the night-shift barges moving out of Dowlais wharf.

"Ach," said he, sad. "Jeremiah eight, verse twenty-two. 'Is there no balm in Gilead?' . . ."

The big shire horses strained to commands: bargees, the morning-shift just come on, laboured in swirling mist; casual child labour, their eyes gummed with sleep in the frosted compounds, stood in shivering groups, waiting to be taken on.

The ironmasters, glutted with labour, worked on a nucleus of the specialist trades, depending on migrant workers for unskilled work. These came in starving, ragged streams across the mountains of The Top, crowding the streets, begging on the pavements; jamming up the cobbles of the taverns and ale-houses.

With no public lavatories, they defecated in the open, these people, exposing themselves along the Taff. And down at the China Wharf, the confluence of export and import of pig, finished iron, limestone, coal, the human misery was at its worst – a rectum of despair that called itself China.

Old Shenks now, powdering his broken nose in a bit of mirror, said:

"Ye've got to keep 'em out, mind, or they'll be in an' eat ye whole, especially when the cholera's around; can't take risks with the old effluvia."

"Right, Mr. Shenks."

"And don't invite the women in – pity do extend to forni-catin', mainly speakin', and the reverend gents don't hold wi' it. The poor old molls come begging at night – it's the cold do get 'em, see?"

I pledged celibacy.

He could remember as far back as 1758, he said, when the iron first came to Dowlais; he saw the first furnace built at Cyfarthfa seven years later: he watched the Iron Bridge go across the Taff and the first, second and third Merthyr riots; he was present when a lad was killed by a cannon on the night Nelson came to Merthyr, and at the race between the Trevithick engine and the horses down to Abercynon.

I marvelled at him. "You saw the first Trevithick?"

"Ay ay, but I didn't hold wi' it, see? Horses breathe, engines fart." He jabbed his finger on the table.

"You collect the tallies off the barges, understand? – and the clerks do enter them in their books. Now I'm best off, you're the night-shift."

"Thanks, Mr. Shenks. If I get it round me neck I'll call at your house."

"You do that, son. Number Three Beehive along the British Tip; I'm digging a hole for me hip with our Jen. Knock twice and ask for Shenks."

"Our Jen?"

"Don't come in wi'out a knock or she'll 'ave ye with the bloody ladle." I gave him twopence and he spat on the coppers. "Ach," said he, "here comes a feed. These days I'm tightenin' me stays."

Poor old lad, I thought. Munching his iced whiskers, he hauled off into night-shift retirement on half pay – sleeping in a hole; yet he had given fifty years to iron. In his prime he had also given an outing to Dai Benyon, Champion, over thirty rounds, who complained about scent in the clinches.

Shenks left behind him a faint fragrance of toilet water.

There was another human commodity abroad around the canal; this was the Rodneys. These were mainly the unwanted or orphans; their parents having been killed in the mines or furnaces, or having just deserted them.

The Rodneys were the lowest of the social order, many of them living in the disused 'hives' that ran the length of the British Tip – decaying coke ovens still warmed by the internal fires of the great cinder mound. Burrowing like moles, the children had formed small networks of underground tunnels into the warm mass; within these burrows the air was sulphurous from the burning tip, the earth floors filthy and puddled with human faeces. The nearest pure water meant a walk of two miles, and every night long queues of women gathered at the wells, centres of gossip and fierce quarrelling. Talk had it that they were also the centres of riotous assemblies, with orgies of drinking and fornication; the respectable inextricably mixed with the disreputable. Virginity and life could be lost at the well heads, it was said, but the journeying was necessary, the four great Works taking the abundance of water coming down from the Beacons.

It was in one of the hives – Number Three Beehive Row – that old Shenks lived, he said; the only adult I knew of being granted the privilege of a beehive guard.

It was Saturday night, I remember: though officially on duty in the tally-hut, I had booked in all the barges: those due out on Monday dawn were tied against the wharf, their horses at feed and the bargees, another isolated community, out on the town with their women.

Locking the door (earlier I had knocked up a wooden bed) I went out into the shivering cold, making for The Patriot Inn up in High.

The Patriot, next door to the Colliers, was but one of a couple of hundred taverns in Merthyr then, conveniently situated close to the police station. Indeed, it was possible, from a window upstairs in its Long Bar, to observe the comings and goings of the law-enforcers, a vital activity during revolutionary Chartism. But watchfulness was not without its sense of humour. On the wall above Sam's head (I saw him the moment I entered) was an inscription which read:

Sweet smiling village, loveliest of lawns,
Thy sports are fled and all thy charms withdrawn.
Amid thy bowers the policemen's hats are seen,
Now desolation reigns where once our joys have been.

"Come you in, Tal," called Sam, and I took my seat at the table among some twenty others.

Colliers, ironstone miners, furnace men and ostlers, Chartists all, they were straight from shift. Two puddlers, their red eyes blinking in their scorched faces, particularly looked me over, then stared ahead in a predetermined eloquence of silence.

They had come, these workers, from the coal workings of Penyard Pit, the Nantyglo Level and Trecatti; one at least was from the Brewhouse Coal and two from the Rhas-Las Drift, they said. Six were from Dowlais Ten, in the middle of the Works, the furnace Brewhouse served, and two came from beyond The Walnut public where the great new Ivor Works was being built. Another claimed he was a roller on the Gardner Big Mill, the pride of Dowlais.

From what was now the greatest iron town in the world they had sent half a million tons of finished iron down the Glamorganshire Canal to Cardiff, and were justly boastful of the achievement.

Within their Merthyr home of thirty thousand people, they valued parenthood and beat their wives but rarely. They worshipped with gusto, in the ale-houses and the Chapels, singing in choirs with a preference for Oratorio.

They fought bare-knuckle for honour, because they loved a fight: but only recently had they discovered the inequality of their existence. Even Mr. Clark, John Guest's agent – but not Lady Charlotte or her husband – conceded that 'Dirty Dowlais' was as bad as the slums of Bombay, the brightest jewel in Victoria's crown.

They had also learned, these workers, that the Dowlais directors were annually banking two hundred thousand pounds while they were burying their children for want of a decent water supply. So now they had joined the national ranks of the Chartists: the employers weren't prepared to give, so they would take: and Chartist leaders like Frost and Henry Vincent, knowing their anger, would put them in the battle's van.

Sam Williams said, "Are all representatives here?" and looked around the room; I was looking for my father; this was to be his first Dowlais meeting, and I was nervous for him: Bosanquet had only to lift a finger and the whole of Brecon garrison would be out on the streets. Some twenty representatives of Merthyr's Chartist lodges were in the room; it needed but one to be a defector – and Napier's spies were everywhere – for the inn to be surrounded. Knocker was reading from a roll, the men answering their names, and Sam said, when this was finished:

"This is a special meeting called at a moment's notice, and I'll tell ye why. We know where Gid Davies is, we think. More'n that, he's being shifted from the police station to Brecon barracks next Wednesday."

There was a hubbub of suppressed excitement; a man called from the back, "Penywern you mean, Sam?"

"I do not – the police station across the road."

"Ye mean he's been there months and we never knowed of it?"

"Christ! What kind of organisation is this?"

"Let's fetch the lads and hook him out of it!" Their anger grew.

Sam cried, "Now easy, easy!" He glared about him. "Would ye have us announce our intentions by the rule of the mob? All right, they've made bloody fools of us, but we're here now to get the fine man back." He looked at his waist-coat watch. "And there's more on the go than Gid Davies tonight, lads. We've Gwyn Roberts, the Northern representative, comin' to address us, an' I pledge ye to the deepest security: Gwyn's wanted as much as Gid Davies, his friend these twenty years – more, perhaps – and if he goes down we all go down."

"Don't tell me there's a union spirit in the North, Sam!" This from an Irish giant with a face like a bunch of laughs.

"Aye, I will! Good shamrock country up there, too – for Welshmen are the same as Irish, Shamus, when it comes to a fight."

"Ach, balls to ye, Sam," said a Welsh voice. "When ye get above Rhayader they don't know bloody Guy Fawkes."

Sam said, and it silenced them, "This fella does. He's just jumped transportation for runnin' guns up in Anglesey, and I'll trouble ye to mind your mouths, for his son's sitting among ye."

The room door came open and Dada came in.

He looked older; compared with the faint light of the Llangynidr cave, this lamp was pitiless. Seeing me, he wink-ed as he took his place at the head of the table.

"Next Wednesday, eh?" he asked Sam, after the introductions.

"Aye, but we can handle it from here – you stay down."

"God no, it's Gid, and I'll be here. But are you sure it's him?" and I replied:

"We can't be sure, but think it is. Sam says all interrogations go on up in Barrack Row, Penywern. This man's held in the police station, just across the road from here. It's a civil crime, and the police are holding him."

"Police?"

"The Specials – the usual; with military backing."

Sam said at nothing, "Months he's been there, perhaps he

anna worth having."

There was a silence, and my father rose, saying, "Listen, dead or alive, every Union man is worth having. And if he's a Chartist, too, then more so. For this is a movement that's spreading its fingers on the throat of the country, and we won't rest until we rid ourselves of this damned autocracy that rules our lives and watches our children die."

The men stared up, shocked, as I was, by his sudden vehemence, and I saw him again, in my mind, standing on the quay at Amlwch. He cried:

"Ay, tub-thumping you may call it, any name you like, but it is time we thumped, not sat on our backsides and waited for the rule of law." His voice rose. "For there is no law in this land save the law that suits the knight, the peer, the Church and the industrial robbers! The Angleseys and Penrhyns up in the North, the Guests, Crawshays and Hills down here."

"Christ, mun, go an' tell 'em that up in bloody Amlwch – one bang up there and the buggers'll be off!"

It rocked them; they shouted laughter, and my father cried, cutting them into silence, "Aye? Sweet Jesus, you have to come down South for scholars and education! Is there anyone here who can count up to five? Do you know your Welsh history?"

"Mind ye tongue," said a voice.

"And you your talk," said Sam, "for it was you who started this, Daio. The man's a guest, so give him a hearing."

Dada said, "It's the old two-nation story, is it not? Well, we up North have a version of that, too – the North for the Welsh, we say, and the South for the Taffs. And all the Welsh are in this fight, not just Merthyr. God Almighty, are you the only ones exploited, then? I've watched families starve to death in copper while you lot were drawing face-work rates and puddler's pay. And we've had the Cornish copper agents on our backs since the slave trade and the Romans before that, before you knew there was iron in Merthyr." He was breathing heavily, now haggard in the face.

"Listen, the moment I stepped foot in this room I knew the hostility. What's more, I expected it, and it is wrong: it's wrong because it divides us at a time when it is unity in manhood we need – Welshman, Northerner and Southerner, Irishman, Spaniard, Scotsman and Hunky. By this time next year two million men and women will be under arms in Britain, and we will call for help from the French, if needs be, to pull these parasites down. It is a call to arms in the name of decency, irrespective of race or creed."

It did nothing for them; we sat among them, Dada and I, but as people alone, save for Sam and a couple of others. And I think I knew then the tragedy of my country; we had allowed greedy foreigners to ravish the land and drive between us an unfathomable wedge.

So we sat, North and South, within an unspoken disharmony, and Sam, knowing it, said:

"Now to the main items of the evening. Meanwhile I say this – one day you'll know the debt ye owe this man. I'm Irish, an' I've no part in the enmity, but I look upon ye all with some disfavour."

Old Nana, the mother of Irish Joe Dido, the shot-firer, who kept The Patriot, came up from downstairs to bring the ale: she was a little scrag of a woman with an air of dislike for men, us in particular.

"Are ye finished puttin' the world to rights now?" She had a tray of pewters in one hand and a big ginger tomcat under her arm.

"Och, Nana," said Sam, "don't you bloody start."

She put down the tray and then came back with the ale.

"Is it right the dear fella's languishin' in the station over there, Joe?" she asked her son.

"He is, Nana," said Joe Dido. "Now will you sod off?"

Sam said, "There's a dozen or so publics on the route the escort will take, see – which will be up High from the station and along Charlotte to the new Ivor Works. After we snatch him we can bed him down in any one of 'em."

Knocker said, "Lest they lift him through Dowlais gardens up to the Gwern?"

"Don't talk stupid," came a reply. This was from the landlord of The Welsh Oak; a revolutionary to his fingertips, his face was parched white from a furnace blow-back and one eye peered from his scalded cheek. "Would they haul him through the gardens in the middle of the town? They'll get him into the open, I say, and meet a troop from Brecon – that's the usual when they go from Penywern."

They considered this, and Old Nana said, stroking her cat:

"Have ye got the wind up, you lot, then?"

"Oh Nana, bugger off!"

"I were only askin', see? Because back in the Wexford Ninety-eight we'd 'ave had the sods on pitchforks, and that were before tea."

"If we snatch him through the gardens, he'll likely end up in the New Inn. That's close," said my father.

"If he's that close he'll end up here, in The Patriot," said Nana. "Meanwhile, you lot sit here sinking quarts and polishin' your arses. When's the revolution, for God's sake?"

"And then?" asked somebody, ignoring her.

"A day or two, then we ship Gid down to China," said Sam.

"Who gets him then?"

"I do," I answered, standing up. "By tomorrow I'll be down on Canal Wharf, tallying."

"You, Tal?" My father looked perturbed.

"Why not?" asked Sam. "He's already up to his neck."

"China?" asked Joe Dido, "that's the first place they'll look."

"Not so. Five go in down there and four come out, Joe, leave it to your betters," said Nana.

The others, I noticed, looked me over with faint approbation, and the old woman said, "And once you've got him, son, he's yours – yours until you get him down to Cardiff docks and aboard the ship to America, understand?"

I nodded.

"That's a tricky sample, Missus," said Dai Tomorrow. "He's only a kid, mind."

"Then now he can grow into a man," came the reply. "We'll spring Gid Davies, house him, mend him – if it be Gid Davies – and carry him down to Dowlais Wharf: the rest is up to you." She clapped her hands. "Right, then – Wednesday dusk, remember, and all report to me downstairs – Old Nana. Socks and pick-handles and hit to kill."

"*Iechyd da i bob Cymro. Twll din i bob Sais*," added Knocker, lifting his pint. One eye was filled up, blood was down his muffler.

"Aye, son – arseholes to all Englishmen," added Nana.

Long after they had all gone I sat there talking to Dada: then Sam returned.

"Time to leave, Gwyn," said he. "By the way, d'ye recall that Mortymer lad working with the gunsmiths? Tell him I delivered the letter he gave me."

Smiling, Dada nodded.

"And tell him that his sister Morfydd's playin' Hell about him being away from home; his young wife, too – they want him back."

I couldn't account for it, but I knew I would see Iestyn Mortymer again.

21

Dai Tomorrow, the five-foot landlord of the Vulcan and Friendship, was doing well these days.

Since he had obtained the Brew Contract for the Dowlais stables, the ostlers, farriers and muckers-out were not only paid out by him in his pub, but were provided with the Allsops upon which to spend it; thus Dai got a two-way cut, though he wouldn't do today what could be done tomorrow.

I don't remember what took me into the Vulcan that night, and as I came in, Fanny, the Guest parlourmaid, went out of the jug and bottle.

"And what have you been up to, you randy old soak?" asked Dai, his face over the counter.

"Don't believe all you hear from her," I replied, and pushed him money.

"Don't sell Fanny short. She's got the feel of things in Dowlais House, and her and your Rhiannon are as thick as thieves, I hear."

"I doubt it."

"Aye? Well, I tell you this. Sam Williams thinks high of Fanny; there's not much goin' on round these parts that she don't know about, he says."

"He's welcome to her."

It was strange, I thought: I despised Fanny for spying on the Guests, yet I'd done exactly the same thing myself.

"Well, a pint on the house, son," said Dai. "We can drink together, can't we, since we're going to die together?"

"If Sam Williams has his way."

*

The stable men came in for their six weeks' pay, and I remembered how my father and I used to get paid at the Oddfellows up in Amlwch. It was the same old greed and corruption, North or South: doubtless, the Guests had shares in the Vulcan and Friendship.

"Been blottin' ye copybook again, I hear," said Dai, and he smiled me a leprechaun smile: Irish was he, with shamrocks in his mouth, but the Taffs liked him and gave him a nickname – proof of local acceptance.

"Just pour the pints, mun, it's all you're fit for."

Over Dai's shoulder, perched like an undertaker's rook on the skew seat by the fire, was Eli Firmament: potent on a hassock and the metrical psalter was he; just out from Correction, having done six months – interfering with children. Talk had it that he popped his false teeth for ale on Monday and got them back on Friday.

"Watch your tongue, Dai." I nodded towards Eli.

"Yes, he's been seen up in Penywern recent," and Dai went on polishing. Barrack Row being the place where the Guests housed their soldiers for putting down the Welsh.

Upstairs they were fighting a couple of terriers later, and the dogs were now on the leash, snapping and snarling at each other. What with them and the shouting you couldn't hear yourself think. And Eli was watching me, a man of evil intent.

Jake Kilrain, the giant puddler, came in, handling people aside.

I shut myself off, thinking of Rhiannon: without her I seemed to be standing within a vacuum of solitude; the bar noise beat unheard about me.

"Go up there and fetch her, then," said Dai, as if reading my thoughts.

He poured glasses for two farriers, big men of furrowed brows and tired eyes, and they brought with them odours of crushed oats and urine: from the furnacemen came stinks of soot and fire, from colliers stale tea and tommy-boxes. You could tell their trades by smells.

"I said go up there and fetch her," repeated Dai. "Hell, mun, imbecility's your greatest talent, so it is; the poor lass must be pinin' to death."

I drank, not answering.

"D'ye love the sweet child?"

Sod him, I thought, he was touching raw spots.

"How ye doin', son?" suddenly bawled Jake from across the room.

"*Dando!*" I gave him some rough Welsh.

"Is it right Sir John has eased ye out?"

"Right and fair, Jake."

"And you're taking old Shenks's tally nights down the canal?"

"Sharing shifts."

"Aye? Well, I'm a second-class fella, too, though I were just tellin' Eli here, temperance is a sacred virtue all the time you're sober."

"Watch him," breathed Dai, swabbing the bar.

"Jake's all right," I said softly.

"Ay ay, but he had a few before he come."

The men were well informed, I thought. Then I remembered Fanny.

Half an hour later the room was full. Jammed against the bar by the night-shift rollers coming off, I was into my third glass and seeing Dai Tomorrow yesterday, for I wasn't used to Allsops. A man beside me whispered into my ear, "I've a darlin' wee Kathleen back home in me cot, and I'm celebratin' for a hooley, so I am." He hammered the bar for ale. "She's a decent piece, my missus, ye know."

The customers roared, and it hit between us. He shouted:

"I said she's a decent little piece. Mind, I wifed and chapelled her proper, oh aye! But I've not seen her in the light since the altar, now would ye believe that?" He drank deep and gasped. "Six bloody weeks I've been down Penyard, I never seen the sun." Turning, he dropped money into Dai's hand, who said:

"Stop bumming up your missus, Mick – Mother o' God!"

"Ach, away to Hell!" The Irishman shoved him, asking me, "Do you know the Rhondda?"

"No," I said.

"She comes from Porth. Tidy folks, ye know, me place is like a new pin, but I've forgotten what she looks like . . ."

"She'll have flat feet, though," said Dai, swabbing up the counter. "They get those in the Rhondda, walkin' up the hills."

The Irishman ignored it. "You got a woman, lad?"

Dai said, "Go easy, Mick – he don't know if it's slated or thatched."

"I asked if ye had a woman. Ignore this dirty bastard."

"No."

"That's a tremendous pity, Taff." His rheumy eyes glistened above his glass. "It's a fine poise woman like mine ye need; she walks around that bedroom like an African queen."

"Ay ay," added Dai, "with the jerry on her head."

"Will you give up, ye palsied wee pixie!" The Irishman swung to him. "I'm raisin' the womanly race, can't ye see?"

"Ach, buzz off!" said Dai, polishing. "He's got his own troubles, ain't you, Tal? – he don't want more from a randy old drunk."

I heard an old man say, "I live wi' me daughter since my Ellie died – her chap's foreman down the Garn. But I can't come downstairs wi' the kids, of course, I 'ave to stay in me room."

A man with a silky red voice like a Bolshevik declared noisily, "Aye, she's narrow-faced and as dry as tinder, mun – lift her skirt and ye'd find a bird's nest – don't you fret, my beauty, she'll be here any minute to see where I am." I swung around, but he was gone as if evaporated.

"Where's your Alfie got to, Joe?"

"Ain't you heard? Killed down Gethin."

"But he were only ten!"

The room fell into a conspiracy of silence, as if conjurors in black were crawling under the tables.

"Holy Jesus, look at that," whispered a man, and I turned to the door.

The babble died; even the dogs upstairs stopped barking.

Rhiannon, in a white cloak, with her long black hair tumbling over her shoulders, was standing there. Seeing me among the men, she raised her face higher, and smiled.

"Hallo, Tal."

It was snowing outside; the market hall, just built, was clad in white; early winter having pulled a bedsheet over the world.

Afterwards, they told me, Jake Kilrain, the big puddler, got Eli Firmament by the coat and lifted him out of his skew seat by the fire.

"You saw nought, remember, Eli? *Nought*, you hear me? If you did, it was the Allsops, understand? A word of what you saw in here and I'll swab the bar with ye."

Dobie was tethered outside. Going to him, Rhiannon said:

"Fanny told me you were down here, Tal. I . . . I just had to see you. Take me up to Dolygaer . . . ?"

"In this weather? God no!"

"Please, Tal, please take me."

Her face was powdered with snow, her eyebrows flecked with it: she looked like a snow maiden come from the forests of Grimm. I looked around; the market square was deserted; the walls of the stables leered down, imprisoning us. When I drew her against me she was trembling, and the trembling came into me also, bringing us to a sudden, intimate warmth. Her lips were scarlet against the wind-bitten redness of her cheeks, her eyes were shining.

I kissed her. What began in kindness ended in snatched breathing, and she tore herself away.

"Oh, God," she whispered.

"Come," I said, and took Dobie's bridle. Together in the saddle, we took the road that led to the lodge.

22

Joe Hitherto used the shooting lodge mainly for cleaning guns before the Twelfth, having his own tied cottage in the grounds of Dowlais House. And since the Guests only used it when the game was in flight, the stone lodge stood isolated and alone, mantled with snow.

It was dark within the lodge.

Rhiannon tidied the flowered curtains against chinks; I lit the single lamp, and a warm, yellow glow searched the corners of the room.

Outside in the snow I gathered loose timber and piled it under the chimney: a fire was soon leaping in the open hearth, painting in redness the four small bunks, the piled rugs, the gun-racks, the sheepskins on the floor. Rhiannon knelt beside me and I blew the wood into a forge-glow; we sat there.

Amazingly, now that she was here beside me, I had no physical need for her; my father's predicament was invading the inner tenement of my mind, stealing desire.

Nevertheless, it was enchantment to sit there with Rhia's hand in mine. Her eyes were bright, as if with unshed tears, her lips bitten scarlet by frost, and the shadows of her high-boned face were deepened by the red light. This beauty enhanced the intimacy of utter quiet . . . wind-sigh, the crackle of the logs. Also, and I recall this so well through the years, there was a lovely smell of tansy and woodruff, which old Joe used to keep the moths away.

The years have gone on a rush of tears, but I will always remember the perfumes of that room, where I made love to

Rhiannon.

"Wait!" I exclaimed. "Poor old Dobie!" and I went outside and put him in the stable, with a bag of oats to keep him warm; returning, I stamped the snow off my feet.

"God," I said, "they'd comb the meat out of us if they found us here. Our tracks in the snow are six inches deep."

It appeared to startle Rhia. She said, making big eyes, "Comb the meat out of us? What an expression!"

"That's what will happen, like it or not." I beat myself for warmth and sat down beside her.

"Would you use such a phrase in Dowlais House?"

"Probably not." I spread my hands to the blaze. "Why, what's up?"

"There you go again," said she, and she stared at the fire with a sloe-eyed indifference, as if she had said nothing.

"What s the odds?"

She shrugged, saying, "You know, I heard you talking to the ostlers once . . ." Uncertain, she hesitated.

"Continue, do not spare me." I grinned at her, kissing her face.

"You . . . you sounded as rough as them – you were actually swearing."

"*Damnia a'i chwythu!*" I said, "is that a fact?"

"But, then you spoke to Lady Charlotte – and sounded very, very different!"

"You don't speak Chinese to a Hindu."

Ignoring this, she said, "Actually, Lady Charlotte mentioned it, also. But she knew why. Welshmen, said she, possess a trick of the soul – one speech for the bawd, another for the bard."

"That sounds exactly like Lady Charlotte."

"Dual identity."

"Aye, the English gentry bring out the best in Welsh beggars."

She should have laughed, but did not. "Don't trifle with me, Tal."

"*Diawch!* This sounds important!"

"Lady Charlotte said you were an enigma."

"Her opinion isn't confined to me – she is, too."

Rhia smiled at the fire. "But I am not. I am uncomplicated. Everybody knows where they stand with me. I tell you that I love you, Tal, and this is true. If I told you that I would die for you, that would be true, also."

I put my arm around her. "And now you are doubting if I love you?"

"Do you?" Her eyes beseeched.

"Of course, with everything in me I possess."

"You'd die for me?"

"Dying would be the easiest part."

"Then why do you keep leaving me?"

The flames were red in her face, her eyes bright. It seemed impossible, but I thought she was about to cry.

"Leaving you?"

"As I said – you keep leaving me. Just when I think I've got you, you've gone."

I dared not tell her about my father. Her possession of such knowledge was unfair to her. She said, in the crackle of the fire:

"Then, if you love me, take me away?"

"How can I, woman? I haven't five guineas to call my own."

"Money isn't the reason – I've got money . . ."

"You expect me to live off you?"

"And that's not the reason, either!" She was abrupt.

I got up, wandering about. Rhia said, "There's something bigger than me going on, isn't there? Nobody has told me, but I know. And you're here in Dowlais because of that, not because you love me."

"That isn't true!"

"And when the right time comes, you will leave for good."

I did not reply.

She added, staring at me with lost, forlorn eyes: "It's to do with the Chartists, isn't it?"

"It has nothing at all to do with the Chartists – why do you imagine such things?"

"Fanny told me."

"Who?" But I knew whom she meant.

"Fanny, the parlourmaid. You're up to your neck in it, she

said. 'You'd best keep off that Tal Roberts,' she said, 'or you'll be landing in politics.'"

I came back to the fire. Beside her now, I took her hands in mine. "Listen, what Fanny doesn't know she makes up. Yes . . . all right, I am involved, but . . ."

She interjected, her arms going about me, "Then why won't you let me help you? Anything to do with you is to do with me."

"You cannot."

"I'm frightened, Tal – please tell me what's going on?" She was crying now. "I'd . . . I'd go anywhere with you. Please give it up and take me away?"

"You'd never survive it."

She became haughty and distant. "That's like a speech you've prepared."

"It isn't; it's a sermon on stones, a genesis of hatred written for the poor, and you know it's true."

"And that's made up, too."

I emptied my hands at her. "You're used to fine things – life comes easily for you; you snap your fingers and everything happens. How can you ask me to take you into poverty?"

She got up, flouncing about, brushing at her tears in disdain. "I'm much stronger than you think, and you know it!" Then she clasped her hands and turned back to me. "Oh God, this is dreadful, we're actually quarrelling . . ."

I held her and there was wetness on my lips when I kissed her: she said, as one holding back a grief:

"Make love to me, Tal, please make love to me?" She stared about her like something trapped. "Let's forget the world, if only for a minute?"

It was a madness, a thriving impulse that we had never known before; it banished all sense, obliterated consciousness. The pillows of the bunk were cold to our faces; it was a celebration of warmth within a world of ice; a cosy play within an uncosy act of dying.

Rhiannon, beneath me, turned away her face and the redness flew to her cheeks.

Her lashes were dark, her lips scarlet with my kisses; her

mouth possessed a subtlety I had never known before. The coldness of my fingers took her breath and she clung to me as something lost, when one with me. With Rhiannon it was as if our bodies had come from twin moulds, fashioned by hands of silk. In the depth of her I knew an exultant strength; she spoke, though at first I did not understand her.

"Gently, Tal, gently . . . ?"

Motionless we lay then, the act consecrated by silence save for our breathing: unified, discontented with movement, Rhiannon stilled me with her whispers. To have moved a finger would have sullied the moments. The stillness of the room, now our pent breath, was like a sacrament; even the night beyond the window was still, a white-furred world awaiting our gasps, the spy: an owl called and it momentarily shocked us, the screech echoing in the frost-laiden air.

"Do not move, darling, please do not move!"

She held me, as one forged into immobility, scarcely breathing.

It was an unmoving joy that transcended anything I have known: by word, touch or glance, I could never express it; it was an impetus unresolved and lost in time.

"Lie still, Tal?"

I obeyed and there was no sound but the beating of our hearts, heart-beats that seemed to fill the room, enveloping us; now moving slowly into a rhythm where one heart only could be heard.

I am old now; I have known many women, but never has this happened, save with Rhiannon: even our breathing was unified, from gasps to small, unvapouring breaths.

I saw beneath me the waves of her black hair on the pillow: the sharp curve of her cheek I saw, and I raised my face and looked around that room, taking in every detail, listening for every sound. Yes, other women I have known, for woman, to a man, is need as well as love. In the business of my plundering manhood, they have made shape as undifferentiated pieces of malleable clay; some noble, others unrefined. But none were such as this, whom I joined to me on that winter night in Dolygaer.

"Please . . . Just hold me?" The request was urgent. We lay together in a sad, fierce oneness, and I lowered my lips to Rhiannon, consummated, with her, in unmoving peace.

Later, again by the fire, Rhiannon said:

"There is a difference between us, Tal; this is why we are apart, although one. I look at you with the eyes of a wife, you look at me with the eyes of a lover. But thank you for that love-making."

She drew from me then, rose, and went to the window, saying:

"It's snowing again. Our footprints are gone. They will never find us now." Then she came back, took my hands and drew me up beside her. "Whatever happens, Tal, you will always be mine, remember?"

"Whatever happens," I replied.

"This . . . this thing between us, whatever it is, will take you away from me, but we will always be one, Tal. Never forget tonight?"

Such was the unusualness of her voice that I held her away, searching her eyes, and she said then:

"Thank you for being gentle with me. And . . . and forgive my stupid apprehension, but . . ." She was smiling. "I'm with child."

23

Mae'r Siartwyr yn dod! (The Chartists are coming!)

This was the new clarion call echoing over the land. Sick of it, the Welsh of the valleys gathered for rebellion, and in the counties of England an army was being formed.

On the night before our attack on the military to free our prisoner, seven hundred Chartists marched around Merthyr in gay colours, with brass bands and the banners of their lodges and benefit clubs; planning, they said, to meet again in a vast rally on Christmas Day, on Heol Cerrig Hill.

The ironmasters, from Dowlais to Cyfarthfa and Pen-y-darren to Plymouth Works, panicked. With the Merthyr riots on their conscience, they alerted Brecon garrison, begging its commander to send a force at a moment's notice.

But we in Dowlais had more important things on to consider: first we will get Gid Davies out of Redcoat hands, said my father, who, despite the initial hostility to a Northern leader, had now taken command in Gideon's absence.

You couldn't see across the bar for steam in The Patriot public, Irish Joe Dido's place, for the wet-pit colliers from the Race Lace Level were in there playing dominoes. Soaked to the skin, they were drying themselves off before Old Nana's hearth fire, which she kept especially for wet colliers, and now the steam from their clothes was smoking up the lamps. Old Nana herself was squatting on a skew seat, warming bed-bricks in the oven. Big Tom, her ginger cat, watched every move.

As skinny as a quarryman's haft was Old Nana, aged ninety, come up from County Antrim these seventy years back. Joe Dido's mother, she ruled the ale-house with a hand of iron, and Big Tom ruled her, sticking his claws into loitering customers. Now, for some unknown reason, he was yelling his head off.

"What's wrong with him?" I asked, coming to the fire.

"He wants me abed," said Old Nana, and raised her ancient face to mine. A revolutionary, this one, since the years of the Irish famines – pull the garters off bishops and strangle the Queen.

"You know about Gid Davies?" I asked her quietly, glancing around.

"I do," said Nana.

"For God's sake stop that bloody cat!" bawled a collier.

"You try stopping him," cried she, and turned her bed-bricks in the oven, saying, "Half-past ten Sam wants you on the job, son. The military convoy leaves with the prisoner fifteen minutes later."

I nodded.

The colliers guffawed, dry-swimming the dominoes. "Can ye hear me above this bloody palaver?" asked Nana.

"I hear you."

"Right. Now, there's a tunnel leading from the cellar downstairs to the grounds of Dowlais House – an old working. And the convoy is taking the lane through Dowlais gardens up to the Gwern Road, we've heard – do ye know the grave of Tancy the Dog?"

"I do."

"Ten yards behind it in the coppice is a brattice cloth entrance to the working – Mark, Mary, Joseph, I've shivered me bones on the face down there in me childhood for the Guests, I know every inch . . ."

"And my job?"

"Get into the tunnel from our cellar, and you'll meet Joe Dido halfway through: help him place the powder charges, for after they fetch Gid Davies through we're bringing that tunnel down – on soldiers, if needs be. Are ye listenin'?"

"Yes."

"Clear the brattice entrance where the tunnel comes out in the orchard, then help Knocker carry Gid Davies back into here."

"Is that all?"

"No, here's the easy bit. Go back into the tunnel and fire the fuse, once my son, the last man through, is back in the cellar. And check that he's brought his powder box back, or he'll have this public down on top of us. He's the best shot-firer in the business, is Joe, but he's as addled as a Chinese egg."

"I fire the fuse," I said.

"You fire the fuse when Joe's clear, then run."

"It's risky, mind."

"It's a bloody sight more risky being ninety." She lit her pipe.

I got up. "What are you drinking, lady?" Talk had it that she could put most colliers under the table.

"Well now," said she, "since I'm communin' with the spirits soon, I'll sink a wee drop o' the hard stuff—raw gin preferably. And then I'm away to me bed, I don't trust meself with six-foot handsome fellas. What about this for a knee?" and she lifted her skirt.

"Easy, Nana, it's hard enough as it is."

"It put the skids under County Clare, I tell ye. Can you spare five minutes?"

"Ach, I'd love to, girl, but we haven't the time."

She fanned me away. "You're more useless than this bloody tomcat. He has me in bed at half-past eight to warm it up, but he don't come up till nine."

I slapped down twopence for her gin, kissed her, and went to the door.

"Don't forget the matches," called Nana.

It was cold on the streets; the night was sparkling with frost. I walked aimlessly, to waste time, thinking of Rhiannon and the dangers encompassing my father.

Nobody was in the yard of The Patriot, and the door of the entrance to the brewer's cellar was unlocked.

Finding a lanthorne on a peg I lit it and went down steps

into the dark; soon I came to the old working Nana told of. Bent double, following the drift for about two hundred yards, I stopped to listen to the traffic of Market Street drumming above me.

Farther on I struck pit-water, but breathed fresher air as the drift shallowed, then the old brattice cloth halted me and through its decaying chinks I saw the moon.

Here the drift sloped sharply upward; I set the lanthorne on the gob and worked swiftly, clearing the entrance of fallen stones. Cold air and moonlight struck my face as I crawled up into the Dowlais orchard, and the coppice where the grave of Tancy the Dog stood was white with frost.

Crippled trees of winter enveloped me with icy arms. Nothing moved. The lane the Redcoats would take sparkled in silence.

For perhaps an hour I sat there shivering, listening to the activity of Dowlais stables; the clattering of hooves, Shire snorts and the shrill commands of ostlers. From Jones's Court, just across the road from the garden wall, came the wailing of babies; a man and woman were quarrelling in a cottage behind the Chandlery: faint music came from the windows of Dowlais House. Another Ball? I wondered. And, if so, would Rhiannon be there, dancing with the cavalry beaux . . . ?

I thought: when this is all over, I am leaving Wales. Once my father is safe, I will go from here and take Rhiannon with me. On the road to tell the tales? – I did not know: nor did I know how it would happen, or when, but we would travel together – away from anything that savoured of Dirty Dowlais. The very night, with its shivering cold, seemed part of the resolve.

As I got to my feet and beat myself for warmth, a man's head and shoulders rose up before me, fracturing the moon.

"That you, Tal Roberts?"

I clenched my hands. "Who is it?"

The head came closer, spurting breath. "Irish Joe Dido – did ye see Old Nana?"

I nodded.

"And is the brattice entrance clear?"

"It is, where the Hell have you been, and what about the mining?"

"All done, son – nothin' left to do but light the fuse."

"How many are we?" I asked, thinking of my father.

"If there's five mad Welshmen in this orchard there's fifty, and they're all three feet between the eyes. God help the English. Listen!" and he put his finger up for silence.

A little hay cart was coming: flanked on both sides by marching soldiers, it was drawn by a white dray and preceded by an officer on horseback.

Now we could see the little procession clearly – four Redcoats and their officer. As we watched, it entered the shelter of the grave coppice, and the trees about it moved, suddenly becoming men. A small army of black figures darted out with raised pick-helves, clubbing, clubbing, and the soldiers went down. All in seconds; there was no sound save the shrieks of the floundering horse as its officer was pulled off and silenced.

Running, Joe Dido and I reached the ambush: red-coated soldiers lay everywhere, their limbs moving stiffly, and colliers were going round them to make sure, tapping the semi-conscious. Knocker was already lowering the tailboard of the hay cart. In the light of the moon I saw the astonishment upon his face.

"Hey, Sam, is this Gid Davies?" He was staring down at the man on the litter.

"Just get him out," commanded Dada, coming up.

With Knocker on one end of the stretcher and me on the other, we doubled back through the brattice cloth and into the old working where Joe Dido was putting the percussion cap into the charge. Running past him in the light of the lanthorne we reached the cellar and clattered through it: men were waiting at the top of the steps and hands reached down, hoisting the stretcher up into the yard.

Men were running up behind us and I flattened myself in the tunnel now, holding high the lanthorne; my father paused to peer into the light.

"Tal?"

"Aye, Dada – get clear, for God's sake, we're pulling down

the roof."

His eyes were steady in the slanting light, and he flattened his body against the wall, like me. "Did ye see Gid's face?" His voice broke.

"Get clear!"

I pushed him aside and ran back into the dark. Joe Dido was scarfing the fuse and we lit the end of it, kneeling, watching it hissing and spluttering sparks.

"Right," said Joe, "*away!*"

We were going up the steps into the Patriot yard when there came a dull thump, and a rumbling as the roof came down.

Men were standing around the stretcher as we reached it; my father was upon his knees beside it. I looked down into a reddened, bruised mask that was no longer a face: the opaque eyes moved slowly in Gideon's swollen cheeks. His lips were split, his shirt tattered and starched with blood.

"But you didn't tell them, Gid? You didn't tell them?"

Sam Williams bent to him; tears were in his eyes, I noticed, but not in my father's: there was upon his face an anguish and hatred that I had never seen before. And I think I knew, in that moment, that I would never wean him from the task in hand; that he would never rest until the task was finished.

Gideon Davies spoke then and we bent to hear him.

"No," he said, "I didn't tell them."

"Right," said Nana, "get him inside quick, before he dies on us."

Never will I forget my father's face as they lifted his friend. And when the stretcher had gone into the house he went to a lonely place in the yard and stood there, and I did not go to him.

24

I was in the checking-office a week or so later, tally-carding the barges, when Old Shenks came in.

"We've got Gideon Davies," said he. "Come," and I followed him along the canal and over the Taff to Jackson's at the bottom of the British Tip.

Here among the rickety courts and alleys was the Pen-y-darren to Abercynon tram-road that skirted the Morlais Brook, and a line of trams I'd checked earlier on were coming down to the wharf: sheet fire from the nearby Cyfarthfa furnaces was playing on the topsy-turvy roofs of the cottages, the threatening glow before the roaring blast: the iron was due for tapping; drop-hammers were beating on the rain-washed air. Splashing along side by side in the filth of Morlais, ignoring the begging children of Beehive Row, we arrived at the very foot of the tip: Number Three in the Row was Shenks's home, he said, and knocked on the door; a battened window swung back and a face appeared.

"Our Jen," said the old man, and stood aside and the door came open.

I recognised the girl before me. She was the tattered child I had seen in Cyfarthfa over a year before, when I first came South. Now about seventeen years old, still bent nearly double, she supported herself on the same cranked ladle, her drum-stick arms projecting through rents in her dress: her eyes, as before, held me; they burned as with fever in her sallow face. Old Shenks said:

"You got a lodger, Jen."

"Ah." She was looking me over. "Who's he, then?"

"Now come on, I told ye he was comin'."

"Ain't he got a tongue?"

She stood aside as we entered, walking on the cinders of the old oven. A broken lantern hung from a semi-circular roof, casting a faint glow through the shadows beyond: along the curved walls were laid filthy straw mattresses. In the middle of the oven was a big black cauldron; a charcoal fire licked up flames, and the air was acrid with smoke.

"Where's Gideon?" I asked.

"Hold hard, son," said Shenks, "ye've got to bargain."

"Have you got honey?" asked the girl, coming closer.

"Money, she means," whispered Shenks, nudging me.

"We don't keep no one free." The girl's small, peaked face stared up. "Everyone pays the Rods, don't they, Shenks Boxer?"

"How much?" I asked.

"Four shilling a week." She smiled at me with broken, yellow teeth. "Even old Peg-Leg paid, didn't he? And Big Buzz and Waspie, they all pays Our Jen – even you pays, don't ye, Shenks?"

"I pays regular. You don't have no trouble with me."

"Four shillin', then," and the girl held out a small, grimy hand, stamping her clogs in a circle about me. "It was our Queen, really speakin'."

"Your Queen?" I asked.

"Well, it was our Queen's idea, see? 'I'll take the old man in,' says Queen, but she had to get me to agree, because it ain't Queen's hive. Understand?" Her small, peaked face peered up at me.

"No," I replied.

The girl said, "Well, Queen reckoned she owed this chap one, 'cause once his friend were good to her."

I nodded. "She lives here too, your queen?"

"O ah! She been here two year come spring Fair Day, and Sam Williams comes down, see, an' gives her a talk."

"She knows Sam Williams?"

"Aye! She's good on all the gents, is Queen."

Old Shenks asked, "Who brought Gideon Davies here?"

"Knocker and old Sam – on the dram-road from Dowlais

Top. He's blind as a bat, this fella, ye realise."

"Take us to him, please."

Reaching up with her ladle, Jen hooked down the lantern and led us deeper into the darkness beyond the coke-oven walls; shadows flung by the wavering light danced her hunchback form grotesquely on the sooted ceiling.

Here, deeper in the stomach of the tip, the air, strangely, was purer: two outlet pipes, shafting upward through the roof, mirrored the stars: beneath each pipe were two wall niches, each holding a palliasse and a bolster: at the head of one such cell hung petticoats and dresses.

"Queen's cell," said Jen, in explanation.

In the opposite cell, lying motionless on his litter, was Gideon Davies, his face upturned. I thought him dead.

His hand was cold in mine, as cold as death.

"He's alive, mind," said Jen, "though I dunna give much hope for him."

"Mr. Davies . . ." I whispered, my face close to his, but he made no reply: clearly a doctor had attended him for the swellings of his cheeks were reduced; one eye was still bandaged, but the other, wide open and opaque, stared defiantly back at me.

"Mind," said the girl, "Queen saw to him before she went out on shift, ye know – gave him milk an' a wash all over."

"He drank milk?"

She grinned at me with a broken mouth. "Yes. Big Buzz slipped over to Creigiau Farm and milked one o' the buggers."

To my astonishment Old Shenks said to her, "This fella, Jen, he's sort of special. You won't kill him, like you did Peg-Leg?"

"Christ, no!"

"Because, if ye put this one in the Taff, like you did him, the queen might fly off."

She considered this, scratching.

"Then the hive would go cold. Besides, he's worth more alive than dead, Jen – how much?"

"Four shillings – now come on, Boxer, I just bloody told ye."

The old man said, "She wants four shillings a week."

I took out the silver and dropped it into her hand, saying: "And you'll keep Big Buzz and Waspie and the others off him?"

The girl smiled, shaking her ladle. "Anyone tries at him gets this."

Old Shenks said, while I stared at them both, "Ye know, Jen, it could be your pa come back – you thought of that?"

"Jesus, no!" She pushed back her hair. "Can't be. This bugger's got two legs, Pa only had one," and she raised Gideon's blanket.

Outside in the Row I said to the old man, "God, she's mad!"

"Maybe. She ain't alone round these parts."

"Who was this Peg-Leg you spoke of?"

"The children took him in because, like Jen's father, he only had one leg. But he became their bully man, their boss: he sent the boys out thieving and made the girls prostitutes. One night, while he slept, they unscrewed his wooden leg and beat him to death with it."

Old Shenks lit his pipe and its fragrance momentarily banished the stinks of Morlais. "Mad, you say? Not as mad as she makes out – it keeps grown-ups away if they think she's a lunatic, an' she's got quite a bit tucked under the mattress, has Our Jen."

"But is Gideon safe with her?"

"Safe as a bank – you and the queen-bee being related, so to speak."

"Related?" I stared at him.

"Ay ay – Sam Williams reckons you've got a lot in common – she being your Cousin Poll."

25

The early winter snows had gone. Gentle October winds were into us, and it was a fortnight or so before I dared to approach Jen's hive again, for China was alive with searching Redcoats.

With Chartism growing in the land, unrest was up and down the valleys; men stopped work and defied the blacklist, furnaces were blown out and production stopped: the Scotch Cattle, gangs of roving unionists wearing animal skins and cow-horns, were beating men who worked on when the Union said stop, or hoisting the guilty ones to the top of pit-heads.

Hillside meetings became a nightly occurrence; with bands playing and flags of their clubs and lodges waving, the Chartists proclaimed the New Ideal, Lovett's Six Points of Parliamentary reform. On every other street corner, new Demostheneses ranted and raved. And the ironmasters, sworn to banish all unions, formed their own – The Association of Employers.

As fast as the prisons filled, new leaders arose to replace those banished to transportation: the treadmills of Usk, Beaumaris and a dozen other towns were never out of use, the cries at the whipping frames never silent. *Agents provocateurs* sent into Wales never arrived, spies among the workers disappeared. The aristocracy and shopocracy were lampooned openly: attacks on the military grew as patriots were smuggled out of cellars and attics to freedom abroad.

But still the transportation ships sailed from the Welsh ports with chained insurgents. Welsh womanhood being among them – sent to the brothels of the Colonies by order of Victoria, now publicly proclaimed by Welsh and Irish as The Royal Pimp. Barracks were built in Welsh towns, English soldiers pounded our streets, and General Napier, on Melbourne's instructions, set up a counter-espionage movement to '. . . examine the state of the districts . . .'

Whispers of Chartism and revolution sent bishops to the country and curates under beds – 'More pigs and less parsons' was now the labourer's toast. The rich lodged their jewels in bank vaults and spent more time in Church: the Archbishop of Canterbury undertook a continental tour in the name of a capricious Almighty, who, until now, had always voted Tory; the Queen herself was indisposed.

All was not well with the Guests, either, according to reports. With a home by the sea in Sully and a London house, they felt the need of something more propitious than Dowlais Manor, and set aside three hundred thousand pounds for its purchase (they eventually settled on Canford Manor, Sussex). Further, Sir John was planning to form the Works into a joint stock company with assets of a million, so they were immersed in a new theology of profit, and that meant keeping wages down. Meanwhile, they were preparing for flight to Grosvenor Square, their haven of escape from the cholera.

Rhiannon, however, was concerned on another account. She begged me, "Please, Tal, please – let me help with your father's friend!"

Fanny, the maid, had been at it again, I thought.

"Darling, no," I replied. "It's far too dangerous."

"Then, at least let me bring him some nourishing food?"

"I don't want you mixed up in this!"

She glared at me, snatching herself away in anger.

"What kind of a woman do you think I am?"

Beside Rhiannon, I had Our Jen to contend with; she was even trickier.

When I took to the hive the food Rhiannon had given me, Jen was sitting in the middle of the floor like a witch on a broom, cross-legged, the ladle across her knees.

"Hello, my lovely," said she.

I said, "I've brought food for Mr. Davies."

"Food?" Reaching up, she snatched down the bundle as I went past. "I does the food."

Hands on hips, I glared down at her, and she smiled up.

"You think I'm mad, don't ye?"

I did not reply.

"You're the mad one to bring that fella here." She jerked her thumb at Gideon. "He's bloody near dead, ye know. Any time now the Lord'll be moppin' his brow. I seen liver ones floatin' down the Taff." She got up. "You'll never ride 'im down to Cardiff, son, the soldiers'll see to him long before that."

I met her eyes, and she winked, adding, "Ye see, lad, I know these parts, an' what comes an' goes. I'm saner than you, really speaking. Just that it suits ole Jen for people to think she's addled." She gestured around the walls and the children's straw mattresses.

"Now, you take this lot – they're only kids, see. So I brings 'em in from the streets and puts 'em in this hive and tell 'em they're bees: I make the bee noises, they make 'em back, and out they go for honey and bring it back to Jen . . ."

I interjected. "Where's Poll?"

"Ach, dear me! Poll, is it? You and her related, eh? These last few nights she don't sleep much, our Poll – just talkin' about you."

I said, "I brought this food for Gideon, not you, and I'm going to see that he gets it," and I strode past her, deeper into the cave. Catching my arm, she hauled me back, the ladle up.

"Listen," she whispered. "I'm boss here, son. Everything's shared, crust an' crumb. Old Poll might be the queen, like the kids say, but I'm in charge, 'cause I got the ladle."

Footsteps sounded outside the door and Jen swung round, saying, "Christ, here they come – Big Buzz first, as usual – with his honey."

Big Buzz, as she called him, was a tall, rangy lad of about

fifteen; there was about him a sinewy strength. Until Old Shenks came to the hive, Buzz was its guard, he told me, eating while the rest went short. Now he was one of a dozen workers; a thimble-rigger by day, a pickpocket by night.

I watched Buzz enter. Seeing Jen approaching, he stood nervously before the cauldron, screwing at his hands. And Jen, with the aplomb of an ancient princess, squatted on the floor beside it, gripping the ladle, saying:

"Hallo, my charmer, what you got for me?"

Excitement struck his thin face. "I got twopence, Jen!" Fishing into his rags he dropped the money into her lap.

"More," said she.

"Got no more, Jen." He was shivering.

"Turn out, Buzz, there's a good boy."

Bemused, he was staring down at her, and she shrieked, the ladle up.

"Turn out!" And then, by way of explanation to me, added, "He's a good lad is Buzz, but sometimes he do tamper wi' it – like thief bees." She made a faint humming noise.

"You been eating it?"

"I only got twopence!"

Rising, Jen struck out with the ladle, the spoon caught the boy's shoulder and he danced about, howling: and she, stooping and straightening, thumped blow after blow into his body. As I leaped to intervene, Jen stepped back, saying:

"He's a thief bee, ain't you, Buzz?" and then she quietened, adding confidentially to me, "He's bigger'n me, see. I 'ave to lather him much more'n the others."

Gideon was asleep, so I sat by his mattress and watched the children come home; bringing their earnings.

There was a bantam hen from Waspie, a shrew-like child with an impish stare: chicken giblets from Song, a tattered urchin with a ready smile: half a rabbit from Hare, a gnome of a child with a deformed lip, aged eight: six sausages stolen from Butcher Heppo's stall in Merthyr market came next, a grubby, evil-looking, half-man-half-child called Doss being the donor: then two duck's feet from Hummer, aged twelve, filched out of the bins of the Lamb Row public, and a loaf of bread from Shrinky, who, cranked-back like Jen from work in the lower levels, was only four feet high. One other worker brought money – a shilling from Fly, who held the horses' heads outside the Castle Inn.

It was then that Poll came in.

Everything ceased.

This was not the Cousin Poll I had known; the harlotry of powder and rouge had painted out the smile that I once knew, and her eyes, once alive with sin and mischief, held the false brightness of mascara: even her voice, when she spoke, had changed: two years on the pave had taken their toll. Seeing her coming, the children rose; even Jen, pinned on the ladle, struggled up.

Unlike them all, Poll was well fed. Dressed in a long, grey skirt, wearing a broad-rimmed hat, she entered with the self-assurance of one who took obeisance as her due. And the children stood silently, their switching eyes alternating between Poll and the cauldron: Shrinky, crying, was silenced by the upraised ladle. Fingering it, Jen asked softly:

"How did ye do today, my precious?"

Poll didn't appear to hear this, but opened a purse and dropped a sovereign; the children squirmished for it on the floor. Biting on it, Jen said:

"You'll 'ave your supper now, Missus? You got someone visitin', look," and she nodded towards me.

Not replying, Poll walked past her, and past me, too, into her cell.

I greeted her, but she ignored me, lying full length on the bed, eyes closed, her hands folded behind her head. And Jen, beating away the begging hands of the children, filled a bowl with choicest pieces from the pot, saying amiably:

"Take ye time, kids, take ye time! You got to feed the Queen, ye know." She approached Poll with the bowl of food.

"Get rid of him," said Poll, her eyes still closed.

"Well now, ain't you two happy to see each other, and you born relatives?"

I said, at the cell door, "Thank you for taking care of Dada's friend, Poll."

"Get rid of him," she repeated.

"Bugger you," exclaimed Jen, "you've upset the Queen." She gathered the children about her, adding, "Best he gets goin', eh, kids, 'afore he gets stung?"

They encircled me, following me to the door. I looked back before I went through it.

Poll was standing with her hands over her face.

26

Within a week of Gideon arriving in the hive, a squad of Redcoats under a Captain Wetton came down to Canal Wharf and started going through the cottages, throwing out people's possessions, poking under beds. And they hooked me out of the tally-hut to take them into the stacking areas and round the moored barges.

They went through the warehouse with a tooth-comb, burrowing like moles into the stacked pig ingots, emptying waiting trams of fish-plates and spikes. Wetton was watching me closely, but did not speak; he was the new English commander of the Penywern garrison, Old Shenks told me, and it was clear to me that he was on a concentrated search for Gideon, their lost prisoner. The last I saw of the soldiers was them marching off towards Morlais brook and Beehive Row.

"Don't worry," said Old Shenks, coming on shift, "if they go into the hives it'll be the first time ever. Adults, not kids, hide wanted people around these parts."

An Irish bargee called O'Reilly came in for his tally-card for his Cardiff run, and Old Shenks waited until he had gone. Then:

"Your dada wants you up at Llangynidr," said he.

"Llangynidr? What for? I was just going to get my head down."

"Reckon ye'll get no sleep today, old son. Knocker says it's important. The boys up there are running a dram load of rough stuff down to Abercynon."

"Rough stuff?"

"Don't ask me, son – that's what he told me." It was the way he looked at me that made me ask:

"Arms?"

"Don't call it names, for God's sake."

I'd heard the term, of course; up and down the valleys arms were being made in small quantities and smuggled down from remote places like Llangynidr into the towns.

"What for, Shenks?" I asked, but he lit his pipe and turned away, not answering. I said:

"All right, there's a revolution coming – but where, and how?"

The old man shrugged. "You ask your betters, lad, not me. Getting patriots out of the country's one thing, a revolution's another. I'm too old for sense, but I reckon Wellington will cut fanatics to pieces, and there's more than one fanatic around."

"Men like my father, you mean?" and he shrugged empty, and waved me down, replying:

"Ay ay, if ye want it straight. But there's hotter heads than him. Best you get up there to Llangynidr, then ye might see what I mean."

He sat at his table and began to write out tally-cards; it was an indication that the conversation was finished, so I stood by the window for a bit and watched the barges moving off; the man O'Reilly, waiting on the tow-path, made a brief signal. I saw Old Shenks nod.

Old men, I have found, often speak with two tongues; one for practicality, another for wisdom. I began to wonder if this old man was up to something he didn't want to share with me.

It was dusk when I went up Dowlais Top on my way to Llangynidr, and it was dark and the stars were like Chinese lanterns as I reached the cave on Dobie. A man was standing on guard at the cave mouth, and although he recognised me, he told me later, he called:

"You – the password!"

"Beanswell," I called back.

"Who do you seek?"

He approached me with his musket at the ready and peered at me and Dobie, and his eyes were sunken in the caverns of his face and his clothes were ragged. I replied:

"Gwyn Roberts. I am his son."

"Ach, dear me! The Captain himself, is it?" He winked, presenting arms. "Shanco Blackbird Mathews I am, honour to ye name, lad. For there's a hundred or more comin' and goin', but if I blew this bloody musket the sods'd vanish. Shall I accompany ye?"

"You can hold the horse," I said, and went past him into the cave.

"Will you tell me when the revolution's starting, so I can get back to Nanty for me supper?" This he called after me, and I went flat and crawled through the light-lock, and an unknown helper seized my arm and dragged me through.

My father disengaged himself from a clutch of men.

"Ah, Tal, good lad. Later we'll be needing you. Meanwhile you're just in time to hear The Watchmaker."

Other men surrounded us; one was Iestyn Mortymer, the lad whose letter Sam Williams had delivered to Nantyglo, the town at the top of Black Rock; he greeted me with a curt nod – not a great deal to say, this one: the others were talkative, and the black-maned giant whom I had seen before suddenly put up his hand for silence, saying, "Listen!"

A low knocking came on the rock door and the big man knelt, listening, and a faint voice called:

"Mr. Edwards?" It was the sentry outside.

"Aye, Shanco!"

"'Tis the revolution committee, Mr. Edwards. Shall I send 'em in or shoot 'em?"

The man Edwards said, "Christ, we can do without comedians – send them in, Shanco!"

There was a pause; whispered consultation behind the light-lock; the men about me stirred uneasily, their faces gaunt and careworn, grotesquely shadowed in the yellow light.

As my eyes became more accustomed to the glow I saw above me the vaulted roof of the cave, and beyond the searching fingers of the lamp a gulf of blackness. The tables I had seen before had vanished.

About a hundred men were in the cave, sprawled in various attitudes upon the earth floor or lying back against the rocky walls; in one corner pikes were roped in bundles like firewood, their rough iron heads dully gleaming: beside these were packing cases, some ten or more, and upon these other men were sitting. Now there was a scuffling at the light-lock.

"Here he comes," whispered Dada beside me, and knelt beside Edwards.

I watched fascinated as a hand and then an arm came through into the light; elegantly decorated at the wrist with lace, the hand waved, disembodied, seeking assistance, and my father gripped it and hauled and the arm became a shoulder and the shoulder a man; they pulled him through unceremoniously into the light, and he stood there, this man, in a fine velveteen frock coat and trews, then bent, beating the dust from his shoulders.

"The Captain?" he asked.

"This is our captain," said Edwards, and indicated my father.

I weighed the man before me.

He was of medium height, and slim; extraordinarily handsome, his dark eyes moved slowly around the scene before him. My father offered his hand in friendship, but the stranger did not take it.

"Your name?" he asked faintly, in English.

"Gwyn Roberts," said my father. "Welcome to Llangynidr," and this he said in Welsh.

The man snapped, "Talk English, man, for God's sake. The Irish are with us one to one; Scots are here, even Spaniards, and the rebellion is more English than Welsh, for it is nationwide. Are you the leader here?"

My father replied quietly, "No man is leader. None here stands an inch above another, Mr. Jones. But I am the captain of the Merthyr contingent, for Gid Davies is blind."

"But safe now, I hear?"

This was William Jones whom men called The Watchmaker, one of the three leaders of the Welsh Chartists, of whom John Frost was its chief and Zephaniah Williams of Coalbrookvale its second-in-command.

Many said that Jones the Watchmaker was the most fervent and fanatical of the three, with his fiery talk of shifting Victoria off the throne and fleshing swords to the hilt in a victorious battle that would fling off the English yoke. Certainly there was an arrogance in his attitude to my father, and the way he held himself was, for me, foppish.

"Yes," said Dada. "Gid is safe, and we will get him out of the country."

"Did he talk?" asked Jones.

"Had he done so, we would not be here."

The man glanced about him, then jumped lightly on to a packing-case.

"I will address the men," said he, and faced them, his feet astride, his hands upon his hips.

"There's a bloody pansy for a half-pint revolutionary," said a voice beside me, and I turned. Iestyn Mortymer sat on his hunkers and I joined him, whispering, "You don't think much of him?"

"God help us if we're dependent on the likes of him to lead us," came the reply. "I've got a sister back home who'd take him while she poured the tea."

"Hush you," growled the big man, Edwards, and gave us a look to kill. Raising high his hands, he said, "Listen, you, listen all. The time has come to hear the plans, and Mr. Jones is travelling round to give it to the Pontypool contingent, of which we mostly are a part. Can you hear me at the back?"

"They can hear ye in Brecon barracks, Ed," called a man.

"Then peg back your ears and give the leader a hearing, for you'll not be hearing it twice," and he gestured to William Jones, who cried, his voice highly pitched:

"In the past ten days I have spoken in Pontypridd and Aberfan; from Crickhowell to Usk and east to the labourers of the Forest of Dean, I have travelled to rally our comrades in the cause of Chartism." He raised a small fist. "And if men of Beaufort and Merthyr march in my Pontypool column, they are welcome. I greet you all."

He paused, breathing heavily.

"The time has come to put these valleys to the torch! No longer will we workers tolerate the ever downward trend of wages when the iron trades are down, for we do not get rises when times are good. No longer will we accept the filthy housing of places like Merthyr's China, or Dirty Dowlais under the benevolence of the scrounging Guests.

"Listen again. I will not keep you long, for I am not here to inflame a rabble, but if we lie down in the face of this exploitation our masters will sink your hopes for another ten generations." He flung up his arms. "So we will tear the crown from the tyrant's head! We will trample their banners in the dust! We'll build a new Jerusalem out of the ashes of the old!"

"Wait," said my father, and came to the fore.

William Jones lowered his hands and there was no sound but his breathing; slowly, he turned.

"God! You dare to interrupt me?"

"Aye," said Dada. "Because, with respect, we've had enough of rampaging speeches about tyranny. We've had enough, too, of words and hotness, for words are cosy old things when they advocate the business of dying, which can't be easy if you're stuck by a Redcoat bayonet."

Jones the Watchmaker shouted, "Mr. Edwards, I am here by invitation. Can you stand by and see your speaker insulted?"

"Ay ay, he can," said Dada, "for I'm the captain here. And it's a bloody sight more insulting, I vow, to sit chained in a cart, for I've had some. So temper your tongue, Mr. Jones, or we'll send for John Frost, the spiritual leader of this mad-cap expedition. Can ye hear me at the back?"

They rose to him, on their feet now in simmering excitement, and Dada said:

"Listen – bad cess, as say the Irish, to any man with no respect for Chartist leaders, but we'll flesh swords to the hilt on our own account. Merthyr has its own contingent – we're miles away from Pontypool: let Mr. Jones poach his marchers from Brecon and Abergavenny, and Blaenafon, the town of mountain-fighters. We in Merthyr will make our own run to Newport, and we don't need salty old talk to send us on our way. What say you?"

They shouted in chorus until Shanco Mathews banged on the light-lock for quiet and Edwards silenced them by bawled commands. My father said:

"Lest Mr. Jones forgets the reason for his invitation, I will tell you it. For, if you are prepared to die in this fight you have a right to know the plans and dispositions. The scheme is this. To invest and capture the town of Newport and to stop the mail coach to Cardiff. The failure of other mails to arrive will alert scores of other towns and cities from here to London. For two million men are under arms in Britain, awaiting the signal to rise in rebellion, and we, the Welsh, have been chosen to be in the van."

"When do we go, Welshman?" shouted a foreigner from the back, in darkness. "Lead the way, and we'll follow!"

My father said, "We move on Sunday, November the third. We march in three separate columns – the first under John Frost, the western men from Blackwood; the centre column under Zephaniah Williams from Ebbw Vale district; the third under Mr. Jones here, driving out of Pontypool: all three columns join forces at Cefn, between Risca and Newport; then they will descend in a body and take the town."

"And after that, mun?"

"After that, comrade, we march on London," shouted William Jones, and he quoted, "'We'll rend their veil, we scorn their steel, we shrink not, nor dissemble. By every burning wrong we feel, cold tyrants, ye shall tremble!'" and he seized a sword nearby and brandished it above his head. "These are the words of our Chartist poet Ernest Jones. If they are good enough for him and our beloved Henry Vincent now in gaol, they should be good enough for us!"

"Aye," said my father, and reached up and took the sword away from him. "But words will not be enough when Wellington brings out the troops that beat the French. Cool heads may win, but men like that will cut the fanatics into pieces." He tossed the sword into a corner. "Listen again, men – more plans and less poetry."

It silenced them.

"Merthyr, it is decided, will supply three contingents, and their task will be this: One squad will be stationed on the heights above Garn on the Brecon Road, and cut the road to Brecon barracks: a second will ambush any troops coming up the road from Swansea: a third, under my command will be astride the road at Llanhennock to repel all military reinforcements aiding Newport from Monmouth. This contingent, swelled by numbers after Newport has been taken, will then march on Cold Bath Fields prison and release the hero Vincent. Before that week is out, my friends, the government of Wales will be run from the tap-room of the Coach and Horses, John Frost's pub in Blackwood!"

I stared at my father as the men rose about him in shouts of exultation, for there was a light in his face I had never seen before: little to choose between him and Jones, I was thinking; both possessed a frightening, tub-thumping eloquence. Iestyn Mortymer, squatting beside me, said above the hubbub:

"A good old boy your da, I'm thinking. I had one like him once; they'd spark a bit if they could get together."

I gave him a glance in the yellow light. His eyes were good, this one, like shining orbs in his square, handsome face. I said back:

"Never seen him like this, though: another couple of minutes and he'd set himself alight."

"The whole business stinks, mind."

"It's a stink, and it must stop," I said.

He rubbed his fingers through his dark hair. "Aye, and perhaps we need such leaders – a pack of whirling dervishes, to get some spirit into the mass."

He surprised me; I had never heard one speak like that.

"You approve of Jones and my father?"

He raised his face to mine. "Jones, no. People don't trust him. Rumour has it that his Pontypool column will never see the skies over Newport. But your father, aye, he's all right, but I tell you this – he'll sell his words with blood." He rose in the babble and shove of the men. "I lost my dada to the furnaces, you will lose yours in this rebellion. Men like him go home in coffins."

Dada, freeing himself from the others, came to us, saying: "Dobie's outside, is he, Tal?"

"Aye."

He gripped Mortymer's shoulder. "Listen, I want the pair of you on this," and he jerked his thumb at the packing cases. "This lot have to be delivered to Turnout Six on the Pen-y-darren tram-road at midnight – two hours time."

"Turnout Six, the tram-road," I repeated.

"Aye. And Sam Williams and Old Shenks will be waiting and fix the load – under three tons of dog-spikes going down to Canal Wharf. A bargee called O'Reilly will be hauling them down to Abercynon in the morning. If you're still on duty then, make sure they're tally-carded through, understand?"

"Yes," I said.

"And Tal . . ." He drew me to one side. "What's this I hear about a girl . . ."

"What about her?"

"A gentry?"

I faced him. "Aye, well?"

"You realise the danger, I suppose?"

"It's not important, Dada."

"But at a time like this?"

The men were pulling at him, invading the affinity with questions; Edwards was trying to turn him into a goodbye with William Jones. I said softly, "I'll tell you when there's time, Dada. Meanwhile, forget it."

"Aye, and meanwhile don't trust her. The daughter of Richard de Vere? You're a worker, Tal, you'll never stand on her side of the chandeliers."

I whispered. "Go easy. Who wants to?"

He nodded. "All right, but if anything slips out you'll be the first under suspicion, remember. This lot wouldn't think twice about tearing you to pieces."

We slid the long, thin packing cases through the light-lock, Iestyn Mortymer and me, and straddled them, three each

side on Dobie, who was watching me with an evil eye
because he was on overtime, and meantime shifting his rear
to get Mortymer into range.

"Watch his hind legs," I said, in passing.

"It's the fillies on two legs you've got to watch," said he at
the moon.

"O aye? What does that mean?"

"Your dada's right, boyo. I heard what he said. It's
common knowledge, did you put it in *The Cambrian*?"

"What's it to you, then?" I came around the horse, and he
said with a dark, lazy smile:

"I heard it in the Vulcan and Friendship. Once Old Joe
Hitherto climbs on, everybody knows. Ye need your head
read, sparking a gentry at a time like this." He nodded
towards the cave mouth. "They'll have your balls for
Spanish castanets." He took a final tug on Dobie's saddle
rope, tightening up the boxes. "Do you love the maid?"

There was an easy strength about him; a manner that
dispelled anger, and he was older than me. The moon
suddenly blazed and I saw him more clearly.

"Aye," I said.

"How old are you?"

"Eighteen."

"Your first girl?"

"No."

"Good for you, but why the English?"

"Who said she was English?"

"Good God," came the reply. "Don't tell me you're
sparking gentry Welsh – she'll sell ye down the river soon as
bloody look at you."

This angered me and I fancied a go at him, yet his careless,
easy charm again placated me. Now he said, as I took
Dobie's bridle and we went along side by side:

"Do you love her, Tal?"

"Aye." I warmed to him because he had used my name.

"And she loves you?"

"Her business."

He made a face at the misted moon, for clouds of rain had
come up. The air was needle crisp and suddenly cold, the

heather flattening in quick buffets of the wind. "Dear God," said he, "you're a tight old boy when it comes to romance – are they all like you up North?"

We walked on side by side with Dobie between us hating every minute, and the sky over Dowlais Top was suddenly a strickening red as the furnaces were tapped: the clouds, fat-bellied with pulsating light, poured down a radiance over the earth.

"What's your wife's name?" I asked.

"Mari."

"Where's she now, then?" and he said, as if to himself:

"Over at Nantyglo in one of the Bailey houses with my mother and sister."

"What are ye doing up here, then?"

"Working for the Chartists – over suspension. We get furnace rates, mind, just to see us over, until we get the Charter."

"You think we'll get it?"

"God, yes. Or why would I be here?"

"When did you see your wife last?"

"Six weeks ago. You know the sentry back by there? Old Shanco Mathews? He slips over to Nanty from time to time to take her money."

"Why don't you go yourself?" I asked, and he stopped, pulling up Dobie short.

"Because if I go, I'll stay the night, and if I do that they might get me. That means four go to transportation, not just one: Shanco's got no family."

The fizz-gig light of the furnace tapping died: we heard the drop-hammers forging the soul into the iron, and Dobie's eyes were bright under the moon. Then rain fell, sweeping over the boulder-stricken country, and I wondered about Rhiannon. Every step now was bringing me closer to her and I knew a small, comforting warmth. Above Garn Caws, at seventeen hundred feet, the stars seemed even brighter, and I imagined her asleep in the bed at Kierton with this same moonlight on her window, this same rain pattering on the glass.

"What's her name?" asked Iestyn suddenly.

"Rhiannon."

"Is she beautiful, as Rhiannon of the *Mabinogi*?"

"I've only got words to use," I said, and it delighted him, for he replied, quoting in Welsh:

"'I welcome you,' said Pwyll, 'for it seemed to him that the beauty of every girl and woman he had ever met was as nothing compared with the beauty of this lady . . .'"

"You know the *Mabinogi*?"

"It is the Welsh soul – who does not?"

Trefil came up on the moors and we saw the lights of Beaufort in the sky. And I knew with this new friend an understanding and nearness I had felt for no man save my father.

A furnace whistle from the valley told us that it was midnight, and we made our way now with greater care, coming to Dowlais Top where the Guest trains were tipping their loads of muck: leading Dobie down a fire-break in the forest, we came to a road facing the railway line.

Here the new locomotive 'Perseverance' was steaming on the wide track, and behind her was a line of trams stacked with dog-spikes for Spain – I knew these tallies now like the back of my hand.

"Wait here with Dobie," I said to Mortymer, and whistled my way down the line, hands deep in my trews: and I saw against a roseate sky two men rise up from the waggons like brooding hulks, and one I recognised as Knocker. I wandered up to him, still whistling.

"Got rough stuff, Knock," I said. "Where's Sam?"

Sam's face then appeared above the side of the same tram; ridged with bumps and bruises, it seemed, fashioned by the strange red light.

I said, glancing around, "Is it safe?"

"Be your age, lad," said Sam. "Is it safe anywhere? With bloody Wetton plunderin' down on Canal Wharf, waiting to knock up our kneecaps? Who's he?" and he indicated Iestyn, who had led Dobie to us. I explained, and Knocker said happily:

"O aye, I remember – the love-letter lad. I delivered it personally, mind – and you got a right old varmint for a sister – she threatened me with the poker, she did."

"That's the least will happen if you get mixed up with her," said Iestyn. "Are we staying here all day, Mr. Williams?"

"Aye, load up," said Sam. "Is this the lot?"

"It isn't. Another load coming down before dawn."

So we loaded the tram and the engine puffed off, down to Canal Wharf where Old Shenks and Bargee O'Reilly were waiting. And we got off back, Iestyn Mortymer and me – he to the arms cave and me down to Dowlais along the Pen-y-darren road, and I knew again, more strongly, that our destinies, his and mine, were linked.

I did not know then that it would be under a hail of Redcoat bullets along the road to Monmouth.

27

The night before the big Chartist demonstration in Merthyr, Poll tapped the window of the tally-hut, just as I was getting my head down. Getting out of bed, I let her in. Rain was splashing down the window.

"Hallo, Tal," said she.

"Ay ay, Poll."

In the lamp-light of the hut, I could see her better than in the dimly-lit hive; she looked even older, and the rain had washed the mascara off her eyes on to her cheeks, giving her a strangely haunted look.

She said, her head low, "Don't think a lot of me now, Tal, do ye?"

"You're all right. You'll always be good old Poll."

"Oh yes?" She raised her face. "Always been good old Poll, hasn't it! But if you'd sparked proper instead of lagged, I'd still be on me feet."

"Somewhere down the line it went wrong," I said.

She shrugged, empty. "Perhaps I just made the mistake of wantin' to be alive." She rummaged under her coat and brought out something I instantly recognised. "I only come to give you this, Lover," she said. "Our pa used to read to us from it, remember?" and she gave me the manuscript of 'The Tale of Delwyn'.

I held it joyfully against me. It was impossible to believe that I had got it back, and said, "I . . . I thought Dada took it when he was arrested . . ."

"No, I took it, 'cause it was his. But then I tried to sell it. Nobody wanted it—only a book, see?"

Dry of words we stood there like strangers.

She added, "So you'd best 'ave it, and keep it for Pa."

I waited. There was more to come, made evident by the twisting of her fingers. I said, "Sit down, Poll," and drew up a chair.

"No, not staying," came the reply. "I'm off directly," and Poll raised her painted face. "It . . . it was me who told old Casanova, too."

"Mostyn Morris – the constable – about Dada?" I peered, perplexed because I was now hearing it from her own lips.

"Aye, Tal, it were me." She stared vacantly around the hut.

"But why, Poll? Why?"

She emptied her hands at me. "Pa were . . . well, he were sharp on me, remember? Over that Andy Appledore. After Meg was on her feet he don't need Poll no more, I reckon, and . . ."

"That's not true, and you know it!"

"And . . . and you, too. You slid up garters wi' anyone but me, you realise?" She held herself. "I boiled for you, Tal, deep in 'ere. A sort of motherin' and frolics, all rolled in one. But nobody cared much for me in them old days."

A silence of awkwardness came between us. She continued, "You think anything much about me now, Tal?"

I had no words for her and she came closer, her hand shaking on mine. "I'd go straight for you, *cariad*, eh, ye sweet thing. I'd go straight, ye know – I'd give up the pave." Then her expression became alight with a sudden radiance and for a moment she was Poll again, in bloom. "Honest I would, Tal, I'd go decent. Say the word an' I'll start again. I ain't ill, ye know – they say I am, but I ain't. I'd keep your place brushed and tidy for you, and I'd wash all over, mornin' and night." She opened her arms to me. "And I'm a steady old boafer, like the lads say – I'd be worth the rent. You listenin'?"

I nodded, and she added, "Be a sport, Lover, give us a chance?"

My mind flew back to the kitchen of Three Costog. We stood in silence, reading thoughts, while the rain poured down, and I lowered my head. Poll said:

"Because of that gentry piece, isn't it?"

I nodded.

"I saw her the other day, an' she's all right, but she's only got the same equipment as me, an' anythin' she can do, I can do better."

I looked at her: head on one side, she added, "Go on, Tal."

I thought: one wrong word here and we are all dead. She had betrayed once, she could do it again. I said, quietly, "Gid Davies first, Poll, isn't it? It's got to be Gideon Davies first, if you want to make up, you see?"

Her eyes narrowed; she was fighting for comprehension. I said, "No good talking about us till we get him out of Beehive Row and down to Abercynon."

"Ay ay, well Old Shenks do come talking last night about that . . ."

"About what?"

"About getting him down to Abercynon. On Rally Day, he said – Saturday, ain't it? On the barges wi' the Chartist bands playin' on their way to Cefn Fair, and banners and flags, an' all that . . ."

I said, "You'll help?"

"Jesus, yes, what d'ye think I am?"

"It's dangerous."

"I don't care none about that."

I took a breath. "First to Abercynon with him, then, and after that to Cardiff. Then we'll talk about us, is it?"

Her eyes became alive. "You promise?"

"No! Can't promise. Who can promise? Perhaps I'll stop a bullet, perhaps you . . . First we get Gid down to Abercynon."

We stood together within our indecision; the rain beat down, drumming on our world, and Poll said, her eyes bright:

"Give us a kiss, Tal?"

I caught a glimpse of the purity of Rhiannon's face: even a kiss, I thought, could mean acquiescence . . .

"Just a kiss, Lover? You won't catch nothin'."

I put my arms around her and kissed her, and she clung to

me gasping and sobbing, like a woman drowning. I said, holding her away, "Poll, you'd best go. The military have been round once tonight, perhaps they'll come again."

She said, "Gawd, I feel clean now! Ain't that wonderful?"

She looked at me within the icy silence of her loneliness. Time was that Poll had a fancy-free piquant charm; in Chapel, a nobility and grace even; but now this had gone. She said:

"The runt of the litter, ain't I?"

"Ach, no! You'll always be good old Poll."

"What . . . what happened? I wonder." She smiled, empty, "I suppose I grew up, is that it?"

Then she collected herself with the little fussy movements women employ before leaving, and said, looking away. "Sorry I hooked out of Amlwch and left you flat wi' Meg, Tal."

I didn't answer, and she added, going to the door. "After I'd done it – gone to Mostyn Morris, I mean, I had to go: I just couldn't bear to see him whipped." Suddenly she began to cry. "God, I couldn't bear to see 'im whipped . . ."

Opening the door she went out into the night: holding the blind aside, I watched her running through the rain to Beehive Row.

Shenks Boxer came into the tally-hut a few moments after Poll left.

"Young Poll was that?" He beat rain from his shoulders.

"Yes."

"What she want?"

"It doesn't matter, Shenks."

"I told you before about havin' the molls in 'ere, mind."

"It isn't what you think."

He grimaced. "Your business. She'll likely do her bit, that one, so no odds to that."

I nodded. "Let's hope so. But it's a pity we have to trust the others," and he replied philosophically, screwing plug tobacco into his pipe:

"Aye, but when the queen bee flies, the hive swarms, don't it? They'll 'ave to come. Mind, Sam Williams don't worry about that, the more the merrier on Fair Days, he says."

"Have you seen the Union lads?"

Shenks nodded. "They ain't runnin' this Chartist Rally for a half-dead blind chap – it's county-wide. But we're getting a few extra banners stitched up, the wives are at it now – 'We Want a Hospital', 'We Want Doctors', 'We Want Stretchers'. Just about every lodge and Benefit Club will be carrying invalids – stretchers and corpses will be end to end."

"I hope to God it works."

"Ach, you're mooney for a funeral, of course it'll work! When poor old Gideon comes out o' Beehive Row, he'll just be an extra body."

"What happens if they lift the blanket?"

The old fighter lit his pipe; the match flared, banishing the shadows and lighting his disfigured face. "Then Gid's a gonner, ain't he? So it's up to us to see no squaddies get near 'im." He licked his knuckles and struck his fist into his palm.

"It's a risk."

He shrugged. "All right, it's a risk. Can you think of anything better? It ain't so healthy in Beehive Row, come to that."

Over a hundred million people crossed the Atlantic that century, and most of them must have visited Merthyr's Chartist rally before they went, said Dada: the town was jammed like herrings in a barrel. Political rallies, like annual Fairs, being the essence of corruption, most people took their morals out of pawn in the morning and sold them back at night: there was bull-baiting, pitch and toss, cock-fighting and thimble-rigging, but one thing was certain: for a rally that was heralding a coming national rebellion against the State, things were circumspect.

The theme for this Chartist march being the need for hospitals in Merthyr, it was the organisers' intention to move the stony hearts of their employers to grant medical facilities: the attempt failed – we didn't get a wheeled stretcher in Dowlais, Cyfarthfa, Plymouth or Pen-y-darren until the 'forties, and the first hospital in Dowlais came ten years later. But the Merthyr Chartists, though a mere two thousand strong, were increased to an army by the valley contingents coming in from all corners of the town.

They came with the insignias of their lodges and the costumes of their Benefit Clubs: they came marching in from all points with flags and streamers waving and banners strung across the roads. In ranks of six abreast they marched, chanting their aims in unison, the need for reform. From Nantyglo and Brynmawr they came, from the Chartist lodges of Blaenafon, Abertillery, Bedlinog, Pontypool, Bargoed and a dozen other iron towns. Some had been marching for days, sheltering on the treeless mountains, crouching soaked in caves and quarries. With hope and aims for fulfilment they marched, shouting their defiance of military authority and employer domination.

They came not with arms, but with music and the poetry of Ernest Jones, now in custody for sedition. In company with their comrades of Sheffield, they had as their slogan, 'March, Death or Glory'. They knew the history of the Plug Plot disturbances of Preston, and by heart the speeches of Rayner Stephens, the attacker of the New Poor Law. 'Let the child take the needle, the housewife her scissors and the men to the knife,' said he, 'aye, and the firebrand, too, if all else fails.'

Rayner's cry was on their lips as they marched to Cefn Fair in Merthyr, the centre of the cauldron that day. And banners they carried proclaimed:

EVERYMAN FOR SECRET VOTE: PAID M.P.'S, NO LANDED ONES: EQUAL VOTING DISTRICTS AND ANNUAL PARLIAMENTS!

They thronged in their thousands, dressed in the colours of their clubs and Societies; the Oddfellows, Ivorites, True Britons and a score of other lodges and Benefits: weavers and bleachers of the North Country, deputations from the woodsmen of the Forest of Dean.

Gentlemen puddlers were there in grey suits and stove-pipe hats, the cream of the trade of iron: Irish luggers and trimmers were drunk at seven in the morning. Waving their beer notes, they flooded into every pub in Merthyr, from the old Dowlais Inn to The Colliers, hammering the counters.

Their women came too; tipsy Irish arming it around with Spaniards, and pinafored Dowlais ironwork girls in their brown woollen stockings and quarter boots. With their black straw hats and brightly coloured kerchiefs on their heads, these marched in hundreds, bold-eyed, picturesque in their black shawls and coloured earrings. And they waved aloft their calloused hands and bawled their bawdy songs, a strident contrast to the official music . . . Buxom, wide-hipped, armoured against weather by their lusty thirteen-hour shifts of piling sheared iron or moulding furnace bricks up Penyard for five shillings a week before deductions . . . they were a part of the official labour market, said a visitor to Dowlais, 'Among whom the young masters played the role of many dingy sultans . . . with promises of shorter hours and higher pay'.

As far as I knew, not many succumbed: these, the 'lower orders' as Lady Charlotte called them, but the beating heart of Dowlais labour, the fulcrum of her obscene fortune.

Quakers and priests abounded in funeral-black procession, chanting from brass-bound Bibles; touts, toughs; medicine men and quacks slapped up their bottles of cures from mange to toothache and ointments for piles. A fat Hereford bull, contentedly munching, was being led to the baiting ring for the sport that would make him tender . . . followed by snarling bull-terriers straining on the leash.

And then, as the column, ten abreast, rounded Canal Wharf, I saw the Beehive Row contingent led by Jen. With her hair hanging down, she was dancing a crippled fandango, using her ladle as a crutch: prancing here and there in her rags, waving to the crowd, her gap-toothed mouth leering into the sun.

Waspie I saw, also Song: Hare of the deformed mouth was there hand in hand with Fly, the horse-holder aged twelve; Shrinky, in her crippledom, was riding a flying-angel on the shoulders of Doss. But Poll was not there, neither was Big

Buzz. The band marched past, the combs and gazooters shrill to the deep-throated trombones and ophicleides. Our Jen cavorted and spun, her spindly legs kicking up. Seeing me, she momentarily paused, then swung the ladle around her head in new grotesque contortions. The sun shone down. The music blasted the calm clear air.

Thumping reverberations were approaching from the other side of the river, for, with the head of the march in China, its tail was still in High Street. Shift-workers of Cyfarthfa dropped their tools to watch: the furnaces simmered in threat. Sprag-men on the long-haul wagons to Abercynon Basin on the rack-and-pinion railway leaped down from the engine footplate; 'Perseverance' steamed and shunted in protest at the stop, clanking her loads: her firebox sparkled and belched relief. As I stood there the first Hospital Column came around the bend of the wharf.

Packed together by the narrowing street, the people came in growing disorder, quarrelling and pushing for room, shouldering each other aside with their stretchers and placards. It was well-constituted chaos, I thought; typical of Sam's organisation. Above the marchers were slung banners proclaiming:

WE WANT A HOSPITAL, ONE FOR EACH TOWN.
WE WANTS WHEELED STRETCHERS.
WE WANT PAID SURGEONS.

Children were running among the crowd, distributing leaflets by Ernest Jones, the Chartist poet; taking one, I read:

The Song Of The Day Labourers
Sharpen the sickle! How full the ears!
Our children are crying for bread!
And the fields have been watered by orphans' tears,
And enriched by their fathers' dead;
And hopes that are buried and hearts that broke
Lie deep 'neath the treasuring sod,
So sweep down the grain with a thunderstroke,
In the name of humanity's God.

Ernest Jones

Minor placards announced demands for drugs, not whisky-dousing, and first-aid centres for accidents. And suddenly, to my astonishment, I saw Fanny, the Dowlais parlourmaid, dressed as a nurse within the crush. About her thronged the litters and stretchers, each carried by two giant colliers, the hewers of the steam-coal faces from Bedlinog No. 1 to the Old Black Vein. Stripped to the waist these stretcher-bearers came, coal-grimed, straight off shift. And on their stretchers and litters bounced the blood-stained actors, among them the 'corpses' of those who had apparently 'expired' on route, for black-gowned priests were giving 'last rites', one of these being Dai Tomorrow.

And then I saw Old Shenks and Big Buzz of the hive: on the stretcher they carried, his face covered with his blanket, was Gid Davies. The marchers spilled over on to the wharf itself, close to a line of moored barges I had just tallied in for Abercynon, and the bargees, furious at the interference, raised whips and foul language: the usual antagonism between bargees and ironworkers.

I watched the anger and disorder. The procession pushed on, the stretcher-bearers now engaged the bargees in wild altercation. Fists were raised, oaths and threats were flung; and when the column reached me – not twenty yards from the tally-hut – Old Shenks, Big Buzz and Gid's stretcher had disappeared.

"*Well!*" said a voice behind me. "Would ye believe that? I wonder where they got to," and I turned to find Sam Williams and Knocker.

"I didn't even see the going of them," I said, softly. "Are the bargees in on this?"

Sam raised his face to mine: as old as a dead crow he looked in that morning sunlight.

"To a man," replied he. "Give it six hours and Gid Davies'll be in Abercynon. You listening?"

I nodded, and he moved closer. "Then listen again. You're being watched, you realise that?"

Sam continued, "By Old Eli over there, probably others." He nodded through the ranks of the procession which had now surrounded us in music and chanting. "Which is all to the good, is it not? For while they're watching you, they're missing Gid."

Leaning on a bollard on the other side of the road was Eli Firmament who used to drink in the Vulcan and Friendship, and the hate in his eyes must have liquified his brain. Not ten yards from him, lounging disinterested, was Jake Kilrain, the giant puddler, and Sam said:

"As I say, there'll be others, but leave that one to Jake. Can you hear me above this racket?"

"Yes."

"Right, now jump one of the 'Perseverance' wagons to Navigation House, Abercynon: she's due down there in three hours, her footplate tells me. Gideon won't arrive on the barge run till well after dark, and the lads'll take him to the stables of the Swan. Understand?"

"The Swan."

"That's it. The landlord's name is Maginty, and he's one of us. Just make yourself known to him – say 'The Devil a monk would be', and he'll get things moving. He's teetotal, but ye can trust him . . ."

"'The Devil a monk would be'?" I repeated.

"That's it. The rest is up to you. Old Shenks will help you handle the run down to Cardiff Sea Lock, it's too bloody dangerous for ninnies like us. All right?"

"Yes, Sam."

"It's not! I lay ye ten to one none of you make it, even with Maginty's help. There's renegade military searching the canal between Abercynon and Cardiff."

"Renegade?"

"Deserters, and they're tougher than the real thing."

"That's pleasant," I said, eyeing him.

"Aye, and make sure Old Eli sees ye hop the Abercynon Wagon, *Number Fifteen*. The wagon number's important because he'll pass it on to the military, and that'll take the pressure off the barge."

Knocker said, "He being a dear devoted comrade of your mate, Captain Wetton."

"Captain Wetton!"

"It could be poetic justice, done properly," said Sam, rubbing his chin. "Don't you owe that one a couple?"

"*Iechyd da i bob Cymro. Twll din i bob Sais*," said Knocker.

"No odds to that, Knock," I replied, "will you do a good turn for a Welshman?"

"If he's from the South."

"Will you take my old cob Dobie up to Kierton Manor in Pontsticill and hand him over to Miss Rhiannon de Vere?"

"I'll do that," interjected Sam. "Likely he'd hit Hell out of him on the way. Any message?"

"Just say that I've left Merthyr, and I can't afford to feed him."

I did this with a heavy heart, not bearing to say goodbye.

"About time, too," observed Knocker.

28

I lay on my back and shut my eyes to the morning sun thrusting down darting rays.

Hidden in a chamber of the stacked ingots on Number Fifteen wagon, I lurched and bumped down the old dram-road route, my world obliterated by the puffing, hissing 'Perseverance'.

Not half a century ago the Dowlais Company built the first railway to Morlais Castle for limestone: the second, Overton's Rack-Assisted from Pontmorlais, linked the Works to the terminus at Pont-Storehouse, where I had my tally-hut. But this, Overton's third ('Ten Mile') railway, from Carno Mill to the Navigation at Abercynon, was the prideful boast of Dowlais.

One horse hauling twelve wagons forty years back was replaced, through the genius of Richard Trevethick in 1804, by the first locomotive to run on rails. You can forget George Stephenson and his half-hinged 'Rocket', my father used to say, *his* first engine arrived ten years later: trust poor Wales to take a back seat in an English roll of honour.

Never before had I done this run by rail: when necessary to make a tally-check at the Navigation, I'd travelled by barge along the route Gid Davies, Poll, Big Buzz and Old Shenks were taking now, which was risky. The twenty-five mile Glamorganshire canal, from Dowlais to Cardiff Lock, worked through nearly fifty locks, all time-wasters; ideal check-points for Captain Wetton and his Redcoats.

I prayed now that, tipped off by Eli Firmament, Wetton would follow me instead of Old Shenks's barge . . . in the hope that I'd lead them to his prisoner. Clearly the military believed that the railway or the barges would be Gideon's method of escape to the sea.

Is there a sadder sound in the world, I wonder, than the *rat-tap-tap, rat-tap-tap* of a train taking you away from the one you love? Or to stand on an empty road and watch a coach entice your lover? Your lips move, but make no sound; you see and hear, but you are not alive.

The sun made love to the earth that morning; the hills of Glyn-dyrys shimmered; a hawk, I remember as we rattled along, was flying against a stormy, pentecostal sky; all was blinding warmth and colour. Yet nothing absolved me from my inner grief at losing Rhiannon.

Perhaps, I thought, one's tenement of clay was bought and paid for at birth; that the dreams we foster are but the dusty myths of tomorrow that never become today; that love, like patriotism, is the hole men crawl into when they are afraid.

The wagons bumped and lurched in a cacophony of shrieks and clanks; down, ever down from The Top. Farm women, high-breasted and robust, straightened from milk churns as we rushed by, their faces astonished by the noise and action; pensive children, drooping in rags, gave sullen stares of greeting, too shy to wave: the stalwart birches of Waunwyllt stood black against the clouds.

Bumping along in the rattling, swaying tram my thoughts were now all of Rhiannon, the turmoil of revolution forgotten. I saw her in my mind against the white cloth of Dolygaer's winter, the place where we made love: I saw her swinging her gaitered boots through its lanes, her cheeks bitten red with frost. In the keen and beautiful air of autumn I saw her eyes large and startled as I kissed her, and heard her say:

"Oh come on, Tal – why delay if we love each other?" and her hands moved over me, making her the lover.

And now she was having my child: the thought both censured and excited me, but what would be the end of it I dared not think.

"What's the time, Tal?" Again I heard Rhiannon's voice.

"Must be midnight."

"A full moon, is it," and she raised herself and looked at the window.

"Not for another hour or so, unless Lady Charlotte's changed it lately."

"O hush, you, the silly old politics. Love me again, my precious?"

But it was not supposed to end like that, with her coming for a baby . . .

She is gone now, my Rhiannon, but I will always remember her.

Then my dream was shattered, for the brakes of the 'Perseverance' went on with a crash, sliding me down the length of the tram: the wheels skidded, sparks flew, and the day exploded into reality.

The face of Captain Wetton stared into mine during a two-hour interrogation: they checked and counter-checked every tally-card and invoice I carried before they let me go.

But, and God be praised, they stopped the search half an hour after the barge carrying Gideon was due at Abercynon.

The Abercynon basin had to be seen to be believed.

Strategically placed as a signpost from the Top Towns to Cardiff port, it carried to the industrial towns like Merthyr, Aberdare, and Quakers' Yard the mineral wealth of the country – limestone, coal and iron ore from Spain for the manufacture of iron; then carried down the finished products from the Top Town furnaces to Cardiff.

The Basin itself was at the confluence of the Aberdare and Glamorganshire canals, roads and tram-roads. Here the River Cynon made a fork with the Taff, vying with it for dirt and disease, both now being mere sewers. Time was, said Old Shenks, when both ran bright and clear through the bluebell woods of places like Mountain Ash. Wild daffodils bloomed along their banks; ragwort and foxglove decorated the halcyon days, with the mountains waving green and the brooks and streams that clean you could drink from them

200

with cupped hands.

But all that had gone with the coming of the iron and coalmasters. Abercynon, once the home of the roe and hart, the haven of wild birds, was now a blackened monument to industrial greed; and the big silver fish that had fought up to the spawning grounds had long gasped out their lives on sands of ash.

The hive of the army of artisans and labourers who worked here in the basin was Navigation House, now the beating pulse of the Welsh Industrial Revolution: standing at the confluence of drovers' tracks, the railways and the canals leading south, it had so far sent this year to Cardiff docks (and 1839 was not yet out) a quarter of a million tons of coal and finished iron, at a penny a ton per mile.

Here on their high stools, bent over their ledgers, were the clerks and tally-men of the Canal Company formed by the ironmasters; the accountants and book-keepers with their plumes scratching, recording the up and down traffic – iron ore from Spain sent up to the furnaces of Merthyr and other iron towns; bearing-plates, fish-plates, dog-spikes and rails bound for India and Argentina, Africa and Peru.

This was the courthouse where legal disputes were settled and summary whippings carried out: here the stone-masons' areas, the wood-yard, dry dock and repair channels: here the smiths hammered and clanked and the '*Quack Quack*' bargees (who mainly lived in Nantgarw) poled and laboured in a forest of swinging cranes.

The Basin, once known as Junction, was a smooth flat sheen of water, a pond where loaded barges were navigated into line for the journeys up to the Top Towns or down to Cardiff port.

Swan Cottages, two lines of single and double-storey homes, served the clerks and resident bargees: the Swan and Boat inns, the Traveller's Rest and Junction served them ale, a few painted ladies thrown in for good measure served them pleasure. You couldn't go wrong if you knocked three times on the door of the Swan, for instance, and asked for Nellie.

I entered the inn after my confrontation with Captain Wetton with an unconcern I didn't feel.

" 'Evenin'," said the landlord.

I nodded him greeting and looked around the room.

The place was full of the hotch-pot trades of transport; bargees, raucous and foul-mouthed, spraggers and plate-layers straight from lifting and packing on the lines, engine drivers and mule-skinning gipsies from the old pack-horse trails, remnants of a dying breed.

Swarthy Spaniards were there, and dark-skinned men from the Mediterranean ports; North-country navvies and West-country men from the hills of China Clay. And with them were their women, most in gay colours, their quarrelling shrieks piercing the fug of ale and tobacco. In a far corner, near the door, sat Eli Firmament, his small, red eyes watching me over the top of his porter: we stared momentarily, then I turned away.

The landlord was pouring pints. Behind him, polishing glasses with dying lethargy, his wife moved within the elephantine slowness of almost total obesity, one eye blinking from the fatted layers of her face. I said to the landlord:

"A pint," and looked past him, adding, "The Devil a monk would be . . ."

He pushed a glass towards me. "O aye? So the Devil's troubled. What troubles you – Captain Wetton?"

I drank, watching him, and he added, "Make mine a quart."

I eyed him. "They told me you were dry."

"Roberts, I were, but you try bein' a teetotaller in Wales. Besides, look what I've got behind me," and he jerked his thumb. "She were a good ride once, mind, but the brewers 'ave a lot to answer for. It were the bloody Allsops – in Paris, of all places." He grimaced. "Got a face like a nun in a movement of cantabile."

"No odds to that." I didn't like him, and he knew it.

"Yes, you're right. Down to business, then – Gid Davies is here, but so's Eli Firmament."

"Aye, I saw him now just."

He went on pouring glasses as if he'd said nothing in particular, then:

"Perhaps he'll 'ave to go for a walk, I don't know. I'll speak to the lads . . . meanwhile, take the second door on the right, it's where the nobs hang out. Poison Ivy will be with ye right away."

I drained my glass and left him. When I looked again for Eli his chair was empty.

A few ancient colliers were champing their whiskers and eating their lungs, and some of them peered over their pints at me as I left. As I reached the darkness of the night outside the back door a light began to dance, supported by an unseen hand. I waited. The light began to dance eerily towards me and I came face to face with the landlord's wife.

Never will I forget that face: grotesquely masked by the wavering light of the lantern she carried, it was monstrously disproportioned, bloated and discoloured; yet her contralto voice was cultured: her accent was French.

"Monsieur . . . ?"

I took off my cap. She said, "You 'ave come down on the railway, I understand."

I nodded assent, and she said, "The great man your comrades have sent – Gideon Davies – is safe, and his companions, the old man and the girl are with him. Their names, if you please."

"Old Shenks and Poll."

"And yours?"

"Taliesin Roberts."

"Excellent. One must be careful, as you know, but we have been expecting you. Do the two with Gideon Davies know about the arms?"

"Old Shenks does, he arranged it, but the girl does not know."

"She can be trusted?"

I suppose I hesitated, for she added, "All must be trusted in this business, Mr. Roberts. One word in the wrong place and all our heads will fall."

"She can be trusted."

"*Voila!*" She made an expressive gesture. "Then all appears simple, but great care is needed, as I said. All day long the soldiers have been searching for arms in the Basin;

they have turned out all the rooms in our inn, and known informers are actually sitting within our tap. Now, if you are ready, I will take you to your people; see to Gideon Davies, and leave the arms to me, understand?"

"I understand."

She raised her lantern higher, saying, "Ah, now I see your beautiful white hair more clearly; how stupid of me to doubt."

She opened a door and I saw beyond her the broad sheen of faintly moonlit water, the Basin, and beyond that to the squat shapes of moored barges. Following her from the Swan, I went along the tow-path of the pond to the front door of Navigation House. Here, in the porch a light burned faintly. Leading the way, the woman entered a hall, and then descended twelve winding stone steps to a cellar, tapping on a door hidden behind stacked furniture.

Old Shenks opened the door, a cudgel in his hand; the landlord's wife raised her lantern.

"Monsieur?"

"Aye, Missus," said Old Shenks, and I pushed forward into the little room. Poll, on her knees beside Gid's litter, smiled up.

"Hallo, Tal," she said.

Before the woman left, I said, "Thank you, Madame. We begin to know our friends. But is it safe here?"

She emptied her hands in an expressive gesture of nothingness. "What better place?"

"But in Navigation House, the canal office? Under their noses?"

She patted me. "But is that not where people rarely look? And what is Fate? *Le Nez de Cléopâtre*, for instance? Had that nose been longer the history of the world might 'ave been different. Long noses we also cut off in Abercynon, as we did at the barricades. And gentry noses mostly.

"Listen more. South of the treble locks before Pentyrch is the lock cottage of Tom Ostler the bargee; he is your last lock resting house before the final run to Cardiff. The emigration ship is the *Erin's Hope*. She clears the Lock on the morning of the fifteenth; eight days' time. At barge speed you will get there early; this is bad. Once in the Sea Lock area there is no escape, you understand?"

"Yes, Madame."

"So rest your passenger with Ostler and his good wife; they will be expecting you and have food and clothes if you need them: he can bring a doctor if necessary, and will serve you well."

I asked, "When do we leave here?"

"When men come for you; another barge and a fresh horse are being made ready. Do not ask more, leave it at that."

"Yes, Madame."

At the door she paused, smiling. "*Bon voyage*, and good luck." Hesitating, she then said:

"Ah yes, but one thing more. A gentry nose was smelling around the Basin yesterday. 'Is one called Taliesin living here?' this nose asked my husband at the Swan."

I did not reply, and she added, no longer smiling, "A beautiful nose, but I sent it on its way to smell elsewhere. Everything in its place, *n'est-ce pas*? Gideon Davies first, this nose later. You will attend to that?"

"Yes, Madame," I said, and contemplated Rhiannon. Had she been near enough to be upbraided, her face, as always, would have been sanctified by its usual radiant innocence. But Poll, in tune with a world of substance and cruelty, said, after the woman had gone:

"By God, if she comes sniffing around on this trip to Cardiff, I'll not be responsible!"

29

It was a night of storm.

For three days we had held Gid in the cellar of Navigation House, hiding by day, coming out for food at night. Now thunder rolled over the roof in reverberating crashes and lightning lit the mountains.

Poll said, "We need water."

Old Shenks was over in the Swan. Gideon lay as still as death on the litter. Earlier, he had tried to talk, his words fumbling on his mouth as if after a stroke, every sense urging him to speak, but he could not. Eventually, exhausted by the effort, he lay back. I said to him:

"Gid, listen. We are taking you south to Cardiff. It is the network, do you remember? It is sending you to the sea for the ship to America, do you understand?"

Poll knelt beside me. "He is dead," she whispered. "Jen was right, he breathes, but he is dead."

"Quiet, he understands every word."

She rose, holding her ragged dress together at her throat. "What's the point of all this if he's going to die on us?"

"He will not die, and if you want to make it up to Dada, this is his friend." I added:

"Look, he has soiled his clothes. When Old Shenks comes back I'll change him . . ." and she cried:

"No, please go, Tal. I want to do him." She was agitated now. Her moods were sliding between expectation of joy and deep despair, and as we faced each other over the litter, I was uncertain of her, and becoming afraid.

For there was a strange light in Poll's face, something akin to madness, as if there was a tapping in the hall of her mind. Perhaps, I thought, once alone with Gideon Davies, she might kill him. Her remorse at betraying Dada had brought to her despair; had my father been the man lying on the litter she could have expiated the pain she had brought him. But the helpless one before her was not my father, and her reaction to him might be different. But through all my fears I knew I had to trust her. Between here and Cardiff she would have a dozen opportunities to do Gideon harm if she intended it.

Outside on the Pool the barges were sliding up and down, their squat hulks alive with dancing, silhouetted figures; earlier, coming from the Swan and Mrs Maginty I'd watched the bargees getting them into line: somewhere among them, I thought, was the man O'Reilly and his family with the cache of arms Iestyn and I had brought from Llangynidr.

Footsteps sounded below the trap-door of the yard then: I heard the scrape of boots in a lull of the thunder, and pushed up the boarded flap: the head of Old Shenks was framed against the flying stars. He lowered a steaming bucket and tossed me a towel. To Poll he gave a small basket of food.

"I'll give a hand," said he, and lowered himself down.

"No," I replied, "We're off back to the Swan, you and me."

His eyes switched from me to Poll and then moved to Gideon on the floor. The question in his face was plain. Poll said, smiling with sudden brilliance:

"My job, Old Shenks. I'm his nurse, ain't I? I got to do 'im."

Gideon's blind eyes, wide open, were staring fixedly at me as I looked down from the trap-door.

It must have been midnight before I left the Swan. I saw Madame and Maginty behind the bar, but spoke no words to them. There was a brawl between a Welsh collier and an Irish bargee whom he called a 'Quack Quack', something guaranteed to start a fight even before opening time, let alone stop-tap.

"You're taking a chance, aren't ye?" Old Shenks had said. I knew what he meant. He added:

"She's puggled. Ye can see it in her face."

The noise of the bar enveloped us; a gaggle of Irish bargees were dancing to the music of a fiddle, their clogs stamping the time, and their women were arming them around in shrieks, and Old Shenks watched them with a cat-like stare of imperturbability; senility, said he, being the last refuge of the old; one thing was certain, it hadn't touched his brain. A harpy with a red mouth like a letter box came dancing up, snapping her fingers and dancing a fandango in front of us, and the bargees roared, and Old Shenks said:

"I don't trust her, that one. If the mood struck her she'd put a knife in poor old Gid, you realise?"

"Ach, you've a shrivelled soul, Shenks, give her a chance."

"A chance is all she wants, I reckon." He stared moodily into his ale. "I reckon you ought to kick her out, mun."

I said, "She'll do it for my father. Poll's all right, I tell you – you didn't know her in the old days, beside, we need her."

"Not as much as all that, and if that gentry piece of yours turns up, anything could happen – that Poll's mad for ye, you realise?" He grunted. "Anyway, how did your fancy piece know where we were?"

I knew but did not tell him – Fanny, the Dowlais parlour-maid; her tongue was inches too long.

Shenks said, with finality, "Ach well, I'm off to bed. But we can do without your well-meaning friend, you know, while Captain Wetton's sniffin' around, remember."

"Wetton? He couldn't track an elephant in the snow." I replied carelessly, thinking about Rhiannon.

"Don't be too sure."

I followed the old fighter to the stairs and he went up to his room.

As I pushed my way out into the darkness I saw the faces of Maginty and the French woman, and they were expressionless.

*

That winter was into us with sweeping rain, but the tow-path around the Navigation pond was still covered with autumn's dross of gold. It was a black pig of a night with the wind in a festivity of temper, charging head down across the valley: one of the Swan characters called Dai-Come-Home-Via-Railings was dancing a jig against the scurrying moon and by the time I'd got rid of him there was rising within me an intuitive sense of disaster, and I cursed myself for my foolishness for leaving Poll alone with Gideon. I actually ran the last few yards to the trap-door, and knelt, levering it open.

The tiny room was empty. Dropping into it, I stared around, whispering, "*Poll!*"

Nothing stirred except the lantern, swinging gently from its big hook in the ceiling.

Suddenly, in a little buffet of the wind, I heard voices.

Opening the cellar door I looked around the stacked furniture into darkness, seeing nothing. Moving silently into the main cellar, I looked up the winding stone steps to the floor above.

"*Poll . . .!*"

Suddenly realising that the voices were coming from another cellar room, not from upstairs, I crept towards the sounds in the darkness, seeing almost instantly a chink of light beneath a door. The voices grew louder, but were indistinct against the background of the storm; I could not identify meaning. Then suddenly there was a scuffle and a shrill outcry; a man's high-pitched shriek now, muffled as with masking hands; I heard the noise of a chair overturning, deep-throated oaths. Then a man shouted, and I heard this clearly:

"Tie him, for God's sake. We'll settle this palaver!"

More scuffles now, a faint whimpering; this grew to a sobbing that echoed around my hiding-place, an eerie accompaniment to the sounds of storm which now appeared directly over the Basin. Now more determinate noises came: a man being bound. I heard the victim's protests grow fainter, dying into suffocating groans as he was gagged. Hobnails scraped the stone flags of the cellar and I im-

mediately retreated to the winding staircase. A door burst
open. A beam of light splayed the floor. Two men burst out of
the room, dragging between them a prisoner, and his boots
trailed the flags, kicking and clattering wildly; behind these
came other men, but I saw only their legs as they pressed on
in whispering commands, to the very cellar in which, but a
few hours earlier, we had been hiding Gid Davies. Descend-
ing one step, I peered around the corner into the cellar area,
seeing in the framing doorway a man's hand go up and a
rope snake high over a bacon hook. The bound man struggled furiously, shrieking behind his gag: the cellar was filled
with his animal panic. Men heaved. I saw their straining
bodies, the taut rope, the condemned man rise, his tied legs
bucking violently.

In the slanting rays of the cell lantern I momentarily saw
the victim's face, bulbous, scarlet; eyes dilated with terror,
suffused with blood.

Silence.

No sound now but men's breathing and the obscene noises
of ritual strangulation. The rope trembled, taut. The body,
arching and bucking, slowly pivoted. The rain sleeted down,
crashing in gusty squalls against upstairs windows; thunder
boomed and cracked, dying into the rim of the world. Slowly
the dying man swung, in gasps . . . into inactivity: his legs
moved slowly now, pathetically twitching; the feet amazingly jerking up and down, his bound hands spasmodically
twitching, fingers clawing . . .

"Right you," said a voice. "*Out!* Back in half an hour and
cut him down."

"What time are the clerks due back?"

"Night-shift comes on after supper – half an hour; tallies
first, the bosses don't come on 'till six."

"Aye, well I want him six foot down long before then.
Dump him anywhere between here and Nantgarw, he's got
the whole county to sleep under, the bastard. I'll be gone
now just, so I will."

A man said, and his voice was as bitter as dregs, "He were a
cough-drop, mind, that one."

"Aye, less diabolical intervention, he'll be playin' dolly

stones wi' St. Peter."

"Poor little scratch, there were nothin' of him, mind . . ."

"Thinner'n Handel's lute."

"Ach, save ye pity! Got a gab on him bigger'n a baby's bum, an' there's only one place for him."

Taking advantage of their hesitation, I descended the stone steps and flattened myself along the cellar wall, waiting there in pent breathing, in darkness. I heard the creak of the trap-door as they climbed out into the night; a careful sound as they closed it from above. For at least a minute I stayed, listening to the noises of the house and the gentle, rhythmic creaking of the hanged man's rope.

The storm had ceased; only whispering booms now were clattering over The Top, and the rain was falling on the roof as if in quiet balm to the night's activity.

Feeling in my pockets I lit a match; it flared in my hand, banishing shadows, and I crept forward with the subconscious urge not to awaken the dead.

The open cell door made shape, framing its slowly revolving burden. The match burned my fingers and I dropped it, momentarily standing in blackness before lighting another.

Raising it, I looked up into the face of the hanged man, seeing the bloated cheeks, the protruding tongue, the bulging eyes. And despite the malefaction of that countenance, I knew it instantly.

Eli Firmament.

"God Almighty!"

As if hearing this, and called by Deity's significant command, there came from the gaping mouth a last strangling gurgle. I stared up. Eli Firmament stared down, and in his dead look I saw his condemnation.

Suddenly the trap-door went back and above me the head and shoulders of Old Shenks appeared, framed against the rain-washed stars like a departing soul. He called softly:

"You down there, Tal? The lads awakened me. Maginty says we're moving early . . . that you, Tal . . . ?"

I could not answer him. I was still staring up into the dead eyes of Eli Firmament.

30

Poll said, "They came soon after you left, Tal – Sam Williams, Knocker and six more waitin' in the cellar with Big Jake Kilrain, and with them was Eli Firmament and he were squealing for a pig-sticking till they shut him quiet. They waited till I'd finished doin' Mr. Davies, then they took up his litter and carried him down the tow-path to this barge."

"Getting Gid away a trifle earlier, they told her," added Shenks.

Poll said, brightly, "I asked what they was up to – just leavin' early, they said, because of the military pokin' around – besides, said Sam, we want the bacon hook."

"To hang a pig," said Old Shenks, softly.

"Funny old time to hang bacon, I said," continued Poll, "and I didn't see any old pig either, except Eli Firmament, and he didn't 'ave no apple in his mouth." She laughed and I saw her eyes in the dim light of the barge aft cabin. Now she stopped and whispered to Gideon like a mother speaks to a child:

"Don't you worry, Mr. Davies, I've got you. First light tomorrow and we're off directly down to Cardiff wi' you. Don't you worry about hanging old pigs."

And Gideon smiled and moved his body. I would have spoken to him then, but I felt the long-boat swing into the wind as the bargees poled her, and they took us along the bank of the turn-pool and out into running water through Isaf Lock into the lower canal, south for Cardiff. The young barge horse took the strain, and with Old Shenks walking at its head, we were away in the first cold redness of a watery dawn.

A cool old lad was Shenks; neither frost nor frenzy in him. I couldn't have done better at a time like this, and got proof of it in the miles to come.

It was a beautiful November morning after the night of storm, with rushes waving at us from the canal banks, and from the fields the great moon-like eyes of cows watched us with stares of bovine queens as we clip-clopped past: goldcrests and tits flew about us, chirping into the watery sun: mallard were flying clear of the staining Industry: a mother coot with a well-grown brood behind her paddled defiantly across our prow, then shepherded them into a feeder-creek to watch us pass, and Poll, sitting on the stern within sight of Gideon's litter in the aft cabin, tossed them bread.

Before us, when the canal lined out, we saw the earlier barges, filled to the gunwales with finished iron; behind us were others. At every one of the forty-nine locks and all through the nearly six-hundred-foot drop between Merthyr and Cardiff, we passed scores more going up, their twenty-ton holds heaped high with iron ore from Spain or limestone from quarries like Llangattock.

Astonishingly, I knew no apprehension now; it was as if my fears had died with Eli Firmament, which was ridiculous because there was more than one informer lying in wait. And I could tell, by the cautious looks and guarded greetings of oncoming bargees, that our presence was no longer a secret. With a casualness that betokened duplicity, all barges gave way to us; every man leaped to the assistance of the lock-keepers to see us through, their women and children cautiously peering from cabins.

The Nantgarw community of bargees, conservative in the extreme, who kept their own customs and resented the influence of strangers, now opened its arms to undercover escapees from Merthyr. It was also clear, from their little gifts to us, that they knew that sickness was aboard . . . a packet of sugar, a can of milk, freshly cooked bread from the wayside ovens.

Always will I remember that journey from Abercynon to

Cardiff: Wales arose, independent, purified.

Women with colliers' caps on, sitting outside their doors, waved gaily as we went down: children ran along the banks pestering to lead the horse. No more were we accused of coming South with Northern airs and graces; we were as one with them, the Southern Welsh, unified in a common task, to get a Welsh hero down to Cardiff.

Down through the bright country we went along the cut. It was as if we had left all our cares behind us north of Abercynon: no sign of military patrols, no talk (from barges going up) of the independent loafers and armed deserters who were the scourge of the valleys. We just floated calmly on for mile after mile: first past the head of Sir Charles Smith's tramroad that served Gelligaer and Quakers' Yard, down, down through the locks with the old Taff, sulking and broody, mooching along beside us with her filth of The Top.

Now past the Dinas and Hafod tram-road, then east of busy Pontypridd with her distant gay market and lines of coloured washing, the home of the mad Dr. Price; along the stretch called The Doctor's Canal, past Treforest collieries and the pits and drifts of Dynea where the canal lapped up to the mouths of the coal levels.

Women, stripped to the waist in the keen sunlit air, swarmed like flies over the waiting barges, carrying head-baskets of coal like Egyptian aristocracy. It was a journey of sun and wind under the open, blue vault of a cloudless sky.

Squatting at the tiller, I stared into the sunset. And saw on a humped bridge over the cut about two hundred yards before us a figure astride a horse: against the red sunset I clearly saw horse and rider. Motionless they were as if carved from black stone, etched against the redness.

I glanced down at the barge horse and Old Shenks on the tow-path; they were marching with the weariness of the day's trudge, heads low, feet dragging. And, when I looked again, both horse and rider had disappeared. Even as I watched, the sun sank into oblivion, its last shimmering rays fingering the empty bridge.

"Did you see that?" I called down to Shenks.

"See what?"

"It doesn't matter."

Night fell. The moon came out, lighting a dull, forbidding country, a world changed. How strange it is that the land smiles in sunlight, and darkness brings threats and shadows waiting to spring. I was filled with sudden apprehension.

The horsed rider I had seen looked surprisingly like Rhiannon, even from a distance.

By midnight Nantgarw itself was behind us, and the great treble locks before Pentyrch coming up. And Poll, who was now at the horse's bridle, called from the towpath:

"You there, Tal?"

Old Shenks, asleep on the floor beside Gideon's litter, did not stir: climbing out on to deck, I called softly, "What's up?"

"Trouble coming, I think," said Poll, and slowed the horse: the barge swam on weigh through overhanging alders where the moon made no light, and I saw her face in that blue light: strangely shadowed, that face beneath the tight drag of her shawl . . .

"I'll come down," I said, and moved to the gunwale.

"Not yet!" commanded Poll.

Two men had emerged from the hedge of an adjoining field in moonlight; wandering in single file towards Poll, and their arrogance matched their tattered clothes and mud stains.

Their feet were bare, their red pantaloons tied at the shins. Upon their heads they wore French cockade hats; over their shoulders were slung Army muskets. Even from the barge I got the stink of them. Feet splayed in the mud, legs wide, the first, a man of gaunt height, pushed back his hat and examined Poll with an impudent stare, and the second cried:

"Manna from heaven, Ben Stripe! Look, a wagger!" and he gripped Poll's arm, while his companion snatched at the other. And they walked her along the tow-path while she led the horse, bantering, swaggering as she fought to push them off.

Renegades.

These were the dregs that hung on to the legs of the Brecon military; gouge-fighters, kick-fighters, the riff-raff deserters from the old French wars. In batches they had come ashore from hired Breton schooners, trained and battle-worn, owing allegiance to neither queen nor country. Taking to the mountains first, they then scavenged in roving gangs, moving into the industrial towns for theft, haunting the highways, tram-roads and canals with robbery and violence. A glimpse of a cockade hat or a pair of French pantaloons and the military shot on sight, but where was Captain Wetton when he was needed? I wondered.

"*Tal!*"

Now one had pinioned Poll's arms behind her back; the other had her skirts above her waist, and in the struggle they were nearly under the horse, which reared up, hooves skidding in the tow-path mud. The smaller of the two came clear, not expecting me, as I leaped off the barge, and I caught him with a right that laid him flat: the other, the bigger, flung Poll aside and came at me low, head down for the butt. I stepped aside and he ran past me, yelling as he toppled into the cut. The barge slid up on the weigh, running him under. I caught a glimpse of him flailing in the rushes: his oaths and curses followed us into the night.

"Jesus," whispered Poll, "did you fix them!"

"Perhaps," I said, snapping up the horse into a trot. "But it's two more worries we could have done without, for they won't forget. I'll take a spell, you get back aboard with Gideon."

31

Poll was sparkling like a new pin that night, as we slid the barge alongside Tom Ostler's lock cottage: it was a night for dormice and owls and hooting things, with thickets waving to unseen hands, and the moon beamed down from rents in the clouds like sun-shafts.

Earlier, we had passed a race of 'coal-holes' – black openings in the hillsides where narrow feeders entered, lapping at the entrances.

Here, by the light of the naphtha flares women and girls were working long convoys of lilliputian iron barges, linking them into trains of six and hauling and heaving them into the entrances: here unseen colliers, less covered than they in nakedness, laboured at the seams. And, as they worked, the women were chanting a bawdy song in Welsh, wagging their bottoms to the rhythm and kicking up their legs in sinuous, provocative gestures and antics that delighted me and shocked Old Shenks, who was knitting off duty.

Poll, hearing the singing, came clambering out of the aft cabin (I was with the horse) and, with clapping spoons in her hands began to dance audaciously, bucking her body in gay vitality. And the other women, seeing her, clapped the time with hilarious joy.

I can see Poll even as I write this, with her skirts up to her highs and dancing to a tattered audience of coal-grimed, bare-breasted women, young and old, who jigged and jogged on the lips of their man-made pandemonium.

Now we slid away into darkness amid the fire-fly lights of following barges, until the tumbledown outline of Tom

Ostler's lock cottage by Treble Locks made shape in moon-light; a twisted edifice of phallic chimneys and Tudor gables: a mute amen, it appeared, to the obscene chorus of the women of Gehenna.

Tom Ostler, the lock-keeper, was a one-armed chap with good Welshness in his face. "He had two arms once," said his missus, "till he had the gate accident – jumped into the lock to save a child, and the gates closed and gripped him – so I hopped in and sawed it off."

"You did what?" I asked, astonished.

"Wouldn't be here now if it weren't for my Jasmine, mind," said Tom, all six foot and sixty years of him.

"She actually cut off your arm?" I stared at him.

"Ay ay – the water were comin' up, see?"

"More'n he'd get from that Dolly Oh-no," said his wife from Wigan, hanging her smalls on the fender.

"Dolly Oh-no?" asked Poll. "Who's she?"

"The fancy piece he were courting. Couldn't slice funeral ham, that one, never said no in 'er life."

"Ach, give it a rest, girl, that were forty year back," said Tom.

"She sawed off your arm?" I repeated in disbelief.

"Made a good job too!" Tom unpinned his empty sleeve, jerking the stump up and down with rhythmic precision.

"Mind, I'd rolled and boned a few legs o' pork 'afore then," said his wife, "being a butcher's daughter. Same job really, though they makes a lot of less fuss and palaver."

"Some woman," said Old Shenks.

"O ah!" exclaimed Tom. "She don't take nothin' lying down, she's after me legs now," which put everyone into stitches, of course.

"Some arm, ye mean," said Jasmine. "It took some saw-ing. The military wouldn't believe it, neither."

"The military?" I asked, looking up.

"That Captain Wetton from Dowlais Penywern."

"Does he get as far south as this?"

"Aye, on patrol after deserters mainly, but don't worry: you and the girl in the barge, Mr. Davies and Old Shenks in the house, to make an early start."

I looked at Poll and she looked at me, and Mrs. Ostler added, "Mind, likely little Poll could share a bed wi' me . . .?"

"That would be best," said Poll, which surprised me.

Earlier, following Tom Ostler's instructions, we had poled the barge into a pool lay-by beside his cottage, and Jasmine, his missus, had helped carry our things from the cabin; she was a lively, bright-eyed woman of candid stock, as dark as sin and big-bosomed, and her mutton stew she ladled boiling hot from the saucepan; we ate like people famished.

Just like a wedding in Amlwch, it was; sitting there in the kitchen while the kettle sang and the cat washed its face by the hob. And Poll's eyes, dark-lashed in her pale face, were rising and lowering at me across the table; I knew she had something under her apron that would come out later by the look on her face. Tom Ostler said:

"I've worked out that if one of ye gets a lift down to Cardiff port tonight he could be there Thursday and arrange with the *Erin's Hope* to take Mr. Davies aboard on Saturday."

"Ye'll need to give the skipper a bit o' notice, natural," said his wife.

"And since it's a three-day barge run down to the Bute Ship Canal, it'll give you a clear four days to deliver Mr. Davies," added Tom.

"Can you keep us hanging around here without some suspicion?"

Tom Ostler shrugged. "A few hours won't rupture us. Who's going south, have ye made up your minds?"

"To Cardiff?" I nodded at Old Shenks. "You'd best; you know that new sea-lock like the back of your hand."

"Then take this wi' you," said Tom, and handed Old Shenks an envelope. "Give this to Skipper O'Shea, and for God's sake don't mention the name o' Tom Ostler or we'll all swing together."

"Do you handle this sort of thing often?"

"Official, you're the only candidates, arrived by chance: unofficial, we run about ten or twelve like you a month . . . to Bilbao in Spain, then cleared to America."

"All Sam Williams's people?"

"Mostly Sam Williams's people, but others are startin' now . . ."

"Coming thick and heavy these days," said his wife. "God, what a country!"

I thought it astonishing that such domesticated people, their children married and gone, should be members of an organisation running escape routes to the sea. Yet it was their household's very normality that lent it strength.

According to Tom Ostler's placid conversation, it appeared a usual occurrence for Captain Wetton to drop in for refreshment while escapees were hiding below stairs. Wetton, it appeared, was a regular visitor when on patrol.

The courage of such people was commonplace at the time: half Wales was at it in one way or another. With the transportation hulks crammed with patriot convicts, families like the Ostlers were getting hunted men to America via Spain by the score.

And leaders of espionage groups, men like Sam Williams of the Union, put their lives in the hands of such as these, for Napier's counter-espionage didn't stop at torture when it came to confessions: one craven down the line could hang a score within the chain's command. And this chain, to my own knowledge, stretched from North to South in Wales. Loyalists like Skipper Rowlands were dependent on the sense and fortitude of the Ostlers, though a hundred miles away: Sam Williams's life hung on the thread of Old Shenks's integrity.

It was a chapter of Welsh history that has never been defined because of the individual secrecy; sacrifices of those who ran the routes, snatching patriots from the gaols of England. It was built on the courage of Welsh men and women: those who broke the rules, like Eli Firmament, paid the price, patriot or traitor.

In the ensuing silence Tom said, getting up, "Best to bed; it'll be a different kettle o' fish in the mornin', and we've got to get Mr. Shenks away."

I think I knew that Poll would come that night. Her passive acceptance of Mrs. Ostler's offer for her to sleep within the house was as much a ruse as my acceptance.

Rhiannon's absence, the uncertainty of the future, was building within me an intemperate demand for escape, both from this nightmare journey and my own male need.

Nothing mattered save the wish to possess Rhiannon.

After Old Shenks had left for Cardiff port, I lay in the cabin and listened to the lapping of water: barge after barge, in a singing of ropes and tumbling water, slipped up and down the cut. A baby cried, strangled by darkness; men's guttural voices I heard, women's gentler replies. And the moon, shafting through the port-hole windows drew etchings of water-silver upon the ceiling. I lay stiffly, every nerve tensed, and my longing for Rhiannon bore down upon me, forbidding sleep until well after midnight.

I sensed rather than saw the white form of Poll standing beside my bunk, and was not surprised.

"Tal . . ."

I opened my eyes.

It was not Poll the street-walker, the wanton of China. Fashioned by need she stood before me then in frail sisterhood; no immodesty touched her, no carnality stained me. Instead, I remembered her as the one who raised Meg; who had come to us in Amlwch at a time of greatest need; washed, cleaned for us, suckled my sister. Who to know? I thought. And who to judge, since life had thrown us so violently together? Was one a cockatrice to snatch at moments of oblivion within the senseless fight?

In that blue light, half-clothed, Poll looked seraphic.

Her breasts were of alabaster whiteness, her hair of deepest black upon her shoulders: serenely beautiful she looked in her tattered petticoat, and her feet were bare.

"Tal . . . !" Again she called, and touched my hand.

I reached for Poll, all guilt abandoned in a senseless urgency; my body moved for her, not Rhiannon. Yet desiring was not desire, nor lusting lust: it was a crisis of the head built upon companionship: a wish to melt in her: to be reborn in dark-sweet-dark or golden girl, her age or shape or colour undefined.

"Please love me, Tal. Nobody's ever loved me, they only took."

I opened my arms to her.

"Listen!" whispered Poll, and drew from my lips, her head inclined towards the door.

"What is it?"

I listened, too, hearing nothing but wind-sigh down the canal, and the creak of overhanging branches.

"It's nothing!" I kissed away her breath.

Now that she was with me it seemed that she had been there all my life; in part or total service, always Poll, a play in my existence. I smelled again the wild thyme she pinned upon her clothes in Amlwch, saw her smiles, and her aggression: all became the whole. Harlot, trull, strumpet? She was none of these. She was a honeycomb woman and her mouth was sweet to me.

"*Listen!* Tal," she rose beside me, her face chalk white.

Her fear snatched at me like a contracting muscle: listening, I heard a low, distant buzzing. A fly around a lamp? Then the strange sound rose to a louder note, rising and falling on the wind.

Now it appeared to be within the cabin.

A captive bee?

Poll's hands made claws of her fingers and she put them in her hair and screamed with all the facial contortions of a scream, but made no sound.

"What is it, for God's sake?" I gripped her shoulders and shook her to rattle. "*Poll!*"

The bee-song grew louder still, now coming from the cabin roof. I raised my eyes to the ceiling. Slithering feet I heard then; the unmistakable clamour of naked feet on wood . . . now falsetto consultations came from the night, then silence.

And in that silence the cabin door crashed back and Big Buzz burst in with Jen behind him. They stood motionless. The hive children crowded in behind them until the cabin was filled: the bee-sound they were making died away.

Our Jen said, saluting with her ladle:

"Well well! I never did. Just look at this, my charmers – the things they get up to!" and she reached out, seized Poll's wrist and twisted her out on to the floor.

Clutching her torn petticoat, Poll shivered before her.

"No clothes, neither? Dear me!"

It was the same old Jen, purposeful, articulate. I leaped off the bunk and pulled Poll aside.

"Get out!" I whispered. "Get out, all of you!"

"Oh no, my lovely," said Jen. "We ain't goin' without our Poll, are we Buzz?"

The children pressed about her.

Waspie I saw, and Doss: Shrinky was there at the back, also the three child cripples, their eyes like saucers. To fight would mean fighting children. Jen said, serenely:

"Mind, we nearly 'ad rag babies, didn't we, Buzz, when we thought you wasn't comin' back, Our Pol. But I've been in this game, girl, since your arse were a thimble. Once you're with Our Jen, there ain't no pissin' off."

She grinned at us, her teeth gapped and discoloured. Poll stood staring, as one mesmerised.

"So now you're comin' home, my honey-pot, ain't ye? Ye see, these little drones an' workers need the loot, and you're their queen."

I took a step, but Big Buzz barred the way, and in the hands of the children were knives.

Poll gasped, "Tal, I'll go. She'll kill us, else; I got to go."

"Ay ay," added Jen, "more'n likely, precious, so make yourself decent. And charge him sixpence for seein' your petticoat. Really, in all my life, I ain't never seen such goin's on, 'ave you, Buzz?" She elbowed him and he chuckled inanely, spit dripping from his mouth.

There was a silence, and then she shrieked:

"*Sixpence!*" and raised her ladle high.

I dropped the silver into her hand.

"Right you, and any more foolin' around wi' Poll and I'll move me backside lively – up to Penywern and the military, and to hell wi' your old Gid Davies."

Snatching Poll's wrist she pulled her towards the cabin door, but before she went through it, Poll said:

"I loves you, Tal. I've always done, remember?"

"Come on, come on!" said Jen.

I stood on the stern of the barge and watched Poll being prodded along the road that led to China.

32

"She's gone, you say?" Tom Ostler peered in disbelief. "That was sudden. Why?"

His wife added, "At a time like this, for heaven's sake?"

I said, "With Old Shenks gone, too, I can't handle the barge now."

We stood in silent perplexity, wondering what to do: if they had any suspicions, they didn't make them apparent. Then Tom said:

"Aye well, son, ye canna stay here. At latest, the military will be round the day after tomorrow and we're done for if they find Mr. Davies here."

"What about the old Star Inn, near the Cow and Snuffers, Tom?" asked Jasmine. "It's the nearest lock with a lay-pool, an' he could hang out there till the old man got back."

"The Cow and what?" I asked.

"The Cow and Snuffers," said she. "Disraeli meets his Mary Ann there, but we ain't supposed to know."

One thing, they hadn't lost their sense of humour. "But how do I get there?" I asked. "I'll need a tow-lad, won't I?"

"No. I can get you that far."

"Right. I'll handle it after that."

"You must," replied Tom. "I got to be back here to handle Wetton."

Jasmine helped us to get Gideon back aboard the barge, then we slipped it down through the trebles with six others coming down behind us and two more going up: with me at the nag's head and Tom on the tiller we rode her down to

225

Melingriffith and the old Star Inn, a mile or so south.

And the last I saw of Jasmine Ostler was her waving goodbye with a little lace handkerchief in the dawn.

Later, I learned they committed her for treason at Cardiff Assizes; fettered her at the Bridewell in Swansea to Mary Ann Brewer, a prostitute, and sailed her on the *Tory* in October 1844 for seventeen years in Van Diemen's Land. She died six months later in a punishment cell in the old gaol at Paramatta, which, spare time, was used as a brothel: typical of Jasmine, I thought; as old Tom said, being Lancashire she took nothing lying down.

A dumpy, ruined place was this Star Inn; an old pub built beside the ancient pack-horse trails when the iron came down on the backs of animals; the days of the fierce drovers who slashed their live animals for black puddings, and fought each other, Hell-bent for right of way. Some queer old boys Wales has spawned in her time, said Tom Ostler.

Aye, dirty old lads, these drovers: romancers have built them into legends, but they were evil; heartless to their animals.

"You'd be best in here, mind," he added, and opened the iron door of a little lock-up attached to the inn. "Time was they put the drover drunks in here," said he. "What better, mun, for a Welsh hero?"

I did not answer, being sick to death that Gid Davies had come down to this.

After Tom had helped me carry him and our belongings the hundred yards or so from the barge pool into the Star Inn's gaol, he took his leave of me, to return to Treble Locks, saying:

"It shouldn't be too long, Tal. Old Shenks'll be with you soon. I'll send word down to him tonight."

"Tell him to bring more food," I called, and waved him off.

It was the last time I saw Tom Ostler: talk was that they hanged him after Jasmine went, but I never got proof of it.

*

After seeing to Gideon, and with the sun high, I walked around the ramshackle rooms of the old public.

In the middle of the shattered tap-room I tried to imagine its activity when droving was at its height in the Vale of Glamorgan; the bull- and bear-baiting, the cock- and fist-fighting: the navigators' randies which, as they pushed the canal through to Cardiff nearly fifty years ago, put every spare woman to flight or in the family way.

And soon, I thought, now that Trevethick and Stephenson were inventing railways, men like Brunel would push the lines all over the country, and the eternal boardroom squabbling, the same old tap-room conflicts would start again: a new era of industry; a score more towns like Merthyr, another fifty Amlwchs. Was there no end to the violation and carnage?

I noticed unwashed plates and mugs on the splintered bar counter; filthy rags in a corner, the remnants of a mattress. Clearly the place had been recently used, probably by tramps.

Strangely, I did not give a thought to deserters . . .

Lighting the barge lamp, I hung it from the lock-up ceiling when dusk fell: Gideon was asleep in a holy quiet; twice I bent to the litter, listening for his breathing . . . but his heart was still thumping with its old defiance.

Before darkness I lit a fire and upon it cooked oatmeal and toasted bread; mixing this with milk I propped Gideon up and fed him.

Feeding him brought us our only small affinity, perhaps because he was in my arms. He swallowed automatically, a man swallowing chaff; he drank clumsily, spilling it down the front of him like an untaught child. His eyes were still upon me when, the bowl empty, I laid him back.

For the first time I noticed a phenomenon.

His eyes, large and blue in his haunted face, seemed opaque, and fixed; unmoving when I moved, unlike the eyes of a portrait. The blank stare of those pale eyes searched me, and I shivered, saying involuntarily:

"Come on, here's a treat, Gid," and I took from my pocket

the tin box holding 'The Tale of Delwyn'. "I'll read a bit from this—things my father used to read to old Poll and me, when we were up at Amlwch," and opening the manuscript at random, I read aloud:

"'Now solve this riddle, Welshman . . .

"'There was living in the land at that time a woman of honey fashioned by bees. Her body was of wax, her head pollen, her face was of bee-bread, and her hands and feet made of larvae, the stuff of queens: she was a delight to men, this woman; her lips were sweet, nectar was upon her tongue. But it was she, the honeycomb woman, who betrayed Prince Arfon to King Maelgŵn as a traitor; and Maelgŵn put out Arfon's eyes and imprisoned and starved him in Castell Deganwy. Later, relenting, she entered the dungeon on wings with her swarm, and fed Prince Arfon. The honey she fed him was her blood, the wax she fed him was her flesh, being in love with Delwyn, his son, by whom she had been rejected . . .'"

I looked up at Gideon in the light of the flickering lamp and knew the fixed stare of his eyes. I read on:

"'But the bees prevailed upon the honeycomb woman to return to them, saying, "You are the prisoner of the hive. Without you we will die. Let us seek a mortal woman whose body is of flesh and whose veins run with blood, and she will serve your Prince." And so, bidden by the woman, a princess came to Delwyn and stood before him, and said, "A honeycomb woman bade me come to serve your father, and I am not of honey, I am real: I stand before you in flesh, not a sweetness that melts in the sun." This the mortal woman said, not knowing that her testing time would come; that soon, at the hands of a priest and a foreigner, she, in her prince's service, would suffer outrage.

"'This is the riddle. Who, then, was the honeycomb woman? And who the mortal who did not melt in the sun? Solve this, Welshman, and you have solved 'The Tale of Delwyn'.'"

When I had finished reading this I shivered, closing the book; for I still could feel old Gid's eyes upon me in the dark.

*

I awoke within minutes of falling asleep, aware of a change in the room. The lamp, flickering low, suddenly dimmed almost to blackness, and, as my eyes grew more accustomed to the faint glow I saw a great black shape looming above me, and I stiffened on the floor. Then I realised that the black shape leaning over me was Gideon; that his form was obliterating the lamp. Sweat broke out upon my face as I stared up into his blind eyes, and he stared back at me in his blindness as if mesmerised by my nearness. A sudden panic seized me and I would have reached up and thrown him off, but he spoke.

"Taliesin!"

His voice broke the spell and I reached up and wiped the sweat of my face into my hair, gripped him by the shoulders and gently forced him away.

"What is it, Gideon? What is it?"

"Go back," said Gideon, in a whisper.

The lamp suddenly flared up and I saw his eyes large and full upon me, and it was impossible to believe that this man was blind, as sightless as Prince Arfon, who had been blinded by his enemies.

Now Gideon gripped my hands, and astonishingly, as I rose, so he rose with me, staring into my face.

"In the name of God, Tal – leave me. *Go back*."

With the knowledge of his strength had come relief and I could have wept for joy that he was recovering; yet, strangely, the sense of foreboding deepened within me; but I cajoled him, whispering to him encouragement as I helped him back to his litter, and he lay there, exhausted by his effort, and I knelt beside him, stroking his hair. Gideon spoke again, and his voice was firm and strong:

"There is evil here, Taliesin. We blind ones are given other senses. Leave me . . . you are too young . . ."

A low tapping came on the cell door and he turned his head to it, saying, "Don't open it, Taliesin."

Going to the door I whispered, "Who is it?"

Rhiannon said, "Tal, is that you . . . ?"

I opened the door and let her in and she said, her finger to her lips, whispering:

"I waited until dark in case somebody saw me come. This morning a girl called Poll came to Kierton with Fanny, the housemaid from Dowlais House – she begged me to come to you, this girl: 'Go to Treble Locks on the canal,' she said, 'and the lock-keeper will tell you where Tal is,' and I did so, and Mrs. Ostler sent me here."

"Oh God," I said.

But Rhiannon didn't appear to hear this, adding, "There is a light in the windows of the inn next door – do you know that two men are in there?"

"Two men?" I stared at her, and I heard Gideon ease his big body on the litter, listening, and Rhiannon whispered excitedly:

"One is a priest. Surely he would help us – he is a man of God, Tal, you'd only have to ask," and she looked at Gideon on the floor.

I kissed her face and drew her within the tiny room, knowing that 'The Tale of Delwyn' was being fulfilled by prophecy, step by step, and that, like me, she would have to suffer it.

Leaving Gid with Rhiannon, I crept out of the cell door, shut it quietly behind me and went on all fours through the tangled undergrowth of the gaol forecourt to the nearest window of the Star Inn next door.

Raising my head, I peered through the cracked, mud-stained glass.

Two men were sprawled over a trap-door in the middle of the decaying floor of the tap-room; they were eating from newspapers and drinking, turning up their bottles.

One man was small. Of evil countenance, he was dressed as a priest in black. The second I recognised as the one I had thrown into the cut. Bearded, of great height, he dwarfed his companion and now said bassly, with a fine French accent:

"Ah yes, I remember her! The wife at Treble Locks? But she is fat and fifty if she's a day." He spat. "Come! Keep your English! I tell you this – it is to my village in France that you should go for beautiful women . . ."

I drew back into the shadows, realisation dawning.

Priest and foreigner!

These were the two of whom the Tale had warned; men who would make an outrage . . .

The little priest said, "We cannot pick and choose. I am a man of God, as you know, but that woman walking the barge horse took my eye . . ."

Said the Frenchman, "I have seen her before, she is a Rodney of China! Lovelier than the Woman of Samaria, is she, yet a shilling would buy her! Oh, to have her within reach of a nudge," and the little priest raised his blue-veined hands upwards, crying:

"Judge not the wild oats of my youth, O Zion! Pester me with her kisses red as wine! Had it not been for that white-haired bastard I would have died for her on all fours."

"Don't worry, Priest," came the reply. "Nobody ever went to Hell on his knees. How old is she, you think?"

"The bargee bride? No more'n twenty, but these water folk come brutal if you lift their women!"

"Yes indeed," replied the other. "Look at my fine red pantaloons, they are ruined. When I meet that one, you can have his female; I will entertain myself by pulling bones from his back." He turned, looking straight towards me, and I drew away instantly. "What time is it?"

The little priest said dreamily, "Eleven o'clock, by the size of the moon. Where did they get to, Frenchy? She could not have travelled far. He called her 'Poll', remember?"

The big man wandered about, drinking from his bottle. "Around these parts, she is, no doubt. There is a loose barge up in the pool – what about that one?"

"Nobody aboard. I looked through the window."

"My poor friend, you are in a bad way," said the French-man. "But it is not laying a woman that brings bad dreams, it is thinking about it that knocks your brains loose. Would you recognise this bargee Rodney?"

"In the dark."

They spoke more, but I could not hear them. On my way back to the cell I knelt upon a ring-bolt, the forecourt barrel access to the cellar, and I nearly shouted with the pain of it.

It was raining now and the wet undergrowth fastened into my clothes, soaking them as I shook myself free. Mud and wetness was on my face when Rhiannon opened the door to me. To my astonishment, Gid was on his feet again, feeling his way around the walls, assessing the room. Rhiannon asked:

"They'll help us, Tal?"

"No. We'll have to get away." I went to Gideon and he leaned against the wall, gasping. I said, "Save your strength, Gid, we've got to get away from here."

It was not the presence of the men which was bringing me to panic; it was the inevitability that Rhiannon, without even being aware of the reason, might be sacrificed in the name of Poll.

With Gideon staggering between us we got out into the night without detection: the rain splashed down, soaking us yet assisting escape. Reaching the barge, we helped Gid into the aft cabin, and there he lay down gratefully, his face sheet-white; he did not speak even when Rhiannon questioned him.

Leaving them together, I poled the barge out of the lay-pool into the cut, and there, to my astonishment, I saw Dobie tethered beside the barge horse, happily grazing nearby and he raised his head and gave me an evil look and a snort. He followed happily behind the barge horse as we pulled off down the cut, his apprehension diminished now he hadn't got to work.

His presence brought to me a warm, undeniable comfort. For if Dobie had brought Rhiannon as far as this, the chances are, if he hung around, he could take her home again . . .

The rain had stopped and the stars looked down, but I remembered again the words of 'The Tale of Delwyn' as we slid along through the night:

'. . . This the mortal woman said, not knowing that her testing time would come; that soon, at the hands of a priest and a foreigner, she, in her prince's service, would suffer outrage . . .'

When, later, with the dawn coming up, I looked down into

the aft cabin, Rhiannon was kneeling by Gideon's bunk, holding his hand: she had washed and fed him, and was speaking to him as if he were her own.

A bright new optimism came with the arrival of Rhiannon: it coincided, for me, with Gideon's sudden recovery of his strength. She seemed to radiate vitality and the joy of our reunion quenched my original fears. Her confidence and gaiety transmitted itself to Gideon, who, now that he was upon his feet, appeared revived. Though still weak from his beatings, he was now getting around the barge; sometimes, at night, sitting in his cloak on the prow, bird-listening, as he called it, returning the called greetings of passing bargees.

And Rhiannon astonished me; no pampered gentility, this one, now she was given the chance to prove her worth: she handled Gideon's dressings like a nurse, cooked and cleaned the cabin, and walked the horse with laughing pleasure. She was dressed like a boy in a sheepskin jacket and wearing a narrow home-spun skirt down to her calves: the incongruity of her appearance enhanced by the little moleskin cap she perched on her braided hair. And old Dobie, in possession of a newly-found mistress, clip-clopped patiently along behind the official barge horse, ignoring me.

Earlier, Rhiannon had said, while Gideon conveniently slept:

"Look – I'm over four months now," and she opened her jacket and groaned to the grip of her skirt, her hat on one side. "Here's an old mule-kicker comin' for the Roberts family."

I asked, quietly, "Have you told your people about the baby?"

"No!" She was affirmative, content to leave it like that.

"Why not? They're entitled."

"Not until I show, and that isn't yet."

"Oh come on, love, they've got to know some time."

"Of course, and when they do, I'll be a long, long way from here."

"Perhaps you won't," I said.

"Oh yes I will, Tal, because you'll take me – you promised, remember? That is why I've come."

A lot had happened, I thought, since I promised her that.

Now, smiling into my face, she said, "You said you'd take me to a place where time did not exist, remember?"

"Yes, I will, but it can't be yet, darling. One's got to be practical – you can see what my responsibilities are. Rhiannon, what did you tell your people?"

She was clearly perplexed. I added, "About you coming down here on this mad caper."

She emptied her hands. "I told them I was going to stay with Mary Pegus."

"In those clothes?"

"Ah!" She was trifling with me. "I looked a lot different when I left."

"There's going to be trouble, you realise that?"

"Of course, I'm not a mental case."

"There'll be fighting. A lot of people are going to get hurt, even killed."

She groaned. "Oh God, why can't we all live in peace?"

"Because there's two worlds, love – yours and mine, and mine isn't doing so good. For God's sake, can't you see what's happening under your nose? The cruelty and the injustice?"

"That's why I want to be with you," she replied. "You think I'm a pampered fool, don't you? You think I haven't given a thought to what goes on, and that if I do, I don't seem to care. But I do care and I hate the inequalities; I hate to see children going to the mines in Dowlais, and women hauling trams; I hate the brickfields and the lime kilns, the rioting, the strikes, yes and the hunger on every side in the middle of wealth." Her voice rose and I noticed Gideon open his eyes. There was a brief silence of wave-lap and the sigh of the wind, and in that silence, Gideon said:

"She shouldn't have to explain, Taliesin. If your father was here he'd say you weren't worth her, and if you've promised you'll take her with you, now's the time to do so."

"In the middle of a revolution, man?" I shouted this. "Talk sense!"

"Aye, most of all in the middle of a revolution, for women make revolutions, fight in them, die in them and put an end to them when they've had enough."

He was breathing heavily. Through the window behind him I saw a woman, one of the bargees' wives: gaily dressed was she, laughing in the cold sunlight. And in a flash vision, the delusion of her face and symmetry called to me, and I thought she was Poll. God, I thought; it would be different if Poll were here, and not Rhiannon. Gideon's voice raked me from my thoughts; he said:

"Listen, Tal, better she takes her chance and stays than go back home with her tail between her legs, because she'll never forgive you for that."

"You realise, don't you, that she's going to have a baby?"

"Yes, I heard, and that's one of the reasons why she ought to stay. Because it is not for this generation that we're fighting, remember, but the next, and the one after that. And if she's going to end as a working man's wife, isn't it right that she could have her say in the outcome of this business?"

"So what do you expect me to do – put her in the attack on Newport?"

"No, but she can tend the broken heads, as she has tended me. She can reload muskets, bring up powder with the boys, run errands – aye, and fight if needs be, as her sisters fought on the barricades of Paris and up the steps of the Bastille. Do ye know, Taliesin, that the men wilted in the fight long before the women? That the first in to free the Bastille prisoners were women? That the French Battalions were more afraid of them than men?" He waved me down. "Ach, read your history! From Ernest Jones to Plato the same tale is told. It's the likes of her who fashion the course of history."

I listened. I was persuaded, and it was a mistake. Much better had I closed my ears to them and sent Rhiannon home to Pontsticill, where she belonged.

Now the winter country ahead came up with cloudy threats of rain and the land seemed subdued, crouching under the threats of deluge.

Once I had seen this land in summer, and it was milk and honey country; of hazel, cherry, blackthorne and dogwood. Birch and elder had grown in profusion here since the Ice Age; fast-growing spruce and pines crowned the western hills. It was ecclesiastical country, the distant environs of Llandaff, and it had escaped the axe of earlier centuries: now it lay flat and fearful under the setting sun in calm, monastic seclusion.

Rhiannon said, "How long are we staying here in the lay-by, Tal?" Miles away in my thoughts, I did not reply.

We were alone now, walking down the deserted cut; Gideon was busying himself about the barge cabin. Earlier he had gathered rushes by pulling them from the thwarts and these he had plaited into intricate patterns and designs, his flattened fingers amazingly dexterous as he bound them into shape with sap-grass Rhiannon had discovered in the water; small, quaint dolls he made, and now was fashioning imitation love-spoons, one for Rhiannon to wear, said he; another, a smaller one, for her baby. We could see him by the door.

"He's better," said Rhiannon, walking beside me in the cold; the evening was arriving with promises of ice; rain was falling over distant Llandaff in faint, thundering booms.

"Overnight," I said. "His strength is astonishing – and it's mainly since you arrived."

"That's the effect I have on people!" She added:

"I asked you how long we're staying here?"

"Until my father comes, this is a rendezvous."

"What will he say about me being here, I wonder?"

"God knows. I don't think he'll agree with Gideon."

"When is your father due?"

"Midnight."

She questioned more: unlike Poll, she had to be in the heart of everything. I replied, "All right, I'll tell you, then perhaps you'll realise why I want you away from all this. Arms are stored in the barge. It's a floating arsenal. The dog-spike load I'm carrying is only there to cover the boxes – cases of muskets, pistols, bayonets and pikes – shot and powder, for distribution among the valley contingents. Men will come with my father and they'll load it out. And whoever is found in possession of such stuff will end in transportation, you included."

"Right. If that's the end of it, so be it. So long as we're together."

"And I shouldn't bank on that."

There was a need in me to hurt her, if, by this means, I could force her to leave. It was not necessary that she should play a role in this; she was not equipped for it, neither was she required. For this was a working-class struggle in which her kind would be rejected, and I resented her presence. Also, I did not trust myself. I loved her, and love could turn a man to cowardice. Yet, had Poll been still with me I would have snatched at her for support, let her run with me, if necessary, into battle. Rhiannon's very femininity, her inability to understand the extent and danger of the struggle ahead, gripped me with growing apprehension, but there was more to my fears than this: there was gnawing at me a timeless, senseless dread I could not shake away, one beyond all reason and comprehension, and it sickened me.

"Perhaps now you know why I want you out of this," I said.

Rhiannon didn't appear to hear this. She said, with a smile, pointing, "Tal – how handsome Gideon looks, plaiting his rushes . . ."

Later, I pulled the curtains of the barge, took the key out of the aft cabin door and gave it to Rhiannon, saying:

"We're nearly out of food, and Old Shenks may be overdue. The village is only a couple of hundred yards away."

"Why can't I go?" she asked.

"You'll be safer here – look I'll be back in half an hour." And I kissed her. Gideon, still busy with his rushes, didn't look up as I left them. "Don't open the door to anyone," I said.

It was a ridiculous decision; almost as if I had been commanded to leave her unprotected. I gave no thought to more than average danger: the moon was coming up, barges were constantly coming and going past the lay-pool. She would only have to shout and a score of men would come.

And so, unknown to me, the Tale was being fulfilled.

As Old Shenks moved north from Cardiff, as arranged, I hurried west to the village. And, with neither of us more than minutes away from 'the moored barge, the irony became complete.

The priest and the foreigner, the two men from the Star Inn, tramped south in search of Poll.

How many times since, I wonder, have I cursed myself for my tragic stupidity. And yet, I repeat, it was as if my absence had been commanded.

33

When I returned from the village I found a great activity around the barge, and ran with my provisions: the moon, beaming down, lit the scene; the stern was crowded with jabbering women and children; groups of people were on the tow-path and around the lay-pool, chattering and gesticulating, and the barges were snubbed nose to stern along the canal.

I ran, and plunged into the crowd by the aft cabin door, and the people fell to silence as I entered.

Old Shenks was sitting on the floor with Rhiannon in his arms and a barge woman was attending her. The body of Gideon, viciously stabbed, was crouched in a corner half under a bunk. And Rhiannon was half naked, her clothes ripped from her body; blood was upon her face.

"Rhiannon!" In growing horror, I knelt, pushed the bargee aside and took Rhiannon into my arms.

All around were signs of a violent struggle and blood from Gideon's wounds was everywhere; the bargees crowded in now, their mute faces staring at the wild disorder. Old Shenks said:

"Christ, man, where were you when you was needed?"

I didn't get the sense of him; Rhiannon's heart was thudding against me and her breathing was laboured. The barge woman said:

"Hey up, lad; leave her!" She looked up at her man standing above us, "O'Reilly, get hot water from our stove, and towels, quick." She called to a man bending over Gideon. "Leave him," she commanded, "that one's dead –

O'Reilly! Will ye get these people out of here?"

I said, "Oh God, woman, what happened?" but I knew what had happened, and Old Shenks replied, kissing Rhiannon's face:

"Two men. They kicked the door down. Somebody saw them runnin'."

"I saw 'em!" called a lad from the back. "It were Priest and Frenchy, I reckon – I saw 'em!"

I said to the bargee. "She . . . she's having a baby, nigh four months gone."

She was businesslike, this woman, fat and grimy, her black hair tousled in the fashion of the Irish; she replied, "Aye, I know, but she'll likely hold it, she's young," and Rhiannon, as if hearing this, opened her eyes, saw me, and said:

"Tal!"

"I'm here, love."

Old Shenks bowed his head, whispering, "Oh Christ, bloody murder I'll do for this . . ."

"Don't worry none," said the man O'Reilly. "If it's Priest an' Frenchy the bargees will have 'em down to the third generation, so they will, aye!" and he made a fist of his hand.

"I'll have them long before that," I said, and rose. "Lie still, girl, lie still . . ." for Rhiannon was twisting and shuddering in Old Shenks's arms. She said then:

"They . . . they were the men at the inn, remember?"

I nodded, kneeling now, holding her hands, and I bent to kiss her, saying, "Look, close your eyes . . ."

"They knocked and we wouldn't let them in, so they broke down the door. Oh, the way Gideon fought! But the little one had a knife. He couldn't see . . . and the big one hit him from behind." She began to cry in stuttering panic, her hands making a cage over her mouth. I said:

"Rhiannon!" and held her, pushing Old Shenks away; I was with her at the start of Time, kissing her lips, her face, her hair.

"And . . . and while they were doing it they kept calling me Poll. 'Lie still, Poll,' they said, 'Keep quiet, Poll . . .'"

The barge woman got up, rolling up her sleeves, crying, "Ay ay, now out of here everyone, come on, come on, it's no

240

place for men. Have you got that bloody water, O'Reilly?"

I went to Gideon. His body was covered in knife wounds, one thrust being through his heart.

"And I want two men," called the woman. "Come on, don't stand there gaping, get this poor fella out of here." She glanced at me. "You, too, mun – out," and she helped Old Shenks to his feet and steered him through the door.

"Don't go, Tal," called Rhiannon, raising herself on the floor.

"I'll be back," I said.

On deck now, Mrs. O'Reilly said, "She's not the first woman, and she won't be the last, do not look so holy. But she's bleeding a bit, and might need a doctor. O'Reilly and me are on the way back up, so we'll take her. You her chap?"

"Sort of," I replied.

She clapped me on the back and grinned wide. "Canal Wharf, then, and I'll try to get Sam Williams. What's her name?"

I told her.

"Holy Mother," she exclaimed. "Gentry, is it? Aye well, she'll be just the same as us when it comes down to the essentials, son – it's the business of being a woman round these parts, see? She'll likely pull out of it."

"Will she lose the baby, Mrs. O'Reilly?" and she threw back her head and cackled at the moon.

"Dear God, no son!" cried she. "Not if the O'Reillys have a hand in it, so to speak. For I've midwifed more down this Glamorgan cut than they've birthed in the cabins of County Cork."

"God bless you, Mrs. O'Reilly," I said.

"Ach, and He will that – she births now, you have the next one."

She was still cackling as I made my way to the prow and went down into the dog-spike load. There I broke open a case and took a pistol, loaded and primed its flintlock; then I pulled a ten-pound bag of quarrying powder and a set of lucifers, which were match-heads and sandpaper. I had just tied the gunpowder around my neck when Old Shenks came in search of me, calling down the hatch:

"Are ye down there, Tal?"

I crouched low in the darkness lest he saw me.

Later, when I was certain he had gone, I left the barge and took along the tow-path towards the Star Inn, to kill the men.

The old inn was nearly a tumbledown now, I thought as it came up through night-mist: it wouldn't need a lot to flatten it, and I found the cellar access trap-door and lifted it, watching the tap-room through its smashed windows, but the place was empty. Perhaps they would not return, I thought; whether they did or not, I was determined to destroy what was left of the inn; it stood as a monument to my own defilement, and I hated every brick and stone of it. But there was also a good chance that the priest and foreigner would come back, for I saw their twin mattresses on the floor, their scattered bottles and tins of food; on a rail above the bar two blanket coats moved lazily in the wind like hanging corpses. Next moment I was in pitch darkness as I closed the trap-door above my head.

Mice scuttled away as I crept through the cellar; cracks in the floorboards above me afforded thin, moonbeam light; broken barrels, the riotous relics of a past age of gluttony, barred my way; from within these came the incessant squeaking of rats in colonies.

I hadn't been in the cellar for more than minutes, fixing the concussion charge, when I stopped work to the heavy tramping of boots overhead; the priest and Frenchman were returning.

At first they spoke only in grunts and whispers, as if the night's work of rape and murder had partly satiated them; then I heard the Frenchman say, his voice raised:

"Was it necessary, Priest, to kill the blind one?"

"What the Hell, mun!" came the reply. "He had me by the bloody throat, and you not lendin' a hand, for ye were doin' the woman."

Irish. It was the first time I'd noticed it.

"But it was not the bargee Poll, my friend, for I heard her making protest. She protested, did she not? But sometimes, I think, in Welsh, for I did not understand."

"Ach, fella, they always protest when their hearts aren't in it, but did you enjoy her? That's more to the point."

"She was like eating honey."

"And me, I can tell ye! Och, while I'm up and breathin' – where do they spawn such women?"

"Some women are chickens, Small One, others are like swans. And this one was a cygnet. But do not swans, in this country, belong to the Queen?"

"Holy Mary, what's the odds?"

"Because any time now the *cuirassiers* will come and cut us to pieces; the girl was a noble."

I heard the little cleric laugh. "Aw Frenchy, to Hell! Swans or chickens, women are ten a penny down the cut, nobles included. Here, sink this an' ye'll feel better in the mornin'," and he tossed the Frenchman a bottle, who missed it, and it went clattering over the floor above my head.

I was in a dilemma.

Hatred of the two men above me had built in me a seething anger I could not resolve by reason or plain sense. I had come to dispose of them: the charge was suspended, the fuse path laid: all I had to do was run the powder in a trail to the outside trap-door and strike the match. Then would follow the snaking blaze and the final detonation that would obliterate the tumbling inn and the two rapists above me; no pain, no expectation, no fear for them: just the instant decimation of the brain by skull splinters. My task would then be over, the revenge for Rhiannon's outrage fulfilled. But I could not strike the match. And I think I knew, crouched there in the cellar, that their deaths in such a manner would accomplish nothing: the sin against my girl could never be erased by so easy a path. She was demanding more – that a personal violence be involved; that these two would know the reason why they were dying, as criminals know when being led to execution.

They were talking again now, their banter mingling with their obscene laughter; I heard her name called – Poll they called her for want of another – and I crawled away from the suspended charge, fighting for calmness amid an inner fury. Reaching the trap-door, I threw down the powder bag that had made the fuse, and pushed up – up and out into the night with the pistol in my hand. Running around to the front door of the inn I burst through it. The men on the floor rose up on their mattresses in the moonlight, their faces astonished by the speed of my entry, their hands reaching for their weapons, and the priest found one, a knife. This he threw, and I ducked, hearing it whistle above me and bury itself, quivering, in the door behind me.

"Right," I said, approaching them. "Up!" and I levelled the pistol.

But I had come too close to them and was standing on the edge of a mattress, and they were professionals. Climbing slowly to his feet, the smaller one suddenly flung himself backwards, pulled at the mattress and tripped me; I fell headlong, the pistol clattering out of my hand.

Immediately the Frenchman was upon me, but I flung him off and rose, hooking him hard to the face as he lumbered in for a hold; and as he staggered I seized a broken chair and smashed it down over the back of the priest as he dived for the pistol on the far side of the tap-room. The big man was at me again on the moment I turned to face him; shouting hoarsely, he caught me in a bear-hug, raising me off my feet. And as he turned me I saw the priest painfully crawling towards the pistol, leaving behind him a trail of blood.

Somehow I hooked my right leg around the knee of the foreigner and we spun, momentarily tottering together in an embrace, before falling with a thud, me uppermost. I saw a flash vision of the man's bearded face, his white teeth behind his hairy lips, and his red tongue lolling as I gripped his throat. But, with astonishing strength he forced my hands away and rose, to face me, stooping, his breath coming in gasps, and I suddenly realised that he was twice my age. Spittle and froth gurgled over his beard as he gasped for breath, and I dived at him head first, catching him in the midriff and pumping out his lungs: grasping his chest, he turned, staggering away like a wounded animal, but I was upon him again, now infuriated by the heat of the fight. In my blind rage I could see nothing before me but the blood-stained face of Rhiannon and the knifed body of Gideon. I struck again and again, thudding my fists into the big man's body, and he slid along the wall of the tap, his knees sagging to the attack. I heard the shrill cry of the priest on the other side of the room, but ignored it; I was intent now on one thing only, the death of the man staggering before me. And then I heard the priest shout again, and turned in the Frenchman's strengthless arms. And I saw, on the other side of the room the little man sight the pistol; instinctively I dropped to all fours as the pistol blazed, and the ball, meant for me, struck the Frenchman in the chest. The impact of the half-inch round flung him back against the wall, and he lay momentarily flattened against it like a crucified doll, before pitching head first across the floor, his big body rolling sideways across the mattress.

"Now you," I said, and turned, and the priest let out a small, wild shriek of fear and lurched towards the door, but I reached it first and slammed it shut.

Cornered against the bar, the man flung the pistol, but I ducked; catching him with one hand, I spun him round to face me and struck with the other fist, and he groaned, and his eyes rolled, then he sank down the front of me, to lay senseless across the dead body of his companion.

I raised my bleeding hands to my face and stood there, staring around the shattered room; at the dead body of the Frenchman, and the unconscious man in black. Yet, despite the sense of victory and the vindication, I felt besmirched by the very essence of the place: all its bawdy past seemed to surround me as I stood there, making me one with its iniquity.

Slowly, painfully, I walked across the broken floor and out into the moonlight. Soon, I thought, my father and his men would come, so I would have to get back: more importantly, I had to get back to Rhiannon and Old Shenks, who would be hunting for me.

So it was but a small surprise to me when I heard him coming; the dust had got Old Shenks and his lungs were bagpipes.

Kneeling, I fired the powder-trail and a little blue flame spurted up, then disappeared under the cellar trap-door.

"Tal, where've you been?" gasped Old Shenks, hurrying up.

"Looking for those two swines, but no sign of them," I said.

"Then come back to Rhiannon, the child's askin' for ye and the O'Reillys are just off up to Merthyr with her."

"Yes," I said, and hurried along beside him.

We hadn't got a hundred yards when the world about us glowed with strickening light: canal, tow-path, forest and hills were instantly illuminated; and all hung in the pulsating light that slowly, reluctantly died into blackness, then the night was split by a clattering roar; the ground beneath us shook.

"Good God," breathed Old Shenks, gripping me. "What the Hell was that?"

"No idea."

Old Shenks peered at me, then wiped his whiskers with the back of his hand.

"Queer old time of night to be quarrying."

Passing the Cow and Snuffers public, we took the towpath south, through Llandaff Yard.

34

It was nearly midnight according to Old Shenks's watch, and I was worried. In my anger I had forgotten the outcome of such an explosion; a blast like that, I now realised, would pull in every Redcoat patrol for miles, and according to the Ostlers, Captain Wetton was already in the vicinity.

So now it was a race against time.

I sat on the bunk where Rhiannon lay in the O'Reilly barge and listened to the lapping of water as the bargee got his horse going along the cut; there was a mystic splendour about the night that belied the coming of a storm. I said to Rhiannon:

"I've got to go, *cariad*, but you'll be all right with these people."

Earlier, I'd got a bottle of laudanum we had used on Gideon, and its effect on Rhiannon was now apparent; she was hovering within the vacuum of consciousness and sleep, but her grip on my hand was strong.

"Can you hear me still?" I asked, and she nodded.

"I can't stay, for there's things to be done, understand? Go back to your people, tell them all that has happened. Up at Treble Locks the Ostlers will fetch a doctor. Do what he says, and as soon as I can, I will come back to you."

Her lips moved. "Don't go, Tal."

"Got to go, love, there's nothing else for it. If a military patrol stops the barge, leave it all to O'Reilly; just tell them that you remember nothing until the bargees found you on the tow-path – nothing, understand, Rhiannon. Our lives are in your hands."

At first I thought she was sleeping, then she said, and her voice was strong, "You're going to fight?" Her eyes were now wide open.

"Aye, girl. Got to fight, see? No alternative."

She didn't reply, so I added, "For you, for me – aye, and for the baby. To make things decent; we can't go on as we are."

In Welsh, she said, before she closed her eyes:

"Mi ddoi di yn ôl ataf. Wyt ti'n gaddo?"

"Yes, Rhiannon. I promise. I will come back to you."

Mrs. O'Reilly came up then with business, a bowl of water and a bedsheet rolled up under her chin. "Away out of it, lad, the girl's still bleeding."

"Yes," I said.

"Holy God, what's the likes of her doin' mixed up wi' the likes of you?"

"Don't know," I said.

"Have ye spoken to her pa?" Her calloused hands were stilled and her black eyes switched over me.

"No."

"Would it be askin' too much to know when you might?"

"When I get back from the march, Mrs. O'Reilly."

"O aye!" Fists on hips now, and she swept stray hairs from her sweating face. "After the march on London, is it?" She glared at me. "After you've put the world to rights, eh – like my big oaf, O'Reilly! Sure, you're a marvellous set o' fellas, so ye are, for swilling ye ale and hammering pikes for a revolution, but you're better at side-stepping your bloody responsibilities." She nodded at Rhiannon's sleeping face. "This one here, for instance. Ye put her in the family way and then post her back to her ma. You know what they'll do to her, I suppose? I know that gentry lot. They'd show more sympathy for a mongrel bitch."

I met her eyes. "Got no alternative, Mrs. O'Reilly."

She was wandering about in pent anger now, picking things up and smacking them down, and she said, over her shoulder, "Right then, go, and good riddance to ye, one an' all. For I'm a woman an' I've got no time for strikes and blow-outs and Union marches. You men are addled, the lot of ye; you've got no chance and it'll only end one way – with your heads on Parliament Square and the rest of you in bloody strips. Now away out of it for I've got a woman to attend to."

The aft cabin door came open and O'Reilly, her husband, came in.

He said, screwing at his cap, "Bengie's on the tiller, Ma, Alice is leadin' the horse. I'm away now, so I am."

"Are ye? Is that a fact?" She approached us, her eyes blazing. "And how am I supposed to handle a barge, five kids and an ailin' woman, for God's sake? Bad cess to ye, Michael O'Reilly, for fetching me out o' Galway into this stink of a country. All right!" She waved her arms and flung the bedsheet at us. "Away with ye and fight the revolution, an' I hope ye never come back, d'ye hear me?"

O'Reilly lowered his head. "Goodbye, Ma," he said.

I closed the door behind us. The stars were big over the moon-lit land. I heard her shout:

"O'Reilly!"

"Holy Mother, what now?" said he, and opened the door again.

His wife was standing beside Rhiannon's bunk with her apron up to her face, but she was not crying.

"Ye'll come back to us, Mick, like this one keeps sayin'?"

"Aye, Missus. I promise. I'll be back."

"Then get goin', for God's sake? Why are ye hanging about?"

But he didn't go back to her.

They got him through the head with the first volley from the Redcoat carts, along the road to Monmouth.

My father had come with his contingent of twenty men, when O'Reilly and I got back to my barge, and Old Shenks was already handing out the arms. It was speedy work, with the hammers rising and falling and the wooden cases splitting under the levers. Look-outs had been posted as the muskets, pistols, pikes and powder were distributed. I found Dada in the aft cabin, and he faced me as I entered.

His eyes were bright.

"Gid . . . they tell me," he said, simply.

"Aye, Dada."

"But how, Tal? For God's sake how?"

O'Reilly fidgeted, restless, and said, "Mister, it weren't his fault. We was waitin' in the cut, and . . ."

"You shut it, I'm asking him!"

I said, "I . . . I sent Old Shenks to arrange things in Cardiff. He wasn't back and we needed food. So I went to the village . . ."

"And left them alone?" He came nearer and his face was sheet-white. "You left a blind man and a slip of a girl alone at a time like this? The bloody barge is full of arms . . ."

"Leave it, Dada," I said.

"Leave it? Gideon's dead, and you say leave it?"

I pushed past him. He shouted, "My friend's dead and your girl's been raped and you say leave it?"

I shouted back, "Aye, so leave it in the name of God!"

"Jesus," he said, and pushed me aside as he went through the door. "Just dish out the arms and get yourself back to Merthyr with your woman, it's all you're fit for!"

Later, my father said, before he and his men moved off:

"Earlier I asked you how it happened, Tal. Now I'm asking why. Can you answer that? Why, why?"

For answer I took from my pocket the tin box containing the manuscript of the 'Tale of Delwyn'.

After my father and his men had gone, Old Shenks and I gathered up the wreckage of the packing cases and buried them on the fringe of a nearby wood, next to the place where the bargees had buried Gideon in an unmarked grave. And I stood for a bit looking down at the newly turned earth, and there was a coldness in me akin to the coldness of death, I think.

"You all right?" asked Old Shenks, coming up.

"Aye."

"Good old boy, mind, that Gid Davies."

I nodded.

"Got plenty o' guts. Blind, see, but not so blind, really speakin'—he knew the time o' day. Your pa's mate, you say?"

"Friends all their lives," I replied.

"Aye, well that's it, ain't it? It do come rough, ye know, when you're on the same toffee-apple. Boys, see, then young men – on the piss together. It's a love, in a manner o' speaking, specially if ye happen to be sparkin' the same women." I didn't reply.

He looked at the moon and whispered as Mick O'Reilly came up, "A man comes sore, ye see Tal, when a love like that goes down. It . . . it's the best sort o' love." He thumbed his face and looked at the moon. "I know, see. In my time I lost a lot o' good mates."

I did not reply.

"That's why your pa said things he don't mean. You understand?"

O'Reilly said, "When are we movin' off, Tal Roberts?"

"Now," I said, and was thankful he had come.

"I'll make ready," said Old Shenks, but I put out my hand to him.

"Not you, Shenks. You go back to the Ostlers, then to Canal Wharf. My father said . . ."

"Did he now!" The old man bristled. "Then you and your pa can get stuffed wi' oat-cake both ends up, you in particular. Not comin', am I? And let a decent fight go by?"

We left the rendezvous lay-by with faint threats of dawn in the sky. O'Reilly had a musket, I had the pistol and Old Shenks carried a pike, and he sat on Dobie like St. George after the dragon. And we hadn't got fifty yards when the rain pelted down: the heavens opened and the clouds shot stair-rods, a cloudburst that soaked us in minutes and sent Dobie curvetting at the onslaught.

"Jesus!" exclaimed O'Reilly, looking around Dobie's bridle with a cold, dishevelled face. "What the Hell's happening?"

"It's revolution day," said Old Shenks. "As usual, God's backing up the Whigs and Tories."

We cut across country from Whitchurch to Lisvane in vicious downpourings of rain which I have never forgotten, and all the time we travelled the sky darkened. The wind rose, tearing hay out of the wayside barns, bringing down roofs and trees, blocking the roads with debris. Brooks and streams, already flooded by November rains, overflowed their banks and swamped the fields: the rivers raged, tossing on their breasts the wreckage of isolated farms. By midday, when we were east of Castleton, thunder and lightning added to the chaos of our lives: soaked to the skin, bedraggled, with our clothes chafing with every step O'Reilly and I led Dobie on, and Old Shenks, mute with misery, sat in the saddle like some ancient patriarch, with his pike spiking the sky, a lightning rod, said O'Reilly.

We struck north after leaving Castleton, making for Llantarnum on the Newport to Abergavenny road, and here the Afon Lwyd had burst its banks and had flooded the fields; the land was one great lake. And it was here, wading up to our knees in water, that we struck Jones the Watchmaker's Pontypool column, and they were marching on Newport, so they said.

Earlier, John Frost's column pouring down from his headquarters, the Coach and Horses at Blackwood, had waited for hours at the Welsh Oak Inn at Cefn for Zephaniah Williams's army coming south from Nantyglo, Newbridge and Abercarn. Now, we heard later, both these columns were waiting again for the one which we struck now, the William Jones's: and long they'd wait, cried O'Reilly above the lashing rain, for these didn't look like getting south of Malpas.

"Have ye ever in your born days seen such a mob?" cried Shenks, lurching in the saddle.

"God help the revolution," I shouted back, "if this is all it can muster."

A man was sitting by the side of the road, clear of the tramping boots: and he gave not a sign that he noticed them, this ragged, dripping army of men and boys: out of step, splashing along in the flood, their lodge and Benefit Club banners hung like dish-rags on their poles. And then he raised his head and looked up as we came abreast, this man, so I stopped at Dobie's head, and asked:

"How many are you?"

He was old and his face was ravaged with work and hunger, his accent, when he spoke, was North Country. "How many, ye ask? Aye, well ye may! There's not more'n six hundred here, marrer, and they promised us thousands."

"And where's William Jones – have you seen him?" bawled O'Reilly.

"Ach, indeed – back in The Green House, sinking doubles and wavin' a sword."

"Not since?"

"Once since, when we stopped at the Abbey for a parley wi' Boxer, the old M.P., who told him the error o' his ways." He wiped water from his sunken eyes. "I come on this outin' for my missus. Leave it to us, I told her, after this you'll live decent, you and the kids. We'll strangle bloody ironmasters."

"What now? Are you going on?"

"Aye," said he, getting up. "To strangle bloody Chartists. What the Hell is a grown man doin' on this mad caper to Newport?"

"They'll be there, though," cried O'Reilly, now beside me, and he shoved away a drunken man staggering against him in the mob. "The spalpeens might be drinkin' now, but come the firing, they'll march on London."

"Look out!" cried Old Shenks, and wheeled the horse. "There's more coming!"

Eight abreast now, they flooded down the road, a mob of mudstained weary men, their ranks a hedgehog of pikes and mandrels. They came in a tattered army, surging along. And, as they marched they were shouting drunken songs and waving two-stick banners. But one man, a leader, I saw marched alone. Inches taller than the rest, he stepped out in regimental style, his military bearing evident, and on his shoulder he carried a musket. Bare-headed in the pouring rain he went, ignoring the banter and jeers of his companions; a ramrod of soldiering, this one, his right arm swinging to his regulation pace. And there arose from the reeling, roaring mob a discordant shout: a hymn of rough voices within the drunken caterwauling, and this came from a group of disciplined men behind their fine leader. I heard the words of Ernest Jones:

> We're low, we're low, we're very very low,
> And yet, when the trumpets ring,
> The thrust of a poor man's arm will go
> Through the heart of the proudest king!

They were abreast of us now, these few soldiers, and I knew then what this attack on a town could have been, had people like Sam Williams, Gideon and my father had their say. But now, said Old Shenks from the saddle, we're being led by a watchmaker, the landlord of the Royal Oak up in Coalbrookvale, and Frost, the draper mayor. God help the town, added O'Reilly, if the men who had fought Napoleon could be here, instead of ballers, colliers, labourers and drunks.

We knew the truth of this when the shutters of the Westgate Inn went back, and showed us professionals.

"Aye, God help us," said the man on the road. "The military will chop us up as they did at Peterloo; what price our wives and children then?"

"Yes, but one thing you've forgot!" exclaimed O'Reilly. "The soldiers are with us, see? Starvation pay and floggings is all they get from their gentry officers."

Aye?

We know better now.

The rain poured down in a roar that sprayed white arms of water over us; the wind tore at our soaked clothes, stung our flesh with the pain of needles.

Cutting through the marching ranks the three of us took east across the flooded fields for Ponthir and Llanhennock to the rendezvous on the Monmouth Road where my father and his men were waiting in ambush. Wearily we marched, and Old Shenks, though riding, was becoming exhausted. Thunder battered the sky in drum rolls, and Dobie was prancing around in terror. From Barry north to Chester the storm raged all that day we heard later: from Shrewsbury to Snowdonia the land was swamped under a turmoil of water.

"I was right," said Old Shenks, "Jehovah ain't voting for the workers no more."

"Ay ay," answered O'Reilly. "The old chap always changes sides when the chips are down."

I did not reply. We were now confronted by the River Usk, a cauldron of rust-coloured water foaming in full spate, shouting at us, reaching up arms as if to drag us down. Above its roar I yelled at O'Reilly through cupped hands:

"Follow this north and we come to Llanhennock."

"Lead the way, lad," he shouted back. "You're young, it's your revolution!"

35

I knew the land around this part of Gwent. Time was, when I was a nip, my father would take me to Chepstow to visit his father; and I remembered now one particular May when the place was all blossom, hitting up for a bun-eared cow-pat of a summer; with coloured birds flying over the Usk and coots and crakes playing leap-frog with spring in a most disgraceful manner.

But now the countryside was forbidding and dull as we came along the Monmouth Road into Llanhennock and the cottages and terraced houses stood shoulder to shoulder in the gloom, locked and barred against strangers, because of the attack on nearby Newport.

"Listen!" said O'Reilly, and we stood on the deserted road. Faintly came the unmistakable crack of muskets.

"The lads are into them," said Old Shenks. "What now?"

"To find my father and his men."

"Did he say what part of the village?"

I shook my head. "This is his rendezvous, but he doesn't even know I'm coming."

"Reinforcement, are we?" asked Old Shenks, who was fading; time and time again I'd told him on the march, why we were coming.

"Well," said O'Reilly, beating water from his hat. "I hope he don't expect a lot from me. The only thing this old musket's good for now is knocking heads in. Look at me powder," and he held up his flask.

"Yes," I answered. "My pistol's the same. Everything's soaked."

"What we want is a housewife's oven, to dry it out," said Shenks.

"Ease up. Have ye brains gone soft?"

"It's true, I tell you – it's an old collier trick."

We laughed, but it was half-hearted, for the rain was lashing us.

Moving south, we were only a mile from Newport, searching for Dada when O'Reilly said, "Heisht! What's that? Listen."

A premature darkness had fallen over the land so we did not immediately see him – a lad of about twelve lying in the roadside ditch, and we carefully lifted him out on to the verge. Shenks asked:

"What you doin' here, lad, for God's sake?" and the boy replied:

"William Jones stopped the lads at Cross-ye-Legs, but a few of us come on . . ."

"You walked from Groes-y-ceilog?" I asked, astonished, for the ball had taken him across the stomach and cut him wide, and the bones of his ribs were stark white and smeared with blood where he clutched himself.

"No, Mister. When the lads come down Stow Hill, George Shell and me went in with them, against the Westgate: George stopped it in the passage and I caught it going up the steps. Christ, mun, you never seen such a mess."

"When was that?"

He was broad and fair, looking more like a man, and he said, "Coupla hours back, or so. Redcoats everywhere – come down from the Workhouse. They was waitin' for us, I reckon. There was dead lads all over the street." He sighed like a child. "You know Tom Callister?"

"No."

"He's another o' my Llanhennock mates. You get back home to your mam, Ianto, he tells me. And the military were there tying the lads up and sending for carts. They'll be comin' by here now just, to the prison in Monmouth."

"Christ," whispered O'Reilly. "The attack's over . . ."

"O aye, Mister. There ain't any fightin' in Newport now."

I closed my eyes, wondering where Dada was.

Old Shenks said, lifting the boy, "No odds to that. We're getting you back home to your mam. Where's your place?"

Ianto pointed. "Over by there – second cottage, but I can't go home in this state, can I?"

"But you can't lie here, either," I said.

"Ay ay, I can – till the rain cleans me up, see? She's got two kids at home, and they're both younger'n me . . ." He looked at the sky and the rain beat fast upon his face; down was upon his cheeks and his lips were red. "Jesus . . ." he whispered. "Ain't it gettin' dark . . ." and he closed his eyes.

"He's away," whispered Shenks, and screwed up his hand.

We knelt in silence. Then O'Reilly said:

"Listen!" He had ears for brown mice, this one.

Across the fields behind us men were coming – twenty, I counted, and my father was at their head; I knew him by his gait. Beside him was the black-maned giant Edwards, the man I had met up at Llangynidr cave. We left the boy and went to greet them.

"It's bad, have you heard?" Dada asked.

We told him about Ianto.

"Yes, the lad's right. William Jones's column never arrived; every gun the lads carried had soaked powder. Under cover, with dry powder, the soldiers mowed them down from the Westgate windows. And the army reinforcements never came through this way. It's my guess they brought in troops from Brecon."

"From Newport workhouse," I replied. "They were holding them in reserve up Stow Hill, according to this boy. Do you know anything more?"

My father replied, "Only that everything's lost. A deserter came through half an hour back, going like the wind, but we collared him. He said that all the columns were late getting in – the weather, apparently. And Jones's lot never got south of Malpas."

A man beside him said, "People like Frost couldn't plan a vicarage tea-party, mun – and Jones wi' his big talk of wading in blood!"

"What happens now, then?" I asked, and Dada replied:

"Chartist prisoners will be taken. Soon the carts will be coming through." He jerked his thumb. "Edwards knows this place backwards. He's found us a headquarters in the wood over there, a quarry. We can lie low in it and make an attack on the road and free the lads."

"Is there a roof to the quarry?" asked O'Reilly. "My gun's useless, we need dry powder."

"So will the Redcoats, butty."

A man spoke at Old Shenks's shoulder: he was a Cornishman by his accent and his face was a pudding of laughs. He cried, "Maister, I'm prayin' they get me first time out. My old Biddy'll kick my arse for comin' on this outing." The men laughed. The wind howled about us; water was running out of my boots, I remember.

"It's the bloody pastor I'm afeared of, son – he be a real Bible-punchin' vandal – and he'll have me out the front . . ."

My father cut them short. "Back to the quarry then, all of us, and wait for the prison carts coming through. If the lads make a run for it they'll still stand a chance. Where's that boy?"

"Here," said O'Reilly, and lifted Ianto.

"Bring him along, we can't leave him here. What about his mother?"

"I know her," said Edwards, and took Ianto from O'Reilly. "I'll take him home."

We stood, all of us, in disconsolate, silent groups, watching Edwards as he carried the boy down the road to the cottages of Llanhennock.

"You," commanded my father, and ordered a man near-by. "Stay and act as sentry," and he glanced at his watch. "Any time now the carts will be through – your mates, remember, so make no mistake about it. Any sign of movement – carts, soldiers – run over the field and shout into the wood, understand?"

"Aye, Captain."

Dada raised his arm. "Right, follow me, all of you," and he led us across the soaked field adjoining the Monmouth Road to the tree-fringe that hid his headquarters, the quarry.

As we squelched along I stole a look at my father.

He was wearing a buckskin jacket and trews of some quality; these I had not seen before. Bare-headed, despite the wind and rain, he walked like a knight from Aneirin's *Gododdin*. This is how I had always seen my father; not with his arms outstretched, bowed behind the whipping cart of Amlwch. Inches taller than any man there that day, save Edwards, he walked with dignity, his head up. Yet soon, I thought – and it was a sudden and terrible vision – that tunic would be stained. And he who was beside me now would leave me an empty shell to venerate. In defeat and death, I thought, he would be one with those who had preceded him; and returning to the courts of his people.

I could have reached out and touched my father then, and the strange thought struck me that, had I done so, I would have touched a myth; one already dead in service to his country.

As we entered the wood my father smiled at me. "Come, Tal – such a face? Smile, for God's sake. What we do today we do for Wales."

36

I counted twenty men within the open quarry cave.

Stripping off our soaked clothes, we were instantly twenty naked men, hopping and shivering in the November cold; wringing out our shirts, emptying water from our boots, we gasped and slapped our flesh to bring back the circulation.

Edwards returned, unspeaking. My father asked:

"You found his mother?"

"Aye, Captain. Do not speak of it."

A man said, "God, what a country, eh? Nigh twelve he was, no more. Wales is forgotten, mun. The devils o' Gehenna are with us."

My father, trying to dry his powder, glanced up. "They are not. At last we're fighting back. This is the best day the country's had since Suetonius, for God's sake."

"Jesus," murmured a man beside me. "Who the Hell's Suetonius?"

I wanted to smile. How often, before and since, I have wondered if my father, so much with the people, was truly of the people? His learning, his nobility of character often removed him, I thought, from the common run. Yet they followed him; this was certain. They followed him loyally, all men who knew him; blindly obeying, without demur. Was this, I wondered, a fault of the Celts? This unquestioning, unswerving obedience to anything savouring of birth and distinction?

Soon, I thought, the sentry will shout and all here will go out to make war. And then they will know, these men, the cost of such obedience. Yet, being Welshmen, they would not hesitate, for it was in their blood.

And then, as if bringing to a conscious end the drama of my mind, we heard the sentry shout, and scrambled into our clothes.

"Steady," said my father. "Do not rush it. Don't begrudge them a little more time to live!" and hands on hips, he grinned around him. "Your powder's wet, but so is theirs. Musket butts and fists, then. Free your mates, but do not hit to kill, remember."

We trooped in single file back to the Monmouth Road and lowered our bodies into the water-filled ditches either side of it.

"Look," cried the sentry, and pointed.

They were coming. Despite the rain we could see them clearly, about ten carts in line, horse- or mule-drawn, and flanked with marching soldiers. And in the carts the prisoners were crammed like herrings in barrels, too tight to fall out.

They were half a mile away, coming around a bend in the road, and we heard their iron-tipped boots ringing in a steady, tramping rhythm and the grating of iron-ringed wheels. Amazingly, from the column of marching men, pent prisoners and heaving animals, a rainbow mist arose of steaming breath and sweating bodies.

"How many are they?" asked Old Shenks on one side of me, and O'Reilly, on the other, replied:

"Some hundred prisoners, I reckon – perhaps more . . ."

"Double that," I said. "Twenty to a cart. And about a hundred soldiers."

"Dear me," said a voice, and I had to smile, "I'd rather be back home in bed wi' my missus – this lot will cripple us."

"Och, Benny," came a reply, "you're no bloody good in there either, mun, she told me."

"I tell ye one thing, son, I could do with a pint."

They bantered, chuckled, laid wagers on their lot. And then my father called down the lines:

"Listen. Let them pass, understand? Lie low in the water and let them go by, then come out when I shout and take them in the middle – the middle, remember, then fan out ither side. It's confusion we want, the lads in the carts'll do he rest."

I watched their rain-washed faces as they stared with unted eyes towards the oncoming convoy guarded by rained soldiers.

They were not trained fighters, these; they were artisans nd labourers. Aye, over twenty rounds up on the Blorenge unch-bowl of a Sunday morning for sport – all right, but ot to the death.

Yes, they fought: they'd been fighting all their lives, but mainly to keep their children fed, or their wives out of debt to he Truck Shops run by the Guests or Homfray. A few had eard of their Celtic past – of the ancient tribes who had ought the might of Rome long after England had been ludgeoned into submission – but most didn't care a jot bout it. The hope was not conquest, but to try to keep off the lacklist, out of the House of Correction at Usk if they were aught paying pennies to the outlawed Union.

Now they stared with vacant faces at the oncoming Redoats, and no leader of that time, including John Frost, could ave commanded a more disconsolate army. The convoy ame on, nearer, nearer. The ammunition boots of the soliers were now thumping the road with cold, military preci-on.

The head of the column, led by an officer on horseback, as no less than fifty yards away: peering through the roadde grasses I could see the prisoners clearly: many were ounded, their bloodstained bandages fluttering in the ind. And then, above the pouring rain I heard a faint, iscordant sound, and realised that they were singing. In Velsh they sang, mostly, which was their mother tongue, ut more were shouting the words of Ernest Jones, our thartist poet, in English:

> Then rouse my boys and fight the foe;
> Your weapons are truth and reason.
> We'll let the Whigs and Tories know
> That thinking is not treason.
> Ye lords, oppose us as you can.

Your own doom ye seek after.
With or without you, we will stand
Until we gain the Charter!

And there arose from the carts then a battering cry in unison:
"The Charter! The Charter! *The Charter!*"

Now they came abreast of us. I saw the horsed officer stare
down at the ditches either side of him, and my father, seeing
him draw his sword, yelled:

"Right, lads! Into them! Get into them!"

Instantly, it was pandemonium.

As we stormed across the road towards the carts, the
soldiers fought to unsling their muskets, and the prisoners,
leaping down on to the road, stopped to fight or fled in all
directions, in wild disorder. I saw the astonished face of a
Redcoat as we met; holding the advantage of surprise, I
hooked him hard to the chin and he fell against me, clutching
me and pulling me down. And out of the corners of my eyes I
saw a levelled pistol; exploding in a shaft of fire, its ball took
O'Reilly through the head, blowing out his brains.

Now, within a mêlée of struggling, cursing men I struggled up, butted one soldier and struck down another, then
stooped to haul one off my back, and Old Shenks came up,
steadied himself and hit the man flat. Edwards, the giant, was
nearby, lifting soldiers off their feet and clubbing them down
like dolls: beyond him my father was fighting with almost
methodical grace, pulling prisoners out of the jumble of men
and animals, striking away those who opposed him. Men
were shrieking, bawling from bloodstained faces within the
struggling mass; some horses were down, their hooves clattering about, carts were overturning. And from the heaving
bodies a wild clamour arose in the fierce downpouring rain.
Locked together, men were rolling about, punching, kicking,
clawing at each other within a howling in English and
Welsh.

And then, floating on a sea of bobbing heads, I saw a face I
knew – Irish Joc Dido, Old Nana's son. And he was shouting
some bawdy song of the Wexford '98 Rebellion and waving
an Irish flag: Knocker, I saw next, climbing down the back of

cart, his head bandaged and his clothes in tatters, and he shouted something incomprehensible as he leaped the roadside ditch in escape.

Now a man gripped me, shouting into my face, "You Welsh bastard!" and he swung me over his hip so that we crashed down together into a forest of stamping boots and legs: astride me, with his red tunic in rags, the soldier was bawling, bawling, and I struck up at his crimson face, missed him and hit another. I covered my head as a fist swung down. The soldier shrieked to the pain of his smashed knuckles as I ducked and his fist hit the road. And I saw, in a gap of the battle a man swaying along the verge. It was Sam Williams; like a drunken man he went, before suddenly collapsing, going head first into the ditch. Fighting myself upright, I butted through the mass of bodies in his direction; in time to see my father fling up his arms. And I saw a soldier's bayonet plunge through his chest and slide, blooded, through his buckskin tunic at the back, impaling him.

"Dada!" I was upon him, hauling the soldier away, and my father stood for a moment, surprise upon his face. Pulling out the bayonet I gripped him around the waist and hauled him away to the side of the road. And I knelt above him while the tide of the fight ebbed about us.

My father's eyes were closed and blood was bubbling down his jacket. And, as I bent to get him over my shoulders to lift him, I heard a voice I recognised.

"Here – you take his legs!"

It was Iestyn Mortymer, the young man I had run arms with, up at Llangynidr, and with him was a man of width and strength; Iestyn cried:

"No, better – get him over Big Rhys's back!" And Iestyn stooped; with his right arm in a sling and heavily splinted, he lifted with me and the big man bent to take the weight at the moment a bright light exploded in my eyes, and I fell across the body of my father.

Later, they told me, the counter-attack had formed a pattern.

Having absorbed the initial impact of our attack, the

Redcoats took command. For these were not the comparatively untrained recruits who had fought so well at the Westgate, but others of the 45th: a hundred and fifteen of Napier's most experienced troops held in reserve for such an eventuality. They were the veterans of Waterloo who had scattered the cavalry at Quatre Bras and shot up the French Imperial Guard under Ney at La Haye Sainte: men whose comrades, with the French, had laid fifty thousand graves in two square miles of country.

Aye, indeed; they had little to fear from us – a bunch of untrained colliers and ironworkers; theirs was a trade of blood and violence.

I opened my eyes to a jolting, searing pain in the back of my head where a soldier's rifle butt had struck me. Green trees and overhanging branches tore at my face and hands as I danced in a dream through the forest. And the man who had carried me laid me down in the same quarry we had left but fifteen minutes earlier to attack the convoy. Others were there; wounded men; men panting from bloody faces; men rocking themselves to the pain of unseen wounds. They were all about me, these, like a pack of gasping, hunted animals. And I saw the face of Iestyn bending over me.

"You all right?"

"*Duw!*" I whispered, and sat up, feeling my head.

"Aye, did he hit you. But Big Rhys got him for it, the bugger."

Realisation struck me.

"Where's my father?"

"Beside you," said Iestyn.

Dada was lying where the man, Big Rhys, had dropped him, and he was dying.

The bayonet had taken him low, up through the midriff muscles and high into his chest, piercing a lung before slanting out through his shoulderblades. But he was still conscious, though his face was death-white; a premature corpse.

"Dada . . ." I said, bending over him.

"You all right, Tal?"

I nodded. Blood welled into his mouth and he swallowed it down.

"Got me this time, didn't they, the sods!"

It was one of the few times I heard him swear.

Iestyn, kneeling beside me, said, "Not likely, Captain. This time tomorrow you'll be back home," but my father did not appear to hear this, for he said, softly:

"Tal . . . the book."

Iestyn whispered, "What . . . what did he say?"

But I knew, and ran my hands over his tunic, and found it, the tin box that held 'The Tale of Delwyn'; I drew it out and held it up in the dim light.

"That . . . that girl you've got—Rhiannon, isn't it . . . ?" His voice was faint and I had to bend to his mouth to hear it.

"Aye, Dada—Rhiannon."

"Give it . . . if she has a son?"

I closed my eyes. "If she has a son, I will give it to him."

There was a silence broken only by his breathing; the men were listening. Then:

"Watch out for Poll, eh?"

I nodded, fighting tears.

"Aye, don't forget her—and Meg?"

A bright crimson stain suddenly widened on his white shirt. He said, his voice so faint now that I scarcely heard:

"'The coming hope, the future day, when Wrong to Right shall bow . . . And hearts that have the courage . . . to make that future now.'"

Then he sighed, turned away his face, and slipped easily into death.

I held him. Even after he had ceased to breathe, I held him.

After a few minutes Iestyn Mortymer came over the floor to me, drew my arms away, and laid my father on to the earth.

"Hush, Tal," said he. "You cannot kiss him back."

Empty I felt, without my father.

37

The quarry cave was open to the forest. For hours – almost up to midnight we could hear the soldiers beating through the trees and the rasp of their bayonets as they thrust into the undergrowth. But after midnight the sounds of their search died away. So we listened for the iron-shod wheels of their carts, the signal that they had continued their march to Cold Bath Fields, the prison, but no such sounds came to us.

"They're still there, boys," said a man. "They'm only waiting for daylight."

"Then they'll bait us like rats in a trap," said his companion.

Easing over away from Big Rhys, who was sleeping, I took my father into my arms, and held him; cold, cold that body against mine.

Moonlight filtered down through the tree-tops: the men slept, snoring; some groaned to the pain of their wounds. They bandaged each other with strips of shirt, comforting one another with a rough, vulgar badinage; you don't need women for nurses, I've discovered, when comrades are around.

Iestyn Mortymer was sitting opposite to me, his head bowed over his broken arm, and he smiled once, opening his eyes to mine.

"Why are you fighting, Mortymer?" I asked him.

He shrugged, but I persisted, to take my mind from grief.

"For my son, and against Cwm Crachen," said he at length, and smiled. "That's the second time today I've been asked that."

"Cwm Crachen?" asked a man nearby. His accent was faintly Scottish.

Iestyn nodded. His hair, I noticed, was as black as mine was white in that dim, eerie light.

"You didn't say you had a son," said I.

"I didn't have one when I saw you last, Tal Roberts."

"What's his name?"

"Jonathan."

"Cwm Crachen?" asked the man again, and Iestyn turned to him:

"The Hollow of the Scab," he replied. "The place where my son was born. Do not ask more, man, leave it at that."

Outside in the forest the rain poured down; the wind was blustering among the little crags and crevices. A man said from the dark in a fine cultured voice:

"They said the Church and Chapels would be with us. They said the soldiers were on our side. The gentry were our friends, they told us. Yet here we are alone."

"Ach, give over, Sol, for God's sake. The Church, did ye say? The Old Testament backsliders? Ranting and ravin' in their pulpits, they're all in it together."

"They piss in the same pot, mun."

"Receive the Holy Ghost, eh? Then they drink a gin and leap a five-barred gate. Don't talk to me about the Church."

Another said, plaintively, "Frost, Williams and bloody Jones the Watchmaker! March on London, is it? They couldn't march on my Aunt Fanny."

There was a silence; then:

"So where did Jones's column get to?"

"Get to? Malpas, no further! A schoolgirl outing, it were – half a mile o' tit in half-inch strips. They were pissin' it up in the Green House, I tell ye, while I was into the Westgate Inn with hatchets."

The wind whispered in the quarry; the brown walls shone with running water. A man said, ruefully, "Mind, they'll make us jump this time for sure. They hung Dic Penderyn for somethin' he never did. Christ knows what they'll do to us."

"Don't talk like that, Paddy, there's dead folks in here,

mind."

"Apologies to their souls, mate, call them bloody lucky."

The night went on, and Iestyn said, "Rhiannon is a lovely name, Tal Roberts."

I held my father closer, for rain was driving in.

"Aye, and your wife's, Mari. There's Welsh in that."

"Yes, but she's English." His eyes were strangely shining, for there was little light. A man deep in the cave said:

"It'll be transportation, mind. High Treason, see?"

"Och, give over, Taff," said a North-Country voice.

"You lot would be wise if you got to sleep," said Iestyn, and rose, and the new leader was born. "You're sitting here with more yap than a pack of women. Are we proud of ourselves, for God's sake? Take it how it comes. The least we can do is keep our dignity," and he knelt beside me and took my father in the crook of his arm, saying:

"Sleep, Tal – lie back and sleep. I will hold him till the soldiers come."

"Is there no chance to get away?"

"No, they're all around us. Sleep, is it?" and he pushed me back on to the rock floor.

"Aye, he's right," said a man. "Sleep," and the place was quiet save for the pattering rain and doleful dripping of the forest.

Near to dawn somebody went around the quarry cave kicking the sleepers into wakefulness.

"What's up?"

"What the Hell's happening?" and Iestyn, standing in the middle of the floor, said:

"Right. Get up, all of you, we're making a break. I want the unwounded in front with me, the old men in the middle and the walking wounded at the back. Crawl, if you like, but we're going out. We're not sitting here like bloody mice."

"Ye askin' for it, ye mad young spalpeen!"

"They're waiting for that – just dying to blast us!"

"Stay if you like, Irish, you're not bound to come," said Iestyn. "Follow me, the rest of you."

With the leader in front we made a break for it, dodging and swerving through the trees, and ran into a half-circle of gleaming bayonets. The sergeant's voice cut through the rain:

"Come on, come on, then, you bloody Taffs. We're just dyin' to let you have it – come on!"

They ringed us with steel, cuffed and prodded us through the forest, and out to the carts waiting on the road for the march to Monmouth.

38

They thumped us through the forest with their musket butts; they prodded us up into the carts where our comrades, recaptured earlier, were waiting in the rain. I was up first and I pulled up Iestyn after me, then the man who was his friend, Big Rhys. Old Shenks had to be lifted in because the cold had got him, being over eighty. Irish Joe Dido, the son of Old Nana, was at the back of our cart, which was third in the line of ten: and he shouted, when they threw him into it:

"Be Jesus – call ye'self lucky. If my Old Nana were here she'd 'ave the bloody lot of ye!

"Easy on me, ye big English oaf!" And he began to sing up at the rain, an Irish revolution song about the hanging of Father John Murphy at Wexford.

The convoy had moved a bit and was now outside some Llanhennock cottages, and the old men and women came out and stood on their doorsteps, staring up with white, furious faces: hatred was in them for the English. And the men bared their heads; the women pulling their shawls over their faces, and we did not look at them, being ashamed.

Gradually they rounded us all up; little groups of shivering, dejected men and boys, uncomplaining under the prods and thumps. Many of them I knew by sight; a few of their faces I had seen in The Patriot meetings or on cock-fight nights in the Vulcan and Friendship.

Standing near me in the cart was Big Rhys, the boxer. And he turned his face to me, this man, and weeping, said:

"O, fy mab; fy machgen bach dewr!"

A man behind me asked, "What's wrong with him, for God's sake?" and pushed a bit in the standing crush. "Something up, Fighter?"

Iestyn said quietly, "Shut it – you asked that before. His son is dead; no more of it."

The big man wept on, biting at his fingers.

I was trying to keep Old Shenks upon his feet. The carts had halted again, but he kept slipping down the front of me. A sergeant went by, his pigeon chest ablaze with medals; grizzled and bucolic, this one, and get these bloody Taffs down to Monmouth quick. I called over the side of the cart:

"Sergeant, this old boy's gone eighty, and he keeps fainting. Can't you give us room to lay him down?"

"Hand him down here and I'll lay him out." He glared up, his moustache bristling. "You bastards!"

"Don't waste your time," said Iestyn to me. "You'll get nothing from them, Tal."

"He ain't fainted, mun," said a voice behind me. "The poor old bugger's dead." And he reached out and turned up Shenks's eyelids.

Jake Kilrain died, I heard later; the giant puddler who had seen to Eli Firmament, who deserved to die. Sam Williams died, too, but later, apparently, and I don't know where. But Knocker did not die; he escaped to Cardiff and took a ship to Brazil, so the tale went; if he did he was lucky, for Zephaniah Williams tried that and they picked him up aboard.

Zephaniah, like John Frost, the Chartist leader – they captured him in the house of Partridge, the printer in Newport – they both went to trial with William Jones and six others for High Treason, which carried Victoria's sentence of hanging, drawing and quartering, the filthy death that every felon feared.

There were some on the attack I never saw again – like Dai Tomorrow, who put off capture until fifteen years later, according to reports, and married a widow with a public in Abercarn, then moved to Maerdy, which they later called Little Moscow.

There was a rumour, too, that Old Cog Costog didn't die in bed, but came South with Skipper Rowlands and a boat-load of Anglesey lads, to fight for the Charter. And they were taken into custody ten minutes after landing in Bute Lock, and went to transportation. God knows why he finished up in Norfolk Island, but he was still quoting poetry, I heard, when they put the noose around his neck.

But Old Shenks, my friend of Canal Wharf, he who had served me, Gideon, and my father so well, died standing up; and I held him.

"Right, whip up the horses!"

The convoy started off again along the road to Monmouth. In the jolting, swaying cart, I held Old Shenks against me, and suddenly the wheels skidded to a stop. The officer on horseback came galloping up, and when he shouted I recognised his voice:

"Roberts, father and son. Are the Roberts pair here?"

It was Lieutenant Wetton, who once was a captain, and I knew instantly that I had heard that voice before – behind red curtains in Dowlais House library.

Recognising me, Wetton reined closer, crying:

"Out, Roberts – down on to the road!"

Big Rhys turned in the crush. "Give him me," he said, and took Old Shenks into his arms. I fought my way to the side of the cart and vaulted down.

"Ah yes!" Wetton smiled down. The rain, blustering in the wind, swept along the road between us. "We meet, I hope for the last time, Roberts. Your father is dead, I understand?"

I did not reply and his mare clattered around me as Wetton drew his sabre. He cried, his voice high-pitched with anger:

"So we're getting some justice at last, are we? You damned Northerners are worse than the Taffs. So far you've got off scot free, haven't you? So take this to remember me by," and he slashed down with the sabre and sliced my face from eye to chin.

'. . . and smote Delwyn, disfiguring him, and sent him to a foreign land, and it was twenty years before he returned to his own country.'

The lads tore the sleeves out of their shirts and tied me up a bit and the carts started off again. And, strangely, after those two days of tempest, the sun came out and the land smiled about us. And it seemed to me, although it could have been a fever, that it was shining for us; because in a break in the lowering clouds a beam of light shone down as if from the Heavens. I raised my face, like the others, for it was dazzling in its intensity. In its rainbow colours I seemed to hear my father's words:

> The coming hope, the future day
> When Wrong to Right shall bow.
> And hearts that have the courage
> To make that future now.

The carts rumbled on, along the road to Monmouth.

Book Three

Tal-y-Bont
1861

39

I returned from the convict settlement in Australia in the summer of my fortieth birthday, and owning nothing save the rags I stood in, made my way from Swansea Docks into a smiling land.

At Tonna, outside Neath, following the canal there out of habit, I worked two days harvesting on a farm for a barn bed and meals, a man who gave a helping hand to returning convicts, paying them half agricultural rates, fivepence a day. I snared rabbits in Rheola Forest and killed a sheep outside Hirwaun, where I worked with Crawshay's ironstone miners; pathetic, half-starved men, women and children who laboured exposed, in bitter winters, under the spray-shot cannons of a dynasty's benevolence . . . until they discovered my identity, and I was discharged.

From Hirwaun I took up over Mynydd Aberdare, and along the ridge to Dowlais Top; to the cottage where Sam Williams and Aunt Mellie had lived.

A child of about five was standing at the cottage gate; neatly dressed was she, in a home-spun frock, a white pinafore, and clogs; and I knew by her white hair that she was of Gwyn Roberts' blood; also the eyes of Meg were in her face. But she shrieked when I greeted her, and ran, this child, and my sister Meg came to the cottage door, her hands white with flour.

"Tal . . . !" she said, and closed her eyes.

We stood in the silence of indecision, friends but strangers, and she said then, holding the little one against her:

"You're back . . . ?"

I nodded. "Aye, Meg."

I saw her not as a prim housewife, the cygnet who had become a swan (for she was tall, fair and beautifully possessed) but like the daughter she now clasped against her: with bright curls, and small fists waving, I saw her, her tiny rosebud of a mouth slobbering upon Poll's breast.

"You . . . you didn't write, Meg?"

She raised her chin. "Not really – Old Sam advised against it, and my man, too. Dunna get mixed up wi' it, he said – he's foreman at Race Level now, mind; we're doin' all right." She frowned, peering at me. "Where did ye get that terrible scar?"

"It doesn't matter," I said. The child looked over her shoulder at me and hid her face again. "Sam and Mellie both gone, are they?"

"O ah!" She brightened, but she was not the Meg I knew: "Old Sam died . . . let me see – about 'Fifty – near ten years back, and Auntie six months later . . . left me the cottage. Sam's friend, Knocker, got killed, ye know?"

"Killed?"

"Shot down Cardiff way, but I ain't sure, really speaking, for some say he got away." She lowered her eyes. "You heard about Dada, of course . . ."

I nodded.

"They buried him up at St. Woolos, you know . . . justifiable somethin' or other they called it."

"Justifiable homicide"

"Aye, that's it." She sniffed and wiped on a little lace handkerchief. "Mind, I do go up sometimes and put flowers on 'is grave. But . . ."

"But what, Meg?"

I fought the longing to take her into my arms.

"Well, my chap don't hold with it. Got the children to think about, he says." She brightened. "He . . . he's foreman at the . . ."

"Children, Meg?"

She held the little girl against her. "This one and another couple inside."

"I'm glad."

The wind moved, bringing between us the old Dowlais stinks, and Meg said faintly, lifting the child. "We . . . we gotta go, *cariad*? Got to get Dada's dinner, 'aven't we?" She peered past me. "He . . . he'll be back off shift any minute."

There came from the kitchen behind her a scent of granny's broth; my stomach, smelling it, too, rumbled for pounce thunder.

"Goodbye," I said.

For all my love of her childhood, it seemed inadequate.

"Goodbye, Tal. Any . . . anything you want you just ask for, mind. You was always good to me, Tal." She waved the child's hand, dying to be gone. "Say goodbye to the nice gentleman, Ceri."

I had got no more than fifty yards when I heard her shriek like a woman scalded.

"*Tal!*" But I didn't look back.

Around Dowlais market the hucksters were at it – bargain boots at sixpence a foot; meat stalls, bread stalls, potatoes for a penny a pound, eggs five shillings a hundred. Macassar oil was being sold by quacks, music sheets and *The News of the World.*

Navvies were in from the outlying railways dressed in their moleskins and gaudy scarves, tipsy already, although the day was young; brawny, insolent, barging the women about with their brightly-coloured waistcoats. The thronging crowds were buying Liver Pills for Biliousness and Dr. Clee's ointment for Skin Eruptions, Rheumatics and Intestinal Worms: dentists were fitting teeth, barbers cutting and shaving outside cheese and butter stalls.

And on the fringe of the crowds sat the derelicts of the gullies – the filthy dilapidated houses, the overcrowded ill-ventilated rooms surrounded by collections of filth. And among these squatted the diseased and maimed; the puddlers, ballers and fillers who would work no more. In line after line they squatted; legless, armless, many with no feet (molten iron had got into their boots) and many blinded: starving, they rattled their begging tins along the walls of the Vulcan and Friendship and the Holywell Hotel, crying hoarsely from their burned faces; they who bought, with their blood, the millionaire pomp of Cyfarthfa Castle and Dowlais House.

It was the same old Dowlais that I had known two decades ago, and I remembered the words of Edward Davies, a Merthyr surgeon: 'There are more wooden legs in this town than any in the country with four times Merthyr's population; our streets are thronging with the maimed and the mutilated.'

If anything, I thought, it was worse than the 1830's.

In such company I could lose myself; in such a concourse of humanity, I was not alone. Nobody even glanced at my disfigured face, the legacy of Captain Wetton.

Now, standing outside the Vulcan and Friendship, I remembered Rhiannon: of how, an age before, I had taken her on Dobie in the snow, and made love to her in Dolygaer forest . . . the memory of her, the place itself, suddenly called me with obliterating force.

Making my way through the crowds in bright sunlight, I hitched up my bundle and took the bridle path I knew so well, up to Hitherto's lodge.

On Dowlais Top I stopped and looked back, seeing below me for the last time the dirty, straggling town amid its sprawling, barren mountains; like a bundle of dirty rags spread out in faintest hope of their bleaching, with belching furnaces and black table-lands of rubbish all around.

Aye, I thought, so leave this pit of greed and sorrow and go where it is clean . . . to the place where you made love to Rhiannon.

40

I walked through the bowers of Dolygaer forest under a bright green shuffle of leaves; above me a kestrel hawk soared in vaporous air-space. Here, I remembered, hand in hand with Rhiannon, I had seen the trailing sword of Orion and the flashing of Sirius amid a wilderness of blossom.

Here sang the robins of winter; there soared young larks in the rafters of heaven; in the hazel wands, where I passed, were the petulant protestations of a redbreast. All was alive with the flame of summer; a reed-warbler chattered to its young: amid languorous blooms of convolvulus, silver-bubbled streams meandered down to the Falls, where danced a sea of dandelion and willow-herb. All was born anew within the seething anguish of our parting.

Following the track that led to the shooting lodge, I walked more slowly, and with care, lest I disturbed Joe Hitherto; were he alive he must surely be eighty, I reflected. And saw him all of a sudden, outlined head and shoulders in the plover field beyond his gate; turning, he cried:

"Well, dang my arse! If it anna Tal Roberts!"

I stood before him gripping my bundle.

He was as old as a dead stoat, with bags under his eyes like the toss-pots of the Casbah; but his brain was up and lively and in his eyes was a wicked gleam.

"You remember me?" I asked.

Closer now, he surveyed me, his faded eyes peering.

"Well sod me! Where you been? – what you been up to?"

"No odds to that, Joe," I answered. "Just passing, and I'm on my way."

A bird whispered sorrowfully, the cadence of its voice rising and falling on the soft, clear air.

He said, out of context, "That girl died, ye know . . ."

"Rhiannon? Yes, I know."

"And Sir John, too – these six year back, an' more. It were jist 'afore goldfinch time, as I recall . . ."

I envied him his articulate sense of time, measuring all by the seasons. He added, screwing at his moleskin cap. "But Lady Charlotte's still goin' strong – married that Schreiber chap, did ye know?"

"I did not know."

His presence, despite its nostalgic sweetness, was also a transgression: I desperately wanted to be alone amid this glowing richness. Joe added:

"Mind, it were a pity about that little de Vere piece, weren't it?" He grinned with broken, yellow teeth. "You were real soft on her, if I remember."

"Yes," I said quietly.

"Went to India, got married, left 'im, came home, and died. Nursing the Old Cholera down in China, she were."

In trackless words, sunless, airless, we stood, just looking. I said, "Joe . . . I've got to go . . ."

"But not directly?" A pathetic eagerness struck his lined face. "You just sod around for a bit, and welcome, eh?" He pushed past me like a man exorcising wickedness, lifting his cap and crying, "Go into the lodge, mun – make yesel' a cup o' tea, I'll be back this minute."

"Thank you."

Alone in the lodge I stood listening to a ring-dove sobbing, a ravishing sweetness on the forest air.

This place, indeed, this room, I thought, was almost exactly as Rhiannon had left it.

Beyond the window where we had watched the snow, March helleborine arose in scents of wild thyme, and the glades were hazed with celandine: within the room were the same, now bald, sheepskin rugs, the faded pictures on the walls; the same, but now faded chintz curtains. And in the silence of the chattering forest, in the mellow-sweet drone of bees, I heard her voice:

"Make love to me, Tal? Please make love to me . . .?"

The room abounded with her presence, and I knelt in the place where she had lain, and knew sounds that were echoes of reality. It was as if, for one undefined moment, I was holding her in my arms and deep within her body, and I raised my face and called her name:

"Rhiannon!"

The forest sounds stopped, listening to a stranger's voice.

"*Rhiannon!*"

It was a heresy of self-deceit: a warped notion of romantic nonsense; I turned to leave, embarrassed by my own behaviour.

A girl was standing in the open doorway, as the kettle boiled.

She surely must have heard me.

"Mr. Roberts?" and she came into the room, smiling. If she noticed my disfigured face, she made no sign of it.

I bowed.

She said, "My name is Marged. Old Joe sent a keeper to the house, and I came straight away. You knew my mother, he says."

Beyond the door stood a little dappled mare; the girl was dressed in brown riding-habit: her face, her form . . . was the epitome of Rhiannon.

In my silence, she asked: "Did . . . did you know her, Mr. Roberts?"

"Yes."

"My . . . my mother is dead. You knew that, too?"

"Yes."

I could not drag my eyes from her face. It was like the crystallising of a hypnotic dream; as if Rhiannon had returned: even the voice possessed the same cadent quality, a dark contralto sound.

"Did . . . did you know her well?" the girl asked.

"Not well."

Her eyes had lowered to my hands and the wrists wasted by the manacles, and I put them behind my back. She said, unmoving:

"She died when I was six years old," her eyes drifted

around the room and she faintly smiled. "She . . . she used to come here a lot when she was young, she told me. She loved Dolygaer forest, this old lodge especially. Old Joe says she was always here, before she married . . ."

"Married?"

"Her people went to India and she married there. My father died out there when I was two, so she came home again, to Wales."

"I see."

"He was an army officer." She raised her eyes and looked at me, then moved with delicate grace, bending to peer through the window. I said quickly:

"You live up at Kierton now?"

"With my grandfather, Sir Richard. There are paintings of my mother all over the house, but none of my father. I'm always trying to find out things about my people – which is natural, I suppose, but nobody seems to know anything. That's why I jumped on old Penny, and came down here."

"Penny?"

She smiled brilliantly. "My mother had a mare called Penny."

We stood as strangers, talking with the inanimate falseness that impedes strangers.

"Yes, I remember," I said, and returned her smile.

It didn't traduce her; her task was discovery, and she was possessed of the woman's subterfuge; later, if this was unsuccessful, she would resort to chicanery; I would have to guard my tongue.

This secret was Rhiannon's, bound by the girl's illegitimacy.

"You used to meet here a lot, Old Joe said." Marged laughed gaily, looking beautiful; like the Princess Marged in the 'Tale of Delwyn' I thought vaguely.

"Joe's a romantic old fool," I replied.

She examined me with the academic interest one reserves for a child, and asked, "Did you ever meet my father, Mr. Roberts?"

"*Diawch*, no! He was an army officer, I was an ostler!"

"But an educated man, nevertheless, aren't you!"

I added, "Anyway . . . your father was in India."

She opened dark, rebellious eyes, replying, "Yes, you're the same as all of them, aren't you! The more I question the tighter you get."

I walked past her. "You shouldn't be questioning me. You should be asking these things of your own people."

It quietened her; she swiftly turned away, and I thought she was going to cry, saying regretfully:

"After my father died in Johore, my mother sailed home, they tell me, and went into Merthyr's slums to nurse the poor. She caught the cholera, and was ill for only two days, my grandfather told me." She groaned. "God knows what she was doing down in that dreadful place!"

I replied, "I am sorry. Now you are telling me things that I do not know. I know only that your mother was beautiful – everybody was in love with her."

She raised her face. "And you, Mr. Roberts?"

"I was a servant."

To my astonishment she approached me, and, putting out her hand, she touched the scar of my face with the tips of her fingers, saying:

"But one beloved, too, unless I'm mistaken. She called you '*fy Machgen Gwyn*', my White-haired boy, did she not? Your hair is white now, but for another reason . . ." and she lowered her hand and stood there, smiling.

I had no words for her. She asked, "And this is where you used to meet, you two?" She looked about the room.

I went past her to the door. "Goodbye, Miss de Vere."

"Why do you call me that?" She raised an eyebrow in admonishment: she and her mother, like the cockatrice, could kill with a glance.

"Because I do not know the name of your father."

Since my rejection by Meg, so total and complete, there was born within me a hunger greater than desire: it was the need to be more than of myself, but part of another; isolation brought an inexpressible sadness. There is a demand in humans to know an affinity with one beloved, and with Rhiannon dead and my father, Poll, and even Old Shenks gone, there was none to whom I could turn for this solace.

And now, standing there in the doorway, I fought the temptation to snatch my daughter into my arms.

She was of Rhiannon's womb, flesh of her flesh, and therefore mine.

"Goodbye," I said.

"My . . . my mother never went to India. You know that, too, don't you, *fy Machgen Gwyn?*"

We stood looking at each other.

"I'll go further. She never even married. You see, she only loved one man."

Every inch of her; her dignity, her beauty, even her admonishment; she was, at that moment, totally Rhiannon.

I bowed to her.

"Goodbye," I repeated, and turning, left her, taking the track past the Falls to the peaks of Gwaun that rose in strickening sunlight.

And I took the road that led to Brecon; turning my face to Amlwch.

And, as I walked, the words of the Tale rose up before me: '. . . and the Princess worked among the villagers of Deganwy, they who were suffering from the Yellow Pestilence; and she caught the plague, and died: first giving birth to Delwyn's daughter, for they had been lovers.'

Book Four

Amlwch

41

I was a week on the road before the weather-cock of Amlwch came shouting through the dusk; a fractured opal moon was rising over the earth.

Tramping over the top of Parys Mountain all was quiet, as if the Devil had cleaned his tools and put them away for night-shift: the whole red land, silent, opened its arms to me . . . in welcome to one returned via Golgotha.

Memories of Dada, Poll and Meg flooded back on that walk down to the harbour, and the nostalgic clip-clop of old Dobie's shoes beat within me a silent rhythm of peace: the deep bass of my father's voice I heard then, Pru Ichabod's soprano incantation in Chapel, Meg chuckling, her tiny fists begging for Poll; the hoarse, howling protests of Andy Appledore as the molten copper bit him . . . and the sultry whispers of Siân Fi-Fi with her drawers down in Cemaes wood.

Nothing stirred in Amlwch; it was as if the Marquis had forbidden human activity between the hours of dawn and dusk. But soon, I knew, the publics would swing wide their doors and the drunks flood in, and the night would be filled with bawling men and the shrill protests of women: the same old Amlwch of drunken ill-repute, yet filled with the sweetness and neighbourly goodness that gave the lie to official historians.

Outside Fifteen Quay Street on my way to the harbour I saw Ida Promise scrubbing out the back, and no sign of Shoni Bob-Ochr, the Flying Dutchman: bent and scrawny was Ida now, pining for him, her only love.

Dora Jewels was sitting in the bay window of The Crown,

weighing up a Guinness, and Dahlia Sapphira, busty and in full song, was giving 'Rescue the Perishing' a going over in the tap-room of the Adelphi, with Tasker Bopper on the accordion, and every dog in Town must have been making for the hills.

Seth Morgan, still alive, which astonished me, went by, dozing on a cloud of Beneficiary Wills; Jacki Scog, still pig-killing, passed with a leer, his brain sharpening knives. And, as if to crown it all, I bumped into Siân Fi-Fi. Wide-hipped and prolific was Siân, done up in vanity flounces, with a floppy hat bouncing on her shoulders and a retinue of followers bouncing along behind.

Vaguely I wondered if any were mine.

She looked right into my face, did Siân . . . and passed me by.

On the cobbles outside the Britannia, I paused, for this was the place where I had first met Rhiannon.

I approached Three Costog, our old cottage above Brickhill, with care, lest people who knew me had taken over. A light in the kitchen window stilled me, and I gripped the fence near Dobie's barn, looking in. A woman (in another age it could have been my mother) was busy in the kitchen, and I wondered if it was old Betsy Costog; then realised that she must long be dead. She raised her face to the window once, this woman, and I drew back into the shadows.

Now, walking along the cliff top, I made my way to Cemaes wood . . . with one last duty to perform. I was hungry, but knew no hunger: tired, yet knew no weariness. For there was burning within me an urgency to achieve one last and solitary task, not only in the name of my father, who had commanded it, but in Rhiannon's name, and Poll's; in Meg's name, and Sam Williams's, Knocker's, Old Shenks's, Aunt Mellie and Old Nana – aye, Lady Charlotte and Sir John, the bards Price and John Jones – even Justice Bosanquet . . . the score or more who had taken their roles and played them in the 'Tale of Delwyn'.

For are we not, as my father once said, mere phantoms in a game? '. . . puppets moving hither and thither, irresponsibly, unknowingly within a play of pawns? And to whom is to be apportioned Saint or Devil?'

I came to the wood where old Brock Badger used to play, and there knelt, looking at the stars. All the sounds of the night were about me; the *chit chit chit* of a bird, the indefinable whispers of things that crawl: far below me I heard the waves crashing on Costog beach.

Finding a piece of elm I fashioned it into a tool and began to dig.

The hole I dug was circular, no wider than the span of my hand, but so deep that, when I had finished I was lying on my side with my arm deep in the earth.

Opening my bundle I took out the manuscript of 'The Tale of Delwyn', wrapped it in oilskin and put it into the hole, carefully replacing and stamping flat the injured ground; upon this I placed a rock.

Thus, as my father commanded (I possessed no son), the manuscript was returned to the Welsh heart whence it came . . . safe from those who would corrupt it into a foreign tongue.

Sitting with my back to the bole of a tree, I slept.

Perhaps I dreamed; I do not know. The night was warm and still, given to dreaming.

In my reverie I saw a tree make shape beside a river; on each bank of the river sheep were bleating: on the near bank the sheep were white; on the far bank the sheep were black. And the tree itself was of the *Mabinogi*; one half being alive with summer leaves, the other half being on fire.

So it is with Wales.

Between cockshut time and twilight my country smiles; her sighs are stilled, her scars erased. In springtime she is beautiful in her white hawthorn, like a Church of England bride.

Spring in my land takes me back to the dandelion days of my youth; the honey-sheen of sun on the sapless rushes; the noonday music of melting ice.

But, come summer, Wales is Welsh best; a mother clad in green finery. The sheepland pastures are her body, the

293

wheat her Brythonic hair. The little streams are my mother's veins, the Teify, Towey, Usk and Wye her arteries, the mountains of Plinlimmon her breasts. She is at once Iberian-dark, prideful, fiercely Celtic.

In her womb she holds the little terraced cottages, in her hands her generations: her right eye is the sun, her left eye the moon, her voice is the wind.

Kneeling there in Cemaes wood the spirit of this mother moved, enfolding me . . . within her arms she holds her exiles.

O, my beloved country, who has raised her sword to the fire of her invaders and brandished her honour in the face of shame! I can see from here the white beam of Lynas, I hear the brooks tumbling through the heather in Dolygaer. Are the black cattle still lowing from the upland farms of Cadwaladr? Does Parys Mountain of Amlwch run with Celtic blood? And is the starlight on Dowlais Top still as bright as when I made love to Rhiannon?

How great my country! Conqueror of the Jute, the Pict, Anglian, Scot, Irish, Dane and Romans – they who came with fire and laid their bones upon the altars of Cader Idris. Cunedda Wledig; Iago the son of Rhun, who fell at Chester; Arthur and Urien, the Splendid Blood of the North; and Owain, the son of Urien! – these are the magic names, the line of my deathless Welsh princes.

This, then, was the part of the tree that waved in beauty.

The other half I saw was the part on fire: the branches that flame between twilight and cockshut time, when the world is dark.

This is when my country burns with the catalysis of an artificial sun, her nights alight with radiant ovens – the tigers of predatory iron that feed on flesh.

Shedding her seasons, she pulls on blackened rags, shovels coal, heaves ropes, digs coke, bakes bricks, becomes illuminary; a mother at the stake, afire with lambent flame. Her hands stir molten iron, her bowels spurt smoke, her eyes calcine. And the summer song within her throat becomes a siren-shriek.

Then she is one with the white-hot chains that bind her; a blackened hag, defiled.

Now the burning tree glowed within its cindering depths, and I saw, as a watching child sees in a grate, the emblem of its carnage.

The stunted fields of my country I saw, the impaled breasts of tortured mountains. And from the pain of the lances in her womb the land cried out as the tree cried now, hissing and cracking in the mutilation.

And in that consuming of tree and land, I heard the protests of my people; the groans and breathlessness of worked-out colliers, the shrieks of entombed children, the screams of women trapped in machines.

Now, as the higher branches caught in scintillating brightness, there arose beams of variegated light that polarised the sun: conspiring to explode into final detonation. The soil heaved up, mushrooms of rock spewed out, and there arose black monuments to my generation.

And over this charred, lunar wilderness stole the smells of Cyfarthfa and Pen-y-darren; of Nantyglo, Risca, Bargoed, Tredegar and a hundred other graveyards . . . and the stink of Dirty Dowlais covered all – putrescent, as a corpse lies putrefying.

Damn you!

My country and my people have been carried off, outraged by you.

Damn you England!

42

I rose in the moon-filled wood and listened to the wave-lap of Costog beach below; the beach where I once saw my father, Skipper Rowlands, and the boat. And the sounds seemed to call me, as a seafarer is called home.

I went down to the beach.

And I saw, on the emblazoned sea, a white bird struggling in the waves . . . and remembered the days of my youth, and Joe Herring, the gull . . . And even as I watched the frantic efforts of the bird, I heard a voice like the voice I heard thirty years before, in the cry of the circling gulls.

"*Taliesin* . . . !"

But this time it was not my mother's voice.

I waited, listening, wondering if it was a trick of the wind, but it was not: so clearly was it Rhiannon's voice. And I remembered the last words of the 'Tale of Delwyn': 'And after twenty years in the hostile country, Delwyn, whose face was afflicted by his captors, returned to his own land. And there was a white bird struggling on the breast of the sea, calling his name. The bird was the soul of the Princess Marged, so Delwyn went into the sea to become one with her, but the honeycomb woman who served his father stretched out her hand to him.'

"*Taliesin!*"

The struggles of the captive bird became weaker. I started forward and was wading through the shallows when a hand caught mine and drew me back.

Poll said: "They told me you was coming, Tal – folks saw ye in Town: then you watched me in the kitchen window, and I followed you here."

I was looking at the white bird. She said, peering: "What they done to ye?" She added:

"Gawd, you look proper ill. Are you all right?"

"Yes," I said.

"What you starin' at, then?"

I said, "There's a white bird dying in the sea."

Poll peered through the moonlight. "There anna! You're seein' things."

I looked into her eyes.

She was older; the matron of her suffering had lined up her face for fifty . . . until she smiled, and then she was Poll. She said:

"Been waitin' all these years. Gone clean, like I said – understand? Take me on, is it? If ye can't 'ave that gentry piece, I'm still around. I'd wash and mend an' be decent, mind – good old Poll, remember?" She hesitated. "I . . . I got some granny's broth on the stove, and . . ."

"Yes," I said.

"Dear me, that skinny and tired ye are . . . Give us a try, Tal? Just a week or so – I won't bother ye none . . . and . . . and see how I get on?"

I looked at the sea. The white bird had gone.

She said, faintly. "Always loved ye, Tal . . ."

I put out my hand to her. For reply she kissed my face; the moonlight was bright yet she made no mention of my affliction.

Together, we walked up the beach, to Three Costog.

FURTHER READING

Public Order in the age of the Chartists, F. C. Mather, Manchester University Press

Dowlais Iron Company Letters 1782–1860, County Records Committee of the Glamorgan Quarter Sessions & County Council and Guest Keen Iron and Steel Company Limited, 1960

The Monmouthshire Chartists, Newport Museum and Art Gallery Publication

The Miners of South Wales, E. W. Evans, University of Wales Press

'In Search of the Celestial Empire', Keith Strange, *Llafur*, Vol. 3, No. 1, 1980, University College, Swansea

'Report to the Board of Health The town of Merthyr Tydfil, 1850', T. W. Rammel, HMSO

'Sanitary Conditions of Merthyr Tydfil', *Cardiff and Merthyr Guardian*, 1847–1855

'Crime in an Industrial Community 1842–1864: the Conquering of China', David Jones and Alan Bainbridge, *Llafur*, Vol. 2, No. 4

The History of Dowlais, Rev. J. Hathren Davies, Trans. Tom Lewis

'A Visit to the Ironworks and Environs of Merthyr Tydfil in 1852, Edwin F. Roberts, William E. Painter, London, Merthyr Public Library

'The Merthyr Ironworker (Toiling & Moiling)', Pamphlet, Merthyr Public Library

'Poor Law Administration in Merthyr Tydfil Union, 1834–1894', Tydfil Davies Jones, Merthyr Public Library

'State of Education in Wales', Merthyr Tydfil Library

Directory of Bristol, Newport and Welsh Towns 1848 – Merthyr Tydfil, and neighbourhood, Merthyr Public Library

'Cholera in Nineteenth Century Merthyr (The Flail of the Lord . . . ?)' Pamphlet, Merthyr Tydfil Library

History of Merthyr, 1867, Wilkins (Subscribers' History (Au.))

South Wales, Thorough Guide Series, 1888, C. S. Ward, M.A., Dulau and Co., London

Copper Mountain, John Rowlands, Anglesey Antiquarian Society

The Industrial Development of South Wales, 1750–1850, A. H. John, B.Sc. (Econ), Ph.D, University of Wales Press, 1950

South Wales Ironworks, 1760–1840: an Early History (from original documents), J. Lloyd, Bedford Press, London, 1906

Guest Keen Iron and Steel Co. Ltd., The Dowlais Story, 1759–1959, Cardiff Public Library

'A Study of some of the social and economic changes in the town and parish of Amlwch 1750–1850', John Rowlands, dissertation submitted for the degree of Magister in Artibus of the University of Wales, 1960, Gwynedd Library

John Frost, a study in Chartism, David Williams, Cardiff, 1939

The Trial of John Frost, shorthand notes

The Diaries of Lady Charlotte Guest (including letters from collaborator John Jones – the Mabinogion translation, and Bessborough Papers) original manuscripts, National Library of Wales

A History of Modern Wales, David Williams, John Murray, 1950

Children Working Underground, R. Meurig Evans, National Museum of Wales

Children in the Mines, 1840–1842, R. Meurig Evans, National Museum of Wales

Official Guide to Monmouth and District, Monmouth Chamber of Trade, 1928

Public Houses, Inns, Taverns & Beer Shops of Dowlais', Pamphlet – B. F. Donelon of Merthyr Tydfil

Merthyr Historian Vol. III, Merthyr Tydfil Historical and Civic Society, 1980

The Industrial Revolution in South Wales, Ness Edwards, London, 1924

Home Office Papers. Bundle Zp 37 of H.O. 17/128 Part 2, Departmental Record Office, Home Office

South Wales Miners, R. Page Arnot, Allen & Unwin, 1967

Welsh Folk Customs, Trefor M. Owen, National Museum of Wales, 1959

Children in the Iron Industry 1840–1842, R. Meurig Evans, National Museum of Wales

The Condition of the Working-Class in England, Engels, Progress Publishers

Hospitals in Merthyr Tydfil (1850–1974), Joseph Gross

The Mabinogion, Lady Charlotte Guest* – a facsimile reproduction of the complete 1877 edition, John Jones Cardiff Ltd.

* Posterity has ascribed to Lady Charlotte Guest the first translation into English of the Welsh *Mabinogi* and other tales from the Red Book of Hergest. In the 1877 edition of her book, which she describes as 'My Mabinogion' she states '. . . for the accurate copy I used [the Welsh from which she translated, Au.] I was indebted to John Jones, Fellow of Jesus College, Oxford . . .'

This statement relegates the bard to the role of a copyist, yet in her diaries, which, presumably, she did not expect to be published, she states that 'John Jones had begun a translation'. Further, 'Taliesin Williams gave me a correct translation to appear in my series.' Further still, she states that 'Mr. Justice Bosanquet translated' and that the Comte de la Villemarqué (an eminent French scholar) gave her a translation into French of the 'first three parts of the Mabinogion'. On her own account she states that the Frenchman claimed that 'I did not write my book myself.'

The Rev. Thomas Price also assisted her, and John Jones was actually teaching her Welsh at the time the translations were first published.

In the light of her own statements, her decision not to share official credit with her many collaborators was unfair and illegal; today, it would be actionable. (It is to be wondered what role Lady Charlotte Guest actually played in the work: the writer believes that her majority contribution was that of Producer.)

Alexander Cordell

HOSTS OF REBECCA

This is a brawling colourful novel of nineteenth-century Wales, with all the passion, humour and Celtic sadness of RAPE OF THE FAIR COUNTRY.

It is the story of a people's struggle: slaves of the coal mines by day, men who unite under cover of dark in a secret host, burning and fighting to save their families from starvation. It is the story of young Jethro Mortymer, striving to keep his family alive, and tortured by a terrible guilty love for his brother's wife.

Royal Mail service in association with the Book Marketing Council & The Booksellers Association.

Post-A-Book is a Post Office trademark

Alexander Cordell

THE FIRE PEOPLE

THE FIRE PEOPLE was inspired by, and climaxes in, the inglorious Merthyr Tydfil riots of 1831 and the hanging of Dic Penderyn, the first Welsh martyr of the working class.

It is a book of great power and vividness, peopled by a host of fascinating characters – Irish immigrants, European refugees, Welsh foundryworkers, whores, soldiers, miners, preachers, policemen – all lending to a backcloth that is alarming and appealing at one and the same time.

But most important is the story of Dic Penderyn – his warmth, his understanding, his dignity, his love for his wife, his loyalty to his friends, his courage in the face of helpless adversity.

Coronet Books

ALEXANDER CORDELL

THIS SWEET AND BITTER EARTH

The men of the North Wales slate quarries lived dangerous, unhealthy and underpaid lives; as a boy Toby
Davies joined them. The quarries taught him precious
truths about poverty and exploitation, but Toby also
learned of love from the two beautiful women in his life
– Bron and Nanwen O'Hara.

Toby came south, to work with coal, but found no easier
future. He was there at the notorious Tonypandy riots of
1910 and the police occupation of the Rhondda, and
would never forget the savagery of the battles between
the men and the bosses.

CORONET BOOKS

ALSO AVAILABLE FROM CORONET

ALEXANDER CORDELL

☐	20509 1	Hosts Of Rebecca	£1.40
☐	17403 X	The Fire People	£2.25
☐	23224 2	This Sweet and Bitter Earth	£2.25
☐	20516 4	Song Of The Earth	£1.50
☐	26675 9	To Slay The Dreamer	£1.60

All these books are available at your local bookshop or newsagent, or can be ordered direct from the publisher. Just tick the titles you want and fill in the form below.

Prices and availability subject to change without notice.

CORONET BOOKS, P.O. Box 11, Falmouth, Cornwall.

Please send cheque or postal order, and allow the following for postage and packing:

U.K.—55p for one book, plus 22p for the second book, and 14p for each additional book ordered up to a £1.75 maximum.

B.F.P.O. and EIRE—55p for the first book, plus 22p for the second book, and 14p per copy for the next 7 books, 8p per book thereafter.

OTHER OVERSEAS CUSTOMERS—£1.00 for the first book, plus 25p per copy for each additional book.

Name ....

Address..

....